PLA~~~

CAT AND

MOUSE

NAZIA JESBERGER

To Diane & Steve

With Love and
Best Wishes

Happy Easter!

NJ

Nazia Jesberger asserts the moral right to be identified as the author of this work. A catalogue record for this book is available from the British Library.

ISBN 979-1-041506-21-7

Cover by Hannah Linder Designs.

Nazia Jesberger grew up in the Poitou-Charentes region of France. She graduated from the University of Poitiers with a degree in English before moving to England, where she earned a Post-Graduate Certificate in Education. Nazia was a Modern Languages teacher for many years, first in England, then in France, where she currently lives with her family and pets.

Playing Cat and Mouse is her debut novel.

For Jade.

And for the men in my life, Martin and Alexandre.

PROLOGUE

TOMORROW, I WILL KILL my neighbour.

I'm neither a killer nor a psychopath, and no, I haven't gone mad. I don't even like violence.

It must be done, period.

I won't dare say something cliché like, 'it's for the greater good', but the village will fare better once he's gone.

My heart feels heavy, weighed down by the usual resistance to change. What a hard step to take. But isn't life a series of steps? The first breath, the first cry, the first word, the first love, the first kiss… and now the first kill.

I bite my bottom lip, scraping my teeth against a loose bit of skin, which falls off, drawing a pinprick of blood. He had been such a fixture in my past, and hating him had been my main reason to live for so long; until love came along. And if you hurt the one I love, it's time to die!

I clench my jaws and tighten my fists until the knuckles turn white.

That's right. Run with the emotions, let them flow right through you.

Sometimes, you need to level the plane; destroy in order to rebuild.

This is much more than a story of love and hate, revenge, and forgiveness. Good things end – often quicker than we expect – but bad things linger; they are annoyingly resilient. Something has to be done about that. So, this is the conclusion, the ending of the story. His story.

I plan to get away with it but getting caught isn't a concern. What's the worst thing that could happen to me now?

But I want to win, to feel the warmth of the sun on my skin, the caress of the wind in my hair, and the sweet lightness of freedom. Knowing he will no longer be part of this world, he'll no longer stand in our way, and with every breath I take, I will feel the elation of being alive when he is not.

And all thanks to me.

So the plan is complete, and the trap is set.

I pour myself a finger of Scotch and raise my glass. The amber liquid catches the light and, for a moment, my heart leaps, and my hand trembles. Eyelids down, I take a deep breath. Inhale, exhale… breathe. I open my eyes. My hand is steady, and my thoughts are clear. Tomorrow, I kill the devil, and out of his ashes, I will be reborn.

Cheers!

MOUSE

1

HIDING, WATCHING. It has been a while since I've done this, but it still comes naturally, and the adrenaline rush pumps me up. I stand there and stare at Cunningham's three-storey mansion. Is it normal for a man on his own to live in such a massive house? All this space, unused, filled with junk... Of course, it's not the house he really wants, but what's in the cellar? The house, like the man, hides its secret in its depths.

I think of the many times I was inside it. Its darkness, the cold, the windowless closet, and the lingering smell of chocolate chip cookies (I can't eat those anymore).

The crisp December air makes my shoulders shudder and carries with it an acrid scent of burning – someone in the village has lit a bonfire.

I scope the area. My villa – the house I grew up in and where we first met – stands just to the left of his. Such a beautiful person, I'd thought, as I forgave my parents' forgetfulness when they had shown up with him instead of meeting my teacher.

The wall that separates our properties looks shorter now. My fingers rub together like muscle memory; they used to scrape the rough stones searching for purchase, arms and legs spread wide before sliding my body over the top. Nowadays, a jump and a heave are enough. The dark patches caused by the ball I sometimes kicked against it form a cloudy pattern on its surface. I'd miss on purpose so it would end up on his lawn. Forever pulled by the compulsion to be near him, to revolve around his world like the moon orbiting Earth. I was young then. That age of innocence and superficiality, when drawing a house meant geometric patterns of square windows inside a rectangular frame mounted with a triangular roof. An age that doesn't yet look beyond the exterior veneer.

A ginger cat sits on the wall licking its paws, and it reminds me of another cat, grey and white, hanging limp from a twine. He had brought this grey-and-white cat to ours once, and I took it as a declaration of war because of my nickname, Mouse. I'd just laughed – and it was perhaps the only time he had ever made me laugh.

Deception, mistrust, disgust, anger, condescension, indifference are the feelings I associate with our relationship. Sneering, tormenting, aggression being the actions. The first two mine, the last one his. His violence, the confinement, the punches, the rope around my neck, digging through my skin...

The orange tabby jumps down and rubs itself against the front wheel of a car: Tommy's Volvo, gathering dust in Cunningham's driveway.

Tommy, wish you were here.

My heart shrivels, crushed by an agonising hand when I think of his delicate face disfigured by the beating, eyes swollen shut, the skin around them purple-brown and puffy, his slim naked body bruised and bloodied and limp.

I take a breath and swallow my anger. Thoughts of Tommy rush in and explode inside my mind like fireworks. The angelic smile, the full lips and straight angle of his nose. His Adam's apple moving up and down. The golden eyes burning with anger. The harsh voice turning velvety soft. His strong hands running through his hair or flipping the cocktail shaker with dexterity.

The sense of loss is overpowering, and I almost kneel on the leafy ground.

Tommy, you once told me the path to revenge is a foolish one that only leads to pain, but I will avenge you now. Today, I kill Cunningham for this.

My hand reaches the pocket of my jeans, and the bumpy feeling of the Swiss Army knife nestled inside it comforts me. His knife. Not much of a weapon, but lethal enough, nonetheless.

Cunningham's house is closed up; he's not yet awake – very likely comatose in a drunken stupor – but spying requires patience. I should know.

A vehicle drives past, and I slither behind a tree trunk as moss stains my right sleeve green. Daniel, on his way to work in my garden and the reason I'm here now, lurking in the tight wooded area surrounding Dad's workshop. He doesn't see me; I'm just another shadow among the gnarled branches and leaves of the oak trees.

The workshop fades into the trees, camouflaged, the perfect stalking ground right opposite Cunningham's house. People forget it's even here now that Dad's gone.

A movement catches my eyes: Cunningham pushes the shutters of his bedroom, and light streams out. He's awake.

Showtime.

I rub my neck with a shaky hand and check the smooth mechanism of the Swiss Army knife. I shove it back inside my pocket, look left, then right, and jump onto the road.

His front door opens with a push, and I slam it behind me. I rush to the living room, turn the door handle with a clatter, stomp upstairs and wait for him by the bathroom. He doesn't immediately follow.

With long nervous strides, I pace back and forth in the dark and cluttered corridor, heart thumping and shoulders tense. I crack my neck, left then right, but the air thins, and it's difficult to breathe – airways constricting, head dizzy, stomach churning – and I realise the symptoms of my childhood have never left but simply lain dormant. The closed wooden doors and the clutter seem to shut in on me. I close my eyes, inhale, exhale, look up and turn around.

His hand is already raised high before it comes slapping me across the face. The sound of the impact is surprisingly loud, like a sharp short roar of thunder. He is still drunk and not in his right mind. The years of pent-up anger seem to flow out of his pores, and rage mixes with the winey scent of his sweat while my cheek burns from the blow. I note the devastating effects alcohol has had on his body.

What a waste.

He had been such a good-looking man, but now his once-perfect appearance is just a blurry caricature of itself: his face is slack, mouth hanging open, replacing the habitual smile with a strange grimace. His skin is red and blotchy, his grey hair is dishevelled and thinning, his hard, toned body has softened, and I am surprised just how old and vulnerable he looks.

Don't get fooled.

His movements are disconnected, giving him a comical gait, but this is no laughing matter. He means harm – I can see it in his eyes – and he is still strong. I am lucky he has only used the open palm of his hand rather than his fist.

He stills, and I realise I may have shaped this man just as much as he has shaped me. I grew to hate him, and he clearly hates me; and I will be his undoing, as he had been mine. We seem to be inextricably and irrevocably bonded, no matter how far apart we try to be. It's as if the invisible link that connects us is nothing more than a rubber band that has returned to its original position after being stretched. The only escape is to sever it.

Dizziness weakens me, but I fight the urge to raise my arm in a protective gesture, not wanting to appear weak but also challenging him, defying him, and that's why the slap hits me hard, sending me to the ground. My hand reaches into the pocket holding the knife, and I grip it tight, its feeling reassuring.

He stands over me, eyes bloodshot and dripping with hatred; then he raises his fists. A thin rope hangs through his fingers – a bright-orange one. My eyes open wide, and my mouth turns dry. I have to take action before it's too late, but he grabs me by the neck and shoves me against the bathroom door, which swings open under my weight.

I fall on my knees facing the bathtub, and the familiar clothes lying discarded inside it distract me.

Tommy's clothes – what? Why are they here?

A stitch pierces my chest, a muddle clouds my mind, and stunned, I forget the figure creeping behind me.

Where am I?

Someone's lifting me, someone strong, and the Earth seems to rotate off its axis. I need to open my eyes to see what's happening, but my head spins, and my eyelids are stuck together.

I feel cold and sore as I try to wriggle out of the person's grasp, but my body is limp and unresponsive. Why can't I move? Why am I hurting? I search through my memories and get scared when my mind faces a blank wall. I recall nothing.

Is this a dream?

I want to speak, but words won't form properly. A low, unintelligent mumble escapes my lips, and a hand is pushed against my mouth, silencing me. The touch is surprisingly gentle.

I will my arms to move, wanting to remove the hand from my face, but my brain seems clogged with a dark, thick fog, and my efforts are in vain.

This is a dream; it has to be.

I feel myself slip into unconsciousness. It might just be the right thing to do to get out of this nightmare, but I fight the feeling, trying hard to stay awake… desperately willing my body to move.

An image appears behind my eyelids, a memory resurfacing… the faces of my parents. The vision isn't clear, but blurry and moving… changing… Liam Cunningham…

The face fleets, disappears… my world darkens.

Soon, everything is black, and there is nothing.

2

I WANTED TO LIVE. And if life was the story unfolding on a page, I was the brief annotation left in its margin – scribbled by a careless hand, unimportant, easy to overlook or quickly forgotten. I knew this even as a child.

My teacher Sophie glared at the clock on the wall and sighed once again. I turned the pages of a colouring book without looking at them, eyes fixed on her, teeth biting my bottom lip with embarrassment. Mum and Dad had failed to turn up to the meeting, and I felt guilty for their lack of interest, always relegated to the bottom of their list of priorities. I imagined Mum was sticking her nose in someone else's business while Dad preferred the company of his car carcasses.

Sophie tapped the desk with frantic fingers. 'Do they speak French?'

I nodded. The question seemed unnecessary – my mother, the councillor, was a well-known figure. Despite my tender age of seven, I saw it for what it was, a desperate attempt to give them a reasonable excuse for their absence.

Mrs Newbury – Mum to classmate Olivia and fellow villager – took me home, and I walked into the house to find an unfamiliar adult in our kitchen. He was as beautiful as he was elegant; I must admit I forgave Mum's distractedness. My mother may have been negligent, but she liked to surround herself with good-looking people.

'Cute kid,' said the man. He ruffled my hair and grabbed my hand to shake it. 'I'm your new neighbour. My name is Liam.'

'Cunningham, like the actor,' added Mum.

Liam asked about homework, giving me a gentle smile, and I beamed, surprised by his friendliness. Adults always dismissed me. I was invisible even to my own parents, and with his attentive manners – and unbeknownst to him – this new neighbour pulled me from the margin and onto the page, breathing life into me. He soon became the object of my obsession.

I longed to be near him, to revel in his presence, but we lived in rural France, and our adjacent properties came with quite substantial gardens. He felt far and removed with his house always closed up, giving him an air of mystery, and trespassing into his home happened by chance.

It was on a hot summer's afternoon – not with skin-scorching sunshine as summers were usually like south of the Loire River, but with a heavy overcast sky that seemed to push me down. I had climbed the thick wall separating our gardens to lie on the cool stones in the shade of the overhanging branches of our neighbour's cedar tree. My favourite spot. A place which revealed breathtaking views of the valley below me.

A jarring note in the landscape made me turn, and I looked at Liam's house. His three-storey rectangular-shaped mansion loomed over me, with cast-iron plates forming crosses on the fascia, small and un-shuttered windows at the top, a high slated roof and multiple chimneys jutting out at either end. Because they faced south, the wooden shutters of the French doors at ground level were only ever pushed into a V shape, and as for the shutters on the first floor, I had never seen them open.

Except for that day.

One window gaped, exposing dark shapes of furniture, and the house resembled a giant who'd lifted an eyelid on waking up and winked at me in an open invitation.

Large branches from the cedar tree led directly to it, and access was but a few scrambling steps followed by a leap. The step from outdoors to indoors, branch to bedroom, was such a quick and easy one to take that I didn't give it a second thought.

I landed on worn-out carpet, perhaps beige, perhaps grey. I wasn't sure because the weather gave everything a greyish tinge. Shabby furniture stood helter-skelter, and I navigated through them along stacks of boxes, piles of old, heavy books, and bric-a-brac. The pages of a children's storybook crossed my mind, with exciting images of secrets and treasures, and my fingers soon danced in and out of dusty surfaces, rummaging through drawers and cabinets.

Getting caught didn't worry me. Small and nimble, I had complete confidence in my skills. I could sneak under the bed with swiftness and ease, hide behind a chest, or even in one of the tall cardboard boxes. I wasn't named Mouse for nothing, and the nickname was a perfect fit – better suited than Taylor, especially in this country, where listening in on people was to be a *petite souris* – a little mouse.

A dozen glossy school photographs lay on top of an opened storage box. Rows of teenage boys stared back at me, wearing sophisticated uniforms: grey trousers, burgundy blazers with a grey trim on the lapels, burgundy V-neck sweaters, white shirts and stripy ties. The name of the school was printed in embossed gold letters at the bottom:

Saint Peter the Apostle
International School for Boys.

Looking at the faces one by one, I hoped to recognise a younger Liam, but he had not been a student. He stood lean and tall, looking young and elegant, and wearing a black gown over a well-cut suit like a distinguished young professor in a Harry Potter movie.

A piece of silver string snaked around a stack of correspondence, letters on yellowish paper between three or four members of a family – presumably Liam's – underneath a wedding photo. It appeared Liam hadn't always been alone; he'd been married to a petite brunette with a broken smile.

I clutched the letters against my chest as though they were the treasure I had longed to find – the only writing we did at home was yearly Christmas cards for Dad's family in Australia. A frisson of excitement ran through me: I had finally passed the invisible barrier, reached the next level and entered the circle of Liam's intimacy.

Bright Post-it Notes caught my eye, brief messages between husband and wife, and the more I read, the more the tone descended into rage. The first few notes exchanged had been romantic, starting with 'my dearest Liam' and ending with 'forever yours' while the last read 'burn in hell' in blood-red letters. It appeared Liam Cunningham had committed some 'great sin' towards his wife, choosing to 'walk hand in hand with the devil' and was 'beyond hope of redemption'.

These messages confounded me; they did not fit with the image I'd had of my neighbour. I had been impressed not only by his good looks but also by his elegant attire. Although he worked at the rural accountancy firm in town, Liam dressed sharply and left behind a trail of a grapefruit-scented aftershave – it kind of smelled like one of Mum's fruit teas. Most Saturdays he volunteered at the local church and, on his return, he would stop at ours, hand out delicious home-baked cookies, and shower me with attention.

These notes would turn out to be the first step, the crack in my youthful and naïve reality. From then on, I progressed through stages of Liam's deceit.

An old passport peeked out from underneath the photos, with the bottom right corner cut off diagonally. Upon opening it, I was surprised to see Liam's face. He'd told us he was Irish, but his passport did not resemble that of the McFarlane family (I had seen Daniel's passport when he had needed it for a school trip), instead, there were the crown, lion and unicorn of Great Britain with the inscription *Dieu et mon droit*.

Liam Padraig Cunningham was born in Belfast, Northern Ireland, yet somehow that didn't make him Irish. My history lessons had only gone as far as the Roman Empire, not yet having learned the difference between Ireland and Northern Ireland, and I thought the man wasn't who he pretended to be: smiling, charming and good-looking on the outside but a devil on the inside; claiming to be Irish, but not really Irish. A fraud, perhaps?

The desire to see him, to pierce through his fake appearance, overwhelmed me.

I tiptoed to the door and turned the handle with a slow rotation in case it would creek, but the mechanism was smooth, and I pulled the door open unhindered. A mouth-watering smell of freshly baked cookies lured me into the dark corridor. I looked behind me at wooden stairs leading up to the second floor. To my right were four wooden doors, with three on my left, including the one I had just come through, all of which were closed. On the landing, more piles of books and newspapers littered the floor, and a discarded chandelier lay shrouded in shadows, giving it a creepy, giant spider look. A stone staircase led down to ground level.

I shivered; the house felt cold despite the heat outside.

The smell drew me further, and I made my way down the staircase, stopping after a few steps when I realised it led directly to a large living room.

Dim light filtered through the partially closed shutters and gave a twilight quality to the space. I watched and listened while holding my breath; the room seemed to be empty, yet a fluttering noise came from it, like the muted sound of birds flapping their wings. Intrigued, I continued until I reached the stone floor of the living room.

Thick Persian rugs covered the tiles, muffling the sound of my footfalls. Wooden crosses of varying sizes lined the stone walls. Drapes of a thick, heavy fabric in an old-fashioned flowery pattern framed the French windows. At the end of the room, behind a long maho-gany table, three winged armchairs with their backs to me faced a lit fireplace. I had never seen a fireplace so large, going from floor to halfway up the wall. Above it, a painting depicted the Virgin Mary with baby Jesus on her lap.

The noise seemed to come from one of the armchairs and, curious, I moved closer. Only two feet away from them, there was a sudden rustle of paper followed by a moan; my heart almost skipped a beat, and I hid behind one of the heavy curtains, trying hard to calm my racing heartbeat. The curtains smelled like dust and linen, and I fought the urge to sneeze. The fabric, worn in places, was almost see-through, and I crouched and bent my back to look through a peephole.

Being able to view the armchairs sideways made me realise how close I'd been to being caught red-handed. Liam sat in one of them, his face turned upwards, eyes closed, trousers around the ankles with one arm moving while the other held some kind of magazine.

It was difficult at first, for the nearly eight-year-old I was, to understand the situation; then I knew, or rather felt, that I'd watched something intimate and that it was wrong.

I closed my eyes and straightened, standing still, but it was too late, and I couldn't un-see what I had witnessed. It left me feeling shameful, dirty, and something else that resembled guilt. Even if I was at fault for trespassing, I instantly hated Liam for it.

A creepy silence stretched, and my eyes reopened. I dared to look through the peeping hole again; the chair was vacant. Moving with the curtain, slowly, I checked out the rest of the room, but it was also empty.

In a rush, eager to leave the place, I came out from behind the curtain, took three steps, and something crushed under my feet – the magazine Liam had been holding. I picked it up, and the images shocked me: bearded men with bulging muscles so enormous they looked deformed. Naked.

Shaken, angered, but most of all scared, I threw the magazine into the fire.

Footsteps approached, and I scurried to take my place back behind the curtain. Liam looked around, perhaps wondering what the source of the noise was, then he saw the magazine burning. He let out an exclamation of surprise, kneeled in front of one of the wooden crosses and started praying, asking for forgiveness.

Seeing him like this, I felt like a balloon lifted into the air, my spirit going from low to high, like he was praying to me, like I was all-powerful, and him the lesser creature, no longer Liam but Cunningham.

No, I thought as I watched him, *I will not forgive you.*

My body inflamed with powerful emotions, and although I was too young to pinpoint what those emotions were, I felt them coursing through me under my skin. I never felt more alive than in that moment.

Yes, I replied to his prayer, *you will be punished.*

And so started my stalking days. Following, spying, tormenting.

I was not a tolerant child and despised hypocrisy above all else, so when the women came a few months later, I felt compelled to watch.

By age ten, Cunningham's persecution was a well-rooted addiction. I crouched by the fire in his living room, tore pages from Cunningham's magazines, took small nail scissors out of my pocket and started cutting pieces to form letters. Strands of blond hair covered my eyes, and I blew them out, working fast to be done by the time he returned. Arts and crafts weren't my strong points, and I struggled to form an 'S'. I had the funny thought that a couple of years earlier, Cunningham would have been one of the rare adults to help me out with such a task.

To think I had admired the man, I snorted at the thought.

The 'S' letter looked irregular but better than expected, and I smiled, proud of my work. Now I had the challenge of an 'O'. The message 'I see you' slowly formed on the floor by the hearth – displayed in the pretence that God was angry with him.

The fire crackled. I shoved the scissors into my pocket, brushed my hands together, stepped into the hallway to peer through the barred window by the front door and waited for his arrival. When a car turned into the driveway, I saw that it wasn't Cunningham but one of his latest girlfriends.

Yep, on occasion, and to maintain the façade, he took a woman home. They never lasted long, though, as he could never follow through, and there were two ways this could play out. Either they would drink themselves into oblivion, and he would pretend something had happened the previous night, face full of fake remorse, smile as mischievous as a naughty kid, or the women acted more persistent, and he would turn violent, as though blaming them for his failures. Even at such a young age, I could never understand or accept this form of cowardice and found the man sickening.

The woman knocked on the door and didn't wait for her call to be answered. She peered inside through the window, under which I crouched down, making myself as invisible as I could. 'Liam, open up!'

A persistent woman.

Didn't she realise Liam's car was not in the driveway? More importantly, didn't she realise who the man truly was?

Three years earlier, I had been as mistaken as her, but then I was young, and I was always in love – one day it might be Antoine in my class, another day it could be Ethan from our village, or his father, or even the guy who delivered the post.

It seemed I wasn't the only one who had been fooled by Liam's impeccable appearance and good-looking features.

'Liam!' she pounded once again.

The engine sound of Cunningham's car roared, and I stood to gaze outside. He came out of the car with a smooth smile on his face, but I knew he was angry. I'd spied on him enough times to know that when the fists stayed closed, something was brewing. It did not bode well for his visitor, a woman whom he greeted with a 'Bonjour, Sabrina.'

Sabrina appeared to be in her late thirties and quite pretty, in a delicate, flowery sort of way. She looked at him with adoring eyes, and I saw what she saw; the handsome face, the easy manners, the gentleman approach, the fit physique from regular exercising and the full head of hair, greying at the sides like a James Bond actor.

They walked together to the door, and I hurried out of the massive hallway. It was the only part of the house that didn't offer a hiding place; everywhere else had clutter, furniture of all eras, boxes, big and small, and piles of old smelly books. I tore through the living room and up the stairs to the dark landing with a grin, feeling thrilled, hoping they would both find the torn pages. At last, Cunningham would be exposed.

They never made it to the living room, though, and I followed them with stealth, creeping near the kitchen where Sabrina sat leaning towards a tall, stiff, cross-armed Cunningham.

'I'm sorry,' he said, 'but I just love women a little too much to be faithful.'

He was breaking up with her! What a load of bull crap! When he was, in fact, a woman-hater.

His two-faced persona angered me. I scampered upstairs and raided his upstairs bathroom, which was baby blue porcelain with a navy-themed wallpaper. A white metal chair sat by the bathtub piled with towels of assorted colours, and a tall white cabinet stood next to a cracked mirror. I found a Swiss Army knife with the initials LPC that I shoved in my pocket, came across some disturbing photos, and moved on to a place so peaceful and quiet I missed dinner.

Cunningham had no pets, and he lived alone. He rarely went to the first or second floor, and it amused me how I could easily move around the place unnoticed, right under his nose. My pranking and tormenting him felt justified. He was a liar and a fraud, and he'd stolen my innocence at a time I had admired him.

Stepping into his house had been my first time trespassing, but it wouldn't be my last. I'd had a taste of life. I got to see who the man behind closed doors truly was, and once you've been pulled onto the page, you never want to go back behind the line of your margin prison. I developed a strange desire to know people through their inner and most hidden secrets. So I learned to spy, to infiltrate, to observe and immerse myself secretly into other people's lives, and this I did for six years until the day before my fourteenth birthday. The day he caught me.

I don't know how he caught me, where I am, or how long I've been here. One thing cannot be concealed, though: my captor's identity. He hides his face in darkness, disguises his voice with strange whispers, but there are things he cannot mask — his touch, his scent, the way he moves, even the way he feels.

I am not tied to anything, and my head is not covered. I am naked, yes, but the room is warm... and completely black.

When I was first locked in here, I dared not move; the darkness was so total that it scared me. Now I am so used to it I fear I might go blind.

It might have been days or weeks since he's been to visit. The notion of time is an alien concept here; it certainly feels like a long time, and I almost crave his return. Almost.

Shouting for help, fighting to escape, crying, pleading, praying, none of that is any use. Believe me, I tried!

Alone in the dark, with only my thoughts, I feel I will go crazy. Perhaps I already have. I try to remember how I ended up here, but I just don't know. Memories of my youth are intact, however, and I let the images run freely, chronologically, in my mind: the very first day of school, with mixed feelings of apprehension and excitement. Birthday celebrations, blowing candles and the rustle of wrapping paper when opening presents. The embrace of a warm towel wrapping me after a bath or the feeling of wet sand between my toes.

One memory keeps trying to push its way out, but I fight it, concentrate on others: helping with the cooking, hands covered in tacky, sticky pastry, or the gardening, mud sticking to boots. Horse riding lessons. Guitar and piano lessons. The light texture of candyfloss on a sweltering summer afternoon, the smoky smell of roasted chestnuts on a Christmas morning, the expanding dark pool of blood on the tarmac and the cries of people dying.

I can't help it. It's like my mind is telling me to return to that moment.

Of course, that's when it all started and the reason I'm here now.

3

THE BLOODBATH ON THE DAY of my fourteenth birthday forever changed the course of my life.

I just stood there, blood pooling around my feet, as a gust of wind plucked the baseball cap from my head and sent it flying towards the trees.

Divine retribution, perhaps, for walking into the church with bad intentions the previous day. The angels and saints painted on the vaulted ceiling had stared down at me – judging me – with austere faces. Some sort of warning. *What was this imposter doing here?*

I'd crept near as soon as Cunningham slipped inside the booth, eyes on the ground and was trying to listen in when a pair of polished shoes entered my field of vision. I looked up and stared at Cunningham's puzzled face, then my eyes shifted towards the confessional and, straight away, he knew what I'd tried to do.

It was a weakness of mine; I couldn't lie.

He grabbed my shirt with such force it tore, exposing my chest, and pulled me along before throwing me onto the cobbled stones outside, in full view of a handful of passers-by.

Face and ears red with shame, I ran to my bicycle with my head down and pedalled home with furious strokes.

He would pay for this.

As soon as I got home, I hacked into Cunningham's account and was excited to see he'd made an appointment for the next day. He had never once met a man here, and this was a rare opportunity. He usually drove miles for his secret rendezvous, and sometimes he even flew to England, so this was a first. *Perfect.* I would follow him and catch him red-handed. The time to expose him had finally come.

On the day of my birthday, I watched his house with my new binoculars (a birthday present from Mum and Dad), but an unexpected downpour lashed at the window, and all I could see was a blurry wet mess – just big drops of water magnified.

I sighed with frustration.

The downpour stopped as suddenly as it had started, and the wind pushed the black clouds away. Cunningham came out of his house wearing brand-new hunting attire and climbed into his car. I unplugged my phone, grabbed my backpack, and rushed through the front door.

I made my way to the park while breathing in the acidic, after-rain scent evaporating from the road, relishing how it turned into an undefined but pleasant taste on my tongue. It got sunnier with every step I took, as if the sun was welcoming me into its warm embrace, pulling me forward. It was late October and unseasonably warm.

'Someone's on a mission!' said a cheerful voice, startling me.

Ethan Wood, seventeen years old, the hunk of the village – the hunk of the entire region – hurried his pace to catch up with me. He lived at the corner of the T-junction, just past Cunningham's house on the other side of the lane, and I was surprised I hadn't seen him sooner. Ethan was around one metre eighty-six tall and possessed an allure not easy to overlook, but my mind was preoccupied and my mood jubilant, knowing I'd soon give Cunningham the punishment he deserved.

As usual, and regardless of the weather, Ethan wore a tight white vest – the kind that showed off his muscular upper body and emphasised the beautiful bronze colour of his skin – and he'd tied a thin brown coat around his waist. He was gorgeous, and he knew it, and I tried hard not to stare at his chest.

'Can you find something out for me?' he asked.

Sometimes I traded information, little pieces of knowledge I deemed unimportant, which came from my mother.

As councillor, Mum supervised our village as well as two others and was the go-to person for dealing with

French bureaucracy. Our village was a community of a majority of British expats, a few Irish, two American families, the Dutch ladies who owned the B&B and a 'young' Belgian couple who had moved in two years earlier.

Villagers were always in and out of our house, and there were many things my parents never paid for: we always had vegetables in season, free grocery shopping delivery services and once, even a fully paid week at a ski resort (we never went). Mum was like a fairy godmother to the community, waving her magic wand and making their problems go away – especially during all that Brexit business. Naturally, she knew a lot about everybody, and people assumed, wrongly, that I got all my info from her.

'Depends. What's it about?' I asked.

'Anna…' He paused. 'Our parents are…'

He frowned, searching for words, and rubbed the palm of his left hand with his right thumb before letting out a defeated sigh.

My ears reddened. I already knew what Ethan wanted to ask, and I had to distract him.

'Instead of worrying about your parents or Anna, shouldn't you put all your energy into your new relationship with Makayla?' I asked with an innocent tone, deflecting the question.

Ethan stopped, eyebrows raised. 'How do you know about that?'

I hesitated, as the two of them had meant to keep it a secret for a while, then shrugged. 'The two of you just weren't as discreet as you thought. Word of advice, if you don't want the donkeys to make such a ruckus, you must feed them first.'

'Jesus! Were you in the barn?'

'No, I was feeding the donkeys.'

Ethan laughed.

It was a lie; I had indeed been in the barn trying to spy on the Van Beers – which had turned out to be quite the challenge. Instead, I got a smooching show between Ethan and Makayla.

'Wow, we were confident no one was around. We sure didn't see or hear anything.' He looked me up and down. 'Your name sure is appropriate, you know that? You really are as quiet as a mouse!'

He had said 'sure' twice, and I wondered if he knew he'd picked up Makayla's Americanism. Anyway, I was proud of myself for having diverted the conversation from Anna to Makayla.

Although I enjoyed knowing everybody's dirty little secrets (they made me feel superior), revealing them was out of the question. Even if I could get them to listen, people didn't like having their inner secret come to light, and they would turn their anger back towards me. Also, just because I knew of a secret didn't mean I wanted to share it. I much preferred to keep it close to my chest in the belief that knowledge is power, and you never knew when the knowledge could become useful.

Ethan walked on ahead of me. I reached the park to find all the village kids – almost a dozen of them, all around the age of seventeen or eighteen – assembled by the children's swings with their bright-orange ropes.

Anna, Makayla, and Juliet sat on a bench watching videos on a phone while chatting with Jamie, his brother Mick and his best friend Owen, who kicked a ball further away. The ball occasionally got thrown towards Jade and Leah, who were practising dance moves, and the smokers, Luke and Daniel, would kick it back while watching them. They formed a strong unit, a solid group of teenagers, not bad, not mean, usually polite and very loyal to each other.

Both my parents commanded a certain respect in the community, and the other kids were all friendly to me, but I was not one of them. Too young for a start, small for my age, and too much of a loner to be part of their world.

I crept towards the wooden bridge leading to the forest – a great big mass of oak and alder trees separated midway by a major road. Daniel, noticing me, detached himself from the group to wish me a happy birthday. He presented me with a gift in the form of a packet of lollipops, which I opened to share with everybody, and with a wave of the hand, this little mouse was off to the deep, dark wood.

I travelled south, following the ramblers' trail covered with early fallen leaves. The half of the forest attached to the park was a common tourist site and well developed with hiking trails, mountain bike trails, chocolate egg hunts at Easter, treasure hunts in summer and mushroom picking in season.

My feet slapped the soft floor as I followed the trail for a few minutes, breathing in the scent of decaying vegetation, then I veered east and cut across the underbrush to shorten the journey. It took a good thirty minutes to reach the main road, but if you knew the terrain, you could shorten it to less than twenty.

It felt cool under the cover of the trees, and droplets of rain fell from branches with a dull tapping sound. The bottoms of my jeans got soaked and started sticking to my legs. I took my cap out of my backpack and put it on, shoving as much of my hair as I could under it to hide it; I had work to do.

On the other side of the road was the *A.C.C.A* forest. I wasn't sure what the letters stood for but knew it meant hunters' territory. I was following Cunningham there despite the danger – it was hunting season, and although my backpack held a yellow reflective jacket, nothing could protect me from a wild boar.

Ruins lay hidden in the forest, part of some ancient monastery with broken stone walls covered in ivy, half a tower, and one small building jutting from a massive rock with a makeshift roof of creepers. People used the place as a meeting point for many secret dirty deeds, and I had no doubt that it was where Cunningham was headed.

Unwrapping a lollipop and popping it into my mouth, I let my thoughts wander. Daniel had presented the sweets as a shared gift, but I knew different. I liked Daniel; he was one of the rare older teenagers who actually saw me. Though the youth stuck together in the village, the age difference meant Olivia and I were often ignored, physically inside the group, yet outsiders looking in, as if an invisible wall separated us.

Daniel had been the only one to attempt to breach that wall, eager to include me despite my aloofness, and unlike others, not angry when I'd organised a meeting with him to share my discoveries about his troubled past. In fact, he had seemed grateful.

Daniel cared for his sick dad and hardly had time for himself, as he sometimes did various odd jobs for the villagers to supplement the family's income. Yet he'd gone to the trouble of buying me a present because that's who he was: thoughtful and kind despite everything he'd endured. His kindness made him beautiful. He had tried to approach the Van Beers and offer his services, but they were a tough nut to crack, and I wondered how to spy on the couple. Despite my best detective work, I knew next to nothing about them except their Belgian nationality.

I prided myself on my spying skills, as well as my extensive knowledge of the local residents and their darkest secrets. Sometimes, they even made it too easy, leaving a door unlocked here, a window ajar there, a laptop on and open or a poorly secured connection.

Here were the things known by all: Andrew Byrne delighted in cross-dressing, and his wife didn't mind (and why should she? He was entitled to wear whatever he wanted, and clothes shouldn't be attached to gender). Widowed Celia Smith had regular, often younger, gentlemen callers. Makayla's family had left the States under mysterious circumstances. Liam Cunningham was a bit of a womaniser, or so everyone thought.

The things only I knew: Robert Wood was both Ethan and Anna Dewsnip's father, and they were to be told on their eighteenth birthdays. Cunningham was a closeted gay man. Daniel had suffered something traumatic in his early years, and Makayla was not the youngest of her siblings, as everyone thought, but had had a twin sister called Mila who had been kidnapped and murdered at age three. Perhaps even she didn't know the real reason for her twin's death.

However, the Van Beers lived in a house on top of a small hill, difficult to approach unseen. They were careful, methodical people, sticking to their routines, never leaving the house empty and keeping themselves to themselves. After two years, they had yet to be seen talking to anyone beyond the exchange of everyday greetings or joining in with any village or town event.

I reviewed the extent of my knowledge about them: the husband was Peter, thirty-seven years old. Lanky with short light-brown hair and brown eyes, he ran every morning at 7.30 sharp for an hour. The wife's name was Gretchen, thirty-six years old, average height with bob-cut blond hair, who sometimes put an easel outside to paint. Perhaps they made money from the paintings – they never left the house to go to work – but I caught no meetings or financial transactions with potential clients or art galleries. No one in the village knew anything about them, not even Mum, and that was a challenge I simply could not resist.

Seconds away from reaching the road, the brutal and deafening sound of an explosion made me jump. The noise was unlike anything I had ever heard before, a bang followed by a loud scraping of metal and a cloud of dark smoke rising above the tree line. We'd had so many drills at school, in case of a terrorist attack, that I knew I should run in the opposite direction and find or call a responsible adult. I did neither and frantically climbed the embankment leading to the road, scraping my bare skin on brambles, moving towards the commotion, curiosity leading my feet, or maybe instinct.

One shoe lay abandoned. A black trainer, Puma, size forty-four, lying sideways on the road. It looked incongruous on its own and oddly familiar. There was a large dark pool of…what? Diesel? Blood? Surely not blood. Surely there was too much of it to be blood! The strong metallic and acid smell made my nose twitch. I moved closer, met someone's eyes, heard her shout and froze. As I stood and took in the scene, a powerful gust of wind blew my cap away and started whipping my hair. Stilled by shock and so many things attacking my senses at once, I felt like I was having an out-of-body experience, as if watching myself observe the carnage, silent and unmoving. Then, quite suddenly, I turned away and ran.

I stumbled through the woods, letting my legs carry me, feet pounding on the wet earth until I stopped to lean against a tall oak tree to catch my breath. My face was wet; was it raining again? Tears. They surprised me. I let them out, and for a long time, I couldn't stop. I wasn't even sure what I was crying for – the haunted eyes? Those ultimate words? Or even the solitary shoe?

The sound of a siren blared in the distance; guilt and relief washed over me in equal measure. Someone had done what I couldn't do: call the emergency services and get help. Eager to move away, I started running again, and as I moved forward, the images rewound in my head, putting themselves together like the assembly of a jigsaw puzzle.

The solitary shoe: Puma black trainer, lying on its side in the middle of the road like an ominous sign, Peter Van Beers' shoe. I had seen him wear the black trainers on his runs, but no sign of Peter Van Beers.

Both cars flattened, misshapen and torn, one of them a dark-blue Volkswagen: the Van Beers' car, the other an SUV, silver, on its side, dark fumes escaping from it.

Glass falling everywhere, and something resembling a metal pole slashing across the sky almost horizontally and piercing through a body inside. A gurgling cry.

A shape in the middle of the road – a headless leather-covered body, arms at a funny angle. I hadn't seen the motorcycle, but the helmet sat close by, upright, as if the rider had just put it down for a moment – *back in a sec –* except it sat in a pool of blood still encasing a head.

A familiar figure appeared to be wearing red clothing. *Except the clothes weren't red.* The blood covered the entire raw-meat-looking body, and the only things sticking out were blue-green eyes and blond hair. So blond it almost looked white, not unlike my own: Gretchen Van Beers. I had just been thinking about her, and the hand she'd raised, reaching out for me in her last desperate moment, looked less like the gesturing of someone asking for help and more like she was trying to express she'd been thinking about me too, which was absurd.

Another woman had been further away, moaning in pain and crying for help. But I hadn't helped. I hadn't wanted to see or smell the blood anymore. I hadn't wanted to see her legs, or the large piece of torn glass slashing through them as efficiently as a guillotine, and those legs falling so abnormally far from her body.

So I fled, trying to put distance between me and those blue-green eyes, but they kept following me, and I could outrun neither her eyes nor her last words; Gretchen Van

Beers' words, uttered in a desperate cry like a dramatic scene in a Shakespearian play: 'To be!'

But what did they mean? To be what? Dead? Alive? Whole?

Those eyes again plunged into mine, calling out for me, pleading, yet some other eyes somewhere were watching me; I was sure of it, and I wanted them to stop!

Paranoia.

I closed my eyes; I didn't want to see, didn't want to remember.

Please!

I felt so cold, and I just wanted to go home – warmth, safety.

The backpack felt heavier with every step, but I didn't want to remove it, and the rhythmic sound of it hitting my back calmed my racing heartbeat. Taking a corner, I slipped and fell on the wet leaves and scraped my chin on a sharp branch; blood mixed with tears and fear gripped me. It was irrational, and somehow I knew it, but it was like the feeling had taken shape and turned solid.

I picked myself up and tried running faster, struggling, as if moving through water, and stopped only when reaching the park, doubled up, hands on knees and panting hard. I had to pull myself together again, couldn't let anyone see me like this, distraught, covered in sweat, tears, and mud, but the park was now quiet and empty. No doubt everyone had gone to check out the accident on the road.

I came out from under the canopy of trees and stepped into a different world. The sun shone bright, hurting my eyes. Its rays caressed my skin, but the wind was cool, and I couldn't get warm – felt I would never be warm again. I tucked my hands under the sleeves of my hoodie, crossed my arms over my chest and made my way from the deserted park and back to the house. Everything was eerily quiet, and no one was around.

Our villa emerged behind palm trees, and I hesitated. Everyone had probably gone to the crash site, but one of my parents might have stayed behind, and, who knows, they might notice me for once. I might have to come up with a story; no one could know I had been at the 'scene of the crime'. Some detective I made! I should have stayed there, taken photos or made videos with my phone, finding out what had caused the accident. Instead, I ran, like a coward.

I clenched my fists. Dammit! People would know I had been there because I had left something behind, my very distinctive hat, given to me by Makayla a couple of years ago. A grey denim cap with the word IOWA on the front and slightly frayed at the edges. It had blown towards the hunters' forest, but what if someone found it? Let's hope not. I could pretend to have lost it some other time and, luckily, no one had seen me wear it that day, but I hated lying as I wasn't good at it.

I reached the front door and pushed on the handle. It was locked. My hands shook so much it took a few attempts before I succeeded in extracting the key out of my pocket and could fit it in the lock. I knew the house was empty, but checked every room anyway before shutting myself in, in the safety of my bedroom.

My body trembled, and I forced myself to take my wet clothes off, shoving them at the bottom of the laundry basket before stepping into a shower as hot as my skin could handle. Even then, I still felt cold, so I donned my most comfortable and favourite pyjamas and curled up under the thick duvet of my bed.

I scrunched my eyelids and frowned; something scratched at my brain. Something I was forgetting.

The Iowa hat, perhaps?

No, not that, something else. Something important.

The image kept to the periphery of my vision, playing hide-and-seek, taunting me, and when I tried hard to retrieve the information, pain exploded inside my head, my fingers twitched, and my body shuddered with cold.

I climbed out of bed feeling sick and rushed to the bathroom.

I feel nauseous and reach for the door leading to the bathroom. I no longer have to feel my way there, knowing every inch of my cell: it is a padded room, and if I stand on my toes and raise my arms high, I just about graze the padded ceiling. The floor is made up of what feels like mattresses, and there is a padded door on one side – the kind of heavy fire door on springs you have to push hard to open before they close in again.

It leads to a tiny wet room with floor-to-ceiling tiles and lit by the most ridiculous faint blue light. Just enough for me to make out the outlines of a toilet and shower knob. No basin, so I have to put the shower on and scoop the water in my hands when I'm thirsty – I refuse to drink the bottled water, probably drugged. The shower head is in the ceiling, so I always end up getting wet, and it is also freezing here, I suppose, to discourage any lingering tendencies. Even the blue light is hurtful to my eyes after a while.

On the other side, a square padded door opens to a cupboard or cubbyhole approximately the size of a small fridge and is filled with plastic bottles of water. At first there was food, but I don't know who delivered it or when. I guess when I was asleep.

If cameras keep watch, it's too dark for me to figure out where they are, as there are no tell-tale blinking lights.

I have felt my way to every single inch of every room, as high as I could reach, but can't find any other door or issue anywhere. How did the food get here? How does he *get here? Does* he *drop from the ceiling?*

Once, I stayed in the bathroom for as long as possible, hoping there was an issue there, hoping to catch a glimpse of my jailer, but I suppose I passed out, maybe from hypothermia.

I woke up in my black cell with a warm body against mine. I fought hard and tried to move away, but my hands were held behind my back, then an arm circled around my neck, squeezing hard, and a strange mechanical voice whispered that I should never do that again.

4

MY EYES OPENED TO DARKNESS; someone had closed my bedroom shutters. The distant familiar sounds of chatter and cutlery reached me, and my stomach grumbled. I turned on a lamp, got up on weak legs and held on to the wall to steady myself. My throat was parched, but the glass resting on my bedside table was empty. I walked to the kitchen with my feet shuffling on the floor. Paper rustled, and I wondered if Dad was reading the newspaper at the table again, something that usually irritated Mum.

'It says here the funeral is next week; you're not making me go, are you?'

'Yes, I am!'

'But we didn't know them!'

'They were still part of this community, and we can't leave that poor boy all on his own. Everybody's going.'

'I'm going too,' I said, and they both looked up at me.

A glass dish held only remnants of a Shepherd's pie, so I grabbed a can of tomato soup from the kitchen cupboard before pouring it into a pan to heat it up.

Dad put his paper down and gave me a fake stern look. 'For two days, you've not been out of bed. Honestly, getting the flu in such glorious weather!'

He looked through the window, and I followed his gaze. The weather was indeed beautiful. Clear blue sky in contrast to the green grass and foliage with warm colours of bright yellow, orange, red, and deep purple. Butterflies fluttered past this late in the season, and I remembered it was Halloween. My breath caught; would the dead haunt me?

'I assume you already know about the Van Beers?' asked Mum as I sat at the table.

I looked down at my bowl, not wanting to meet her eyes and mad at myself for having made such a stupid mistake. They couldn't have found my hat. Mum would have known and mentioned it.

'I guess I must have heard.'

The news had likely spread through the village like wildfire.

'About the funeral—'

'I'm going.'

She nodded; there was no need to argue, and my parents knew this. I had come at a late stage in their life, a life with no thought or desire for children. They were fifty when they discovered they would be parents, and one could imagine their sense of panic, their feeling bewildered and unprepared. I had been raised on the side-line of their relationship, always feeling like an intruder, and I grew up being quiet, managing myself, and staying out of their way. In return, they asked little of me and argued none of my decisions.

'His name is Tommy…'

Mum picked up the conversation where she'd left off while I cut up bread to dip in my soup.

'He is twenty years old, so it was obviously a teenage pregnancy, and he's studying at a university in England. Lancaster, I think.'

Dad snorted, something he did whenever Mum found someone attractive, and I assumed the son was good-looking. I dreaded seeing him, still trying to keep the red figure with haunted eyes at bay, but I had to go regardless: no more cowardly behaviour.

A week later, I stood looking up at a gargoyle outside the church. Luckily and in spite of the sun, the weather had turned cold, and my trembling shoulders didn't draw attention. As expected, no other children appeared – the autumn holiday was over – but the village was well represented, considering no one had known the Van Beers. I suspected people had used the event as some form of social gathering. I had never attended a funeral and didn't know what to expect, except perhaps for other adults to frown at my presence. People had greeted my parents with warm words and handshakes, as they usually did, and either greeted me inadvertently as part of the package or ignored me as if invisible.

Cunningham had a strange, guilty look on his face as he came to shake my parents' hands. He gave me a weird malevolent grin and placed himself in my line of vision. Lately, Cunningham seemed to hate me just as much as I hated him. I stared at him while mentally picturing him on his knees, reciting a prayer, and I don't know what he saw on my face, but he eventually moved away.

A young woman with sleek straight hair approached us, and she looked so out of place in her royal-blue suit and high heels that all eyes turned to her. 'Mrs Robbins, hello, my name is Nikki Smet; perhaps you've read my article about the accident? I hear you're the go-to person when it comes to the village of *Les Vallées*, I would love to meet with you, perhaps later this afternoon if you have time? That would be perfect. I hear the son is on his way now.'

She hardly drew breath, and I must admit I was impressed.

The woman must be a great journalist!

She didn't look much older than Anna or Makayla, and despite her strong Belgian accent, she knew how to get what she wanted, even when dealing with a pro like my mother. She'd spoken quickly and with confidence, and instead of waiting for a reply – and perhaps giving Mum a chance to refuse – she'd turned everyone's attention to the road where the hearse would soon be coming.

She was right, too, as a few moments later, a vehicle appeared, followed by a dark van with tinted windows. A tall blond man wearing sunglasses hurried out of his car; he faced away to speak to the pallbearers, and they walked together into the church while the young journalist followed. I didn't get to see his face, but a strange resonant thud knocked in my chest, like a feeling of *déjà vu* I could not comprehend. I looked around, confused and wondering about this weird feeling, but maybe it was a simple case of Tommy Van Beers resembling his parents. I didn't get to dwell on the thought as the small crowd of villagers closed in on me, pushing me towards the entrance of the church. Cunningham suddenly rushed in the opposite direction, shooting out of the crowd as a voice behind me said, 'I don't think he feels well.'

'Is he hungover?' asked another.

A brief altercation held us up at the threshold, and Tommy Van Beers looked like he didn't want a journalist around as he argued with the young woman in a Germanic language. I wasn't tall enough to see him, and the journalist blocked the view. She seemed to want to put an arm out in a comforting gesture, but he pushed it away, and she left in a huff.

Then, before I knew it, we all stood behind pews waiting for the priest to begin. My parents settled in the second row, next to newly appointed Mayor Isabelle Boireau – Mum's best friend – and I positioned myself immediately behind them. Perhaps, at the time, feeling a little lost and insecure, I had wanted to use them as a shield; but it had been no use because when the priest informed us that 'we may be seated,' Tommy Van Beers chose that moment to turn around just as a ray of sunshine hit his blond hair through the stained-glass window, and his eyes met mine. His mother's eyes, the same haunted eyes, but where hers had been the colour of the ocean, his were the colour of honey, and where hers had been conveying despair and hurt, his were full of light and hope. His face and hair shone with a dazzling aura, and, for a moment, I believed in God and angels and all things bright and thought he was the most beautiful person I had ever seen.

I stood breathless, like after receiving a punch in the solar plexus. My heart was no longer beating to pump blood around my body but was melting inside my chest. I could almost hear the oxygen circulating in my veins, like a refreshing breeze on a hot summer evening. Particles of dust danced before my eyes, shiny and floating like stars in space, and I couldn't take my eyes off of his.

His look pulled me into his invisible bubble, as if he had always expected me to be there or as if I was meant to be there.

The service started, and my eyes shifted, staring at every corner and every intricate detail of the church to calm myself. A church that had previously seemed hostile, where I had felt out of place while getting caught.

But now, the building had a serene quality, filling me with a sense of belonging and acceptance, as if God had joined us to grace us with His presence.

My parents were not religious; I had no clue what a service entailed, especially not a funeral, and this was a novel experience. A little disoriented, I followed when at the end of the service, we were asked forward to dip a stick in holy water and sign before each coffin. A queue formed in the aisle. It was a rather straightforward process of signing and leaving through a side door, and then it was all over, no wake.

Most people moved on quickly, as they had gotten cold from the three-quarter-hour service, but I hung around the doorway: the Van Beers son was a solitary figure sitting upright, eyes unfocused but dry. He looked thin, cheeks sunk in, as if he hadn't been properly fed, but this did not take away from his beauty: high cheekbones, straight aristocratic nose, full lips, well-defined eyebrows and startling amber eyes. He should have looked sad, with trails of tears marking his face, or that's how I had imagined him to appear, but a strange placid look was pasted on his face, like a character in a video game: the valiant hero at the end of a war, who has gained the wisdom of a sage.

The church emptied. Father Prichet whispered in Tommy's ear and walked past me. I hesitated, shifting on my feet, and although he hadn't glanced in my direction since that first time, something about him seemed to pull me in, like an attractive force. I took a deep breath and sat next to him. He failed to react, but he did not push me away or tell me to get lost, so we sat together in silence, and quietude embraced me. A moment later, he rubbed his palms against his thighs, and his right hand brushed my left one. An electric jolt flashed throughout my entire body, and I looked up to see if he'd felt it, but he just stared impassively ahead.

The priest returned accompanied by eight pallbearers, all dressed in black suits with black ties and behaving so professionally they looked more like FBI agents. They worked in sync and lifted the coffins without a word; then it was an odd procession of two coffins, four pallbearers to each, then Father Prichet, followed by Tommy Van Beers and, a few steps behind, me.

We walked slowly to the cemetery a few metres away under the eyes of the remaining few who fell silent. Mum gave me a quizzical look, but I ignored her, and we marched on to the graves, two rectangular holes sitting side by side, each with a marble tombstone that seemed to have been mechanically slid aside. The coffins were lowered by two pallbearers who each turned a crank, grabbed spades and covered them with soil, and all the while, the Van Beers boy and the priest looked upon them in silence. I stared at the two mounds of earth. Father Prichet whispered some words of comfort and took Tommy's hands into his, but Tommy immediately slid them away and into his pockets as if he couldn't stand to be touched, yet there was no issue when each pallbearer shook his hand. They offered their condolences before leaving in silence.

I moved closer to be next to him, and we stood still and silent for so long that the both of us shivered with cold. I had never much liked physical contact – so unused to it as I was – and yet I longed to touch him, to grab his arm, to hold his hand, to hug him even, and found that I had to restrain myself. Tommy took his sunglasses out of the inner pocket of his coat and put them on. He whispered a 'thank you' while staring at the graves – and I wasn't sure who the words were meant for – then he left with a quick pace back towards the church car park.

A head popped up, and Cunningham rose from behind a low mausoleum, eyes stuck on Tommy, watching him leave with a pensive expression.

What was he doing? Was that his idea of spying?

He saw me looking.

'Graveyards, there's always something spooky about them,' he said.

You're the only spooky one here.

He came closer with a sardonic smile on his face and put his tall menacing frame right next to my small one just as black clouds covered the sun, turning my world dark.

Darkness, blackness, blue lighting – that's all I know now.

That first time I opened my eyes to darkness, I still knew nothing. I thought it was night, not fully awake yet. My head had felt woozy, but a gentle hand stroked my hair, a warm body against mine, a familiar scent, and lovely thoughts in my head. Was it a dream? Can you smell scents in a dream? I certainly did not want to wake from this dream.

I must have stirred because the hand stopped stroking my hair, and I felt disappointment: the dream will end.

The hand caressed my face, soft fingers feeling their way from my forehead to my eyes, nose, lips, then lips on my lips, a kiss. Heaven. The kiss deepened. The hand that was on my face was now on my body, naked body, warm hand leaving an imprint of fire where it went, and then my whole body felt on fire.

Love.

This is the person I love; I don't have to see him to know. I had waited so long for this moment. Was this real? Was this a dream? If so, I hoped not to wake up, not yet. I never wanted it to end. I wanted to feel more, to feel everything, deeper and forever.

Tears.

They fall so easily these days, but it's only because I know better now. If only time had stopped at that perfect moment. But the dream turned into a nightmare, and I am here in the dark, alone and in despair. I cry like I have never cried before, and it seems like I will never stop crying, body curled up on the padded floor, trying to make itself smaller and smaller.

I wish to be a baby again, to feel my parents' embrace, two people who had always been so removed from me; how I long to see them now! To feel their love, pure and easy, and I sob even louder because I will never see them again, and I am guilty, guilty of what I have put them through, guilty of what is happening to me; it's all my fault, and I am being punished.

I am lost in hell, and there is no way out.

5

I WANTED TO LOVE. My heart overflowed with generosity, and I skipped on the road as I followed a couple of squirrels gambolling ahead. I stroked Celia Smith's cat and buried my nose in the soft ginger fur, clapped to echo the flapping sound of pigeons flying away at my approach, tickled the ears of Anthony Dewsnip's Yorkshire Terrier, and waved at the cows grazing in the valley. The warm breeze plucked a red leaf from a sycamore tree, and I stopped to watch it twirl and sway as it fell.

It seemed hate wasn't the only driving force of my existence: Cunningham might have been my Geppetto, but Tommy Van Beers would be my Blue Fairy.

I ran to the barn and whistled to the donkeys, which brayed in response, distressed by my exuberance.

A truck was parked in front of the Van Beers' house, and people were loading furniture and other miscellaneous pieces into it, but no sign of Tommy. I did not dare approach, even if I was desperate to see his face again.

The problem with the Van Beers' house was that it rose off a lane in the middle of fields, with no trees surrounding them and no other house nearby. While my dad joked it was open to the elements and looked desolate, it meant that anyone approaching in any direction would be seen immediately; it had thwarted my spying on them. The house remained empty, and I felt its pull like a silent beacon, but it took weeks before I got the courage to break into it.

It had been winter then, and nightfall came early. I had put on my darkest and warmest clothes and made sure to charge my phone. I wasn't sure what to expect, but just like there seemed to have been some kind of connection and a message in the haunted eyes, I had hoped for the same inside the house.

The front door lock was old and basic, and it took less than three minutes for me to enter. I felt a surge of adrenaline, but my excitement died down as soon as my phone light switched on: the house had been stripped bare. The beam lit nothing more than stone walls and tiled floors, no fitted kitchen units, not even a toilet, just pipes coming out of the floor where, presumably, a bathroom had stood. Peter, Gretchen, and Tommy Van Beers had departed my world as mysteriously as they had entered it. Seeing their house like this left me feeling empty and disappointed.

Every morning I woke in a sweat; nightmares would haunt me at night, and I stayed up later and later, refusing to sleep so as not to see the red woman with her haunted eyes.

In the past, whenever I needed calm and inspiration, I would visit the Byrnes – though they didn't know it. Watching the couple and their ritual had soothed me: three or four times a week, often after 6 p.m., they would go through the clothes together, decide which outfit and what make-up Andrew Byrne would wear, then he'd transform himself to look like an elegant woman while his wife prepared tea. They would sit together at the kitchen table and eat triangular sandwiches and cakes while discussing all sorts of topics. Although their behaviour might have looked comical to an outsider, they displayed such mindful respect and gentleness to each other, and unlike my parents' relationship that shut everything and everyone out, their mutual love engulfed me even as they were unaware of my presence. It had a calming effect on me.

After a vivid nightmare, I attempted to break into their home as usual but found it difficult. I ran through the woods surrounding Dad's workshop, which bordered the north side of the Byrnes' large property and jumped over their small fence to access their garden. No sooner was I on their land than my palms sweated, my heart started palpitating and red and grey colours danced wildly behind my eyes, making me feel nauseous. I turned to the Van

Beers' house instead. Although it was an empty shell, I had felt the same serenity inside as when sitting next to Tommy, and I imagined that somehow the two of us were connected. I would sit cross-legged on the cold floor and let myself relax, doing breathing exercises and sinking into such peaceful rest that I often fell into dreamless sleep.

On a Friday morning in spring, before the Easter holiday, heavy rain lashed down, forming large puddles on the road, and we all huddled together in the shelter at the bus stop. A dozen hormonal teenagers in close quarters was a sure way to create tension, and Olivia Newbury kept running her mouth, boasting about her new relationship. Because the two of us were younger, the other kids ignored us, so Olivia's attention turned solely to me.

To say that I disliked Olivia would be an understatement. I detested her. It all started with an innocent remark I'd made in primary school about marrying Cunningham, and I never heard the end of it. We had been copying a poem, and Olivia kept giving me the cold shoulder, either upset or jealous about my upcoming move – I would be skipping the year after Christmas – and I had worked while ignoring her before sitting staring at Antoine's curls.

'I'm going to marry him,' she had said.
'Hmm?'

'When I grow up, I will marry Antoine. Who will you marry?'

'My new neighbour.'

It was so perfectly obvious that I didn't think twice, but my statement had Olivia laughing so hard she'd almost fallen off her chair. She had the entire class joining in with her mockery before telling me to stop being silly because, of course, *I* couldn't marry *him*. I was suddenly glad I'd be leaving her behind.

It turned out Olivia was mean and a bully. The sort of person who needed to make others feel inferior to boost her own self-esteem. I dismissed her, but Olivia never gave up on me because of Mum's influential character. Although she resented the fact that my parents were well liked when hers were barely tolerated, she occasionally stuck to me, pretending to be friends, chatting incessantly about this or that while trying to undermine me with little digs and taunts.

Her ranting about her new relationship with Antoine gave me the onset of a headache, and I eventually roared: 'Why are you telling me this? Just shut the fuck up and leave me alone!'

All the other conversations stopped, and Anna looked irritated. 'You really should show more respect, Mouse! That's no way to talk to her!'

I raised my eyebrows at Anna, surprised not only because she'd gotten involved but also because she seemed to take Olivia's side when, in fact, everybody disliked Olivia.

'I will talk to her whichever way I like; what's it to you?'

'It is that I don't like your attitude! She's done nothing wrong as far as I can tell! Perhaps if you had better manners, you'd actually have friends!'

What the fuck! Was the girl burning me right there and then? Who did she think she was?

I might have uttered a flippant retort, but sometimes it was best to judge the situation first: Anna was all beauty and no brains, but she had Ethan on her side, and that meant she had pretty much all the others on her side too. I glared but let it go.

The bus arrived, and I pushed past to be first on. I sat by the window and searched my phone for soothing music – Linkin Park. I put my earphones on, fuming inside, and tried to give off an aura of 'do not approach'. It can't have been successful because Daniel dropped on the seat next to me. I ignored him, leaned my head against the window and closed my eyes, but as soon as I removed the earphones, he said, 'That wasn't about you. Anna is into things like feminism, equality, and tolerance these days.'

Is that right? Isn't her eighteenth birthday coming up? Let's see how tolerant she is once she discovers she's been lied to her entire life!

Not long after, the 'Anna and Ethan business' was uncovered, and it became the topic of the town since it was like the formula of a bad telenovela: siblings raised as best friends who grew closer, check. Both sets of parents best friends since childhood, check. Short affair between one's mum and the other's dad, check. Cuckooed parties consoling each other in each other's arms, check. Things back to normal, but both women pregnant, check. Same father as one dad turned out to have low sperm count, check!

In the village, tension flared between their parents and Robert Wood's children. At school, a few kids made jokes behind Ethan's and Anna's backs, but they died down quickly as Ethan was an admired figure, and something else happened.

The school had gotten new automatic sliding doors during the weekend, and perhaps the work had been rushed because they were faulty and the mechanism was slow. One of the high school juniors – a guy named Alexis, built like a rugby player and renowned for his troublemaker antics – kept going back and forth in and out and making quite a show of himself. It was a Monday morning, just before the first bell rang, so a lot of pupils happened to be around, and the two supervisors on duty were busy elsewhere. Alexis walked at a normal pace through the doors instead of waiting for them to open, and his friends cheered and laughed every time he bumped into the reinforced glass door.

Then arrived Mademoiselle Chaumont, science teacher, old woman, always harried, stick thin in her pencil skirt, with a neck as long and flappy as a turkey's. Alexis stopped, and everybody went quiet. She gave him the usual telling off with all the dignity she could muster and was going to leave it at that, but with his back to her and thinking she'd already gone, Alexis muttered to his friends something like 'she's just deprived and needs a good seeing to', at which point she turned red and shouted at him to follow her in, then hurriedly turned towards the doors.

Maybe the mechanism had tired at this point because the doors did not open, and she bumped face-first into the reinforced glass. The rebound sent her spinning round straight into Alexis. He fell flat on his back, and she fell on her knees on top of him, her head buried in his crotch and both moaning in ways that could be misinterpreted. Hands holding phone cameras were raised, and shortly afterwards, a video entitled: *a dedicated teacher making a student happy* went viral.

Though the principal found a way to remove it, the damage had been done, and Alexis did not show up at school for a week, but Mademoiselle Chaumont took it in her stride. She turned up and declared to her students that, yes, they'd had a good laugh at her expense, but they came to school to learn about science and prepare for their exams, business as usual. It was a lesson to learn, and I mentally noted for future reference that it was best to confront problems head-on.

And problems came sooner than expected.

Problem number one: I got caught. It was always bound to happen, and I seemed to have lost all my abilities. I had been swift, agile, invisible, and had never felt guilt breaking and entering a home before. However, since the accident, a strange heavy weight pushed on my chest, making me sluggish, shaky, and uncertain. The only place I felt fine was at the Van Beers' house.

Practically setting up camp there, I had brought in a large floor cushion (from our garden shed), a small square pillow (from the living room), a blanket, a scented candle, and my favourite book (from my bedroom), as well as bottles of water.

On my way, I stopped first at Cunningham's, hoping to leave him a special little 'God' message by defacing the 'bodybuilder' magazine he'd bought earlier that day. It proved difficult, and I no longer felt joy in doing it, but the habit was difficult to break, and I resembled a junkie who would never get the same high but kept on taking the drug, trying to recreate that very first feeling. He kept the magazine in his bedroom, and as I grabbed it, a noise from up above caught my attention. Cunningham never went upstairs; he lived on the ground floor.

My head was getting dizzy, and a weight constricted my airways, but I pushed through and crept to the first floor.

A door hung open, which was unusual. I peered in and saw that the only bedroom free of clutter had been prepared for guests: Cunningham expected a family visit, it seemed.

He had never had a visit in the seven years he'd lived here.

I walked around the bedroom. The double bed had been freshly made and the sheets smelled of fabric softener. Logs burned in the fireplace, and an open laptop rested on a desk; I searched my pockets for a USB key – usually having one or two on me – and plugged it in. I loved technology; it made spying so much easier, but I had to work quickly, as I felt nauseous.

Night had settled by the time I got to the Van Beers' house. I entered furtively and closed the front door, but as soon as I turned, a bright ceiling light came on, and a voice said, 'It's you!'

I let out a yelp and backed up against the door.

He walked towards me and leaned both arms on the doorjamb, encircling me. 'What's your name?'

He was tall, and I was in shock. I hadn't expected to see his beautiful face again. He came so close that I could recognise the ingredients of his shampoo (coconut and sweet almond oil with an apricot fragrance). His blond hair was combed back and still wet, as if he'd showered recently. My eyes met his, and I couldn't look away: such beautiful eyes! The colour of golden syrup. The artificial light of the naked lightbulb above outlined a green tinge around the pupil, and his long lashes were so blond they looked almost invisible. I was mesmerised by his enquiring eyes, such captivating eyes. But they suddenly turned hard, with flashes of lightning in them.

'I said, what's your name? I won't ask nicely again!'

'Mouse.'

'Don't try to distract me, that won't work.' His voice sounded gruff and hard, but his English was flawless.

'N-no, m-my name is Mouse.' I was ashamed to be stuttering, feeling intimidated by his good looks, angry at myself for getting caught, and pondering why the only thought in my head was me wondering where he'd showered.

'How odd. What's your real name, Mini Mouse?'

'Robbins, Taylor Robbins.' My voice cracked and came out as a whisper.

'I see.' He looked me up and down, and his eyes caught the magazine in my hand; realisation dawned on me, and my cheeks burned. I tried to hide it behind my back, but his reflexes were quicker than mine, and as he leafed through the pages, my shame turned to humiliation.

'Well, well, well, you little freak!' He raised his hand, and I thought he was going to slap me, but he stroked my cheek before grabbing my face, then pushed my head against the door, pinned me down with his body, and murmured in my ear, 'I do not appreciate people breaking into my house and using it as a fantasy fuck pad, do you understand?'

The sudden cursing and violent behaviour shocked me. I tried to reply, but fear kept me paralysed, and his thumb was painfully digging into my neck. He pushed harder, and I let out a pathetic whimper.

'Do you understand?'

'I didn't, I swear I didn't!'

'Let go,' he said, and for a second, I didn't know what he meant, then my eyes followed his to see that my hands had instinctively grabbed hold of his arm. I hesitated, and he squeezed my face harder. 'Let. Go!'

I let go of his arm, and his hand released my face, then his features softened, and it was an incredible thing to watch, from demon to angel in an instant.

He snickered. 'Seriously? A little thing like you being turned on by this sort of thing. Who would have thought?!' He patted my head and stroked my hair as if I were a pet. 'Do it then!'

'W-what?!'

'What you came here to do, let's have a show, call it repayment for invading my home. I'll sit right there and watch.'

He pointed at the cushion and blanket on the floor, and I stood speechless. He sighed, pointed at his body with the magazine, opened his arms and raised an eyebrow. 'Or do I have to take part? There's only me, though. Clearly that's not enough!' His fingers paged through the magazine again, and he snorted. 'And I look nothing like those freaks!'

Realising he was mocking me, my fear and humiliation turned into rage, and I found the strength to push him away. 'It's a misunderstanding, asshole!'

I turned to open the door, but once again, he was quicker than me and caught my arm.

His face and tone turned serious and menacing. 'Careful there, you still broke into my home, remember? You'll need to face the consequences.'

'Please, I—'

He put his index finger on my mouth, interrupting me. 'Shh! Don't squeak, Mini Mouse. You're a Robbins. Isn't your mother cosy-cosy with the mayor?'

I nodded.

'So, I'll tell you what I'll do: I'll let it pass this time, and, instead, you will do something for me when I ask. And you will do it unless you want Mummy dearest to know about all this…' He gestured towards my stuff with the magazine and opened the door wide with an evil grin. 'Run along now. I'll be in touch.'

I ran home in the night, anger and shame burning in my heart. I had never been so humiliated in my life.

At home, I slammed my bedroom door, threw books, kicked furniture, punched my pillow, and screamed with rage. Had it been anyone else, I would have used one of my little 'secret' bombshells to retaliate, just like I had done with Anna, but he was as equally mysterious as his parents, more so, in fact. And what was even more frustrating was the fact that I felt attracted to him. I deflected, turning my anger towards Cunningham and searched my pockets for the memory stick, but it was nowhere to be found!

The next day, my anger had subsided, but Olivia – problem number two – irritatingly sat next to me on the bus ride home. I seldom saw Olivia at school, as we were not in the same class; in fact, because I had skipped a class, we were not even in the same year and were taught in different buildings – though we shared the same playground. She also usually sat far from me, towards the back of the bus, but Anna's remark must have given her confidence, and she joined me to mess with me.

She kept quiet throughout the journey but as soon as we got off the bus and while the seniors walked on ahead of us, she relished giving me the tiniest details of her and Antoine's relationship. I tried hard to ignore her, but after two minutes of hearing about 'Antoine this' and 'Antoine that', I told her to shut up and leave me alone.

She pounced on me like a predator on its prey. 'You want to kiss him, don't you?'

'What?!'

She'd completely lost her mind if she thought I'd be interested in an oaf like her boyfriend.

'Oh, I bet that's what you were thinking.'

She had a smug look on her face. I tutted, shrugged, and tried to resume ignoring her, but she pressed on. 'Antoine is pretty, isn't he? I remember how you used to stare at him, and I have noticed how you look at pretty boys, especially Ethan and his bulging muscles. He is dreamy, isn't he?'

'You're off your rocker!'

She'd got it wrong, making it easy for me to dismiss her. Yes, Ethan had classic good looks and the body of a Greek Adonis, everyone admired him, but before Tommy came on the scene, the person I would most likely have had a crush on was Daniel; he was... beautiful. There really was no other way to describe him. His beauty shone through from the inside. He may not have had a square jaw or a fit physique, but he was kind, mature, considerate, reserved, tender but strong, the epitome of a proper gentleman.

Olivia's face displayed a look of satisfaction, and I realised I might have given myself away.

'Bet you find it hard to sleep at night and just fantasise about him.' She put on a mock plaintive voice. 'Poor, poor Mouse, who's never been kissed, dreaming all night long of kissing boys.'

I considered pulling on that ridiculous short plait of hers or pushing her into the stinging nettles that bordered the road, but a moan startled the both of us.

'That's not very nice!'

Tommy Van Beers. He stood in the middle of the lane, arms crossed, looking more gorgeous than ever with his blond hair swept to the side, young Justin Bieber style. Even Olivia, who always had something mean to say about everybody, was speechless and looked impressed.

He put his tall frame in front of her and leaned down to face her. 'I hope I'm wrong, but it sounded like you were dissing my mini mouse here?'

'I—who, huh, y-you…' Olivia flustered and looked petrified.

Although my cheeks had turned red for getting caught at my worst again, it was satisfying to see that it had not happened only to me. Perhaps he had that effect on all people; perhaps that was his strength, I thought, the confusion between his warm angelic face and his cold, harsh voice.

He turned away from her and put his hands on my shoulders, leading me on. 'Come on! I'll walk you home; you and I have business.'

The red of my cheeks spread to my ears, but I was happy to leave Olivia looking jealous, stunned, and… was that water pooling in her eyes or just a trick of the light?

We rounded a corner, a few metres from Daniel's home, and Tommy leaned an elbow on my shoulder. I didn't expect the move and tripped; my shoulder bag fell, and we both leaned to pick it up, bumping heads. His face almost grazed mine, and I stared straight into his eyes. Next thing I knew, my lips brushed against his, soft and warm, hesitant at first but firm after realising he had not pushed me away. My body pressed against his, and my eyes stayed open, watching, mesmerised, the sensuous movement of his jaw as I kissed him.

He pulled away, our bodies parting, and mine felt cold, as if plunged into icy water.

'I've kissed a boy now,' I said with a trembling voice.

'Yes.'

He turned on his heels and stalked off.

I remember it well, the first kiss we shared. It had felt like breathing air, like my entire life had been spent under water searching for breath, and he gave it to me, the kiss of life, invigorating, sensuous, moving, and wonderful.

I get lost in the memory while warm hands massage my body, the scent around me a strange mixture of baby powder and antiseptic.

Wait! There really are hands massaging my body. He is here. How did that happen? Was I drugged again?

I make sure never to drink from the bottles, forcing myself to endure drinking the lukewarm water from the shower.

Was it the food?

I can't even remember the last time I was fed. In order to keep me weak, I was given very little. Yet he is here now, oily hands feeling their way around my muscles, kneading them, easing the pain and stiffness away.

Oh, how I want to hate him! I hate him!

Except I don't! So grateful for his presence, and I am so alone in this world like he is.

And I need him, want him, love him for eternity.

His words echo my thoughts as he whispers, 'I love you' again and again, and I don't recognise the voice, but it doesn't matter because he's been using so many voices. I know who he is.

He kisses me, and I want to tell him I love him too, that I am sorry, that I want to see his face, and we could be happy together if he let me go, but I dare not.

The fights are rare but terrible. They hurt not only my body but also my pride. Today, I will not fight. Today, I need his love. I want him to take me into his arms and hold me tight, to kiss it all better and never let me go. I want him to never leave, and I make a silent wish: take me with you, don't leave me here, alone and in the dark.

Take me away. Please.

6

HOW COULD I POSSIBLY CONCENTRATE?

I had a history essay to write, maths exercises to complete and a science report to finish. I also had to read a French literature book and prepare for a Spanish oral test. Teachers were so annoying. Why did they all give copious amounts of homework at the same time? Did they have special meetings where they plotted while rubbing their hands together to make the students' lives as miserable as possible?

Sitting on my bed, staring at my open laptop, words and images unseen, I replayed the scene of the kiss in my head, over and over, trying to give it meaning.

Whatever possessed me to do that?

His eyes had pulled me in like an enchantment, unable to stop myself, and I'd longed to do it. I'd caught him by surprise. He hadn't wanted this, had he? Was he attracted to me? Or had he pitied me? Should I apologise? Round and round it went, hour after hour. Oh, such torture!

I had no choice but to go see him; he said he and I had business, but he never got the chance to tell me what, and that was the perfect excuse.

After supper, when both my parents were at the other end of the house in their bedroom watching something on Netflix, I left through my bedroom window like a thief in the night. Tommy was home: light seeped through the gaps of the brown aluminium shutters. I knocked at his door, but he didn't answer, and I knocked harder again with no reply. I turned the handle, and the door opened.

It took a few seconds for my eyes to adjust to the bright light, its source coming from a massive chandelier hanging from the ceiling. That was new, yet I had the feeling I'd seen it before. Directly underneath, Tommy sat in a small baby-pink armchair with his head down, unmoving, with half a dozen empty cans of beer at his feet as well as two other empty bottles of alcohol.

I called out his name, but he didn't move. His fringe hung loosely, sheltering his eyes, and I couldn't see his face. Was he even breathing? I moved closer. Behind him was a large wooden table covered with plans and designs for the interior of the house. After calling out again and failing to get a reply, I crouched in front of him and put a hand on his shoulder to shake him. His head popped up like a jack-in-the-box.

'You shouldn't be here!' He was drunk and slurring his words, eyes bloodshot, his English slightly accented. He grabbed hold of my sleeve. 'Do you know what I study at university? Psychology, ha! Do you know why?'

He tried to get up but fell back down on the chair, and having glimpsed my small sofa cushion behind him, a small bubble of happiness rose inside me. I looked around and saw that my blanket, book, and bottles of water were still where I'd left them while the candle rested on the table.

I reached for a bottle and handed it to Tommy, but he didn't take it; instead, he grabbed my jumper. 'Do you know why people study psychology?'

I shook my head.

'Nine times out of ten, it's because they want to know what's going on inside their own head. That's what I wanted to do too; I always had a feeling there was something twisted inside there.' He pointed at his head. 'Why else was I… but this, this is… I must have gone crazy for a second.'

He stood up with difficulty and made a retching sound. I looked around for a bucket, bowl, or rubbish bin, but there was nothing more than the table and armchair. I held his waist to support him and directed him outside, but we got stuck trying to open the door. He leaned on me, and we found ourselves in a similar position as the time he caught me trespassing, only this time my cheek rested on his chest.

I lifted my head to look up at him; his forehead butted against the door, eyes closed. My body was sandwiched between him and the door, and, after a while, my back started aching, but I didn't want to move. He wore a navy woollen jumper, and the rough fabric tickled the right side of my face, but I didn't care. I gripped him with both arms, encircling his waist, and listened to his heartbeat. I held on tight and wished to stay in his embrace for ever, but I got greedy and slipped a hand under his sweater to stroke his back. My hand must have been cold because he came back to life.

'You shouldn't be here,' he repeated. 'But I knew you'd come. I've been waiting all day.'

'You have?'

'Either you or the police. I'm happy it's you, or maybe not. Maybe they should lock me up!'

'Why?' I knew as soon as the question was out. I had been so self-involved, so concerned with my own thoughts and feelings it hadn't occurred to me to see things from his point of view. 'Is that why you drank?' I asked.

'How old are you, anyway?'

His eyes filled with such hope: perhaps I looked much younger than he realised, perhaps he was not the monster he feared. For a split second, I considered lying to reassure him, but that wouldn't be fair. Besides, I wanted him to know everything there was to know about me, in its whole and simple truth, so I told him. 'Fourteen.'

He fell into a crouch, put his face in his hands and let out a desperate cry, half animal, half human, which turned into a sad laugh. Unsure what to do, I kneeled in front of him and ran my hand through his hair – it felt as soft as I had imagined.

'It was just a kiss,' I said eventually. 'No big deal.'

'No big deal? No big fucking deal?!' he shouted with sarcasm. 'I molested a… underage…' He squeezed his eyes shut.

'It's alright. I kissed you, not the other way around.'

'You don't understand!' He raised both his voice and his head. Tears were running down his face, and I thought: there were no tears at his parents' funeral, but there are tears now.

'That first time I saw you at the, the…' He hesitated.

'The church?' I encouraged.

'Church…' he repeated inanely. 'Do you know how much I hated that priest touching my hands?! Oh, the church, yes, yes, you're right. Anyway, you were such a vision, your hair pushed back by the wind, I thought, you can't be real… I thought…'

He was either drunk or imagining things. The church hadn't been draughty, and the day of the funeral had been a crisp, cold, but windless day. It made me smile.

'You looked so… surreal…' he repeated, then pointed at his chest. 'I'm a perverted idiot! A fucking molster!'

Perhaps he meant to say monster, or molester, maybe both. He started muttering while punching his own chest, and I moved my head closer to hear what he was saying, but he mumbled in a language I couldn't understand, probably Flemish or Dutch or whatever it was called. I grabbed his fist to stop him punching himself, and he threw me an aggressive look. 'No! I'm not a paedophile!'

Taken aback by his outburst, I tried to keep a cool head and reasoned with him.

'Of course not,' I replied. 'That's your heart you were pointing at. Love does not discriminate, and paedophiles are perverts who want to do dirty sexual things to kids. Is that what you want to do?'

He stilled, looking almost sober as he dried his face clumsily with the back of his hand. 'Actually, no.' That threw me because the whole time he had been lamenting, I had wanted to take him in my arms, console him, kiss him and do many other things.

'You're right.' He grabbed the back of my neck and pulled my face close until our foreheads connected, and I could smell the alcohol on his breath. 'Yet there is some kind of connection between us, isn't there?'

'Yes.'

He let out a sigh. 'I don't know why I returned your kiss today. I shouldn't have! It was a stupid thing to do and… I'm sorry.'

'Don't be sorry,' I said in my gentlest voice. 'I love you.'

The words were so sincere they slipped out of my mouth before I even realised.

Tommy stood up, ran a hand through his hair, and agitatedly started pacing. But he couldn't walk straight, and he lost his balance. He leaned against a wall to steady himself, pointed a finger at me, but he was swaying like a ship in the sea, and the words came out of his mouth with difficulty.

'See, see! Oh my God! What have I done?! One kiss and you already think you're in love. What would a fourteen-year-old know about love?'

My blood boiled, but I had to calm myself. Now was not the time to react impulsively, to reinforce my youth and immaturity in his eyes, no. I had to behave like I thought an adult would, so I grabbed his arm to still him, looked him in the eye and tried to keep my voice as steady as I could.

'Okay, look, sorry, but it's true. I fell in love with you the moment I saw you in that church, giving me the same look you're giving me now, it had nothing to do with the kiss. What you felt there…' I tapped his chest. 'I felt it too. Why would the love of a fourteen-year-old not be as valid as that of a twenty-year-old?'

'Because it's illegal, that's why!'

'It's illegal for you, the adult! To touch me, to kiss me, to do anything to me, but what if I, the child, took charge?'

'Huh?'

I was surprised by my boldness, but my determination was fuelled by desire, and I started unlacing one of my boots. 'Put your hands behind your back,' I told Tommy.

'What are you doing?'

'Just trust me, or are you scared?'

Tommy's bloodshot eyes opened wide, blinking at me. He put his hands behind his back, and I used my shoelace to tie them together, then I sat him in the armchair and told him to stay still and close his eyes. I took his face in my hands and put a gentle kiss on one eye, then the other, then on his nose, then on the lips.

'See, what can you be accused of when you are drunk and powerless, and I'm the one taking advantage?' I whispered.

I kissed his ear, lightly bit it, then kissed his neck, moving downwards, kiss by kiss, to his collarbone, then up again to his chin, exploring with my lips, my tongue, grazing, scratching with my teeth. I kissed his bottom lip, sucked on it; he let out a soft moan, and my mouth was on his, harder now, going in for a deeper kiss. I wondered how far I could go, wanting to do more, but he was drunk, and it was wrong to take advantage. I knew that much, at least.

I untied his hands, sat on his lap, put his head on my shoulder and stroked his hair until a deep breath escaped from his mouth. It felt so right and so peaceful to be with him that I never wanted to leave.

We slept in each other's embrace for part of the night until the cold woke me. I covered Tommy with my blanket, put my shoelace back on, and walked home in a cloud of euphoria. The moon was a small crescent with a light orange tinge, and I felt like howling like a crazy, happy wolf.

Once home, I lay on my bed, arms behind my head, with a smile on my face and closed my eyes, but I didn't feel like sleeping anymore. Instead, I wanted to replay the past events in my head, over and over.

My smile turned into a grin at what Tommy had said – about seeing me with the wind in my hair – and I visualised us both as anime characters facing each other, me with the wind blowing my hair away and him with a bright aura shining behind him. However, the image immediately disappeared to be replaced with another: the massive shiny chandelier with its sparkling lights, and I remembered where I'd seen it, looking like a dark spider. It had been in Cunningham's house.

Liam Cunningham. Why am I dreaming about him now?

It's the smell of cookies, the same that always lingers in his house, and it taunts me. My stomach grumbles and contracts so much it hurts. I move toward the cubbyhole, feeling like I'm floating, when there is a snickering sound, and fear paralyses me. My captor is here. Has he been watching me? This has never happened before; I have always awakened to find him touching me.

I hesitate, unsure of what to do or what he expects of me and scared that if I make the wrong move, I might be hit; I wouldn't see the blow coming, unable to protect myself. He is quite capable of anything; I am sure of it, but my stomach is torturing me, and the need for food is greater than my fear.

I give a hint of a forward step but sense him moving, and I stop. Plastic wrap sheet crinkles, and now he is by my side; he has moved like a ghost so swiftly and easily that I am sure he can see.

He feeds me slowly despite my hunger. The cookies are warm — they've been freshly baked — and I am surprised he's feeding me these cookies. Perhaps he wants me to choke on them. However, I suspect this is a reward. It's been a while since I've been troublesome.

I eat cookie after cookie, trying to count how many, but it's like I can no longer count, and I lose track; then a container of milk is pushed against my lips, and he uses his hand to wipe my mouth and the crumbs off my face.

His mouth rasps against my ear. 'Now shower, you stink.'

I know better than to disobey.

I push the door to the wet room and make a show of how hard it has become and how weak I am now. If there's still compassion left in him, he might feed me more. Unlikely, but you never know. I look back and try to catch a glimpse of my captor, but my prison has been well designed; when the door is open, it blocks the blue light behind it, and my cell looks black and empty.

7

I DIDN'T FALL ASLEEP until the early hours of the morning, and even then, a nightmare woke me. Blood-covered bodies with deformed oversized blue eyes had moved towards me like puppets on a string, opening their mouths to scream, but no sound would come out and instead, they swallowed everything in their path, chanting, 'to be, to be, to be...'

I walked to the bus stop with my head down, irritated because the bright weather didn't match the foggy sensation inside my head. My feelings were conflicted every time I remembered the events of the previous night. On one hand, it had been the best night of my life, yet the sight of that stupid chandelier had spoiled it all. How did that thing end up in Tommy's house? Did he buy it off him? Was it just another one that looked the same? So preoccupied with Tommy, I had neglected my usual spying activity. I didn't know anything anymore.

There were only two things I was certain about: I loved Tommy, and I hated Cunningham.

The sound of footsteps made me turn my head, and Jade ran past me, brushing against my sleeve before joining the others at the bus stop. I paused to look at them all and noticed an almost imperceptible divide between the boys and the girls: the boys sat or stood under the shelter, at a distance from each other, with Ethan and Jamie towering over everybody else, while the girls stood on the road huddled together, chatting.

Undecided, I hesitated before sitting next to Daniel and regretted it straight away as he reeked of tobacco. Leah was helping Juliet readjust the hood of her jacket while scolding Jade. 'We always meet early. Why are you so late?'

'Some guy had an appointment with Dad about building work, and I had to keep the pets away. I thought he might be some useless city person, but once I saw him, I didn't want to leave. His face is a work of art! He's the son of the Belgian couple from the village, the ones who died. Have any of you seen him?'

Jade's dad was a builder, while her half-brother worked as a woodworker/cupboard fitter. They lived close to the bus stop at the north end of the village, which meant they didn't get the view over the river, but they owned the most beautiful house in the village: a large conversion-barn property on two acres of land and many outbuildings, all renovated stonework. Her family was big on environmental issues, and they produced their own organic food. They had a large permaculture garden, a small vineyard, paddocks with horses, a hen pen, two goats, two cats, and a blue-eyed husky dog.

'That must be the guy I saw yesterday on the road; he's going to be my future boyfriend,' replied Juliet, clapping her hands together.

Jamie snorted. 'Doubt it, the dude is totally gay.'

'You think everybody's gay!' laughed Makayla.

'I was right about Pelletier, wasn't I? I have an excellent gaydar.'

Guillaume Pelletier was the school janitor and had recently married a local firefighter.

'Maybe you're the one who's gay, then,' pointed out Juliet.

'Fuck off, I'm not! Take your clothes off right now, and I'll prove it to you!'

'Mouse knows him,' interjected Olivia.

They all looked at me, and my cheeks reddened.

Owen hunched closer to them and hissed in his raspy voice, 'Uh oh, speak of the devil, I think that might be him coming this way.'

All heads turned left and peered at the end of the lane, where Tommy's figure advanced with energetic steps. Why was he here now? What was he going to do? The divide between male and female disappeared as everybody flocked together on the road, even Daniel, who had been rolling a cigarette with a questioning look on his face that said, 'What hot guy?'

I remained on the bench, solitary, making myself as small as I could while Owen declared, 'This could be the moment of truth! Put Anna in front; if he checks out her rack, then we'll know he's not gay.'

'Dude, that's my sister you're talking about!' said Ethan in mock anger.

'Sorry, still can't get my head around that.'

Jamie put an arm around Ethan's shoulder. 'You do it, then. You know gay people like you; take off your jacket and flex your muscles as soon as he's near.' He turned to Juliet. 'If I'm right, you'll owe me a kiss.'

She rolled her eyes and shook her head. They waited with expectation, curious to see what Tommy would do, and I bit my bottom lip with apprehension, wondering what would happen. I couldn't help but look but dared not move.

Tommy nodded at Jade and walked past her to go straight to Ethan – as if there was no one else but him – and introduced himself. He seemed quite fresh-faced and showed no exterior signs of a hangover. For a moment, my mind buzzed with fuzz, as if I had been the one drunk the night before. It took a few seconds for my hearing to clear, and I didn't catch the beginning of his speech.

'… This Saturday, I'm having quite a lot of trees delivered, and I'll need a workforce to dig holes; four or five of you will do.' He looked at the boys surrounding Ethan. 'It will be hard work, but I'll pay, and I have beer – Belgian, of course.'

Jamie nudged Ethan and Ethan took his jacket off. 'Is this the kind of muscle you need?'

Tommy laughed and gave Ethan a pat on the shoulder. 'Perfect! I'll count you in.'

'Can the girls help too?'

Juliet approached him, twirling a strand of her curly red hair with a finger, and froze, leaving everyone perplexed. Tommy had his back to me, so I hadn't seen his expression, but I'd had first-hand experience of how quickly the look in his eyes could turn lethal and perhaps she'd seen it too.

'No girls. They tend to distract men, and the work will be slow. See you Saturday at nine sharp,' he said to Ethan and Jamie before leaving.

No one talked for a long time as we watched him walk away until Owen broke the silence. 'Okay, is it weird that I couldn't stop staring at him?'

'Told you, a work of art,' said Jade in contemplation.

'I know,' replied Ethan. 'He sure is a pretty boy. He looks like a doll.'

'He has that androgynous thing going on, I guess,' added Makayla.

'Well, that doesn't mean he's gay!' said Juliet with a pout, but Jamie stuck to his guns.

'You heard him, no girls!'

'Yes, exactly. He doesn't want to get distracted!'

'Wow! Some people really hear what they want to hear!'

The bus arrived, putting an end to their argument – one I could so have easily ended. Bags were picked up, and we readied to get on. I gave a last glance at Tommy's figure receding in the distance; he hadn't even looked at me. When I turned back, Olivia was staring hard at me, and she sniggered before climbing on. Had she seen us kiss?

The day felt too long, and the lessons didn't go well. In chemistry, while distractedly changing the ink cartridge of my pen, I got ink all over my desk, my white lab coat, and my hands and spent most of the lesson washing everything off. In French, Mr Dupuis asked us to analyse a passage in *Les Fleurs du Mal*, and I mumbled to classmate Dimitri that Baudelaire had smoked more opium than usual. My whispered words weren't as quiet as I thought, and there was a look of shock on the teacher's face. Not because of the remark, which I'm sure he'd heard many times before, but because I was an excellent student, making no waves, never getting into trouble, my motto being to go along to get along. He reprimanded me lightly, then forgave me with an indulgent smile, and the lesson resumed.

Lunch consisted of a blurry mess of meat and lentils, but it looked like things might pick up when I saw Antoine standing on his own in the school playground:

people on their own made easy targets. I looked around to make sure Olivia was nowhere near and pounced. 'How are you doing?'

He hesitated, throwing a quick look over his shoulder to make sure I was addressing him and not someone else, and I didn't give him time to respond.

'I'm sorry, all right. I know break-ups can be tough, but hey, I'm sure you can do better. No, you deserve better.'

'What are you talking about?'

I put on my best act as if discovering I'd let the cat out of the bag by inadvertence. 'What? Oh nothing, sorry, I… sorry, bye.'

I tried not to smile as I walked away. Inflated ego, always so predictable. It was a crass thing to do, not to mention childish, but that would teach Olivia not to mess with me.

I kept losing focus in PE. We played badminton and rotated partners, and each one of them scolded me for being distracted and missing the shuttlecock. They let out grunts of disappointment because I normally excel at sports, but every time I looked up, thoughts of the chandelier would pop into my head, and my reflexes slowed.

When we got to the engineering lesson, Madame Rigaud already appeared to be in a bad mood, then she kept on sighing and glaring at me while droning on about firewalls. It wasn't until she removed the ruler from my hand that I realised I had been hitting my book, making a constant, irritating tapping noise.

'Would you please stop it and concentrate on what I'm saying, it's essential information you will need!'

I almost replied that I would never need her lesson, that the school's firewall was so weak anyone with basic computer skills could hack into the system in less than fifteen seconds, but I managed to keep my mouth shut. When the last bell rang, I leapt from my seat and rushed out the door without a word.

A regular school day finished at 5.30 p.m., and because of the many stops, the bus journey took a good thirty minutes (appalling, as it would take a normal car just around ten), but the sight of Olivia in tears cheered me up, the rumours being that Antoine had dumped her. I hadn't expected my remark would go that far, but I felt pleased and not at all guilty, thinking that if their pathetic little relationship couldn't stand a tiny misunderstanding, it wasn't worth much to begin with.

Not being particularly fond of lentils, I got home just after 6 p.m. quite famished. I hoped there would be something good for tea but found the house deserted. Dad was probably in his workshop tinkering with an old Renault Alpine model he was rebuilding, and Mum was God knows where. I made myself a sandwich, annoyed at my parents for not having prepared food when I needed it.

At a younger age, I had contemplated the idea of what it would be like to have normal young parents. Parents who would show an interest, ask 'how was your day?' or 'what did you do in school today?', take me on picnic outings, have energy for the amusement park, the zoo or camping holidays, but I quickly stopped dwelling on it. Truth be told, the independence and freedom their lack of parenting gave me ended up suiting me to a T.

I resisted the urge to go straight to Tommy's house, it being too exposed during the day. As it was April, I had a few hours to wait until night and, for the first time in a while, I had nothing interesting to do. I watched music videos on my phone.

Later, the dark shadow of Tommy's house hung over me; no light sipped at the windows, no sound came from within. Where was he? I sat on the steps by the door, waited and unfolded my stiff and aching body around midnight to walk back home.

The next morning, I called the school to let them know I couldn't attend because of a cold. It wasn't far from the truth, as the night had seen me tossing and turning in my bed, unable to sleep. I skipped lunch to sneak to Tommy's house, lunchtime being a suitable time to move unseen as people congregated around kitchen tables or appliances to prepare and eat food.

Our villa lay in a corner plot, right at the south-east edge of the village, and we got a view of the valley on both the east and south sides; because of this, the front garden was much larger than the back, and the lane didn't officially start until Cunningham's and Celia's houses. I walked out the ever-open front gate and turned west, past Cunningham's house on the left and the junction after, the Wood and the Dewsnip houses on the right, a barn and small paddock with donkeys and further along, in a solitary plot and surrounded by open fields, was Tommy's home.

A white van idled in front of the house with the inscription *Moreau's plumbing and bathrooms,* and I waited outside, sitting in the exact spot as the night before. After a brief time, two men in black-and-grey uniforms came out and greeted me, unsurprised to find me sitting there, then they climbed in their van and left.

Tommy stuck his head out, then stood at the threshold, arms crossed.

'You saw me arrive, then,' I said.

'What are you doing here? You should be in school! Go home!' he replied, frowning, but I squeezed past him and entered his house.

The pink armchair had been moved and no longer sat under the chandelier. I walked to it, slid my hand on the fabric, then along the edge of the table, leafed through some plans, picked up a paper cup that had held coffee before putting it back and looked at everything except Tommy. I wasn't sure of how much of the previous night he remembered, if he remembered anything at all, and there was no clear sign from Tommy.

'You're upset,' he said. He came closer, moved to take my hand, but stopped the gesture. 'I'm sorry about what happened before; it was a momentary and stupid thing to do, and I take full responsibility, but there cannot be anything between the two of us; you are just a child. Actually, we shouldn't even acknowledge each other. You understand, don't you?'

I nodded. 'If that's what you want. I will always do whatever you want.'

I raised my eyes to gaze up at him, watched his Adam's apple moving up and down as he swallowed hard, then moved away to stand directly under the chandelier and pointed at it. 'Where does this come from?' I had tried to keep my voice as neutral as possible, but my tone still came out sharp.

'Oh this; it's quite beautiful, isn't it? Liam gave it to me.'

Liam. Not 'Cunningham' or 'Mr Cunningham' or 'your neighbour', but 'Liam'. He threw the name like an arrow piercing my chest, and I felt light-headed.

'Are you okay? You look awfully pale. Here, why don't you sit down.'

Tommy directed me to the chair, looking both concerned and helpless. He looked so adorable it hurt.

'I didn't know you knew Cunningham?'

'What?'

Tommy ran a hand through his hair and looked at me sideways. 'I don't, not really. He's just been kind to me.'

I bet he has.

'I don't want you anywhere near him!'

I was as surprised by my outburst as he was, and upon seeing the questioning look in his eyes, I wanted to justify myself. In a split second, these thoughts ran through my head: 1. He likes men, and you're the most beautiful man I've ever seen. 2. He'll corrupt you because that's what he does. 3. He wants to harm me somehow. 4. I hate him, I fucking hate him! But none of these reasons would seem reasonable to him, who had just arrived in the village and knew nothing about anything, and so, despite what it made me sound like, I lamely settled for, 'He likes men.'

Tommy tilted his head, raising his eyebrows.

'You remember that magazine you found me with?' I explained. 'That was his!'

Tommy laughed. 'Well then, I'm definitely not his type.' He made a show of raising his shirt. 'No, not enough muscle…' Then he pretended to look in his pants. 'No, too average.' He kept laughing, not realising how serious the situation was for me.

'Please, stay away from him,' I pleaded. 'Please, stay away from his house or anything to do with him!'

He heard it then, the concern in my voice, and he crouched in front of me. I hated the gesture; I had seen parents do that, putting themselves at eye-level with their kids when speaking to them, and it made me feel insignificant.

'Mouse,' he said, putting a hand on my knee, 'I can't do that.'

'Why not?' I knew everybody knew everybody in our small village, but all he had to do was keep his distance.

'Because I live there.'

I feel hot, and it's unusual.

Normally I don't enjoy showering; there is only one small hand towel to dry myself, and, afterwards, it always takes a while for my body to warm up, but I do it anyway just for something to do. Boredom is the worst enemy. Today something has changed. The room feels hotter than usual, making me thirsty, and a dull tapping sound irritates my ears.

It comes from above, and it's the first time. There's never been a sound before, and it gives me hope that maybe I will be released soon. I always knew I would be released; this strong conviction never left me, kept me going whenever I was on the brink of abandoning hope because of one undeniable truth: my kidnapper loves me. His love is flawed, of course. What does one really know about love? But I believe him when he says he loves me; he always has, right from the start, and this love has been the raft I've held onto in my sea of despair.

I wonder what the tapping sound is. It's quite regular. Is it possible someone is trying to rescue me? I should do something.

My fist thumps the padded walls, trying to echo the rhythm of the tap-tap outside. I yell as loud as I can, but I have difficulty finding my voice at first, and when I do, it is hoarse and weak. I keep hitting and screaming, but, eventually, the tapping sound is no more. What happened?

It is quiet now. I let myself fall to the floor, spent and sweating. Tired, I lay my head down and close my eyes.

Perhaps I was wrong all along, and there is no hope.

8

I WOKE UP LATE to a concert of loud screeching sounds: birds were fighting. I slammed my shutters open, and the magpies and crows flew away, flapping their wings in anger at my intrusion. It was a beautiful morning, sun already high in the sky, with no cloud in sight, but a hundred metres next door loomed Cunningham's house. It felt like torture knowing Tommy was so close yet out of reach. I sighed and stretched my arms; he'd left the house, anyway, and I imagined him with the other village boys, shirtless, sweaty, and bending over digging work.

In the kitchen, Mum and Ann Byrne had set up an assembly line preparing sandwiches, no doubt for Tommy and his helpers, while Dad was on tea duty. He filled up a Thermos, praising him. 'He's more sensible than his parents, at least. Not to speak ill of the dead.'

I found the expression silly, as he had done exactly that.

The entire village buzzed with the news of Tommy and his tree-planting feat. I angrily slammed two pieces of bread in the toaster while Dad handed me a mug of milky tea, oblivious. The whole village would hang around Tommy's house at some point during the day, with an excuse of checking on the progress or helping out, and I made the decision that I was not going to be one of them.

'He must feel odd living in his parents' home without them and so lonely,' said Ann while buttering a piece of bread. She wore surgical-looking gloves that stuck to her hands, giving them a glossy doll-like look.

'He's living at Liam's at the moment,' replied my mother.

'Is he?'

'I don't think that young man is used to living on his own. Liam recognised him from the funeral, and they got chatting. Tommy said he wasn't sure where he would stay, and Liam offered a room.'

'Oh, that's our Liam, how very Christian of him!'

I snorted at the same time as the toast popped out. Dad, who stood closest to me, heard it and gave me a warning look. I frowned, unaccustomed to seeing my dad look at me that way, or in any way, as my parents were just the extras in the movie of my life.

In the past, whenever I got reprimanded – which seldom happened and just for show in front of outsiders – it had always felt fake, like they had been going through the motion or reading from a script of what it is a parent should say on such-and-such an occasion and they would leave it at that, job done. But this time, my dad's eyes flickered with irritation, and I wondered if I'd missed something. After all, I had been out of it lately, other thoughts occupying my mind, and I didn't care. I found nothing interesting anymore, not my spying, not my extensive knowledge of people's secrets, and I'd stopped all that.

All I thought about was Tommy. The contrast between his blond hair hanging in front of his amber eyes, the mole on his left ear, making it look like a piercing, the high cheekbones that gave him a young Elvis look when he smiled, the lips so full they made him look feminine, the protuberant Adam's apple that would move up and down as he spoke and the smooth pale skin free from stubble.

The doorbell rang, pulling me out of my reverie, and just in time too, as my body had started to shiver and tighten with excitement.

'Must be Andy, I'll get it,' said Ann, and she removed the gloves on her hands and went to open the front door. It wasn't Andy; instead, Juliet and Anna walked in looking like they'd gotten dressed and made up for the catwalk.

'Hello, girls,' said Mum. 'Don't you two look lovely!'

'Thanks, Mrs Robbins.'

'Is that in honour of our new resident?'

Anna emitted some sort of non-committal sound while Juliet pretended to deny it, and they both asked if it would be okay for them to be the ones to hand out the sandwiches. Mum agreed with a smile and dropped her voice. 'Listen, I don't mean to burst your bubble, but I think that young man already has a girlfriend.'

Whatever Anna or Juliet replied, I didn't get the chance to find out. The tea I was sipping went down the wrong way, and I started coughing, fighting to catch my breath while Dad slapped my back as hard as a blacksmith hitting hot iron, not realising he made it worse by hurting me.

The girls left with the sandwiches and Thermos, and I glanced at Mum, surprised she had let it go so easily. This would have been her opportunity to 'infiltrate', 'spread her roots in' and 'lord over' Tommy's life like she had done everyone else's; she must have had another card up her sleeve.

And what was that about a girlfriend? I stared at Mum, trying to get past the short fashionable dyed-blond hair, the roundish smiling face that gave her a youthful, innocent look despite her age and tried to catch her blue eyes. However strange this might sound, I had always found it difficult to look Mum in the eye. There was something too bright about her face, like staring at the sun. Dad didn't have this problem, on the contrary, and as a small child, I had often caught the way he looked at her and understood he was madly in love with her. I would imagine their fairy-tale meeting, love at first sight and happily ever after; she would stare back at him, and the intimacy between them seemed to shut out the entire world. It made me feel uncomfortable, like I had no right to witness it and no right to share it, and I would make myself scarce.

Looking at Mum then, while she chatted with Ann, I wondered if she was pretty or if I looked like her. I'd inherited Dad's eyes, our best feature, vibrant blue eyes framed by long dark lashes. People always commented on them.

A desk drawer in my bedroom secretly held photos of my parents as a young couple: early eighties hairstyles, short shorts in summer, thick turtleneck woollen jumpers in winter, but the quality of the photographs was poor, and the faces always seemed slightly blurry, as if my parents could never stand still long enough for whoever took the picture.

Mum remained a bit of a mystery even to that day. Although my knowledge of other villagers was quite extensive, I had never attempted to learn about my own parents, as though they were taboo subjects. Where exactly did she get all her info? Did she spy on people too?

I pondered for a moment and went back to my room, deep in thought. It was odd that Cunningham, a closeted gay man who had spent his life hiding, would welcome a young man into his house. From his point of view, this could become a potentially dangerous situation, and tongues wagged easily. And had he, in fact, made it to the funeral? I remembered he had left looking sickly, only to reappear at the cemetery once Tommy had gone.

I shook my head to clear it and looked around my room at a loss for what to do: my favourite pastime had always been to spy on people; it had occupied me every day outside of school, and I knew who smoked weed or who stole alcohol from their parents – and it wasn't always the ones you would expect. Some spent most of their free time in front of a screen playing video games, while others were hooked on TV series, manga books, podcasts, vines and memes or fangirling over the latest pop/rap/K-pop star. I had experienced all their interests by proxy.

What to do? Go out – to the park, the forest, or the cinema in town – or throw myself into work? The assigned French literature book lay on my desk, and I picked it up: *The Outsider*, Albert Camus. I read the first sentence: 'My mother died today.' Well, that was cheerful! I opened my laptop and checked out the list of movies for the day, but nothing took my fancy. My phone beeped, and I read the WhatsApp message – Don't forget! Entire class invited to mine today, 2 p.m. – followed by emoji balloons, a party face, and an address. Salvation!

After a quick shower, I checked my reflection in the mirror, popped a spot on my chin and brushed my longish hair. I hesitated about what to wear as it was hot out but stuck with jeans and a T-shirt and headed to town on my bike in search of a birthday present.

***

'You're on your own?' asked Marjorie, one of my classmates, throwing a look behind my shoulder as soon as I walked in.

'Don't mind her!' said birthday boy Baptiste as he pulled me into an outer room with a long table pushed against a wall covered with sweets and snacks of all kinds, piles of paper plates, plastic glasses, and an assortment of fizzy drinks. 'Help yourself and come out, everybody's by the pool at the moment.'

He rushed away, and I barely had time to wish him a happy birthday or hand him his present. *Oh boy, what have I let myself in for?* But despite my aversion to crowds and the silly drunken behaviour of a few who had smuggled in beer, I had an enjoyable time, as my classmates were nice. I managed to almost not think of a certain someone. Marjorie stuck to me like glue, hoping I would soon introduce her to 'his hotness Jamie' (her words). She then joined a small group of people who jumped in the pool, leaving me free to enjoy the afternoon chatting with whoever stayed on dry land.

I got home around dinner time, stomach full of birthday snacks and cake, and went straight to my room. Without kicking my shoes off, I dropped onto my bed, exhausted. A knock on the windowpane startled me awake. Clouds covered the moon, and I couldn't see out, but nobody had ever knocked at my window before, and it was an easy guess as to whom it could be. I turned on a lamp and walked to the window; Tommy stood in my mum's flowerbed, a few inches below me, and stared straight into my eyes. His hair was wet and combed back, and the smile he gave me almost knocked me sideways. My hand trembled as I opened the latch.

'I took a chance,' he said instead of a greeting. 'There was no light, but your shutters were open. So were the gates, so presumably, no pets?'

'The gates are never shut, and my father is allergic to… pretty much everything except his cars.'

He laughed, and a thousand tiny bells jingled in my heart.

'I… Er…' He hesitated and slid a nervous hand through his hair. 'I worked hard today.'

He wasn't boasting, and it wasn't a reproach either. His eyes displayed a tinge of insecurity, maybe disappointment too; after all, the look said, every single person from the village had been to see him work, except for me. An uncomfortable silence stretched. I turned around and grabbed my phone, turned the torch app on, and switched off my bedside lamp, then jumped past him out of my room.

'Show me,' I said, and we walked side by side in the night, bats flying overhead and donkeys braying as we passed, all the way to his house.

Even in the dark, it looked immediately different. Unfamiliar shapes and shadows emerged. A small hedge now surrounded the entire rectangular garden, and a large number of trees had been dispersed throughout; it must have taken all day to plant. The smell of garden compost and animal manure lingered in the air, a light breeze pushed the clouds away, and part of the moon appeared.

Tommy sat on a patch of grass, arms on his knees. 'It doesn't look like much now, especially in the dark, but give it a few years, and it will look much more like a garden.'

He yawned, stretched his arms, and lay down flat with his hands behind his head, and his shirt rose, showing a hint of a flat white stomach. My heart thumped, my mouth dried, and my body tingled. I ran my tongue over my lips. I wanted to do so many things just then: reach out and touch, feel, smell, taste. Did I dare? I kneeled next to him and laid a hand on his chest.

He sat up, startled. 'What are you doing?'

I said nothing and kept looking in his direction, but only saw an outline of his face, and I couldn't read his eyes. My hand slid up to his neck, then to the side of his face, and his breathing became loud and ragged. I moved my head closer.

'No,' he whispered, and I froze. But what did he expect, lying down in front of me like that? Surely, he wanted this too. I forced him down with my body and pressed my lips hard on his while sliding a hand under his shirt, but he was stronger than me and pushed me away none too gently. I fell back on my butt.

'Mouse, no!'

He sounded like a dog trainer scolding an unruly pet, and dejected, I almost wanted to cry.

We both sat in the dark in silence.

The moon didn't cast a light strong enough for me to see his expression, and it meant he couldn't see mine either. A jumble of emotions ran through me: hurt at being rejected; frustration at my desires being unfulfilled; elated because I had felt him harden against my body, but also surprised because I had feared Cunningham had traumatised me forever. I realised that when unwanted, something could fill you with disgust, but when desired, it was the most beautiful and natural thing on Earth.

The rejection had stung, though, and my pride was wounded. I threw a distressed look at Tommy and wondered what he was thinking, when his body moved closer.

He grabbed my head with gentle hands and murmured close to my ear. 'You're so impatient, but you have to wait. It's the only thing you can do… wait until you're a grown-up. You may not like hearing it, but you're just a child, Mouse, and nothing will happen between us. I can be nothing more than a friend… or a brother figure… at best. But if as an adult this is something you still want, then I'm prepared to wait, however long.'

I am waiting, waiting to die.

I'm in the shower, squatting on the tiled floor with my head between my knees, and I sit here for a long time. The shower was on until the water turned freezing cold, and my skin wrinkled. Eventually, something or someone turned the water off, but I haven't moved, and my body is shaking uncontrollably. I don't know how long I've been here, and I don't care. Nothing matters anymore, not the cold, not the hunger, not the pathetic blue light, nothing.

I am prepared to die. I want to die. Who's going to miss me, anyway? The only person I love — the only person I've ever truly loved — has betrayed me, sequestered me, degraded me to this useless wilted pathetic creature that I have become; what possible reason is there to live? If I weren't so weak, I'd let out a snort of derision: so this is what my life amounts to.

I suppose I deserve this. Wasn't it my fault? Didn't I start it all? Did I make the first move? Or did he?

Memories form a confused jumble inside my mind, and it's hard to think. I raise my head and turn to look at the blue light until it becomes fainter and fainter. My vision tunnels and everything turns black.

Hands and knees scratching at the tiled floor, I crawl back to the padded room, but the ground suddenly disappears under me, and I'm free-falling. A bruised hand rubs my aching back, and I see my reflection in a darkened window. My face has morphed to look like an old man! I scratch at the rough beard in wonder when a figure appears behind me. There's no one there as I turn around. I stare back at the blackened window until, once again, the world disappears.

I wake up lying on my back on the warm sand, and the sun is so bright that I raise an arm to cover my eyes. The tide comes in, and the seawater licks my toes, in, out, as if nudging me to move.

A shadow stands above me, blocks out the sun, and brings with it the familiar citrus scent of an aftershave. He holds out a hand, and I try to grab it, and that's when I come to.

Back to black, but I am wrapped in a thick duvet, and a warm body embraces me. I stiffen, expecting the worst, but he holds me tighter, possessively, and whispers, 'Silly, silly, you scared me.'

9

I STOOD WAITING AT THE usual kids meeting point: a small crossroad with the statue of a silver Jesus on a wooden cross at the north-end side of the village, right between a small copse of trees where bees were building a hive and a field of pungent rapeseed that made my nose run.

My back leaned against a tree trunk, but not for long, as I couldn't stop fidgeting, filled with anticipation as I was. I had organised a little day trip to the seaside, and Tommy mistakenly thought others would be joining us. He had said to treat him like a big brother, and I had taken advantage of his ignorance; because, of course, he didn't know the comings and goings of the villagers like I did, and I had made it so it would be just me and him. Just the thought made my heart so full it seemed like it would overflow.

We'd already spent a few nights of the Easter holiday together despite his reticence, talking until the early hour of the morning and getting to know each other. Every time, he started by pushing me away, trying hard to send me back home, but I was persistent, wearing him down with relentless visits until he gave in – I wasn't going to let a little thing like age get in my way.

Tommy and I had quite different tastes: I liked maths and logic, while he preferred the arts. He said that if he hadn't chosen psychology, he'd have studied literature and poetry instead (despite his tough demeanour, he had a very gentle soul). He liked old-fashioned movies like *Psycho* and *Citizen Kane* while my favourite movies were *The Prestige* and *The Shawshank Redemption*. I liked alternative music, preferring guitar sounds when he enjoyed classical and piano-based music. Tommy had a hypnotic presence, and my mouth ran almost despite myself, disclosing minor secrets about the villagers. One evening, we were sitting side by side on his lawn, one earphone each, listening to a murder mystery podcast when he asked, 'Why "Mouse"?'

'According to my mother, I was a toddler who crept around "as quiet as a mouse", and the nickname stuck. For five years, I thought it was my name, then I started school and discovered my official name was Taylor. It came as a shock.'

A bee circled my head, dispersing the memory, and I swatted it away. I peered in the distance, anxious for Tommy's arrival, and checked the time on my phone. My heart raced, and I hoped my plan would work. Just me and him, away from here and far from prying eyes. My head was spinning at the thought, seeing a million stars and rainbows in a bright blue glittery sky.

He pulled up in an old black Toyota Celica, and I jumped in.

'Where did you get the car?' I asked, trying to distract him.

'Friend of a friend, you look nice.'

My ears burned. I had spent an unusual amount of time trying to decide what to wear, wanting to look 'cool and sexy but not in an obvious way', which had turned out to be more difficult than expected. Tommy seemed to have paid extra attention to his choice of outfit as well, and a warm bubble of happiness spread all the way up from my chest to my brain, making me light-headed. He wore dark-blue chinos, a dark-blue shirt with a small cream flower pattern and a light-brown suede jacket, which looked expensive. He had combed his hair back, was clean-shaven and emitted a faint spicy and musky smell. For a moment, I wondered where he'd had time to make friends close enough to lend him a car but let it go.

'Where are the others?' he asked as he looked around.

I shrugged. 'They can't make it.'

Tommy threw me a suspicious look and hesitated. I prayed he wouldn't cancel and let out a discreet breath of relief when he put the car into gear to drive away.

Tommy drove fast on dual carriageways, irrespective of the speed limit, and aggressively on other roads, overtaking slower cars as soon as the opportunity presented itself. His face was filled with concentration, and his eyes fixed on the road, now and then looking up at the sky as if to check on the weather. It got cloudier as we advanced west, but no rain was forecasted, which meant little, as the region had its own microclimate, and, to me, weather was inconsequential. There could have been a heat wave or a snow blizzard. As long as I was with him, nothing else mattered. I almost longed for rain, imagining us stuck in the car, windows misted over, seats reclined, me shivering with cold and Tommy leaning over after taking his jacket off and covering me with it in a caring, protective manner.

'What are you smiling about?'

The question snapped me out of my reverie, and I looked through the side window to hide my reddening cheeks. We had left the main road and were passing through a small seaside village. Pine trees bordered the road, and each house had a name. The sea was not yet visible, but its salty, fishy smell filtered in through the air con.

'Where are we?'

I suppressed a yawn and supposed I had fallen asleep. Tommy looked to park the car, and the twisty, winding motion had woken me. The sun shone through an opening between fluffy grey clouds, the sky seemed to shine like sparkling silver jewels, then I realised I was staring at the sea, and it faded straight into the same-coloured sky, leaving just the faintest of horizon lines.

As soon as we got to the beach, the wind whipped my hair in all directions, lashing my face with salt and sand. I took my shoes off and ran on the wet sand like a child. Tommy laughed, his face bright and his eyes shining with happiness. It reminded me of the first time I'd laid eyes on him in church, and I wished I could have clamped him in my arms like smooth softwood in a vice, smothering him with a thousand kisses.

We walked on the beach, barefoot, pant legs folded over, kicked freezing seawater at each other, unearthed a few seashells before throwing them back on the sand and searched for crabs or other sea creatures in rock pools. Time passed like in a dream. The sky turned dark and the air filled with humidity; we retrieved our abandoned shoes and walked along the coast to an open crêperie. I had had a vision of us sharing a large seafood platter, but it turned out Tommy wasn't fond of shellfish.

The restaurant was large but felt cosy with its dark interior. It had a view over the sea on one side and a small harbour on the other and was already half full of patrons. We found a secluded spot in the corner, and it started raining outside; Tommy left to use the facilities just as a smiling waitress arrived at our table. 'Can I get you anything, or would you prefer to wait for your big brother?' I stared at her, speechless. She'd made an assumption, and to her defence, it was an easy one to make – we were both blond and pale in a part of France where the locals tanned easily, and we'd conversed in English – but she'd echoed Tommy's words, and it left me with a strange feeling of inequity. I dismissed her with a wave and moved to another table, to an area with a different server.

Tommy and I took our time with our meal, ingesting a large amount of food while self-mocking our own appetites, and it felt comfortable to be with him. He finished a dessert crepe smothered with caramelised apples, chocolate sauce and whipped cream, then raised his head. 'When's your birthday?'

'October 29th.' I rubbed the back of my neck. Did he want to know when I would be fifteen and legal? It was six months away, and although he had said we should wait, it still felt like an eternity. I looked at him with uncertainty, but his face remained neutral, then his gaze fixed on the blank wall behind me, spacing out. It dawned on me that my birthday had also been the day his parents died.

'Do you miss them?' I asked, but his gaze remained on the wall, and a long silence stretched between us.

'I shouldn't. My parents abandoned me.'

My eyebrows rose, and he explained. 'My mother was only sixteen when I was born. Her parents were strong Catholics, and they disowned her, pretended that neither she nor I ever existed. My father's family came from money, and we all lived together until the day my parents disappeared, leaving me with a grieving grandfather. But he was in no condition to look after a child, and Grandfather sent me from one boarding school to the next, far away in England.'

Tommy ran a hand through his hair, and I wasn't sure what to say. I tried to imagine the words of comfort my mother would have given in this situation, but he added, 'My parents never visited me once. I spent my childhood waiting for them, hoping they would come get me one day; instead, I spent my life abroad in private schools and summer camps… and not once did they visit… I hardly saw them, so I never really knew them at all. Parents are supposed to love their children unconditionally, but I'll never know if mine did.'

Nothing showed on his face, no sadness, no bitterness, no emotion whatsoever, as if he had just been recounting the story of a stranger. I was suddenly angry at his parents; I had tried to spy on them and hadn't learned much, so there hadn't been many feelings towards them, but how could they not love him? It was unimaginable.

'What about your parents? How did they meet?' he asked, and I shrugged.

'Before they took early retirement, Mum was CEO of a big cosmetic company in London while Dad was in the marketing department.'

I hoped Tommy wouldn't ask more than that because I would have been quite incapable of answering. That was as far as my knowledge went. Tommy gave me a dazzling smile, got up from his chair, fished out a wallet from his coat pocket and gestured for the bill.

'Let's go! I want us to take pictures, first in front of the islands, and then we'll drive to the house of former president Clemenceau.'

The strange request made me smile, and despite his revelation and the gloomy weather, we left the crêperie in good spirits. It had stopped raining, but large puddles on the uneven surface of the car park reflected a feathery sky, and we each took a convoluted way to reach our respective sides of the car. I smiled, imagining that from up above, we must have looked like the spasmodic spin of insects on their backs trying hard to flip over.

We drove north along the coast and stopped at a market in the next town; the holiday was ending, and Tommy would go back to university soon. He wouldn't return until August, and I wanted to get him a little something special. While strolling among the stalls, I racked my brain for an excuse to separate from him, and, although feeling like a spoiled child, I asked him to fetch me a Coke from a drink dispenser further away.

As I watched Tommy leave, a hand tapped my shoulder. 'Excuse me, little girl, you might like this.'

I turned around to face a short bald man standing behind a jewellery stall.

'I'm not a little girl, I'm just short like you,' I pointed out. He looked startled but just gave me a condescending smile.

Jeez, what was it with these people? It was lucky Tommy wasn't around, or how could he take me seriously?

Something on the market stall caught my eye, a small silver pendant with an angel and demon intertwined. I had never seen Tommy wear any jewellery and wasn't sure if he would like it, but it was very fitting, and I bought it.

On the drive back, I couldn't help but think about what Tommy had said about parents and unconditional love. Did my parents love me? They had never said so. They did everything they were supposed to: fed me, clothed me, put a roof over my head and bought me everything I asked for, so I supposed they did. Did I love them? I wasn't sure as it is hard to love what you don't know, and yet… I looked at Tommy's profile; he was so handsome, and it felt so right to be with him, but what did I really know about him? Not much, yet in the short time I'd known him, he'd shared more about himself than my parents ever had.

I realised why my own parents had never been the subjects of my spying: I'd have preferred for them to communicate with me, share with me, and pay an interest to me. I hadn't wanted to find things out for myself. They should have told me their story themselves, but they never had. My parents were so in love with each other, so used to living as a couple, that they had created an impenetrable bubble that shut everything out, even their own child. They were so consumed with each other they had no more love to spare. I could understand that; I could accept that. I had just discovered love myself and knew it was difficult to put the feeling into words. It was like Tommy was an extension of me, as if I had lived my entire life with a limb missing but unaware of that fact until he came along.

The journey home felt far too short; soon Tommy would be gone, and I wanted to savour every second with him. He stopped the car at the drop-off point, and I sat gazing out, reluctant to leave. Tommy ran a hand through his hair, and my eyes refocused. I gave him the gift I'd bought earlier, which was in a tiny purple-and-turquoise paper bag. He took great care in opening it and lifted the pendant to the light, then he thanked me with a smile and moved closer. Thinking my luck was in and that he would kiss me, I leaned my head towards him, but he just patted it, and I thought, what the hell was that? Then he grabbed his jacket from the back seat and dropped it on my lap. 'I have something for you, too.'

'Which pocket?'

He laughed. 'No dummy, my jacket. I'm taking far too many things back with me already, and it won't fit in my suitcase, now it's yours.'

I stared at him. Forget the silly pat on the head; this was the best present ever! The fabric looked expensive, as did everything I'd ever seen him wear.

Tommy had style, and he seemed to like quality, preferring natural fibres, always 100% cotton, wool, silk, linen and even cashmere. Wouldn't it be too shameless for me to accept?

I was going to hand it back when he smiled. 'To be honest, it feels a bit tight. I probably got a size too small, and you're doing me a favour by taking it. I think it will look good on you.'

I walked home with the jacket on, holding the lapels tight around my neck. Cunningham stood in our kitchen with his back to me. He turned around, saw the jacket, and frowned, and I saw he had a big purple bruise on the left side of his face, going from his ear to the bottom of his neck. I heard a hiss, and something pawed at me.

What the hell!

He held a small grey-and-white cat in his arms. 'This is my new pet,' he stated, rubbing under the chin of said pet. 'Cats are very good at getting rid of rodents. He's still a bit wild right now, but I will train him to eliminate the vermin that hangs around me.'

Subtle.

I laughed aloud: poor pathetic Cunningham. He was declaring war, and he thought his best weapon was a baby feline!

Dad sneezed and coughed.

'Sorry, Clay, I forgot you were allergic. I'd better skedaddle.'

Once he'd gone, Dad stopped sneezing, and he rubbed his chin. 'I wonder how he got that bruise? It wasn't made by a kitten, and it looks nasty.'

'He probably messed with the wrong *man*,' I replied, and Mum gave me an exasperated look.

'Shut up, you've been gone all day; now go get changed, and you can help us with the cooking. You'll peel the potatoes, and we'll have chips tonight.' She turned to Dad. 'It couldn't be… that young man, could it?'

Wait, wait. She wasn't talking about Tommy, was she? He wouldn't do a thing like that, would he? Is it possible Cunningham came on to him, and that was the price he paid?

Yet it seemed unlikely.

Cunningham wouldn't take the risk of exposing himself so openly, and he had a type: big buff bearded men; and while Tommy felt strong, he had a feminine look about him. Besides, despite his age, Cunningham kept fit, he'd be able to take on a skinny lad like Tommy, which is precisely what I told my mother. But doubt is insidious, and as I peeled potatoes, half a dozen scenarios ran through my mind.

Doubt fills my mind. That voice – the one that kept calling me silly – sounded like it wasn't disguised, and I've heard it before. Although I can't place the accent, it is familiar, and yet it is not the voice I expected.

I slowly regain consciousness and realise things have changed; there is so much noise, and it takes a second to place the sound: birds singing. I am so happy to hear them that tears have inadvertently formed in my eyes. I move to wipe them, but my arm is stuck.

I try to move my body, but I have been tied spread-eagle on a soft surface, like a mattress or a bed. My wrists and ankles are shackled, and as I struggle to free them, I realise my head has been covered with a cloth, and my mouth has been gagged. I panic and in doing so, struggle to breathe. There's not enough air reaching my lungs through my nose, and the cloth sticks to my face, rubbing against my eyelashes. I let out a shout, but only a low moan comes out through the gag. My heartbeat is now galloping, and a pounding starts in my head.

I don't want to die! The thought creeps in and surprises me, and I realise there is still fight left in me. I have to live; I have to calm myself. It's just another form of punishment. He is trying to break me, but I won't, I mustn't.

A faint light comes through the dark cloth, and I concentrate on it; it is less dim when looking to the left. As I wonder what it could be, my heartbeat slows, and my breathing gradually returns to normal. I try to get a sense of what is happening, but the hammering going on inside my skull is making it difficult. Why is my head covered? Why have I been tied down? But most importantly, what does the change mean?

The creaking and clanking sound of a door interrupts my thoughts. I turn my head to the right, toward the noise; there's a movement of air followed by the soft sound of footsteps. As they get closer, the space around me turns frigid, and the hairs on my body rise. I hold my breath, trying hard to listen to catch the tiniest of clues, but the birds outside are oblivious to my fear and irritatingly keep singing their merry tunes.

A hand touches my leg, and I scream.

10

'YOU'VE GROWN.'

He grinned and ruffled my hair, and I was so happy to see him that I forgot to mind.

'Shall we?' said Mum, pointing at the door, and the three of us entered. The house looked good, so different from the empty shell it used to be, and I hoped Tommy would like it. He hadn't been able to return in the summer – something to do with an internship at one of the branches of his grandfather's company – and he'd left the last additions of his re-decorating project in the hands of my mother. A clever move as Mum was a member of the community with connection and influence: not only did it ensure the best artisanship and a job done to his specifications, but in trusting Mum with the job, he'd also earned her respect and loyalty.

As in our home, the front door opened directly onto the living space. To the left, a country kitchen with a bar and a wooden sideboard, still empty, the dining area in the middle with the wooden table from before and six padded chairs. The living room was to the right with two large leather sofas at an angle, side tables, a large wooden bookcase, and at the end of the room, stairs leading to the bedroom and bathroom above.

Three of the Petersons joined us before checking the upstairs floor: Jade, holding a basket of fresh fruits and vegetables, her dad, Elliot, and her brother Jack (technically, Jack was a Smith and not a Peterson as he was born from Jade's mother's first marriage). Tommy appeared to be popular with the locals.

Unlike his parents, who had been discreet and never got to know anybody, Tommy had involved many of the neighbours in his affairs. Mum had had the key to his house and collected his post – which read Mr T. B. Van Beers. She'd also been in charge of supervising the work and receiving deliveries of his furniture. Elliot had done some renovating work while Jack installed the fitted closets, Daniel was given the job of mowing the lawn and looking after the garden, Ethan and his dad had rewired the internet and dealt with other various electrical fittings, and Tommy had always used the Wilkins' taxi service – Leah's family – to go back and forth to the airport.

It was annoying to see that I would have to share him with many people that day, but no matter, because the next day was my fifteenth birthday, and we would finally be together.

My parents were eating breakfast when I walked into the kitchen. 'What do you want to do on your birthday tomorrow?' Mum asked.

'No need to plan anything. I'll be spending the day with my boyfriend.' The toast that Dad was about to bite into never reached his mouth. Instead, his hand stopped mid-air while the toast dropped on the table, butter-side down, making a soft wet sound. Mum paused; she had a certain sparkle in her eyes.

The thing about my mother: she loved attention, and she loved drama, whether positive or negative. She savoured hearing about incidents happening to someone she knew, but even better if it came from me, the uninteresting and neglected child.

There had been that same sparkle back at primary school when my parents, having failed to turn up at organised meetings with my teacher, were summoned to the headmistress' office, and Mum had almost skipped with glee wondering what trouble I'd gotten myself into. She'd walked on air for a short while as the news spread that my IQ was high and I would skip a year, but then I let her down: I adjusted and integrated well into my new class, made no waves, and didn't even have the decency to be properly bullied.

'Boyfriend, huh?' Mum cleared her throat and moved closer. 'Does this boyfriend have a name?'

I looked my dad straight in the eyes; his were open wide, face so pale one couldn't help being reminded of Harry Potter's owl.

I faltered before replying. 'Tommy.'

They shared looks of confusion, then Mum stuttered, 'Tommy? What Tommy? Tommy who?'

Crash! Dad stood up so savagely that he sent his chair flying backwards. 'I'll fucking kill him!'

He ran in a flash, leaving both our mouths and the door open, and I had never seen my dad move so fast! He had almost reached the junction in the lane past Cunningham's house before Mum and I caught up with him, and as luck would have it, a few people happened to be out putting up Halloween decorations.

'Dad, wait!'

He heard me and stopped dead in his tracks. Dad turned around to face me, fists clenched so hard the knuckles had turned white. His face was red, his eyes filled with fury, and the aura of rage surrounding him was so strong that it reached every person in proximity. There was a sudden, tangible silence as all eyes turned to him. He looked at me, and his face softened, then he lowered his head as he stuttered, 'W-w-what has he done to you?'

I couldn't quite understand the sudden interest he showed towards me and sighed. 'Sadly, nothing.'

It was the wrong thing to say, combined with the wrong attitude. His right hand came slapping so hard across my face that I started falling sideways, but he'd grabbed me by the collar.

'What the fuck, Taylor! WHAT THE FUCK!'

Gasps of shock and exclamations of surprise erupted, and my father, realising what he'd done, let go of me and stared at his hand in bafflement. For a moment, nobody dared approach. My father had always been a mild-mannered man, a cool-tempered man who seldom swore. I had never seen him angry – never heard him call me Taylor either – but he was tall, and tall people, willingly or not, cast a menacing shadow, even more so when angered. Eventually, muscle-boy Ethan came running and asked if I was okay while his father put himself between me and Dad, acting as a barrier.

'Clayton, what's this about?'

He got no reply from Dad, who still looked dazed, and turned to my mum. 'Elaine?'

Before she could reply, Dad grabbed hold of his arm. 'Give me a hand,' he said, dragging Robert Wood with him, and I rushed to take hold of Robert's other arm to slow them down, knowing they were on their way to Tommy's. In turn, Mum pulled on my shirt to stop me, then everybody else followed, and, despite the gravity of the situation, it all looked quite comical because we somewhat resembled the unruly procession in the fairy tale of *The Golden Goose*.

Almost a dozen of us reached Tommy's house. On the way, I tried to block out the questioning murmurs of curiosity and wondered why there were no clamouring responses from my mother. I thought hard of a way to stop my father from murdering my future boyfriend, but there was no chance of stopping Dad, who advanced quick-paced and determined.

Without knocking, he slammed Tommy's front door open so hard it bounced back. We hurried behind, but Dad stopped short in front of the dining table. Robert and I crashed into him as we walked through, and the three of us met with the most romantic and domestic scene.

Tommy wore jeans, but his feet and chest were bare. He held a coffee pot and stood next to a young woman with sleek straight hair who sat at the end of the dining table wearing nothing more than a large man's shirt and socks, holding a mug up. It looked as if Tommy had been about to pour coffee when we barged in. Soft piano music played in the background, and if it hadn't been for the wide-eyed look of shock on their faces, they would have looked like the idyllic couple in a breakfast ad.

Wind knocked out of us, we stood speechless, and the young woman looked familiar. After what felt like an eternity but probably was a few seconds, Dad muttered a 'sorry' and dragged both Robert and me out of the house. He started laughing, and the nerves must have gotten to him because he couldn't stop, and other people laughed too because he sounded like a donkey cross-bred with a wild puppy.

'What's going on?' asked Mum while the others looked on questioningly.

Robert shrugged in a 'don't have a clue' manner before glancing at me, leaving it to me to answer. I held my head high even though a giant hand was crushing my heart into a shrivelling raisin and wittered a 'just a misunderstanding' while longing to crawl into a small dark place to hide. Once again, I'd been humiliated.

The small crowd dispersed, and Tommy came out just as I started leaving. He had put on a shirt and seemed to want to tell me something, but he looked past my shoulder and his face contorted into a grimace – Cunningham hadn't left. A strange look passed between them, so quick I almost missed it, and when Cunningham's eyes met mine, they seemed to convey something odd: it looked like sadness mixed with regret and tenderness, very unlike the smirk I was used to. But whether a friend had turned into a foe or a foe into a friend, I was hurt and too confused to deal with either of them.

I rushed home. The front door of our house was ajar, either on purpose or by mistake, and the voices of my parents reached me before I entered.

'You should have told me.' There was a low tone in my dad's voice.

'You left like the wind; you really didn't give me a chance! Besides, you were there that day when I told the girls.'

'I didn't realise you were talking about her.'

'I felt it as soon as she started asking questions, pretending it was background information for an article, my foot! It sounded more like a girl wanting to know more about her boyfriend's parents.'

So that's who the young woman was, the journalist at the funeral; no wonder she had known the exact timing of Tommy's arrival.

'You realise you struck your own child – our child. You must apologise.'

'I know, I can't believe I did that.'

He sighed. I pushed the door, shut it behind me, and the voices stopped. My parents sat facing each other, Mum on the sofa, Dad in one armchair, and both their faces turned towards me. Dad looked crestfallen and shameful, and he lowered his eyes. Mum, on the other hand, gave me a one-hundred-watt smile. I had made her day, and she looked proud of me. I ignored her and just stared at Dad.

He kept his head low and rubbed his chin with the back of his hand. 'About hurting you, I… I shouldn't have done that, I'm sorry.' The last word was just a whisper, then he raised his head, his expression turned stern. 'Boys?!'

I just stared, and his eyes were distant for a moment, then his voice grew firmer. 'Boys, not men!'

We locked eyes in a staring contest, blue against blue, but he knew he couldn't win; he never had. He could stare into Mum's eyes when I couldn't, but he could never hold my gaze. Dad had acknowledged me, though, had shown interest for the first time in my fifteen years, and it was therefore important that I let him win. And so, just before he lowered his eyes, I let out a non-committal grunt and left to go to my room.

Once alone, I plugged my EarPods in and let the music empty my mind. Half an hour later, I checked the screen of my phone, even though there had been no ping from it, and it only confirmed what I already knew: no text, no apology, and no explanation. Fucker!

Anger clouded my reasoning, so I supposed my thinking wasn't on par, yet something felt wrong. Where did this girl spring from? If she'd been with Tommy from the start, why hadn't she stayed until the end at the funeral? What was their argument about that day, and why keep their relationship a secret? And what about the kiss, his promise, and our moments together?

Despite returning my kiss, Tommy had been reluctant to touch me, true; but as I thought about it, I realised the act we had just witnessed had been picture-perfect because that was all it was: an act. Why though? What was Tommy trying to tell me?

I recalled and dissected every minute we shared, every word, every nuance, but the brain works in its own mysterious ways, and the memories they led to were not the ones I expected: a shared look between Tommy and Cunningham, Tommy speaking about his time in English boarding schools, Cunningham in a school gown and rows of light-haired boys on school photographs.

Jesus!

I sat upright on my bed.

They've known each other all this time!

No, surely not! Maybe my crazy mind was putting two and two together and coming up with five. After all, it had been a while since I'd seen these photos, and I had never witnessed Cunningham speak to, or even acknowledge, the Van Beers. Still, I had to make sure and knew only one way to do it, break into Cunningham's house to have a proper look. Where would Cunningham be on a Saturday morning? He sometimes volunteered at church, but his car remained in his driveway, and it was later than his usual morning exercise routine, which meant he was at home, either in the kitchen baking or in his bedroom or study. I grabbed my laptop and hacked my way into his webcam; nothing. I also checked his account, but he'd made no appointments.

I stepped outside, took a breath, and brushed my hair back to hide it under a hat – I had learned early, when playing hide-and-seek with my peers, that blond hair was too conspicuous and caught the light. Hands on hips, I kicked the stone wall, hesitating, then climbed over it and ducked under the kitchen window, feeling rusty and slightly nauseous.

I slipped my fingers inside the gap of the V-shaped shutters and lifted the latch to peek inside. No one was in the kitchen. Bent in half, I moved around the house to the front door and pushed it open. The fact that I found it unlocked meant Cunningham was somewhere inside. One of my shoes squeaked on the stone floor, and I took the pair off, tiptoed inside, and wondered why I'd never bothered to put a tracking device in Cunningham's phone. Perhaps because I hated him so much.

A clock ticked on the wall, but no sound of a human presence and nobody was in the living room. I took the stairs two at a time, stepped carefully along the dark corridor to not bump into piles of books and cardboard boxes, and reached the last door on the right. I tried to remember if the door handle creaked and turned it in slow motion; it was smooth and quiet, and I slipped in, then switched the light on my phone. The room remained as I had left it so long ago – it seemed nothing had changed. I found the box with the photos, picked them up one after another and stared at every teenage face until I found it. There stood Tommy, looking younger and slightly different but still recognisable, with an innocent grin, hair covering his ears and an arm wrapped around the boy next to him.

Devastation. The blood drained from my face, and my heart ached. I clutched at my chest; I couldn't believe it. Such lies! Such betrayal! Terrible anger stemmed from the pit of my stomach and raced through my body like a raging fire. With shaky fingers, I tore the part of the photograph that had both Tommy and Cunningham on it: it was time to confront him. I had been too hasty earlier, leaving without demanding an explanation because the sight of 'sleek-hair' had unnerved me, but there would be no getting away with it this time. I shoved the photo into the back pocket of my jeans and left the room.

As soon as the door clicked shut behind me, something leapt and clawed at my skin, and I yelled in surprise. A ceiling light came on, and a grey cat bit my feet. Cunningham picked it up and sneered. 'Gotcha! I told you he'd be good at catching rodents.'

Bloody hell! I really had lost my touch!

'As you broke into my home, I am entitled to do this.'

He let go of the cat, grabbed the shoulder of my hoodie, and dragged me along down the stairs. I considered taking it off to escape but wore nothing underneath, and I didn't want to expose my chest once again. I tried to fight him off and hit him with my shoes, but he caught them and threw them away without letting go. My feet flailed to kick him, and he grabbed both my arms, pinned them behind me and pushed me into a large dark cupboard, locking me in and shouting: 'I'm calling the gendarmes!'

I knew exactly where he'd imprisoned me, a windowless laundry closet. My hand lifted instinctively to grab the handle but only met air: the door could only open from the outside. My phone light switched itself off, and I was plunged into darkness. I tapped on it to get it going again and tried slotting my nails through the gap in the door for any kind of purchase – there was none. I searched my pockets for a paperclip, inserted it and applied pressure, but it bent, and the door refused to budge. Digging through the shelves, I looked for anything that could help me escape, but they were all stacked with towels, napkins, tablecloths, and bedding; it looked like I was done for.

Who could I call or text for help? Mum and Dad rarely answered my calls, letting me go to voicemail instead, and they were a last recourse: who would want to involve parents in this? Out of all the teenagers in the village, Daniel and Ethan were the closest and the most likely to come to my aid. However, Daniel would never set foot in this house – and I would not ask it of him – and I was not in the best position to ask Ethan for help. That left Tommy, but he had betrayed me, and hadn't I been humiliated enough in front of him?

I leaned against a wall, ruminating. I couldn't let Cunningham get the better of me, no way! But all four walls were smooth, providing no escape route. I was as powerless as a mouse caught in a mousetrap, and Cunningham left me in the dark cupboard for hours.

Before my phone ran out of battery, I swallowed my pride and dialled Tommy's number; it rang many times, but no one answered. I pounded on the door with my fists like a maniac while shouting threats of outing

Cunningham to all and sundry, until my hands bruised and my voice turned raw.

When the door finally opened, I came face to face with Dad; behind him stood Cunningham, then Mum, then a man who looked somewhat familiar, and he introduced himself as Adjutant Moricheau. I winced, hoping he wasn't related to Dimitri Moricheau in my class, but what were the odds?

They marched me to the kitchen table, forced me to sit on one side; Dad sat on the other while the others watched on, like a criminal in an interrogation room.

The silence stretched, then Dad said, 'So… two years in a row now and once again a day before your birthday. Last year, your mum convinced me to say nothing and let it go, and I did because at least Liam caught you on public property, but this time he found you in his home.' He turned to Mum, and a look of complicity passed between them, as if amused by the situation. He stared back at me and continued. 'Would you like to tell us what it's all about?'

I looked at my nails leisurely. 'Did you know that he's gay?'

Mum and Dad didn't look too surprised. Cunningham shouted, 'I am not gay!' He looked like he wanted to hit me, and Moricheau said nothing but crossed his arms over his chest.

I smirked. 'Not only that, but he used to be Tommy's teacher; they've known each other all along.'

Boom! I had dropped the bomb. They all turned to stare at Cunningham, who glared at me with a murderous look in his eyes.

'That's not true! I didn't know who he was when I first saw him.'

'Be serious now!'

'Do you know how many kids I've taught over my twenty years of teaching? Do you think I remember them all? Especially when I last saw them as kids, not as adults, they change!'

'Maybe, but not their names, and Van Beers isn't exactly common around here!'

'He didn't go by that name.' Cunningham had lowered his voice and was no longer addressing me but facing my mother. 'I knew him as Tommy Bakker then. He was only twelve the last time I saw him, and it's true that I did not recognise him; he's changed so much. In fact, Mouse looks more like—'

'That's beside the point,' interrupted Moricheau. 'I've come here as a friend and fellow councillor to Elaine, but if you'd like to press charges, I'll be happy to put my policeman hat on.'

'For what?' I asked, appalled.

'Trespassing for a start, breaking and entering—'

'I didn't break in. I knocked, and there was no answer, so I walked in and looked for Cunningham. That's how I ended up in his house.'

As far as I was concerned, my lie was perfectly valid; I hadn't broken anything and had come in through the front door.

'You took your shoes off!' pointed out Cunningham, holding my pair of trainers.

'Of course! I didn't want to dirty your beautiful home.'

Mum and Dad threw me a suspicious look – I never took off my shoes at home – but even if I had sounded sarcastic, it was my word against his, and they all knew it.

'Harassing people on account of their sexual orientation is a serious offence!' scolded Moricheau.

'I couldn't care less about his "sexual orientation"! He can go fuck goats if he wants! Only if the goats are willing, mind you,' I added, and nobody laughed. 'And I've definitely not been harassing him!'

It was the truest thing said so far. Obviously, I didn't hate Cunningham because he was gay; I hated him because he was a hypocrite and a woman-basher, and it was infuriating that nobody else realised. Anyway, I had been so consumed with Tommy that Cunningham had faded into the background; he'd had a full year of respite from my former intrusions.

'So, what did you want to see Liam for?'

My mother, always the practical one, always straight to the point. Her face was open, filled with an innocence that belied her years, and I lowered my eyes.

'I wanted confirmation that he and Tommy knew each other, and I wanted to ask why they kept that fact hidden.'

All eyes turned to Cunningham with expectancy. He was red in the face, but he crossed his arms and took a deep breath. 'I believe this is between me and him and none of your goddamn business!'

I dream that Liam and I are both teenagers and we are best friends. He smells of wine and cookies, even as a kid, and we tell each other everything, going as far as discussing boys. The two of us always hang around together, at school, outside of school; we are inseparable and so close that I know this is a dream.

We sit in a grassy court, lean against the legs of an umpire chair, and my body itches everywhere, especially in my private areas. I want to scratch, but Liam makes fun of me and when he laughs, I wake up.

The itchiness is real, and I remember I was shaved all over, and I mean all over. When the razor was on the inside of my thigh earlier, slowly going up, I had trembled, and then I had tried hard to stop myself from trembling for fear of being cut.

And now I want to scratch so badly that I pull hard on my binds, but there's no give and the material — it feels like thin rope — starts digging into my skin. Soon drops of blood run down my wrists. I moan in pain and realise I am no longer gagged. I shout for help as loud as I can, through the fabric of my hood, and my voice is raspy; but however loud and long I scream, it heeds no result. Now I have a dry throat; it feels like my tongue has doubled in size, and I'm gasping for a drink.

11

I RECEIVED PUNISHMENT for the first time in my life. Not allowed to leave my room for the remainder of the day, I didn't make it to Tommy's until the next day, too late. He hadn't answered my calls, had left no messages, and had sent no birthday wishes. Tommy's house showed no sign of life when I knocked on his door; either he was gone or lying low. I dialled his number and heard the ringtone coming from inside the house, yet it looked deserted. I pushed a shutter slat up with great difficulty and looked through the gap; the phone lay on the dining-room table, but there seemed to be no one around. I searched through my pockets for paperclips before unlocking the front door. This time, I *was* breaking and entering.

The rooms looked tidy and spotless, and everything was set in its place except for Tommy's phone lying next to a birthday card. The front of the card read 'forget about the past, it can't be changed, forget about the future, you can't predict it, forget about the present, I didn't get you one', but inside, it had been left unwritten. I walked upstairs to his bedroom; he had made the bed, emptied the closet and chest of drawers, and I didn't see his suitcase anywhere. He was gone.

Happy birthday to me.

Fucking Cunningham! Why, why, why did he always catch me? When all I wanted was the truth!

I kicked the leather sofa, hurt my toes, grabbed my foot, skipped, and swore in frustration. I'd left Cunningham alone, no longer trespassing, no longer tormenting him, and this is the thanks I got? He kept ruining my life, putting himself between me and Tommy one way or another. It was his fault I didn't get to see Tommy one last time before he left, and I clenched my jaws with determination, the familiar desire for revenge resurfacing.

Jade threw a Halloween party two days later, an opportunity for all the village kids to gather one last time before leaving for their respective university, internship, or apprenticeship. My parents pushed for me to go. Either they felt guilty after my one-day lockdown birthday special, or more likely because they wanted to be rid of me. It was a dress-up party, and Mum turned up with a strange white robe and clown mask. She looked pleased with herself as she held it out to me, as if it were everyone's dream to be a clown on Halloween night.

'It's Pennywise from the *It* movie,' she explained.

'Are you going to the party?'

'It's for you.'

'Great, you want me to be the evil creature dressed as a clown who lures kids and kills them.'

'I don't need your sarcasm! It's actually very fitting for Halloween, don't you think?'

I sighed and took the costume from her.

The weather was all wrong. It should have gotten colder on approaching November, especially as the day drew to a close, but it felt as hot as a summer's day. I walked to Jade's house as the sun lowered, leaving traces of pink and purple in the sky, and was soon sweating in my uncomfortable costume and mask. Armed with two large bags of sweets and chocolate bars, I negotiated the gated entrance awkwardly and almost dropped them when Jade's husky greeted me with a loud bark and a lick.

I couldn't tell what time the party had started, but it was already in full swing. One outbuilding had been specially prepared with all the usual Halloween paraphernalia, the music blared, and mountains of food spread out on orange tablecloth-covered trestle tables.

Jade had dressed as Luna Lovegood, Juliet was Hermione, and Leah had gone full Harry Potter with a short-hair wig and a lightning scar. Owen wore a Darth Vader costume with Jamie and Ethan as tall Storm-troopers by his side; Luke, on his first permission out since he'd enrolled in the army, was the Grim Reaper; Daniel had a simple skeleton suit on; Makayla was Cat

Woman; Anna resembled some kind of ice princess or white witch, and Olivia had dressed as Dracula.

Soon after my arrival, Jade turned the music down and declared it was time to feast. We grabbed china plates from a pile, cotton napkins from a woven basket and food from colourful dishes. Plates full, we settled in small groups, some on deck chairs while others sat on the grass. Daniel, with his usual kindness, approached me and wished me a happy belated birthday while discreetly handing me the tiniest of cards. Makayla complimented me on my *Pennywise* outfit, saying I looked scary, and the three of us sat by the lit pool.

It was a relief to take the mask off to eat, even if the sun had gone down and it was getting cold. Anna challenged Jamie and Ethan to imitate the Stormtroopers of *Britain's Got Talent*, and a hilarious moment of watching them make fools of themselves ensued.

After the meal and when it was dark, Jade handed out eco-friendly pumpkin bags, and we left to go trick-or-treating. We all had good fun walking through the village like a pack of wolves, failing to scare each other, competing to get the largest number of sweets and swapping masks before abandoning them altogether. At some point, the *Star Wars* set started a fight with pretend laser swords because Jamie argued he was, in fact, a Mandalorian hiding under a Stormtrooper outfit.

We passed a crossroad with a streetlight, and something came barrelling down, pushing Makayla so hard she tripped over, taking the thing with her. She screamed at the top of her lungs; dogs nearby barked in answer, and we realised the *thing* was an actual person.

With no apology, Cunningham picked himself up and dusted himself off with slow, unprecise movements, as if dazed or drunk.

He looked at each person until his eyes found me and pointed. 'You, you, you little—You're gonna pay for this!' He rushed at me, and I thought he'd tried to grab my hair, but a sudden rope pulled at my neck, cutting my airways and strangling me.

Daniel stiffened. The look of shock and fear on his face mirrored mine, and I felt sorry for him; then he got hold of himself, sprang into action and intervened, always the gentleman. 'Cunningham, stop!'

He tried to remove Cunningham's hand from my neck, but Cunningham pushed him hard, and he fell on the ground, instinctively rolling himself into the foetal position. The others immediately rallied: how dare he mess with Daniel! He was the angel of the village.

Daniel cared for his dad, who had bone cancer. Before that, he had cared for his mum until the age of fourteen, when he lost her to organ failure from advanced scleroderma; but all that time he'd gone to school like any normal teenager, did his work and looked after his parents, never once complaining, always with a smile or a kind word to the nurses who visited. Not one kid in the village would ever fail to stand up for him.

It took three strong boys to restrain Cunningham and take the rope from him. Cunningham let go of it, a few clumps of my torn hair stuck in his fists.

'What's wrong with you? Why are you attacking Mouse?' demanded Ethan, but Cunningham was not listening. He stared at me with rage, almost foaming at the mouth like a wild dog, eyes wet with tears and giving off a strong smell of wine.

'I think he's drunk,' said Leah.

'I'm not drunk!' he barked at her before hitting my collarbone with a finger. 'I'm gonna report you to the gendarmes, you little shit, you mark my word!'

'Haven't you tried that already? Call them, I'll report you for assault!'

'You fecking—'

He tried kicking me, but Luke, Ethan, and Jamie still held on to him. Jade tried to calm him down with a soothing voice. 'Listen, I know you're mad about finding Mouse in your home. That would make me mad too if somebody was found digging through my stuff…' She gave me a pointed look that I ignored. If only she knew. 'But that's no reason to—'

'It's not about that! My cat is dead!'

He fought to release himself from the others' grip to have another swing at me. 'You killed him; you killed my cat!'

'Woah! Easy, easy.' Ethan settled Cunningham with a strong hand. 'I understand you're upset about losing your cat, okay? It's super sad, but pets die sometimes.'

'What, by hanging themselves!'

A stunned silence followed.

Cunningham had given in and was no longer trying to hurt me; he was panting hard as he uttered, 'You look like him, so I knew you might be just as bad, but you're actually worse!'

Ethan looked at me. 'What's he going on about?'

'How the hell would I know? The dude is crazy! He thinks I killed his cat, for fuck's sake!' But I knew he was talking about Tommy and was suddenly eager to find out what had happened between the two of them.

'Did you kill his cat?' asked Makayla with her typical no-nonsense attitude.

'Seriously?!' I couldn't believe they needed to ask, but they all stared at me, expecting an answer. 'No, I did not kill his cat.'

'Liar! You lie all the time, but I know it was you, all because my cat found you in my house; who else could it be?!'

'Anybody!' I shouted. I'd had enough of this, and how dare he call me a liar when he was the one who lived in hiding. 'It could be anybody. Maybe it's one of those men you like to fuck. Maybe they weren't happy with your services!'

I saw the fist come towards my face in slow motion, and perhaps it was by that miracle that I managed to dodge it, but Luke, who stood next to me, did not. Because he was tall, the unexpected punch hit him in the chest. He went down flat on his back while the arm holding the pumpkin bag shot straight up, and a shower of sweets fell on and around him. His eyes opened as wide as dinner plates, and his mouth gaped like that of a fish out of water, struggling to breathe.

Cunningham, feeling apologetic, moved to help, but Jamie and Ethan pushed him out of the way while Jade and Leah helped Luke sit up to catch his breath. I wasn't sure who had called the police, but they seemed to appear out of nowhere – no sign of Adjutant Moricheau, thank goodness – along with an ambulance that took Luke to A&E.

The whole affair had put a damper on Jade's party, and she returned home with only half the guests but plenty to talk about. Daniel had stayed behind with me, in a show of support, and he stood next to me, hands in his pockets, scuffing his old Timberland boots against the tarmac. 'It could be Tommy,' he said.

'Hmm?'

'Maybe Tommy killed the cat.'

I whipped my head to look at him. 'Why would he do that?'

He snorted. 'He can't stand cats.'

'Nonsense! Who doesn't like cats?!'

'Tommy definitely doesn't! You should have seen him that day when we planted trees. Old Celia's fat ginger cat appeared by his side, and he leapt almost six feet away. He looked like he wanted to murder the poor thing!'

'He must have been surprised.'

'Okay. To take revenge for you, then. He is your boyfriend or something, right?'

'Nothing happened!'

'You don't have to go all defensive on me, I understand.'

He took out a flat tin of tobacco from his back pocket, licked a thin piece of paper and started rolling a cigarette.

'What makes you think he's my boyfriend, anyway?'

'I have eyes, Mouse. Just because I spend most of my time looking after my dad doesn't mean I don't notice things, and since he's arrived, you've been different. You may pretend not to know each other when there are people around, but your bodies don't lie, your eyes don't lie, and there's something… electric… I don't know, something in the air when the two of you are nearby.'

I had always liked Daniel. He was the likeable kind, beautiful inside and out despite everything he'd endured, but I liked him even more after that.

'It can't be Tommy,' I said. 'Tommy's gone.'

Luke did not press charges against Cunningham; however, he liked showing off the blue-and-yellow bruise on his chest, giving him the opportunity to flaunt the rippled abs he'd got in his army training, and when he explained to people what happened, Cunningham was treated like a pariah and had to lie low – which he did anyway, not too eager to answer questions about his sexuality.

Things settled, and I thought the matter was over, but the holiday ended, and as soon as we got off the bus, I realised something was off: people whispered while casting discreet looks in my direction but stopped as soon as I approached. I had an inclination that Mum had been tongue-loose around town. Sometimes, in her need to get attention, she didn't realise the hurt she caused and who knew what others might have said. But I'd always had thick skin and didn't care about other people, so it just washed over my head.

In maths class, however, Dimitri walked in and dumped his bag noisily on his desk before looking at me, smiling from ear to ear. 'Hi, Mouse,' he clamoured. 'I hear you're into *mature* men, is that true?'

I thought of Tommy, and my cheeks reddened; the entire class fell silent, and his voice grew louder. 'So much so that the guy caught you in his house.'

Our old maths teacher, Monsieur Garais, walked in unaware and asked me to wipe the board.

'Careful, sir, you don't want to get too close. Mouse is into old men, apparently.'

The whole class sniggered, and Monsieur Garais thought the insult was meant for him; he shouted for silence and sent Dimitri to the vice-principal's office.

Things quietened down for a while, but it didn't last, and I spent the day hearing whispers behind my back, listening to insults, being called a freak, and generally being given a wide berth on account of my supposed deviant and disgusting tendencies.

Before the last lesson of the day, the principal called me into his office, only for me to be told to wait when I got there. He had called for me, not the other way round, so why was he making me wait? After eight minutes of waiting, I decided that if by the tenth minute his door remained shut, I would just walk away. I put the timer on my phone, watched the clock and was told to enter with forty seconds to spare.

'Hello, Taylor, sit down.'

I sat and waited for him to speak. He was looking at a folder on his desk that had my name on it. He closed it and put both arms on the desk, hands clasped together. 'How are you feeling?'

The question surprised me, and I didn't know how to respond; what did he mean? How did I feel in general? Or how did I feel about being in his office? And if it was the latter, I wasn't feeling anything particular – maybe I was curious, but was curiosity a feeling? I just stared.

He cleared his throat and measured his words. 'I have read your file; you are a remarkable student. You had a recorded IQ of 140 at age seven, and you have excellent results all round; you have never had problems or created problems, or so I've been told by your teachers, and except for twice recently, you've never been absent.' He paused; perhaps it was my cue to speak, but I had nothing to say.

'As principal, I strive to ensure I always know what is going on inside my school, and there have been a lot of rumours circulating today. Now, I want you to know that I will not tolerate any kind of harassment here, sexual or otherwise, so, if you find you are being stigmatised or persecuted, just know that my door is always open, and you can come to me anytime. As you may already know, I have a military background and rest assured that I will deal with any troublemaker swiftly and efficiently.'

'Yes, sir.' I thought it was the right response, on account of his 'military background', and it had been the first thing that came to mind as his speech had gone in an entirely different direction from what I expected.

'Now, I also heard you entered the home of a neighbour uninvited.'

It wasn't a question, and I remained silent.

'Whether true or not, it should not concern me as it happened outside of school, but I would like to remind you that breaking the law is another thing the school will not tolerate, regardless of who your mother is. Not to mention the potential danger you have put yourself in.'

He gave me a pointed look, and I nodded, all the while trying hard to keep a straight face because a famous line from an old TV series the Byrnes used to watch had popped into my head: *'I am not in danger, Skyler, I* am *the danger!'*

'Good. I repeat: if you have any concerns, feel free to come see me. Anytime.'

He never mentioned a dead cat or the fiasco of the Halloween party, so that was something, at least. When I got to the playground, Dimitri was waiting for me, red-faced but beaming. 'Mouse, listen, I didn't mean any harm; I was just curious.'

'Was it your father? Do you realise he broke confidentiality, and I could sue him?'

'My father didn't tell me anything, and he wasn't even on duty. But he is a cop, so I've picked up a trick or two on finding things out. You're not the only one with brains, you know!'

'Well, you got it all wrong, so the jury's still out.'

We walked to our last lesson – what was left of it – side by side. After a lot of sighing and looking at me sideways, Dimitri asked, 'So what happened?'

'Nothing! I knocked on my neighbour's door, there was no answer. I entered, and because he's paranoid, he thought I'd broken in; the end.'

'Okay, but... I mean... why did you knock on his door? You don't fancy him, do you?'

'Are you fucking mental?!'

'Okay, sorry, it's just... that girl Olivia from your village said you wanted to ma—'

I gave him a death stare, and he shrugged. 'Yeah, well, she is a nutcase, that one!'

It had been a stressful day, to say the least, but what frustrated me more was Tommy's disappearance. He'd left his phone, and I couldn't get hold of him; he'd even deleted his Instagram account. I tried sending emails, but they just sat in my mailbox, *unable to deliver to recipients*. It was only a matter of time until he registered with a phone company, and I thought I'd catch him then, yet I couldn't find him anywhere, neither on Belgian nor English lists. His grandfather, on the other hand, was chairman of an international corporate banking company and easy to find.

I decided I just had to be patient; Tommy would resurface eventually, and in the meantime, I had to return to my old detecting ways. Ignorance was not bliss after all, and I should never have given up on spying. Now, I had to uncover the story between Tommy and his former teacher Cunningham. Just the thought left my mouth dry.

I am dying of thirst; it's been so long since I've had anything to drink. Or eat. I shiver with cold and pain; my captor left me lying in my own filth, and it hurts! You cannot understand the pain unless you experience it: It burns, like when you lean too long against a hot radiator, and it stings, as if ants were biting, eating through my skin. I pull on my binds and wriggle, but it only intensifies the pain, and I have no strength left.

Because of the effort, sweat has formed on my upper lip, and I stick my tongue out as far as I can to lick it. Even this simple task is painful; my lips are cracked, and my tongue feels dry and foreign. I wish to be back in my black cell; the thought makes me laugh, but I cannot laugh, and my chest hiccups, sending more waves of pain throughout my body.

I realise how good I had it there, in my black prison. I was deprived of light, of clothing, but I was free to a degree. Free from pain, free from the cold, free to move around, to drink when I was thirsty, and to wash when I was dirty. And I was loved, cared for with gentle strokes and massages and kisses and tenderness and whispers of I love you. Where is he now, my lover? Why has he abandoned me? Come back, come back.

Come back.

12

UNLIKE BREAKING INTO someone's home, hacking into computers didn't have adverse reactions. I had found pieces of the puzzle but was still missing the major elements and couldn't form a full picture. Cunningham had been 'Master of Mathematics' and had left the teaching profession of his own volition, but two incidents happened around the time he left. A student by the name of Christopher Jennings jumped or fell to his death from the widow's walk of the main building two days after Cunningham's departure, and a priest who officiated at the school chapel was defrocked about four weeks later. However, I couldn't find how these two elements fit with Tommy or Cunningham.

Christopher Jennings might have been Tommy's friend as they were the same age, but they were not in the same class, and I couldn't find a connection with Cunningham – he had not been one of his students. An article in a local newspaper mentioned Christopher's distinctive artistic skills but nothing more, and that information led nowhere. As for the priest, he had been a man in his late twenties named Philip Watson and not even the regular vicar at the local church but a low-level replacement who occasionally officiated in the interim. The only common factor between them all was their shared religion. It seemed the only way to get the full story was to go to the source and ask Tommy directly upon his return.

But Tommy did not return.

I waited for him at Christmas, then at Easter, and still waited in the summer, but there was no sign and no news of him. His house, fully renovated, stood vacant, and I felt just as empty as it looked. The nightmares returned, and I would walk to it at night for peace. So long as no *For Sale* sign was exhibited, and despite the giant hole in my heart, I kept hoping.

Cunningham hadn't handled his coming out well and had turned to drinking, even more so than usual. His resentment towards me grew worse. He considered me fair play since I had been the one outing him and appeared to be under neither Mum nor Dad's protection. He often tried to pick fights with me.

Stories of violence from his ex-female conquests resurfaced, and he would get picked up by the police for drunk and disorderly behaviour. Once, they found him wandering the village off his head after cutting the bright-orange ropes of the swings and climbing frame in the park. He even lost his job at the accountants for reasons of poor attendance.

On my sixteenth birthday, I went to town and hung around the graveyard. Tommy still hadn't registered with any phone company and didn't appear on any social media, so I hoped to catch him there. I once again sat waiting for him by his parents' grave. It was frustrating to be a minor; I couldn't drive, couldn't leave the country without parental authorisation, and there still was that whole pandemic situation. I could do nothing more, and I felt like the patient waiting for an organ transplant, desperately clinging on to hope, to survival, to life.

I left the churchyard and came face to face with Liam Cunningham.

'I know you,' he said.

Although his body stood straight, his words were slurred, and he reeked of wine.

'Yes, you're my neighbour.'

'Rats!'

'Actually: Mouse.'

He got closer, unmasked, and wore a crooked smile on his face. I glanced around, reassured to see that there were people milling about even though I didn't want to be associated with this old drunken fool, however handsome he might have been once upon a time.

'There it is…' he slurred. 'That arrogant tone of yours. You think you're clever… and funny… but do you want to know something?'

That was as far as the conversation went, from my point of view anyway, as the next thing I knew, I woke up on a hospital cot with a busted lip, two fractured ribs, three stitches on the left temple, and one hell of a headache. They kept me overnight for observation, and despite a night of pain, broken sleep, and constant nurse check-ups, I slept soundly, knowing Cunningham would be arrested and would rot in a cell for quite some time.

I was wrong, however, as the bastard was lucky to find himself an excellent lawyer, as well as having a small church congregation to vouch for him. Instead of jail, they sent him to a substance-abuse recovery clinic. Later, I would be appalled to discover that my mother had not only used her connections to let him off – as a favour to one of Cunningham's cousins who was an old friend of hers – but she'd also been the one who had originally suggested he move to the house next door.

On my seventeenth birthday, I had more or less given up on the graveyard. I couldn't go on a weekday, and not only had I started studying at the University of Poitiers, but I was also taking driving lessons.

Cunningham reappeared the next summer but rarely came out of his house; he looked just about presentable, and his whole demeanour was still odd. He was walking to his mailbox when I broke into his cellar, grabbed a bottle of red, opened it in his kitchen, set it up on the table along with two wineglasses and sat waiting for his return. He stopped at the threshold and almost dropped his mail in shock when he saw me.

'What the—'

'Welcome back!'

I poured wine into the glasses and watched how Cunningham couldn't take his eyes off the vermillion liquid.

'What are you doing? Put that away, you little—'

'Except I'm not little anymore. I'm almost eighteen!' I paused. 'Don't you have something to say to me?'

He swallowed hard, but his eyes wavered, looking in all directions except for mine until, at last, they came resting on me. 'I'm sorry I hurt you; now get the hell out of my house!'

'That's not much of an apology,' I replied with a smirk. 'But I'll take it, let bygones be bygones, moving forward. Now that is worth celebrating, don't you think?' I picked up a glass and raised it. Cunningham's hands began to shake, and he hid them behind his back.

'Cheers!' I exclaimed. 'No? Just me then.'

I took a sip of wine and put the glass down before walking out of the room past Cunningham, who stepped back as if I were contagious.

I left the house without looking back. The open bottle remained on the table, and it was up to him to deal with it.

Shortly after, on a hot sunny evening, the council threw a big party at the town hall that Mum and Dad attended. Mum had had a few councillor meetings, and alcohol must have flowed. She looked unsteady as she walked to the Audi, and Dad had to help her to her seat. Even more curiously, she waved and blew kisses at me as the car drove off.

It was the last time I saw her: she suffered a massive stroke and never recovered. According to the people at the party, she was chatting happily one minute and lying dead on the floor the next.

Dad's family in Australia made the journey for the funeral, and the house vibrated, filled with bleached-haired, sun-kissed-skinned foreigners with an accent. Dave and Johnny, Dad's nephews, were tall, slim, energetic, and spoke with booming voices. Dave came with his pretty wife Debbie and handsome twenty-three-year-old son Dylan. Johnny was accompanied by partner Isobel and their daughters, Mallory, twelve and Mabel, eight.

I had never met these people, yet from a different continent, they must have known Dad. They had foreseen the devastation and desolation he felt and understood that to leave him alone would be catastrophic, and they were right. It felt like Dad had had the stroke, like he was missing part of his brain and could no longer function properly. He meandered around the house, had a vacant look in his eyes, refused to eat, struggled to dress himself, and seemed unable or unwilling to form proper sentences. I was grateful for the help and surprised to find I missed Mum.

Not used to living surrounded by so many people, I sometimes needed to isolate myself and would go to Tommy's house. I missed him so much! I needed him; I needed his support, I needed his embrace, and the sound of his voice, but where was he?

Mum had not been religious, but the funeral was big business because she'd been a well-known figure, and many people were expected to show up outside the church. I only wanted one person to be there, to help me through it like I had him, and I prayed he would come, that I would get to see him again.

On the day of the funeral, raindrops spattered against my bedroom window, and I smiled, thinking it would dissuade people from attending, but I was wrong. The crowd outside the church looked larger than anything I could have imagined.

I searched for a familiar visage, blond hair and amber eyes, but too many people had gathered – with too many open umbrellas acting as limits of social distancing – and Dad collapsed beside me. Dave and Johnny stepped forward to grab one arm each and supported him all the way inside, while Dylan grabbed my left hand and patted me gently on the back. We sort of walked into the church holding hands.

The family stayed a week longer than they had planned, even though the girls would miss school, but lockdown measures had been lifted, and they wanted to use the opportunity to visit the country. They took Dad out with them, and their presence seemed beneficial; he was slowly coming out of his shell.

Daniel often visited. He was one of the few who had remained in the village, having gone straight from secondary school to a job at the hardware store in town, and we'd spent a lot of time together: I had him register as the official adult to accompany me on my drives. I had to clock-in quite a substantial number of hours before my eighteenth birthday and certainly couldn't have relied on my parents for the job. Daniel never came to the house – too many strangers, he said. Instead, we would meet at Tommy's. He'd lost his father six months earlier, and he would give me little pieces of advice that he thought might help me with the grieving process.

'You're allowed to cry,' he said to me one evening as we sat side by side on Tommy's lawn, watching a buzzard glide smoothly above the forest in search of nourishment while the crows flew high in formation to chase it away. I remembered how perceptive Daniel had always been, but what he didn't know was that I was less upset by the loss of my mother than by the loss of Tommy.

He grabbed me by the shoulders to shake me. 'Let's shake those tears out of you, yeah? Come on tears, get out!'

Instead of tears, he made me laugh. I rubbed my face with the palm of my hand, turned to look at him and stared straight into his blue eyes. He moved closer, hesitant, and brushed his lips against mine. They felt warm and dry and tasted like cigarettes, and I immediately pulled away. He didn't insist but rolled a cigarette and started puffing away. 'I've always liked you, Mouse, ever since you came to see me about… well, you know. You are smart and independent and beautiful, and I knew you would always be out of my league. Did I ever have a chance?'

Four years earlier, I might have reciprocated. Daniel was someone special, and if anything, he was the one out of my league (far too good for me), but then Tommy had entered my life and taken my heart hostage. It didn't matter that he'd left; as long as he still had a house in the village, it meant I would get the chance to see him again. That was all I needed, a chance.

'I still love him,' I said with a heavy sigh. 'I will always love him.'

Daniel nodded. 'Maybe that's for the best. I've been seeing someone lately, although nothing's happened yet.'

'Really, who?'

Daniel crushed the end of his cigarette on the ground, took a paper hankie out of his jeans pocket, rolled the cigarette butt inside it and put the whole thing back in his pocket. 'Makayla.'

'Makayla?!'

That seemed like an unlikely union. Daniel was gentle and reserved, and his family situation had made him antisocial. Makayla was kind but bubbly, full of life, and she liked to surround herself with people. She had returned with a degree from a prestigious business school and had bought into an insurance company in town, while Daniel had never left, becoming a mere employee in the local hardware store. They seemed the complete opposite; she was as to night as he was to day. Not to mention the fact that he had just tried to kiss me.

'Are you sure she is the one for you? You're not trying to use her to—'

I stopped myself as I realised how stupid my words sounded. Daniel didn't use people; he was too upright – some going as far as calling him uptight – to do that.

'I'm not trying this or that, that's not the issue,' he said gently. 'She is incredible, good to me, generous, caring, bright and funny. We share the same vision of life as a couple and even with our future together, but she has a past with Ethan, and I want to make sure it's all okay with him before we start anything.'

Like I said, upright.

I returned home to a quiet house. Dad was asleep in his bedroom while the family sat outside around the garden table. They'd left the patio door open and were in deep conversation about my and Dad's future. I crept near to eavesdrop. They agreed that, for his own sake, Dad would leave with them and live with his older brother Harrison, but there was hesitation and indecision when it came to me. I had no choice but to come, according to one, I wasn't yet eighteen. What about my law degree, asked another, I couldn't just up and leave, hadn't my student accommodation already been paid for? And what about my friends?

'What friends?' said the girls in unison, and I felt like I was once again the superfluous element in their lives.

The next day, they had made a decision. They sat me down and explained how Dad and I should leave with them to live in Australia. I could transfer to a university over there or study online. I refused and hid in Tommy's house for two days. How could I envisage a future that would take me so far away from Tommy? I hadn't given up on him. I would never give up on him.

In the end, Dad had to stay until my eighteenth birthday as my legal guardian before moving to Australia because it turned out the house had been in mum's name and would be bequeathed to me while the both of us shared quite a considerable fortune through Mum's life assurance.

***

I woke up late and missed my first lesson of the day. Dad's flight had been in the early hours of the morning, when the trains didn't run, and it had been a ten-hour drive to Paris airport and back the night before. Though Dad's saloon was a comfortable car, I had not enjoyed the drive back home, not because it had been illegal –

until I went to the actual driving test, I was not supposed to drive unaccompanied – but because I did not enjoy driving. Dad was currently on his way to Brisbane via Dubai, and I was officially an adult.

I looked around my small student room and thought perhaps I should buy a comfortable apartment in a newish *Résidence Universitaire,* somewhere with private parking and close to both the campus and the shopping centre. Even if I wouldn't need it for long, it would still be a sound investment and easy to rent, as Poitiers was a student town. I shook my head. *Best not to squander money away.* Mum had made it so I would inherit according to British taxation, but I still had to pay for my education and the day-to-day cost of owning a house.

After a lecture on torts, I went to grab lunch at the university restaurant. Since the beginning of the academic year, a science student by the name of Enzo – who pompously preferred to be called a 'fundamental and applied science student' – would join me for lunch every Thursday. He usually walked in with four or five raucous friends, the kind of noisy, lively blokes full of themselves who would go to the gym or play team sports like handball or rugby – Makayla would have called them jocks.

They always caught everyone's attention, but once they'd filled their trays and settled, Enzo would abandon them to sit opposite me. He was discreet but transparent in his flirting with me, making it clear that a sincere relationship wasn't the end goal, and I imagined he enjoyed collecting conquests just as much as trophies. I grabbed my soda, and he grabbed his glass of water, clinked it against my drink and whispered, 'I'm taking you out for a drink this week.'

'You are not.'

He was the persistent kind and never seemed offended by my rejections, his good looks giving him the confidence (or arrogance, depending on the point of view) to approach whoever he fancied without fear.

'When are you going to give in?'

'Never, you're not my type.'

'I've never heard that before! You want to see the goods first, is that it? I'll lift my shirt and show you my six-pack if you follow me somewhere… quieter.'

I sighed and shook my head but instinctively looked at the stomach area of his shirt, and he puffed out his chest. We finished eating in silence, and I picked up my tray. He smiled and waved goodbye, but instead of leaving, I just stood staring at him. The look on his face transformed, his grin getting wider.

He thought he'd taken down my defences and stood to face me. 'I'm glad you've changed your mind.'

'I haven't.'

I left, but as he joined his friends behind me, I heard him say, 'I'm almost there', and there was some high-fiving.

No, you're not almost there, but I'm human after all, and I'm eighteen now, isn't it time to gain some sort of experience?

But I wouldn't have been able to go through with it, it just wasn't me. There would always be only one person for me.

After classes, I walked to the supermarket and wandered down the aisles. It was my birthday, and I wanted to treat myself to something good but found nothing inspiring. I went back to my dorm empty-handed, thinking about ordering pizza, and found a hooded figure in designer blue jeans and a stylish black hoodie standing in front of my door.

He turned around and removed the hood. 'Hello, Mouse.'

I blinked and froze, wondering if I was dreaming, then I had the urge to grab him hard by the neck, but I wasn't sure if it was to kiss him or punch him in the face.

We stared at each other for what felt like an eternity until I got my voice back. 'What are you doing here?'

'I'm here to give you your birthday present.'

He slid a nervous hand through his hair, and the familiar gesture nearly brought tears to my eyes. A couple came out of a neighbouring room laughing, saw the awkwardness between us and passed us in silence.

'Should we go for a drink?' he asked in a shaky voice. I nodded and followed him to a sparkling brand-new dark Volvo like an automaton. It was only once I was sitting in the car, going in the opposite direction of the town centre, that I thought, what an idiot! He'd been right there by my door; all I had to do was push him in, turn the lock behind us and…

Tommy drove less than a kilometre before stopping in front of a little house; I followed him like a pig to slaughter and eventually exclaimed, 'This isn't a bar!'

No shit, Sherlock! It seemed my IQ had plummeted within the last half hour.

'We can still get a drink here.'

We walked into a sparsely furnished living room with a drinks cabinet. Tommy took two tumblers out, dropped ice in them and poured an inch of whisky in one and half an inch in the other before handing it to me. He raised his glass, and I watched in wonder how the amber of the alcohol matched the colour of his eyes.

'Happy eighteenth Birthday!'

He took a large sip, rested the glass down on a side table and rubbed his hands against his thighs. I gawped at him, unable to tear my eyes away and trying hard to restrain myself as I realised how much I wanted him, how much I still loved him. But would he want me? I had changed so much! I wasn't the mini mouse from three years ago. I had grown tall, filled out, had shorter hair now, more yellow than white, and I was no longer a child.

Tommy looked up and saw me staring. A smile brightened his face, and he suddenly had the aura of an angel.

'Now, your present,' he whispered as he took off the hoodie.

The silver pendant sparkled on his pale smooth chest, angel and demon intertwined, and a small, cute clipart mouse was tattooed on his heart.

It was all the encouragement I needed. I put my glass down and pushed him against the wall, and we locked in a passionate kiss.

It wasn't clear who led who to a bedroom or how we got naked, but I remember that despite my inexperience, I was the one who pushed him on to the bed just after whispering, 'You left me.'

He left me.

He's abandoned me.

There is nothing for me now. No love, no pain… Just a vast emptiness, and I'm floating in it… in and out of consciousness.

I thought I heard noises behind the door on my right, sounds of thumping or scuffing, and something heavy dropping on the floor, but it's probably just my imagination or the echo of a memory. I don't know what's real anymore.

I am dreaming when the smell wakes me. I recognise the stench: dead things. Death is coming for me, or am I in its embrace already? I pull on my bind, and the pain shoots up my arm. Not dead yet, then.

Why am I dying? Why has he left me to die?

I thought I knew why he'd locked me in the dark: I was being punished. But this? This I don't understand. I want to understand before the light goes out. Somehow, I must not let go yet… not just yet.

But my eyelids are heavy, and the numbness of nothingness beckons.

13

THE FIRST TIME HAPPENED QUICKLY, but after that we took our time, testing, feeling, discovering each other's bodies until we lay side by side holding hands, spent. As we lay there perfectly happy, I knew why I was on this Earth and understood my purpose in life: to make him happy, please him, protect him, care for him, support him, and love him until my dying day. I turned and put my left hand on his chest, ran my fingers over the tattoo, kissed his shoulder, and whispered, 'I love you.'

My stomach replied with a grumble. Tommy raised his head, smiled and got up to put shorts on, then threw a bathrobe at me.

'Someone needs feeding. Come on, I'll cook you something!'

'What is this place?'

I looked around the small, sparse kitchen with its gleaming white units and black marble countertops. I was sitting at a small round glass table while Tommy scrambled eggs and fried bacon.

'It's my house, well, it's a rental, and it's close to the campus.'

'The campus?'

'Who knows? I might do some more studies, perhaps literature this time. After a painful three years of business school, it will be good to read a subject I'd actually enjoy! Only a few hours a week at most, and I would be almost next door to you.'

He was referring to the proximity of the buildings, the law faculty building being only about fifty metres away from the literature department.

'I had to negotiate with Grandfather, who wants me to work within the company and "give up that silly artsy nonsense". I got two years of freedom, so you'd better not fail.'

'Have you been keeping tabs on me?'

'I told you I was prepared to wait; didn't you believe me?'

'You just disappeared, Tommy, on my birthday. Without a word or a way to get in touch.'

I didn't want to darken the mood and raise my voice, but it was impossible to hide the hurt and disappointment.

Tommy put a plate filled with bacon, eggs, and toast in front of me, prepared another one for himself, and sat opposite me. 'Eat it while it's hot.'

I looked at him; he slid a hand through his hair and sighed.

'You were just a child, Mouse, an impressionable teenager, and it seemed I was leading you down the wrong path. Who knew what you really wanted at that age? And you seemed so determined! I found it hard to push you away, and I knew the best thing was to leave. So when Nikki turned up, and you saw us… I could see how it looked, the two of us half-dressed and sharing breakfast, and it wasn't quite how I had planned it, but it turned out perfectly! I thought it was for the best: you deserved a chance at a normal life.'

Normal.

What did the word even mean? I looked it up on my phone, and it defined normal as 'something expected, usual or average'. None of these words defined me. I was definitely not expected, born to indifferent parents who, at almost the age of some of my peers' grandparents, were neither eager nor willing to have me. There was nothing usual or average about me: I was more mature than people my age, and my IQ was way above average. I was born in one country but also had the nationality of another. I studied in one language but spoke in another. I was a loner, sometimes described as pedantic, and I fell in love in my teens with a boy six years older than me.

'I was never normal,' I replied. 'And I've always known what I wanted. You disappeared for my sake and just ended up wasting three years of our life together.'

Tommy lowered his eyes and picked at his food. 'I didn't do it just for you. I did it for me too.' He raised his head and looked at me. 'They liked me in the village, Mouse. They appreciated me, and it felt good, and I knew that being with you then would have jeopardised that, even if it was just as a friend. I wasn't strong enough to withstand people's judgement or their antagonism toward me and the label that would have stuck to me for the rest of my life. I couldn't do it!'

So that's what it was. I had never cared what people thought of me, but Tommy cared; he liked attention. Mum had also been someone who cared – in her own way.

'I needed you when Mum died,' I whispered.

'I was there, Mouse. I came back from the States especially.'

'You should have come to me.'

'Believe me, I wanted to, but… I knew I shouldn't. I shouldn't even have returned in the first place, and anyway… you were with someone.'

I remembered how Dylan had had his left hand squeezing mine for support and his right arm around my shoulder as we walked into the church.

'My cousin.'

He was, in fact, the son of my cousin, but I didn't know if there was a specific term for him other than 'relative'. Growing up in France meant that my knowledge of English vocabulary was sometimes limited.

Tommy nodded. We finished eating in silence and rose in sync to put our dirty plates in the sink.

'Would you do it now?' I asked.

'What?'

'Come out as a couple to the entire village; would you do it now?'

It was fine being together there and then, in the city's anonymity, but would his behaviour change in the village where everybody knew everyone else's business? It seemed I was worried over nothing, as he replied without a hint of hesitation. 'Yes, I would. A hundred times over.'

He untied the belt of my bathrobe, and, for the very first time, he was the one who initiated the kiss.

Early morning came with a dark, heavy sky. People rose from slumber with croaky voices, shop shutters slid open with a rumble, car doors creaked open and slammed shut, keys inserted in front door locks jingled, and the sounds of footsteps and traffic swell with each passing minute.

Tommy had woken me to take me to my morning lectures, but I'd refused to move. He'd disappeared on me once, and I wasn't going to let him go again. He tried his best to coax me out of bed, but I was having none of it, and we were both tired from lack of sleep and other bedroom activities. He gave up and got up to put the kettle on.

We sat in bed side by side, sipping hot milky tea, eating buttered toast and chasing breadcrumbs off the duvet.

'No more disappearing?' I asked while putting my hand on his.

He nodded and repeated, 'No more disappearing.'

'You promise?'

'I promise.'

'No hiding our relationship, either.'

'That's right.'

'No secrets?'

There was a slight pause, and I looked into his beautiful honey eyes. Tommy sustained the look and repeated. 'No secrets.'

'What about Cunningham?'

'What about him?'

'I know he was your teacher; he said he knew you as Tommy Bakker.'

Tommy nodded. 'The name Bakker Van Beers was too long for school registers; they always recorded it as Tommy Bakker.'

'What happened with him?'

He sighed, shrugged, and brushed his hair with a hand. 'Nothing much. One day we discovered he was gay, and he couldn't face our class anymore. This was an all-boy Catholic school, so you can imagine the jokes, the name-calling, the verbal abuse, and the pressure from parents and school councillors. I guess he had no choice but to leave.' He snorted. 'Who knew he'd end up living in the same village as my parents? What a small world!'

He got lost in the memory and something crept over his face, like some slight malaise, and I had a feeling he'd left something out. He was still hiding something.

'Did you hit him?' I asked, remembering the massive bruise on Cunningham's face.

Tommy's cheeks reddened. 'That was an accident.'

'What happened?'

I couldn't contain my excitement, imagining the love of my life hitting Mouse enemy number one, but Tommy was hesitant.

'What happened?' I repeated calmly.

'It's not something I'm proud of!'

'Just tell me,' I encouraged.

'I had... sort of blackmailed him.'

I tilted my head, and Tommy explained how he had needed a place to stay while his parents' house was being renovated. He would force his old maths teacher's hand in offering him a room for free, or his secret lifestyle would be revealed.

'He wasn't happy to be manipulated by an ex-pupil, and his revenge was to get a cat. At school, everyone knew I had cat phobia, students and teachers alike. He carried that small cat with him everywhere he went, even when cooking, which didn't seem very sanitary if you ask me.' Tommy grunted and ran a hand through his hair. 'Anyway, he'd only recently got the cat and kept waving it in front of my face, but the cat was still wild, hissing, and trying to scratch at me. I panicked and threw punches all over the place until my fist connected with something. That something just happened to be his neck.'

I started laughing, but the laugh got stuck in my throat. I felt weird; there was something missing in his story.

No, that wasn't it.

I had been wrong, as simple as that. When Cunningham had turned up at ours with a cat, I had assumed it had been some sort of weapon against me. A simple pun, cat versus Mouse, when, in fact, it had had nothing to do with me. The 'vermin' Cunningham had meant to eliminate wasn't me but Tommy. The realisation left me slightly deflated, and my cheeks burned. That cat had been short-lived, and even with my excellent memory, I couldn't recall its name. Perhaps I had never known it, yet it seemed to have had a major impact on our lives: it had pushed Tommy out of Cunningham's house, had unmasked me as an intruder, and ultimately, had been the reason for Cunningham being outed to the villagers.

'Guess he learned a lesson that day. The path to revenge is fruitless, always leading to more pain,' Tommy said before changing the subject. 'So, reading law! That's a surprise, I must admit; out of all the subjects you could have chosen, I was expecting math, or science, or computer programming, or… well, I wasn't expecting that.'

I shrugged. 'It just felt right.'

I didn't want to tell him that ever since witnessing the death of his mother, I'd felt a strange sense of guilt over my former lawless behaviour. And I enjoyed studying law.

In the few weeks that followed, we fell into a routine: Tommy would pick me up at the end of my lessons, we would sometimes go to the market for groceries, then spend the rest of the evening together. He would cook while I studied, and we'd do the dishes together. Most times I would spend the night; my small student room had become a place of transit where I would just grab a change of clothes and the occasional shower.

Tommy moved some of his clothes from his closet to make space for mine. The closet took one whole side of the wall with two large sliding doors, and everything was hung and folded neatly – even the shoes had their own special shelves. A white cardboard box lay in the bottom corner, full of old written research notes that still hadn't been digitised. It was stressed to me that the work and research had implied a certain level of confidentiality and that this box was, therefore, out of bounds.

Tommy hadn't bothered to register a phone on purpose, as he'd been in the States using those prepaid phones instead. His grandfather had forced him to study business and finance in Chicago to prepare for his future at his side in the company. Tommy said he hated business studies and struggled with it, but life wasn't too bad because his best friend Nikki stood by him until she moved to Tallahassee to be with her boyfriend.

I had a driving test in mid-November and miraculously passed, then it was already the Christmas season. Shopkeepers put up decorations and hung flashing lights, and the same repetitive Christmas music played everywhere.

'What would you like to do for Christmas?' asked Tommy that evening as we were in the kitchen preparing spaghetti bolognese. I hadn't really thought about it; this would be my first Christmas on my own. In the past, Mum had given Dad and me specific tasks; Dad's duty consisted of putting up Christmas lighting outside while I prepared the mincemeat pies; he sprayed the windows with fake snow while I wrapped small presents for each villager, and we would all decorate the tree together before going back to our separate lives. To me, the excitement of Christmas had always been more about the preparations than the actual Christmas Day.

'I could take you out somewhere nice,' said Tommy.

'Aren't you going to be with your family?'

'I have not had a family Christmas since I was eighteen years old.'

'Why not?'

'Quite a few things happened then.' He brushed sauce off my nose with a finger. 'But I have been strongly advised to attend Grandfather's annual New Year's Eve party. I'm one of the two major shareholders of the company, and he insists I should spend time with his friends and acquaintances. Grandfather is just a figurehead, but he says he'll be done for good by his seventieth.'

Tommy had explained to me before that although his grandfather was chairman of the company, he didn't get involved, having given his trust entirely to highly efficient CEO Joanna Marshall – a woman in her forties who Tommy had described as 'a distant cousin with fiery red hair but an ice-cold personality'.

He poured us a drink while the bolognese sauce simmered; red wine would have been what Mum would have served as the perfect accompanying drink, but Tommy was not a wine drinker. He liked whiskey, he liked bourbon, and sometimes he would make cocktails. With a glint in his eyes, he said, 'I could take you along and introduce you to Grandfather. I'd love to see the look on his face when he sees you.'

'You don't think he'd approve.'

He gave me a mischievous smile. My cheeks reddened, flattered that he would want to introduce me to the last remaining member of his family, but he always seemed tense when mentioning his grandfather, and I didn't want our first day of the coming year together spoiled by family drama.

I went back to my student room to think it through, and as soon as I walked into the main entrance/common room, my neighbour Manon called out. 'Your father was looking for you!'

'My father? Impossible, my father's in Australia.'

'Are you sure?'

I raised my eyes. *As if I didn't know my own father's whereabouts.*

'He asked which one was your room. He looked and sounded English.'

I checked my phone; did Robert or Andy try to contact me? There were no missed calls and no messages, and I was about to dial Robert's number when she added, 'Tell him he shouldn't wear so much *eau-de-toilette*. It's not unpleasant, but the whole corridor reeks of grapefruit now!'

I looked up at her. She had said 'English' but, of course, that's what the French do – they generalise – and whether you're from England, Scotland, Ireland, or Wales is the same to them, you are simply labelled 'English', the same way a person with Asian features is immediately called 'Chinese'.

'Where is he now?' I asked.

'Gone.'

They're gone.

My parents.

They were here. I saw them, standing together in the distance, holding hands and looking down at me.

Smiling adoringly.

Have I ever seen my parents smile at me like this?

The outline of their figures had shimmered, started losing consistency, edges slowly disappearing.

No!

I'd run toward them as they'd become translucent.

I had almost reached them.

Wait! Don't go!

But I was too late… too late…

14

THE THIRD DAY OF DECEMBER was such a crisp and sunny morning that I walked to uni. I had left Tommy staring at his reflection in front of the full-length mirror in the bedroom, frantic and fussing over what to wear for meetings with some of his grandfather's business acquaintances.

I came out of an intense two-hour lecture to find him standing outside in the sun, looking more beautiful than ever. He wore a pure silk single-breasted jacket with a rust and beige herringbone pattern of faded blue-and-green check on top of a light-blue shirt and matching light-green silk scarf. He stood twenty metres directly in front of the entrance, positioned to be noticed. Needless to say, a lot of glances were cast his way, and a lot of smiles were restored on dark, depressed faces.

Tommy enjoyed all the attention. I, on the other hand, did not. I had always preferred staying in the shadows – something that was already quite the challenge with my very blond hair. When he saw me, Tommy gave me a dazzling smile, and his entire being lit up like a beacon in a dark sky. He moved towards me, and the crowd parted in murmurs of admiration, like a god walking on water. My cheeks reddened as he stopped in front of me, and I was grateful for his dislike of public displays of affection. In a drama, he might have grabbed my hand or kissed me, but this was real life, and we walked to his car side by side.

'How did your meeting go?' I asked Tommy as we sat at a far table in the university restaurant. We were finishing our dessert when a loud crowd walked in, and I remembered it was Thursday. Enzo and his friends, as boisterous and noisy as usual, turned quiet when they saw my companion. With a quick tilt of his chin, Enzo directed the others to get food while he stepped to our table and raised his hand for a handshake towards Tommy.

'Hi, I'm Enzo, Mouse's…' He looked at me and winked. 'Mouse's special friend.'

Tommy stared at the hand, looked Enzo up and down and gazed at me. I couldn't quite read the expression on his face.

'This-this is Tommy, my boyfriend,' I stammered.

Enzo grinned, strangely triumphant, and turned away to join his friends.

'It was fine, but I have one more meeting this afternoon,' Tommy said as if nothing had happened.

'You'll have to walk home, I need to drive to Tours, and I don't know how long the whole thing will take, so don't wait for me to eat.'

He pushed his tray aside and opened the email icon on his new phone.

Taking both our trays, I put everything away and pushed through the round-windowed door to the facilities, which had a long corridor that ended with the women's logo drawn on the left door and the men's one on the right. I came out to find Enzo in the corridor, leaning against the eastern wall, thumbs stuck in his belt like a cowboy in a Western movie.

'I see what you're doing here. Trying to make me jealous, eh?'

'I'm not trying to do anything.' I tried to walk past him, but he stood to block me.

'Come on, Mouse.' He leaned close to me, his tone so smooth he was almost purring. 'There's no need for such games; just tell me when and I'm yours.'

'Games? I don't play games. Now let me pass!'

'Or what? You're going to send your big brother on me? I reckon I can take him!'

'He's not my brother; he's my boyfriend.'

'Don't treat me like an idiot, Mouse. You two look too much alike to be anything else.'

'Get out of the way!'

I shoved and tried to skirt him, but he grabbed my arm and pushed me against the wall with a snigger.

'That's what I thought, you may be tall, but you're not very strong.'

The smile on his face did not reach his eyes, and I saw exactly what was going to happen as if I could read his mind. All the times I had rejected him, it seemed he had minded after all; his pride was wounded, his patience had reached its limit. My eyes automatically looked at the door; someone would walk in, so many people on the other side who could come at any moment, and Tommy, perhaps wondering why I was taking so long, but the door stayed shut.

'Don't even th—'

I didn't get to finish my sentence as his body pressed against mine and against the wall. His mouth violently pressed against mine while his hands held my head still. My arms were free, and I grabbed at his sides to push him away, but he was heavy and strong, and it took what felt like a quarter of a minute to get him off me. Then he raised both his arms in surrender but left with a smug, relaxed smile on his face. I wiped my mouth and face with the back of my sleeve, disgusted, went back to the toilet to check my reflection in the large mirror on the wall, and readjusted a few wild strands of hair.

I came out to find our table empty, looked around, but couldn't locate Tommy. Enzo's friends were eating and talking among themselves while Enzo queued for food. I looked up and checked the CCTV cameras just as Enzo turned around and saw me. He gave me an arrogant, satisfied smile that I really wanted to knock off his face. He knew what he was doing, having cornered me where he couldn't get caught, and I could do nothing now, not unless I wanted to be caught on camera.

But revenge was a dish best served cold, and his time would come.

Tommy stood leaning on the wall outside, speaking Dutch on his phone. Seeing the frown on his face, I assumed he was talking to his grandfather. He cut the call short as soon as he saw me. 'There you are. Come on! I don't want to be late.'

He walked ahead of me and hurried to the car. The engine was running, and he'd already reversed out of the parking space by the time I reached it.

'Was that your grandfather?'

'Yes, and I don't want to talk about it.'

Perhaps his morning meeting hadn't been as good as he'd thought. When Tommy was in a mood, it was best to leave him be; he became cold and distant. We might have been next to each other in the car, but it felt like an ocean sat between us. I knew his mood wouldn't last long, though, and we drove on campus in silence.

His Volvo stopped in the law faculty car park, and just as I opened the car door, he exclaimed, 'Wait!' while removing the house key from his keyring before handing it to me. 'I don't know what time I'll be back.'

Tommy drove off with a rev of the engine and tyres screeching on the tarmac.

***

He hadn't returned by the time I went back to the house in the late afternoon. The sun was setting, taking with it the last remnants of warmth, and the house felt cold. I made myself a hot cup of tea and cranked up the thermostat. Tommy, who was a tidy and organised person, had left clothes strewn all over the bedroom. In a bout of domestication, I tidied up the mess.

Tommy was meticulous when it came to housework, and I tried to do a decent job of folding his clothes, hanging his shirts the way he preferred, with a decent gap between them. I was holding three shirts ready for hanging when I tripped over a shoe, went headfirst into the closet, and landed on the white cardboard box. The lid flattened, and the box got destroyed, spilling its contents left, right, and out of the closet. Something caught my eye among the blackened notes, something oddly familiar. A touch of grey in a sea of white.

I pushed the white papers out of the way to reach the object, no longer caring about making a mess. When the folder was in my hand, I already knew what I was looking at and feverishly pushed the elastics aside to open the flaps. I hesitated; my chest constricted while my heart beat like a tambourine, and my palms started sweating. Slowly, hands trembling, I grabbed the item, pushed on the fabric to reshape it and there it was: a grey denim hat with large denim IOWA letters sewn on the front and frayed at the edges. A hat that brought back terrible memories.

I hadn't seen it again after that day and thought it had been lost, but it seemed to have been misplaced among the Van Beers' recovered things from the accident, ending up with Tommy. But why was it on its own? And why had it been mixed with Tommy's research notes? I checked the folder and noticed it was missing a label. The file was thin, holding only a typical French heavily lined double sheet of school paper.

Recognising Tommy's handwriting, I slid it out and opened it, but these were no notes from any research. I blanched while reading, and the tea in my stomach felt its way back up my oesophagus. I couldn't believe it, and yet, it was all there, in black and white and in all its details, as if I'd written the words with my own hand.

I rushed to the bathroom but didn't make it to the toilet in time, and I vomited milky tea in the basin; sweat poured off me, and my head pounded. Feeling nauseous and achy, I wondered if I was getting the flu. The house was too hot after all and turning up the thermostat had been a mistake. I rinsed my mouth, splashed water over my face and stood in front of the mirror, looking at my reflection.

It made little sense. It was impossible. Tommy had studied psychology, but that didn't make him a telepath or some sort of Avenger; he couldn't read other people's minds. Then how did he know? How could he have described the events of that day with such precision as if he'd been there?

An image popped into my head: as I stood amidst the destruction and death, looking further towards the hunters' forest, a lone figure appeared, leaning an arm against a tree. A vision of an angel who looked right at me, hazel eyes full of life unlike the blue-green ones that had just closed forever; then he closed his eyes too, and I knew I had to flee.

I was sick again, and this time more violently. As I flushed the toilet and rinsed my mouth, I wondered where the vision had come from; wondered if, after having read the vivid description of the accident, my mind had played a funny trick on me by pasting the figure of Tommy into a scene in which he didn't belong. Yet something niggled at me.

I walked back to the bedroom, picked up the sheet of paper with shaky fingers, sat on the bed and took deep breaths before re-reading it. My heart pounded, and I felt ill. He had been there. And I had just remembered it.

Disbelief.

Could it be true? Had I somehow erased that fact from my memory? Re-reading his account of the accident confirmed it; it was not written from my point of view but his. How could I have forgotten seeing him there? How and why was he there? Why had he never mentioned it to me? And what kind of sicko witnessed the death of his parents and said nothing?

Confusion.

Strange connections formed in my mind: Tommy at the edge of the hunters' forest. Cunningham meeting someone in the forest ruins for the very first time. Me following Cunningham. Cunningham's guilty look at the funeral and his sudden departure. Tommy looking straight at me inside the church. Cunningham watching Tommy leave the cemetery. Tommy and Cunningham.

Tommy and fucking Cunningham again!

Anger.

Something violent came over me, a sudden urge to inflict pain and destroy things. I emptied the cardboard box of its papers before sending it flying across the room; I tore notes, pulled at shirts from hangers and trampled on them until, spent, I sat on the bed exhausted and hot, nervously kneading my Iowa hat.

I had been deceived.

Not only by Tommy but by my own desires and emotions. The clues had been there all along, but I'd refused to see them. People kept secrets, a fact I'd learned at an early age. So why should Tommy be any different? And why would he care for me when no one else ever had?

Folding my body over my hand, I clutched at my chest, heart in such pain I thought I might be having a heart attack.

My eyes looked up and met Tommy's glare. I hadn't heard him come in, and he looked furious, lightning flashing in his eyes and a vein pulsing red at the temple. *He* was mad at *me*! I almost laughed at the absurdity of it. He had taken his blazer and tie off, unbuttoned his shirt, and the silver pendant hung from his neck, the angel and demon mocking me. *My* pendant! He had no right to it! I charged at him to grab it, but blood rushed to my head, a curtain of red fell over my eyes, then everything went black.

A muffled voice pulls me out of the darkness. It is demanding. It wants me to wake up and open my eyes just as my eyelids flutter open. Blurred colours. Blurred faces. I am flying on a magic carpet, and it's going too fast past walls, furniture, clocks, crosses, people, and my head is spinning. I want to close my eyes, but every time I do, the voice won't let me. There is a flash of blond hair. No, I must have imagined it. Just like I imagine the body bag being lifted into a van. It must be a dream. It's all too much: too much light, too much noise, too many faces and too many voices.

'Is he dead?'

'Oh my God, he's dead!'

'Mouse? It's not Mouse, is it?'

'What's happened?'

Something is pulled over my head, something is pushed on my mouth and nose, and my arm is being lifted. I want to struggle free, but I have no strength left, and the flashing blue lights are too bright and confuse me. Doors are pulled closed with a metallic clang, and the light, the noise, the faces, and the voices recede.

Peace.

A face leans toward me, an angel with ebony skin and black irises. He tells me to hang on, he tells me that all is well, he tells me I am safe, and I want to believe him.

TOMMY

15

THE NOISE WAKES ME. A sound like a tyre being inflated mechanically, and the bed moves. I yank my right hand up as hard as I can, expecting to be shackled, but it rises straight up and to the left, pulling my body with it, falling to the ground. Something tugs at my left arm, pinching me, and the blinding lights make me scrunch my eyes. Everything around me seems to be shiny and white, and I hardly have time to wonder what new hell this is when a man touches me, trying to lift me up. I yell and fight him off, punching and kicking, but my body feels weak, and now there are more of them, men and women, lifting me up.

Something pricks my arm. The energy drains out of me.

'Leave me alone! Don't touch me... please... don't hurt me.' My voice is stuck between a croak and a murmur, and my eyelids feel heavy.

'Hush, it's okay now, nobody's going to hurt you, you are safe. You're in the hospital, and you are perfectly safe.'

The female voice is so soft and reassuring that my eyelids close. I'm not sure how long I sleep or if I sleep at all, as I don't remember waking. My body seems to be floating, and my eyes are stuck shut, but I hear everything.

'Patient in Room 134 has regained consciousness; best not to involve male caregivers yet. Solid food will be introduced today, so keep a close watch.'

'Rooms 135 and 137 have spent the night fighting, disturbing others; they should move as soon as other rooms are available, which leads us to the patient in 136. She doesn't have long, and the family has requested a visit from their priest sometime today. That's all from the night shift; doctors on call are Dr Provost and Dr Vargas.'

I feel sorry for the person in 136 and wonder if she heard it all; the nurse speaking wasn't being particularly discreet, and I feel outraged. Being a patient shouldn't mean one is not entitled to one's dignity.

When my eyes open, the sun has reached its apex. Pigeons stand on top of a grey building, pick at feathers or take flights into the blue sky. The window is shut, and they make no sound, but I am mesmerised by their grey colours, distinct and vibrant. The blue of the sky is bright, and I squint, turning my head to the left toward the door. I concentrate on the murmur of voices, the rolling and squeaking of wheels, the bell of an elevator, and the swish of its doors opening. Is it real? Am I really in the hospital? I try hard to remember, but a haze saturates my head.

A slow death, that's what I remember. A shout, bulging eyes, and a female voice pronouncing three brief words: he is dead.

He is dead. The three words resonate in my ears and rebound inside my skull like a logo bouncing from side to side on an old computer screen. He is dead, he is dead, he is dead… the leitmotiv does not stop, and a tear slides down my cheek. He has put me through so much that I am angry at myself. I should be relieved, but I am not. All I feel is hurt and despair, and I want to wallow in it.

The door opens, and a junior nurse enters. 'Good, you are awake. How are you feeling?'

I understand her words, but I'm not sure if I speak the language. My mouth moves to reply, but no sounds come out. She checks my pulse, shines a small light in my eyes, takes my temperature, asks me to open wide and stick my tongue out, then takes my blood pressure. The nurse works quietly and efficiently, avoiding my eye, and writes something on a sheet that I hadn't noticed was lying on a hospital cart.

She lifts her head to look at me. 'Dr Vargas will check on you this afternoon; in the meantime, it would be good to see you eat by yourself. The food will be here shortly.'

She is gone before I know it.

Half an hour later, a mixed odour of fish and potatoes reaches me before the meal arrives, but my body does not react. No stomach rumbling, no salivating at the mouth, yet it's been a while since I had a proper meal. Two caregivers bring in the food; it's a couple of middle-aged women and they are as noisy, warm, and vibrant as the previous nurse was cold, quiet, and abrupt. One of them has short curly hair and lifts me up to a sitting position like I weigh nothing. The other is a dark skin beauty who sets up the tray and pushes the table in front of me. 'You need to eat, dear. It will speed up your recovery.'

She has the typical lilt of a Caribbean accent, and I croak: 'Jamaica?'

'Guadalupe, and you know how creoles feel about their food. You need to eat!'

She gives a short throaty laugh, and the other one laughs too before saying, 'Take your time, dear, we're here to help.' She points at her name tag. 'My name is Estelle, and this is Justine.'

They smile, and I like them both already, so I want to please them and eat, but I look at my meal – fish pie, a yoghurt on one side, and a diced apple on the other – like it's an alien creature.

'I'm not hungry.'

It is strange but true, as if I've lost all senses or no longer need sustenance to survive.

'Just one mouthful,' says Estelle.

She gives me the sort of smile that is supposed to melt my defences. I grab the fork with a timid hand and push some of the mash on it, look up at the caregivers, who both give me an encouraging nod, and shove the food in my mouth. Pure nectar! It's like being a baby and discovering food for the first time. No, it's better than that. Like being a smoker who had quit and has just had his first puff in a thousand years. Once I start, I just have to have more; if it hadn't been for the nurses slowing me down, I would have finished it all in seconds.

As they both stand up, Justine pats my hand. 'Very good! Dr Vargas will be pleased, and so will your boyfriend.'

It takes a while for the words to reach my brain, as if my mental capacities have been diminished, and it's only once they're packing up, tray in hand, putting the trolley away, and preparing to leave that I frown and whisper: 'Boyfriend?'

A look passes between them, and Justine hesitates. 'I meant no offence, dear, that's just what he calls himself.'

'It's only been a couple of days, but he's been here to check on you like clockwork; he's quite fussy about your well-being, too,' adds Estelle, pursing her lips.

They see the look of confusion on my face, and awkwardness settles between us; they're about to disappear, too, and I rush to ask, 'Who is he? What does he look like?'

'I didn't catch his name…'

She looks at Justine questioningly, who shrugs her shoulders and says, 'Tall, blond, beautiful eyes, the whole ward is envious.'

They giggle like schoolgirls as they leave.

Tall, blond, beautiful eyes. I can only think of one, but it can't be! I don't understand, and eating has tired me. For a long time, I am apathetic.

Later, after taking the full measure of what they said, I become frantic, and it doesn't occur to me to press the call button. Instead, I lift the blankets and rise. My feet are unsteady, and my weakened body can barely support itself. I crawl to the door and use the handle to lift myself up. The corridor is empty, so is the nurses' station. I walk with a slow, erratic pace with one hand on the wall – less for support but more for the comfort of its feel. The paint on the wall is a very pale pink, and everything else looks white, shiny, and clean. I feel nauseous, and there goes part of my lunch all over the floor; the nurses will not be pleased. Where are they?

I reach the elevator, push the button, listen to the smooth whir of the mechanism as it comes up, hear a chime, watch its doors part, and there he stands in all his splendour, tall indeed, blond indeed, and very much alive. I pass out and fall straight into his arms.

When I come to, the sun is lowering in the sky, and a hand touches mine.

'How are you feeling?'

It wasn't a dream. He rises from the chair, leans over me, and my necklace, with its angel and demon pendant, slips out of his T-shirt. A look of concern crosses his face; is it real, or is it fake? It looks genuine, but I'm not sure of anything anymore. He clasps my hands in his, but I pull them out. He gives me a questioning look and, with a resigned smile, takes a step back and settles in the easy chair by the bed. I sit up, and he moves to help but halts when he sees me flinch.

With measured movements and without a word, I walk to the bathroom, push the door shut, turn the lock and let out a breath. I turn around and almost jump in fear, thinking there is someone else in the room, but a mirror on the wall faces the door, and I hadn't recognised my reflection. I look awful. My hair has been cut short and sticks out in tufts, and dark purple rings circle my eyes, which seem too big for my thin shrunken face. I almost resemble a skull on a pirate flag, so skinny that tears fall on taut, stony skin.

I come out to find him sitting unmoving and watching my every move. My body reacts before my brain does and is drawn to him; there is an inexplicable tightness and ache within, as if it remembers him, as if a seal of ownership has been stamped on it and only he can remove it. I fight and ignore my betraying body and get back to bed, sitting up, and look him straight in the eyes. His beautiful eyes, shaded by long eyelashes but always so inexpressive, are difficult to read.

'Why?' I ask. One word, but everything is in that question, a question I leave ambiguous on purpose as I watch his eyes.

'Because I love you…' He hesitates, looking so candid, and the pain on his face so genuine, so moving, that I fight the urge to embrace him. 'But do you love me?'

And the sad truth is yes, I love him too, but where did that get us? The look in his eyes turns intense, and my heart melts. I live for this look. I would die for this look. I fell in love with it the first time I saw it in that little gothic church, when I shouldn't have, when it was wrong. I didn't know then that it was a look only reserved for me, a look of longing and desire that seemed to burn bright and make the colour of his irises clearer, like the flame of a blowtorch. I thought I'd never see it again, but here it is, still vibrant, full of love, and I'm about to surrender to it when someone knocks on the door.

A couple walks in wearing light and dark-blue uniforms with the words *Gendarmerie Nationale* emblazoned in white on their chests. They both look to be in their early to mid-thirties. The man is short but stocky, with short brown hair and pale blue eyes, while the woman is taller than him, with hard brown eyes that belie her girly appearance.

'Monsieur Van Beers,' she says gravely as my visitor rises from the chair in anger.

'How did you get in? This is a private clinic!'

'Young man, we represent the law. Please step outside for a moment.'

'Please,' she insists while pointing at the door.

Our eyes meet, but his are unreadable, and he leaves the room without a word.

The officer holds a paper folder in one hand and an electronic device in the other. He steps forward and introduces himself with a deep, gentle voice. 'I'm Officer Ahmed, and this is Officer Bouvier. We are here to discuss the events of the nineteenth of this month; I believe we have most of the information we need, but there are some unanswered questions. We understand this might be difficult, so take your time answering.' He pauses and licks his lips. 'What exactly was your relationship with Liam Cunningham?'

'Liam Cunningham?' I don't know why I repeat the name the way he's just pronounced it – with a French accent. It's really not my intention to make fun of him, and I add, 'He hates me. Why?'

'Was there—I mean… were the two of you…'

He makes some strange hand gestures, and his voice trails off, leaving a silence that perhaps he hopes I will fill, but I just stare at him questioningly. He clears his throat. 'Were the two of you involved in a sexual relationship?'

'Me? With Liam Cunningham?' I laugh at the absurd question, but the officers' faces remain stern. 'No, of course not; the guy is like fifty, for God's sake!'

'Ah.' He nods and frowns, opens the folder, and scribbles something on a sheet of paper. 'Was it some sort of revenge, do you think? We were told there was an incident between the two of you in the past… when you were a child; could you tell us about it?'

I wonder how they know about that and find myself unable and unwilling to respond. The silence stretches, and the lady officer steps forward. 'My apologies! Although my colleague and I understand his mental state was not stable, Liam Cunningham was very intoxicated, and he didn't leave a note, you see. Perhaps you could enlighten—'

'What's he got to do with anything?' I interrupt, and they both stare at me with astonishment, even a hint of alarm.

'What do you mean?'

'I don't know,' I reply with irritation. 'I'm just wondering why you're asking me about Liam.'

They share a look of incomprehension, then the woman nods, and the officer states, 'I'll take it from the beginning, then; this might clarify things. Feel free to interrupt or add input as needed.'

He reads from his tablet: 'At approximately fourteen hundred hours on Saturday the nineteenth of December, Father Alexandre Prichet went on a regular visit to the home of Liam Padraig Cunningham, residing at number 33 Les Vallées. He found his call unanswered, but the front door was ajar. He entered and called out, found no one on the ground floor, took the stairs to the first floor, and saw the body of Mr Cunningham hanging from a rope attached to a hook in the ceiling. A fallen chair lay close by. Father Prichet redressed the chair, climbed on it, detached the body, and laid it on the ground. The body was pale and cold, but he checked for a pulse anyway and found none; he then called the emergency services; while doing so, he heard a low moan coming from behind one of the closed doors and went to investigate.' The officer stops reading and gives me a warm, gentle gaze. 'You were found in his home in one of the first-floor bedrooms, hooded, and tied to a bed with ropes. You were naked and suffering from severe dehydration. There were bedsores on your lower body, faded bruises on your face and upper body, and lacerations on your wrists and ankles.'

His tone is apologetic, as if he were to blame, but that might be because tears cascade silently down my cheeks. I let them run. Liam is dead, and I always hated him, but I'm not sure he deserved such a lonely and dramatic death.

I look up. 'Wait, what are you saying? Are you saying it was Liam who held me captive?'

'Is that what happened? He held you captive?'

I nod, blinking in confusion; all this time I thought I knew my jailer. 'I was kept in the dark and never saw his face; I thought... I thought...'

I remember the voice, the Irish accent, the cookies, and the citrus scent of aftershave splashed on sparingly to cover the smell of his drinking. The blood drains from my face, and the room spins. I lose my balance and tilt to the left.

The officer grabs hold of me. 'Monsieur Van Beers, are you okay? Tommy?'

'I'm okay, thank you,' I reply, patting him on the shoulder as I sit upright in a fake show of strength.

The severe-looking nurse walks in, and I see she is not a nurse, as her nametag reads *Intern*. Behind her is Mouse.

My mini Mouse.

Of course, there's nothing mini about him anymore, he is tall and handsome. He sees the tears rolling on my distraught face and runs to me as I open my arms.

'I'm sorry, I'm sorry, I'm so sorry,' I whisper to his chest.

16

'WHY TIE YOU UP in his house and starve you almost to death for three days? What would warrant such hateful behaviour?'

Officer Ahmed is back. He has come to drop off my phone and the clothes I wore when I was taken, and he still has questions for me. They found the clothes in the upstairs bathtub, and they were stained with dried blood – my blood – but I cannot tell him why. I don't remember. I presume the police want to close their case, and they need a reason, something neat and simple that can tie everything up. But life isn't neat and simple, neither are people, and I can see that he knows it.

Three days; that's what he said, but what about the other days before that? What about the black padded room? He doesn't mention it. I want to know but don't want to ask. The padded room was something else, something separate, something I am reluctant to reveal, especially if they don't know about it.

'Is that how long I was there, three days?'

'Approximately fifty-five hours, according to the doctor. A few more hours without a drink and you could have died, but you may have been in Liam Cunningham's home longer if we're to believe a certain…' He checks his tablet. 'Taylor Robbins, aka Mouse, your… boyfriend, I believe.' He hesitates and clears his throat on the word 'boyfriend', and it's obvious he's not comfortable with same-sex relationships.

'Was there anything else?' I ask.

'They took your blood and ran some tests. There were traces of benzodiazepine in your system.'

'I meant at the house; did you find anything?'

'Drugs, LSD tablets.'

He doesn't ask if I know where they come from, and I assume they've already ascertained their origin.

'Anything else?' I ask.

'Like what?'

He watches me, and I put my poker face on.

They don't seem to know about the padded room, and I can see what they've been thinking: if crime isn't about money, then it's usually about sex, especially if drugs are involved, and I can imagine the headlines. At worst: *Lovers' sex games go awry*; at best: *Lovers' quarrel turns vicious*. That's why they asked about 'a sexual relationship', but they'd assumed wrong.

We might have gained some freedom over time and be allowed to live more openly, but there will always be prejudice. If I'd been a woman, things might have been different. They might have asked about a relationship, but they wouldn't need a reason; the whole affair would have immediately looked suspicious. Did it even occur to them to question the age difference between Liam and me? But I'm being unfair; look who's talking, I tell myself, what claim do I have when I fell in love with a teenager?

Liam wanting to hurt me does not sound far-fetched; he hated me. He could turn violent at a snap of the fingers, and I can think of three reasons why he'd want revenge. None of these reasons I want to disclose, but the officer won't leave empty-handed, and I have to give him something. He mentioned a childhood incident, and that's what I'll give him, even though, out of the three, it is the flimsiest of reasons.

I take a breath. 'I was twelve years old when I cost him his job, his marriage, and his baby. I took his "perfect life" away from him,' I tell the officer. 'And that is why Liam hated me.'

He clicks his pen and gets ready to take notes.

Two students always watched the others leave the boarding school during the half-term holiday: 'The unclaimed', as we called ourselves, or the 'leftover duo'. A few classmates left later, and others returned earlier, but there were always a couple of days in between when it would be just the two of us. A handful of teachers stayed to supervise, but the rules became laxer, their attention turned elsewhere, and me and Chris – full name

Christopher Paul Jennings – roamed the school as we pleased. More or less.

We usually stayed in the arts room, our favourite room, and were often left unsupervised for extended periods of time. Unlike other dark and stuffy wood-panelled classrooms, the arts room had a bright, airy space and lay at the top of the main building, just under the widow's walk. I walked to it with quick but heavy purposeful strides, knowing I'd find Chris at his usual spot, sitting by the window and momentarily lost in the creation of one of his beautiful drawings.

My intention was to confront him, even if it meant getting a beating. Chris was not as skinny as me; he was no pushover and had powerful fists. I was angry because I'd found out he had betrayed me. All this time I thought we were kindred spirits, the two abandoned children of the school, the unclaimed, but it had been a lie all along. I had overheard teachers speaking in the corridor and discovered Chris stayed out of choice. His parents had driven all the way from London to collect both him and his sister – a pupil at the nearby school for girls – to go to their holiday home in Spain, but he'd refused to go with them.

I entered the arts classroom and slammed the door shut. Chris's hand jumped from the paper, and he blinked as I stood glaring at him.

'All this time, you lied to me! Your parents haven't abandoned you here. You choose to stay here!'

He jumped up, threw the pencil on the desk, and closed his hands into tight fists. I prepared myself for the inevitable fight, and we stood glaring at each other like in a movie stand-off, but the fight never came. Instead, the hard eyes filled with tears, and they gushed down Chris's face in silence. He reminded me of a grieving person at a funeral, sniffing and wiping his nose with his sleeve.

First, I thought it was an act, a ploy to get my defences down. Then, I wondered if it was some sort of mockery, but when the crying eased up, the pain in his eyes seemed genuine. Confused, I didn't know what to do, and my anger never lasted long.

Chris looked shifty and hesitant, and I stayed on guard, wondering what he would do; then his face hardened with resolve. He loosened his tie, pulled it over his head, removed his maroon sweater, and started unbuttoning his shirt.

'What are you doing?' I asked, but he ignored me and proceeded to take off his shirt.

I didn't want to see his body; none of us did. We had all heard of his classmates' habitual exclamations of disgust whenever he undressed for games. They said his skin was blotchy, looked unwashed, and some of it had a strange texture.

Chris turned and pointed at a patch of raw meat-looking skin on his lower back. 'This happened the summer I turned six; punishment for talking too much and asking too many questions. I was held over the barbecue and told I'd be cooked like a sausage unless I stayed still and quiet.'

I laughed, thinking it was a terrible joke, but something too serious in Chris's breaking voice stopped me, and I stared at him in horror.

He pointed at the strange scratch marks under his left arm. 'Here, I had to keep my arms raised while I was being whipped with a branch from our cherry tree; I was eight and had started eating without being told.' He then pointed at his shoulder. 'My shoulder got dislocated when I was pushed and locked into my sister's rabbit cage, I'm not sure how old I was or what I'd done wrong. This mark here was done with a hot iron, and this lot on my arm were darts; I could go on, but you get the picture! So yes, I *choose* to be here.'

I stood unmoving, speechless, and petrified. I had heard of child abuse, of course, I had heard of it! But it was for other people somewhere else, poor people perhaps, ignorant people. Not rich politicians with a big house in Chelsea, a second home with lads and stables in Devon, a Bentley and other sports cars in the garage, and enough Cartier jewellery with a value that would feed a small country! It was beyond my understanding. And yet there it was, displayed before me: the signs of his ill-treatment like the evidence at a crime scene.

My vision turned blurry, and I wiped my eyes – face wet with tears – I hadn't even realised I'd been crying. It hurt. Somewhere inside me his demonstration hurt, and I decided on the spot what I would later study at university. I'd always wondered what sin I'd committed for my parents to abandon me, but what could possibly go on in someone's mind to keep hurting their own child?

Chris and I locked eyes. He knew I had felt it, and I knew he knew, with no need for words. He'd always known my story, and now I knew his, and there was a deeper, immediate bond between us that made us even closer.

Chris put his clothes back on, but I no longer feared his unsightly body. It was as much a part of him as the absence of my parents was a part of me, and when he spoke again, the tension lifted like in a puff of magic. 'I'm done drawing. How about we try to go up to the widow's walk?'

For obvious reasons, access to the widow's walk had been condemned. The staircase leading to it was in the storage room at the back of the classroom and blocked by a heavy, reinforced door. Even if we somehow managed to break into the storage room, which the janitor kept locked outside of art classes, it was quite impossible to get past the reinforced door fitted with a security code and an alarm system. We tried cracking the code but got distracted by our rumbling bellies and left to go to dinner.

Friday evenings were the best, as most teachers would go drinking down the local pub, and so long as we didn't break curfew, we had free run of the school grounds. We sauntered to the tennis courts, where Chris stopped me and gestured to be quiet.

'What?' I mouthed as he pulled me into the bushes.

'There's someone there.'

A beefy man wearing casual clothes leaned against the umpire's chair, looking nervous, and I didn't recognise him.

'A stranger at school? How did he get in? I suppose we should tell someone,' I whispered.

I moved to leave, but Chris grabbed my sleeve. 'Wait, look!'

I turned and saw Master Cunningham, my math teacher, approach with careful steps, barely swinging his arms. He joined the stranger on the court, and they seemed to know each other, but they spoke in muted tones, and we couldn't catch what they were saying. After a brief exchange, the two of them walked together to the equipment room.

'Why is Cunningham meeting his mate here and not at the pub?' I asked.

'Maybe they're having a game; should we stay and watch?'

I shrugged. 'I've got nothing better to do.'

We sat and waited on the grassy court for the two to get changed. The sun was angling down, and we expected the lights to come on, but they stayed off, and there was no sign of our two players.

Chris got up and dusted himself. 'What's taking so long?'

'You don't think they've gone, do you?'

'We would have seen them.'

We ran to the equipment room, and both grabbed the handle at the same time. I let go, and Chris pressed on it, but the door was locked. Grunting sounds reached our ears, and we climbed on a rock to peek in through a high side window. My first thought was that they'd started to wrestle, but who wrestles naked? Then Cunningham expertly flipped the stranger over on all four while the latter exclaimed, 'Oh, Liam!' and both Chris and I covered our mouths with our hands to stop ourselves from laughing out loud.

We jumped down. Chris grabbed my arm to lead me away, and once we'd put a safe distance between us and the 'wrestlers', we screamed with laughter, doubled over, hands on our bellies, chanting, 'Oh, Liam!' over and over.

'Pity we're not allowed phones,' said Chris as we strolled back to our dorm. 'I could have made a video and charged others for viewings.'

Chris often had some weird money-making schemes, but the school had one very strict rule: no mobile phones on school premises.

'We can still make a video, you just have to draw it, like in a comic book.'

'Dude, I think you're overestimating my artistic skills!'

I never overestimated his skills, and we both knew it. Chris worked on the drawings all weekend; he drew only two still images, more precisely: caricatures, and a bubble caption with 'Oh Liam!' had been added to the second one. We then uploaded them onto my laptop, used Moviemaker to make them repeat, and sent the short video to friends.

In hindsight, it was a stupid thing to do since the drawing wasn't proof of anything. Over the following week, the video reached parents and staff alike. It must have been easy to trace it back to us, and we were soon called into the headmaster's office.

'Mr Jennings, Mr Bakker, did you or did you not sign a code of conduct upon entering this school?'

Chris and I exchanged a look. 'We did, sir.'

'You know, therefore, that any form of libel will get you immediately expelled?'

'Sir, we did nothing wrong—'

'You have tarnished the image of this school, made a mockery of the church, and you have lost me a valuable member of staff! Master Cunningham quit over this matter as he felt he would lose all respect with his pupils, and you are lucky neither he nor Vicar Watson wish to sue!'

'Vicar?' I exclaimed as Chris shouted.

'It wasn't us, sir!'

'Mr Jennings, do you take me for a fool?'

Chris lowered his head. 'No, sir.'

'Then, if you do not wish to be expelled, you will write formal letters of apology to Master Cunningham, Vicar Watson, as well as the board of governors. The drawings have been removed, but you are suspended for two weeks, effective immediately.'

Both Chris and I stood silent, unsure of what it meant to be suspended; we were the kids who never left.

The headmaster saw us hesitate and raised his eyebrows. 'Your parents have been notified, gentlemen; I suggest you go pack your bags.'

'Do you mean we are being sent home, sir?'

'That is what suspended means.'

Chris blanched, and I felt bad for him, yet I couldn't help the hint of excitement at the mention of parents and asked, 'My parents, sir? They are coming?'

He put his eyeglasses on and checked his notes. 'Your legal guardian, Mr Timothy Van Beers, he will send for you tomorrow. As for you, Mr Jennings, your father's personal assistant, will collect you on his return from Spain the day after tomorrow.'

I could sense that Chris was trying not to cry as we walked to the grassy playground, and I felt guilty for having suggested the video. If he were cooked like a sausage for talking too much, I couldn't imagine what they would do to him this time.

'You could leave with me tomorrow and stay at my house,' I suggested.

Chris stopped biting his lower lip and smiled, but it was a vacant smile because we both knew it was an empty offer. Grandfather didn't even want me around, let alone someone else's child, and Chris's parents would never allow it.

Grandfather had taken away my phone and laptop in punishment, and the news about Chris did not reach me in Brussels. I did not find out about his demise until my return two weeks later. It seemed he had found a way to access the widow's walk, after all. Accidental death, said the official report, but I didn't believe it. It took years for me to stop grieving, and although I blamed and hated Liam for the part he played, I will always carry the responsibility for Chris's death with me.

When I recount the story to the officer, I leave much of Chris's part out, telling him instead how, thanks to our little prank, Liam's wife found out her husband had deceived and cheated on her and how she left, along with their unborn child. The school later heard the baby was stillborn, and because Maeve Cunningham was a religious zealot, she saw this unfortunate fate as God's punishment for her husband's sin.

'You think that's why Liam Cunningham harmed you?'

'Yes, that's exactly what I think.'

Officer Ahmed's eyebrows rise, and I have a feeling he knows there's something amiss. I try not to avoid his eyes and hold his gaze: I want to – no, I have to – convince him. Nobody can ever know the part we played in my parents' death. He taps the tip of his pen against the notebook, and the noise is distracting. He stares ahead, face blank for a few seconds. 'Why wait twelve years to take his revenge? That seems like an awfully long time.'

It's clear I haven't convinced him, and that's an excellent question; why, indeed? Would Liam really sequester me? I'm not sure how and why I ended up tied to a bed at his house, but I'm pretty certain he wasn't the one who locked me up in the dark.

Best keep my doubts and questions to myself, though. I want to find out the truth, but I don't want the police involved. 'I only recently returned from the States, and he was an alcoholic. I guess he had his demons. Who knows what the drink made him do?'

Officer Ahmed stares at me for a long time and hesitates.

'What's wrong?' I ask.

He shrugs. 'You might as well know; the general theory among the villagers is that it was a case of mistaken identity.'

My eyebrows furrow, but I understand why he stared so hard at me. He might not see it now because I don't look my best, but there is an undeniable physical resemblance between Mouse and me. I sigh with frustration: the bloody police! What was he playing at, letting me recount the story when he already knew what it was all about?

'It is entirely possible you weren't the one targeted. Liam Cunningham had a well-documented history of violence, and there was a previous incident involving Taylor Robbins; there were many witnesses, and as you pointed out, he was an alcoholic. He may have killed himself once he realised his mistake.'

The officer leaves me with this pondering information, and I realise I have to rethink everything.

A previous incident involving Taylor Robbins.

Mouse never mentioned anything, and I thought being detained in the dark was his way of punishing me. That's what Mouse does; he likes 'punishing' people if he thinks they've done him wrong, but try as I might, I could never think of what that could be. If anything, Mouse was the one who did me wrong: he kissed someone else right under my nose!

I still get angry when I think about that day. The nerve of that guy Emilio, or whatever his name is, calling himself Mouse's special friend. And him being so handsome with his Latin good looks and bulging biceps! And him winking at Mouse right in front of me! It took all the strength and acting skills I had to remain unaffected and play it cool, but then I witnessed the two of them kissing, and I had to force my feet out of the restaurant, resisting the urge to separate them and rearrange Latino guy's handsome face.

My afternoon meeting had lasted no longer than an hour, but I hadn't wanted to go straight home, driving around aimlessly instead and eventually stopping in the deserted area of a supermarket car park. I stayed out for as long as I could, prolonging the time before facing Mouse, trying to dissipate my anger. It had taken longer than usual, even after doing breathing exercises and trying to refocus my mind like Mouse had taught me. I had waited for him. I had come back for him! What was he playing at, looking at me like I was the most precious creature on Earth, whispering the words 'I love you' as easily as breathing air, and yet kissing other guys on the side? I had screamed in frustration and bruised my knuckles, punching the steering wheel. The memory of that day has me in a panic, and I start hyperventilating.

He had left me.

I had walked into the overheated house to find him sitting on the bed, surrounded by shambles of shirts and torn sheets of paper, all strewn around the place. He'd looked up at me with eyes an unusual icy blue, devoid of passion and desire, and his face was blank. He was still for a moment, then he'd sprung up, and his right hand had moved toward my throat, but he lost his balance, falling on his knees.

When I'd looked down, my necklace hung between his fingers, the angel and demon swinging and catching the light. He was taking it back, the little couple he had gifted me, and he walked out of the house with them, taking his love back, too.

I have to breathe, in, out. I can't. Because the little couple still hangs from his neck now. Perhaps he hadn't confined me to that cell to punish me; perhaps it had been a ploy to discard me, to make me hate him, to push me to the edge like he had pushed Liam. Oh God, Liam, is he really dead? Did he really kill himself?

I have to breathe, in, out.

I still can't.

The thought of Mouse leaving me is unbearable. I don't care if he kisses a thousand guys or if he locks me up again. I don't even care about my own life and will gladly give it up for him. Just please, please, don't abandon me. Not again. Not you.

Mouse pushes the door of my hospital room so hard it crashes against the easy chair behind it. 'Good news!' he exclaims with a smile. He sees me struggling to breathe and rushes to my side. 'What's wrong?'

'Bad dream,' I lie, and he sits on the bed and pulls me into his arms. I calm down and breathe again, but when he pulls away, I hold on to his sleeve. 'Don't leave!'

'Of course not, I just got here.'

That's not what I meant, and I repeat, 'Don't leave me!'

There is a pause, and I stare into his beautiful blue eyes. They are as glassy and vacant as usual, but, over time, I have learned to read his face in different ways. When he is angry, he clenches his jaws, and the skin around his mouth tightens. When shy or nervous, his ears turn red. When he is happy, his smile is bright, and his laugh childlike, and when he lies, it's easy to tell from the vibration of his voice: he sounds like he's making a bad joke.

I observe him as he replies, 'Never!'

He pronounces the word so fiercely that it sounds less like a promise and more like a threat. He takes my head into his hands, wipes tears off my face with his thumbs, and kisses me. It's like breathing pure air; the kiss, almost tentative, with his warm lips pushing against mine in an instinctive movement, then gradually, I feel his tongue, first against my lips, and then searching for mine until he gives himself completely.

The way Mouse kisses me is unique, and that's how I know he was the one with me in my padded cell.

17

I'M GOING HOME FOR CHRISTMAS. That was the good news Mouse wanted to share with me as we roll south toward Les Vallées. My legs are tense, feet pushing against the floor of his Audi: Mouse only passed his test recently, and he is not a confident driver. I stare through the swinging motion of windshield wipers and watch the soaked road with a sigh. The one-hour drive will feel longer. I'd offered to drive, but Mouse refused, declaring I was 'in the recovery period and still too weak to drive.'

'Whose fault is that?' I reply.

Mouse casts a quick glance at me without a word. He must know that I know. What he doesn't know is it's why I'm staying at his rather than at my parents' house. First, and though I would never say, I am a little scared of being on my own. The clinic had its quiet moments, but there was always someone catering to my every need, and I've never liked being alone in that house. Second, I have to stick to Mouse so he doesn't leave me for someone else – that guy Emilio, for example. Third, I am on a mission to solve two riddles: the first one is the padded cell – and I will dismantle every house and check every basement in the village if I have to – and the second is to find out what really happened to Liam.

I peer at Mouse while he's busy watching the road; his face looks bright and peaceful, but there's a dark side to him. He's not good with lies, yet he can get quite crafty when hiding something. But once I've found the padded room, there will be no escape, no excuses, and I will confront him with it.

As we get closer, the rain has become a drizzle. I glimpse the roof of my house in the distance, standing alone in its rectangular plot and dominating the rest of the village, and I remember the first time I saw it. No cypress hedge surrounded it then, and you could see the whole desolate place in one go.

I was on a recon mission and didn't yet know the house belonged to my parents. Having located them in this village, I needed to proceed with caution. My parents had not seen me since I was six years old, and I wanted to plan a strategy before meeting them. I had considered staying at the B&B, but realising how small the village actually was, I knew I'd have to find an alternative. My parents couldn't know their son was closing in on them or they might disappear – even if by then they had wanted me to find them.

I had been driving around the village at leisure, following the GPS directions, when a figure I recognised waved an arm at his neighbour. The two of them were so engrossed in their conversation that they never even glanced at my rental car. I slowed the car to make sure, and it was none other than my 'Oh Liam' old math teacher.

He had barely changed, slightly grey at the temples but still trim and elegant, and as a pre-adolescent, I had not realised how handsome he was. I drove away feeling happy, already forming plans in my head. They lived in the same village, so he would know my parents, and I had the means to make him talk without their knowing.

I found a hotel room in the nearest town and sat in their restaurant, waiting for my meal. I opened the search engine icon on my phone and entered Liam's full name. It was pretty much a dead-end as he shared a name with a famous Irish actor, then inspiration struck. I went on the local church's website and bingo! After a few well-placed phone calls, I got what I needed. Back in my hotel room, I'd set up a Facebook account under a false name, added the blurry picture of an older model, then took quite some time phrasing the right message – I wanted to make sure not to come across as too young a person.

Hi Liam, Remember me? We met in St Albans about five years ago (or was it ten? Time flies so quickly!). I happen to be in your neck of the woods, just passing through, and wondered if you fancied meeting again, we had such a fun time last time (winking face).

Let me know!

The fishhook was cast. All I had to do was wait and see if Liam would take the bait. It worked, and we were to meet a day later in a forest car park. I couldn't help but snigger at his message: it seemed, after all these years, that 'Oh Liam' hadn't changed his ways.

The sound of the handbrake brings me back to the present, and Mouse has parked the car in his front yard. I unfold my stiff body out of the vehicle, shake my legs, and flex the fingers that had been gripping the handle. I look around at the manicured garden and stare at Mouse's house. It is a Mediterranean-style villa that looks like the succession of three small, attached bungalows, each with a roof at different heights and in a descending pattern from right to left. Each window has two sets of shutters, and I expect the push-open ones are for aesthetics. The front garden matches the house, featuring palm trees, olive trees, banana trees, New Zealand flaxes, lavender bushes, and other Mediterranean plants. Water trickles down a stone amphora-shaped fountain. A garden that was designed to impress.

Mouse has grabbed both our luggage and has already unlocked the door by the time I reach it. I hesitate at the threshold, aware that I'm entering the lion's den by my own choice.

It's my first time entering the villa, and once inside, I realise how deceptively large it is. The kitchen and living areas are open-plan and in the central block. To the left is a door leading to the parental suite with its walk-in closets, large en-suite bathroom and a small office. Mouse has the right 'wing', perhaps the biggest, with two bedrooms, a large shower room with its own washer-dryer, and a door leading to the attached garage.

Mouse has dropped my suitcase next to the closet by the front door.

I grab it and ask, 'Which room is mine?' I want to make it clear that we will not be sharing a bed, not after what he put me through.

He spreads his arms. 'Your choice, my house is yours.'

Although he looks like a young man now, Mouse smiles at me with such an open face I am reminded of the boy I first saw four years ago. We stare at each other, and, for a moment, I think he's going to rush to me and rip my clothes off right there and then, but, instead, he turns away. 'I'll put the kettle on.'

Staying in his parents' bedroom is not an option; it would be inappropriate, and the other end of the house is too far from Mouse. Although I don't want to share a bed, I still want him near me. I settle in the spare bedroom next to his, leaving the shutters open, but come nighttime, I toss and turn, unable to sleep.

There's been a shift in our relationship, and it's not coming from me or what I have been through; Mouse is different. Less needy and more distant.

Even though our relationship is new, Mouse and I have always felt comfortable with each other. He has always been a very touchy-feely person, always stroking my hand or my neck, resting a hand on my lap, or his head on my shoulder, or running his hand through my hair, but since the kiss at the hospital, he has not touched me once. I miss it. I miss him.

I tell myself not to be daft, turn over, and close my eyes, but sleep eludes me. If he'd wanted to get rid of me, Mouse would not have taken me in. He has always known what he wanted, even as a child, and he doesn't waste time on unnecessary stuff. So why did he lock me up? What had he said when I'd asked?

'Because I love you, but do you love me?'

He doubts my love. I feel the heat rise in my face, realising he's never heard me say the famous three little words. And yet, how many times has he told me? How many opportunities did I miss to reciprocate? And how many times in the past have I pushed him away?

Is that all it is? And if so, does the punishment really fit the crime? I reach out a hand, but, of course, there is no one by my side. Staring at the three-quarter moon through the window, I wonder if I'm regretting my decision to sleep in separate bedrooms. It was my decision, yet I don't like that he is not by my side, or the distance between us and the feeling of cold war it's creating.

I get up and tiptoe out of my room.

The doors are open, the shutters up, and a bright moon casts long shadows across the tiled floor. I wander around the house, and something strikes me as strange: there are no photos of Mouse, no family photos on display except a small wedding photo in Mouse's bedroom. The rest are artful tableaux of picturesque countryside.

Mouse has kicked part of the bedding off and is sleeping with one arm above his head and his hair in his face. I grab the comforter and pull it over his body, then sit on the bed and push his hair up high on his forehead and away from his eyes. He looks peaceful and handsome, with his long lashes creating shadows over his cheekbones and his mouth slightly open in the shape of an elongated heart. I resist the urge to kiss him.

His eyes dart from left to right under their lids, face scrunching up in pain, and his hand twitches as if to fend off something, and I know that he's not dreaming but having a nightmare. I lift the comforter and lie against him. He settles down, and now that he's at peace, I close my eyes and go straight to sleep.

I wake up and run a hand on the sheet. The spot next to me on the bed feels cold and empty.

Scuffing sounds reach me from the living room, and I get up to find Mouse fully dressed and putting on his hiking boots.

'Morning; where are you going?'

'To the Petersons for supplies, and they should have pre-prepared a turkey for us.'

'A turkey?! For the two of us?'

'Only a small one and two friends will be joining us.'

He leaves before I can ask, and I'm disappointed that he didn't give me a parting kiss. Walking back to my room, I wonder who the two friends are. Mouse is a loner, but this is a tight community, and during my brief stay here, I quickly discovered there were two people who would always get help and protection from the others, whether or not they were aware of it. One of them is Daniel, and I'm not sure why. Perhaps it is his gentle nature, or perhaps he's not as strong as the other boys, although I had seen him digging and planting trees with as much gusto as the others, but more likely, it had to do with his sick father. The other one is Mouse.

Involving others in the making of my garden had been a way not only to get to know them but also to gather information about my parents. It was dismaying to realise none of them had known my parents at all, as if they'd been invisible, leaving no traces behind, but planting trees together had been a bonding experience, and conversations had flowed. They may have known nothing about my parents, but they certainly knew Mouse, and the information about him came later when the boys had left and Leah and Jade turned up with a picnic basket full of homemade dishes, courtesy of Jade's mother.

'Mum wanted to invite you for dinner, but with the pet situation, we thought a picnic would be best,' Jade had declared before proceeding to set the table with tablecloth, napkins, and dinnerware. The food had been delicious, the conversation easy, and I had liked them both very much. They were genuine, kind, and unlike the other girls, had not tried to flirt with me.

I had held my tongue all day, trying not to ask about Mouse, the boy I had to ignore and stay away from, whose deep soft voice didn't match his long-haired appearance. The boy who had had the daring to tie my hands behind my back and tell me that *he*, the child, would take advantage of me. The boy who had seemed so confident and unafraid of who he was and the only one who hadn't come to see me work.

Jade was being helpful in telling me who was who in the village, and I tried so hard not to mention his name – I had to get him out of my head – but there had been such a strange connection with him, as if we were kin, and I finally let it out: 'That boy Mouse is a bit weird.'

I saw it immediately in the way they looked at each other, the same way people rally for a common cause, so giving them my killer smile, I added, 'I like him, though.'

I don't know what it is about me, but people find it easy to open up to me, and my smile never fails to charm.

It didn't fail me that day, and Jade said, 'I suppose he is a little weird, but that's because he grew up all by himself.'

'Oh?'

'His parents are old, and his mother is always busy with her councillor duties. He's always alone, and he fends for himself.' She hesitated about what she was going to say next, and my smile widened. 'One time, I was with my mum in their house, and in comes Mouse with his legs covered in blood. He'd fallen from a tree and scraped his skin quite badly; he must have been about six years old, but he didn't cry. I was only ten myself, so I looked at his mum, thinking she would get up and deal with him, but she never moved. She just asked if he was okay, and Mouse nodded, then he went straight to the medicine cabinet, cleaned his wounds, and tended to them all by himself. I was both shocked and impressed that day.'

'He impressed my parents too,' added Leah before ramming a massive salad leaf into her mouth. Jade had looked at her knowingly. I could tell she knew what Leah was about to say, and I suspected they all knew.

'What did he do?'

'Dave Newbury was about to take his brother-in-law and family to the airport when his car broke down, so Dave called my dad; but it turned out that his brother-in-law was racist, and when my dad turned up, he refused to go, shouting, "I'm not getting in there with a Black." Mouse was there filling a colouring book with Olivia – he was about seven or eight, I think – and he replied, "He's not a Black, he's a Wilkins." At which point, the brother-in-law shouted, "Go home, kid!" Mouse put his colouring pens down, stood up, held out his hand for my dad to shake and asked, "How much to take me home?" According to my dad, he sounded dead serious, as if trying to make a point. A mere eight-year-old kid,' she'd scoffed.

The memory of the conversation has me smiling, and I feel sheepish. I had told myself to stay away from Mouse, and yet, a few moments later, I'd been at his house knocking on his window.

It would be great if the people sharing our Christmas lunch were Jade and Leah. I wouldn't mind Ethan being one of them either; he is stunning with his fierce Asian eyes and perfect body. I shake my head and admonish myself. I shouldn't be dwelling on the identity of our guests; instead, I should concentrate on fulfilling my mission.

I put on some loose sportswear and reach for my phone. After Mouse left my house on that fateful day, I thought he would soon come back. We were both angry and needed to cool down, but he didn't return, and I went to find him at his accommodation only to be told he wasn't there. I try to remember what happened after that, but the memory eludes me. All I have is the strange sensation of my weakened body carried away by brawny arms. Between that moment and waking up in the dark is a complete blank.

I'm almost certain the padded room is not in Mouse's house; he wouldn't be that reckless, but I check everywhere anyway, and it goes quick as there's no cellar and no hidden rooms.

On my way to the garden shed, I glimpse Liam's house in the distance, all closed up, and I'm not sure what I'm feeling. A blanket of glistening dew covers the grass, and the air is humid, but the weather is mild, and I stand staring at the house for quite some time. The fact I was found inside it seems surreal – almost like moving in circles – yet it will be my next place of investigation. It's difficult to imagine Liam wanting to keep me trapped inside, not after the trouble he went through to chase me away. I'm not sure how far the police went, but it seems they never found a padded room.

I need to see it. I need the physical proof it wasn't a figment of my imagination because I know what the police would have said if I'd mentioned it and they had found nothing. That I had been drugged and confused, that my mind had played a trick on me, that my mental state was fragile, and they would have had me consulted by a psychiatrist. Not going to happen. Nobody's going to look inside my head.

A hand on my shoulder startles me, and Mouse gives me a hug. I am glad at the embrace; perhaps I had imagined our cold war. He peeks at Liam's house and squeezes my hand. 'It's okay, he's never going to hurt us again.'

He pulls me inside and presents me with two beautifully wrapped presents. 'Merry Christmas!'

I stare at the gifts, not knowing what to say, and Mouse encourages me to open them. I start with the small one, which is a pocket watch; the second is a beautiful, navy-blue, perforated leather jacket.

'It's a summer jacket, so you won't be able to wear it yet, but look, you can fold it into a small headrest.'

My fingers stroke the delicate texture of the leather, and I am touched; Mouse has grasped my fashion sense. I don't go for big labels or follow fashion trends but prefer tailor-made and rare items.

'I… thank you, Mouse, you shouldn't have. I don't have anything to gift you in return—'

He waves my words away. 'Your presence here is enough, and you did give me a gift of sorts: you reunited me with something I thought was forever lost.'

'Really? What?'

He doesn't reply but turns and walks to the entrance closet and pulls out a grey denim baseball cap that he adjusts on his head.

I swallow hard and blanch at the sight of it.

18

MOUSE AND I GET BUSY preparing the Christmas meal. Mouse says it's a combination of both French and British tradition, so there's foie gras and salmon for starter, as well as oysters and shrimps, even though I hate seafood and, apparently, Makayla can't eat it, but Mouse assures me there will be other savoury snacks for the two of us.

I tried not to show disappointment when told that Daniel McFarlane and Makayla Cohen were the ones joining us. I have had little interaction with Makayla in the past, so I don't know her very well, and as for Daniel, he may just be one of my least favourite people. He's too nice to be normal, and I wonder what his kindness hides. Maybe he'll explode one day like one of those crazies who walks into a school and starts shooting at random. To top it all off, I think he has a bit of a thing for Mouse. Mouse knows it too, as he flashed a hint of a smile at the mention of his name, as though he were both aware of making me jealous and pleased about it.

I sigh, casting short peeks at Mouse, who peels Brussel sprouts, denim cap turned backward on his head, and I can't help but think about the first time I saw him. Not at church like he believes, but at my own parents' crash site.

I had been waiting for ten minutes when Liam's compact car pulled up in the forest parking lot, and my rental had misted over. Ours had been the only two vehicles there, but he had not looked my way; neither did he get out of his car after killing the engine. I had waited a beat, and he eventually stepped out to walk toward the back of the car. I got worried when he pulled a rifle out of the trunk, but then realised he wore khaki cargo pants and some sort of fisherman's vest over a T-shirt, perhaps in the pretence of going hunting. He looked around and, without a glance toward my car, stepped into the forest.

I hurried out of my rental to follow him, desperate not to lose him. He walked ahead of me for a few feet, then stopped. He turned and seemed startled to see me. Liam mumbled a *bonjour,* and I reciprocated, sticking my hand out for a handshake, which he took distractedly, throwing an anxious look over my shoulder.

'There's no one else,' I said. 'I'm the one you're expecting.'

He frowned at me. 'Who are you?'

'I guess you don't recognise me. Weird, considering I might be the reason you live in this country.'

'Is that so? Or you're just a silly young man with a big ego. Anyway, I'm not interested, and you're too young for this sort of thing. You should have stayed home with Mammy and Daddy.'

He side-stepped me, and I said, 'Come on, sir! I was suspended from school because of you. My friend died because of you!'

He stood still for a few seconds, then turned around and stared at me. 'You're the Bakker boy?'

'So you do remember!'

There was a moment of stillness when we heard nothing but the buzzing of insects and the distant sound of vehicles approaching. I couldn't help but stare at the rifle in Liam Cunningham's hand, mentally cursing myself for my stupidity in challenging a man holding a weapon, but Liam was not looking at me. He dashed to walk past, but I blocked his way, and he charged toward the road instead. I followed, not wanting to let him get away so easily.

We had just reached the road when I grabbed his arm, but quickly let go as a vehicle was approaching fast, and the tarmac was still wet from the rain. We both looked in its direction, and it was just as it drove past, avoiding us, that I saw my father at the wheel. The final look on my parents' faces before their death will forever stay imprinted in my brain: a look of recognition. I had no doubt they had recognised me, as if they had watched me grow all that time, and it was perhaps this shock of recognition that had my father's car veer off course to the left, straight onto an oncoming SUV and the motorcycle behind it. Neither car barely had time to brake, and the crash was tremendous.

My memory is sketchy at this point, it's like a succession of images: Liam raising his hands to his head and falling on his knees, rifle by his side on the road, one car sort of rolling over the other and leaving it flattened before flying and crashing on the tarmac, fumes and gasoline and blood everywhere, a body being catapulted against a tree at the same time as a cracked windshield, another body, headless and lying at a funny angle, and one covered in blood with white-blond hair in the middle of the road: my mother.

I'd rushed behind the nearest tree and vomited my lunch.

Liam had grabbed his phone to call the emergency services, facing away from the crash as if he couldn't stand to look. I didn't want to look either but had to force myself – it was my parents who were dying – but when I raised my head, I couldn't see anything as a thick cloud of smoke engulfed me, followed by a powerful gust of wind, pushing it away, and taking the cap off someone's head.

It was then that things became surreal because the person who had lost their baseball cap and stood in front of my mother was... me... or rather... a figure resembling my past self of when I had been about fourteen or fifteen years old. My mother must have thought so too because she raised a hand and called out my name. 'Tommy!'

I closed my eyes and shook my head, but when I looked again, the vision had disappeared. I was sure I'd imagined it. I ran toward my mother and checked her pulse, but couldn't hear anything, and she didn't quite look... whole. Tears covered my face, making my vision blurry, and I had the stupid thought that because I couldn't see well, I couldn't hear well either. I kept holding on to her wrist until Liam pulled me out of the way, pointing toward the sound of the sirens. 'It's too late for her! Don't touch anything, you've done enough damage! Let them do their job; you can't do anything for these people now.'

Under normal circumstances, I might have slugged him, but grief had numbed my senses, and a realisation kicked in: Liam didn't know who I was in relation to my parents. He had never met them at school, had always known me as Tommy Bakker. To him, I was just a stranger who'd witnessed a car crash.

Disoriented, I moved away in search of my father but couldn't find him, and I knew, deep down, that I wouldn't because he was still encased inside his flattened car.

Mouse opens up an oyster, and I feel nauseous. I excuse myself to go to the bathroom and splash water on my face.

Although I hadn't seen that cap for a few years, seeing it now on Mouse's head fills me with a strange sense of loss, as if I were losing my parents all over again.

I had walked through the cataclysm of the accident, despair overwhelming all other feelings, and looked for my father's body, hoping he had escaped his car somehow, hoping he was still alive, but all I saw was death. I was on the verge when I stepped on the cap, picked it up, and ran my fingers over the IOWA letters several times, just to make sure it was real. Then I'd held on to it for dear life and walked along the road, not knowing where I was going, not caring either. I just kept on walking, sometimes on the short wet grass, sometimes through brambles and stinging nettles until my body ran out of tears and pain and sorrow, and I'd let myself fall on the leafy ground and curl up into a ball, hugging the cap like a baby holding their blanket until one of the ambulance drivers found me.

Water sputters out, splashing onto the basin, and I turn the faucet off. When I get back to the kitchen, Mouse has finished arranging the seafood platter and is wiping the countertops. He points at the fine white china in the display cabinet, asks me to help him set the table up, and pulls a red tablecloth out of a drawer. My hands feel clammy, and I brush them against my thighs before carrying the dinnerware to the table.

When we are done, the table is beautifully set with silverware, crystal glasses, crisp red-and-green cotton napkins folded into some sort of crowns, and red candles in silver candlesticks. I'm surprised at how much care Mouse has put into it all; he didn't strike me as the type to worry much about Christmas. I wonder who exactly he is trying to impress and secretly hope it's me.

'I'll go in the shower first, if you don't mind,' he says as he steps out of the living area.

A few minutes later, I follow. The denim cap lies discarded on the bed, and the silver pendant rests on the bedside table. I fight the urge to grab them both, feeling possessive toward them, and laugh at myself for looking almost as crazed as Gollum and its 'precious'. Still, they were both mine once, and I have to get them back, which means I have to regain Mouse's love and trust.

His words echo in my mind. 'Because I love you, but do you love me?' I grab my phone to call Nikki and ask for her advice – without telling her about the ordeal I went through – but I remember it's like 5 a.m. for her in Tallahassee. I don't feel up to talking to anyone else just yet, and I already know what Nikki would have said. 'Just tell him you love him!'

But do I? The voice in my head says yes, but why am I incapable of actually pronouncing the words? I suppose I have never said the words before; to anyone. I may have told my parents before my sixth birthday, but if so, I do not remember and until Mouse, no one had told me either.

I have even less reason to tell him now. He locked me in the dark for... I count the days on my fingers; I was found on the nineteenth, and the last day I remember, the day I went to his student room, was the fifth: eleven days, not counting the three days in Liam's house. It felt like more. It felt like a lifetime. I should hate him now, but I don't because I know I deserved locking up: I kissed him when he was just a child, corrupting him. He had every right to punish me for my transgression, and I want his love; I need his love. I crave his love as strongly as a baby craving her mother's milk, and I have to take a leap of faith.

The sound of running water rushes, and I think, I could go to him, join him in the shower, and whisper the words 'I love you' as his lips kiss my neck.

A leap of faith. I hesitate, undress, and open the bathroom door. His figure detaches itself through a warm cloud of coconut-scented mist, and I get close enough to stand in front of him. He is shampooing his hair with his eyes scrunched shut and doesn't see me.

Whenever I see Mouse's body, I can't help but stare in wonder at the outline of his perfectly shaped abs; as long as we've been together, I have never seen him exercise. Not a hint of a push-up or sit-up, and he doesn't feel that strong either, so I have no idea where they come from. Perhaps it's genetic.

He opens his eyes and jumps, startled to see me, and my mouth moves to speak.

'…'

The words won't come out. Not the right ones, anyway. I am meant to say, 'I love you', but instead, they turned into 'I want you' in my mind. I take a deep breath, mentally push myself to make the effort, and try again. 'I—'

Mouse pulls me against him and kisses me as the hot water hits my chest, and the words die in my throat.

My skin feels raw as I shave. After raiding Mouse's bathroom cupboard for a strong moisturiser – the water in this region is hard – I try to style my hair with a left parting, wanting to look sophisticated, but it's frustratingly short, and I can't do much with it. With just a towel around my waist, I walk into Mouse's bedroom to find him dressed, wearing a light-grey suit and a simple white shirt. His blond hair has been smoothed, parted, and stuck behind his ears, and he looks terribly handsome.

He strokes my cheek with the back of his hand as he brushes past me. 'Don't take too long, they will be here soon.'

The bed is fully made, and there is no sign of the cap, but the angel and demon necklace still lies on the bedside table. I pick it up and rest it on my palm, staring at the intricately detailed wings, then I tie it around my neck and go to my room to get ready.

I am dressed to kill, wearing my shiny charcoal suit over a light-grey shirt with my favourite silk olive-green waistcoat and matching cravat. The suit pants are normally tight-fitting but having lost quite a few pounds, I have to wear a belt to stop them from falling at the waist. I feel frustrated, but when Mouse sees me, the blue of his eyes burns bright, his pupils dilate, and a wave of warmth rushes through me.

I readjust my sleeves and run a hand over my hair as he opens the front door. Makayla is the first to enter, hollering a season's greeting and slipping me a bottle of Jameson Black Barrel in hand. I barely have time to register the simple black dress moulding her petite but curvaceous body before she engulfs me in a tight hug and moves on quickly, trailing something behind her and leaving me in a cloud of strong heady perfume that has me slightly dizzy.

'That's what I thought!' she exclaims.

She pulls food containers, a small, folded Christmas tree, and decorations out of a black canvas shopping trolley and gets to work. Meanwhile, Mouse and Daniel share one of those silly handshakes, holding arms, brushing palms, bumping fists, and I try not to show any annoyance at this.

Daniel puts himself in front of me. 'I'm sorry about what happened to you.'

I nod coldly and stick out my free hand. He grabs it and pulls me into a soft embrace, and, although I have to bend my back because he is shorter than me, his warm hug feels comforting. He then joins Makayla in the living area, puts a hand on the small of her back, kisses her on the head, and that's when I realise they are a couple. It seems I was wrong about him.

I thank them for the bottle and offer them a drink; I'm surprised they're not spending Christmas with family and tell them as much.

'We had a big turkey dinner on Thanksgiving, and my family is Jewish,' replies Makayla.

'But you just brought a Christmas tree!'

'Yes, the tree is a secular symbol of the season, not a Christian one.'

I help her with the tree and find that she is lively, funny, and easy-going. When she smiles, she is extremely pretty, with a dimple on her right cheek and dark freckles dotting her tanned face. I'm not sure what she sees in Daniel. He is very banal, and the only interesting things about him are the flame tattoos crawling up his forearms, but now I know he doesn't have any design on my mini Mouse, I feel much more relaxed and lenient toward him.

We are comfortable around each other, and thanks to their presence, this turns into the best Christmas dinner I've had in years. Mouse is not very good with small talk – he tends to go straight to the point – but he has known these people all his life, and he is a superb host, witty and talkative, expertly corking and decanting wine, knowing which drinks to serve and when or how long to wait between courses, and it's easy to forget he's only eighteen and the youngest among us.

I suppose, though, that the awkward moment was inevitable. How long can you go on with a conversation without mentioning the obvious? I drink far too much, and there's a lull in the conversation. 'What do you think will happen to Liam's house now?' I ask.

Silence fills the room, and it's like time stopping. I'm aware I have made our guests uncomfortable as heads look down toward their plate, but I can't help myself and push on. 'Will it be sold?'

I look at Mouse, who sits across from me, but it's Daniel next to him who nervously picks up his glass and replies, 'I'm not sure, but after' – he glances at Mouse – 'what happened; I suspect it might stay empty for a while.'

'Good.' I nod, and Makayla's hand comes resting on mine.

'I'm so sorry.'

'Don't be, it's not your fault.'

'Perhaps it is, perhaps it's all our fault. We should have seen this coming after the way he had it in for Mouse; he put him in the hospital for God's sake!'

'He what?!'

I sober up quickly and whip my head to look at her. Makayla's mouth forms an O as she realises my ignorance in the matter, and Mouse whispers, 'It was a long time ago.'

But Daniel seems like he can no longer contain his anger. 'It was only two years ago! And what about that

Halloween night when he was hell-bent on harming you, nearly strangling you, or the few days before when he locked you up in a dark cupboard for hours?! We should have known he was not right in the head!'

This is too much information all at once and too shocking to contemplate. I take my cravat off – the damn thing feels like it is suffocating me. I stand precipitously, pushing my chair back with a scraping noise, and stare at Mouse, speechless. I shake my head and my voice trembles. 'He, he—he locked you up. He physically locked you up?'

Mouse nods and my right fist hits the table, making the crockery shudder and an empty glass tip over. 'Why didn't you tell me? WHY?'

Makayla jumps, and I see they are all taken aback by my outburst. Mouse rises from his chair to put a hand on my arm in a calming gesture and looks me straight in the eye. 'Help me clear the table, will you?'

'Actually, Daniel will help you with that,' declares Makayla. She rises too, takes my hands in hers, and pulls me back down on my chair. Mouse and Daniel get busy going back and forth, clearing the table. She waits until they're both in the kitchen and tells me to take a deep breath – and I do as she says.

She takes a deep breath too. 'You can be quite scary, you know!'

'Me?'

'Hell, yes. Just now, when I saw the storm in your eyes, I had the urge to take all the knives on this table away from you. You have this air about you sometimes, like… you're hard.' Her cheeks redden as she realises what she said has a double meaning. 'I mean tough, sorry, the bane of being bilingual and thinking in French. Sometimes words are being translated literally.'

I laugh. 'I know what you mean; I speak four different languages myself. And I went to an all-boys school: you quickly learn to stand your ground. Sorry if I scared you.'

'It's okay. Are you okay?'

'Yes, no, I don't know. He should have told me.'

'I think you'd already left when the assault happened, and knowing Mouse, my guess is he didn't want to worry you about things that are in the past.'

'So that's what the "previous incident involving Taylor" is,' I whisper inaudibly.

I lean my elbows on the table and rest my head in my hands; once again, my world has been turned upside down. I recall Mouse's words said earlier outside, *he's never going to hurt us again*. Not *you*, but *us*, and I should have known; Mouse had tried to warn me about Liam right from the very beginning. Is it possible Liam was indeed the one who held me captive?

The other two return to the table, and a silence stretches. I raise my head. 'I need to see it, Liam's house. All of it actually, where he locked you up, where I was tied up, everywhere, everything, I need to see it.'

'I'm not sure that's such a good idea,' replies Mouse. He rests a gentle hand on my arm. 'You still need to recover, and anyway, the house is all locked up.'

'Actually…' Daniel hesitates. He is stroking and scratching the tablecloth with a finger as we all look at him. 'You could see it as early as tomorrow if you want. I happen to have a key.'

I lean back against my chair with an enormous sigh and exclaim with happiness, 'Outstanding! Then it's settled.'

I glance at Mouse with a smile, but his eyes glower at Daniel. His jaws are tightly clenched, and there's a strange, intense expression on his face.

19

MOUSE HAS GIVEN ME the silent treatment for the best part of the evening. He is taking his anger out on appliances – slamming their doors – and on other inanimate objects which are treated none too gently. I stand with my hands behind my back, staring at the lights of the small fake Christmas tree Makayla set on a sideboard, when a hand on my shoulder forces me to turn around.

'I'm not happy about this,' he says with a frown on his face.

'I don't care.'

His finger comes pointing hard on my chest. 'What the hell is wrong with you? Have you forgotten what he did to you?'

I push his hand away and grab his neck hard, fingers digging into his skin, thumb lifting his chin, and I get all up in his face. 'What about you? What did you do to me?'

'What?'

'Did you lock me up? Did you enjoy it, making me your plaything, having me at your mercy, all starving and feeble and compliant?'

'What are you talking about?'

'That's your thing, isn't it? Being powerful and dominant and taking charge, perhaps you even enjoyed hurting me.'

He pushes me away, sending me cannoning into the couch, and I let myself fall sitting on it.

'You've gone crazy! I would never hurt you, never! How could I hurt you when I love you? I love you so much that sometimes I can't breathe when I look at you. I love you so much, so fucking much, but all you care about is "Liam"! That's all you've ever cared about! And I hate him! Even now he's dead, he still has a hold on you! I hate what he did to me, and I hate what he did to you; I hate that you met him in secret, that you have a past with him you still haven't shared with me, I hate that you want to be in his house, that you still feel close enough to call him "Liam", you have no idea how much I hate that word in your mouth!'

I have never seen Mouse cry, not even that day at his mother's funeral when he could have used the rain as cover for his tears. He had remained face dry under the open umbrella, head held high, looking aristocratic in his dark suit and almost peaceful. But now tears slide down his cheeks, and the sight of them is both shocking and heartbreakingly painful.

I grab his hand to pull him onto the couch next to me and hold him tight, burying his head in my neck and stroking his hair. 'I'm sorry, I'm sorry, I love you too, Mouse, I love you.'

It took Mouse's tears for me to be able to say the words, and now that I've said them, I wonder why it was so difficult; it feels like they're tumbling out of my mouth. 'I love you too, don't cry, mini Mouse, don't cry, I love you, don't cry.'

And now he sobs harder, chest hiccupping against me, and I keep kissing his forehead and stroking his back until he's all out of tears.

He lifts his face to kiss me; his lips move down to my neck while a hand unties the buttons of my shirt. Mouse's tongue teases one nipple, then the other. His mouth moves further down, and my mind goes blank, swimming in a sea of pleasure.

Mouse is 'feather' stroking the fold of my arm with a finger, and the gentle touch makes me shiver. He grabs the sofa throw and covers us with it at the same time as pulling me to lean against him. 'I never thought age mattered,' he says as he strokes the palm of my hand. 'I didn't care that you were six years older than me. It meant nothing to me, but now I see that there's a whole world about you that I don't know.'

'What do you want to know?'

'Everything, I suppose.'

'But you have something specific in mind?'

'No, I really want to know everything, perhaps starting with why you and Cunningham had a secret meeting on the day your parents died.'

I blink, surprised Mouse knew about it, though I shouldn't be. He had opened up to me in the past, revealing some of the villagers' darkest secrets, and if he'd found out about these, then there was no reason he wouldn't know about my meeting with Liam.

I sit up, exhale, and brush my hair with my hand. 'You're not the only one who hated him. I hated him too, Liam. Sorry, Cunningham. Perhaps not as much as you, but I hated him too. I know you don't like me calling him by his first name, but that's what we called him ever since Chris and I caught him with the vicar; he was no longer a "Master" or a "Sir" after that…'

I tell him everything, from the time I first arrived in the village – as well as some background information about that incident at school – to when I turned around in church, expecting to see Liam and wanting to witness him realise whose son I was but meeting Mouse's gaze instead.

'Chris was your best friend?'

I nod. Mouse gives me an intense look, and I know what he's getting at. 'Just a friend, nothing more; I wasn't… I didn't know then.'

'So you've been with girls?'

'No. I mean, I had girlfriends when I was young; peer pressure, you know. But in truth, until I was eighteen, I was pretty much interested in neither boys nor girls.'

'Then you met someone?'

I nod. 'Then I met someone.'

Or rather, someone met me. The funny thing was that it was Grandfather himself who'd introduced us that summer: Niels Pierson was to be my driving instructor.

I had never seen such an ugly man. Niels extended a hand so hairy it looked repulsive, and I was loath to take it. Perhaps he had been told to present himself wearing formal clothing because he looked uncomfortable in an ill-fitting cheap suit. I watched as the ape-like hand moved to his neck to loosen his tie, and the gesture awakened something in me.

Looking at him more carefully, I saw that he wasn't ugly exactly, just that he had unusual features, and I gave him my best smile, suddenly desperate to make a good impression. I knew nothing of his age, marital status, or sexual inclinations – in fact, I wasn't sure of my own inclinations, just that I was attracted to him.

Although I had the gift of charming people into doing what I asked – it only took a bright smile – I had zero experience in flirting. Whether boy or girl, others had always made the first move and been rejected, so I wasn't sure how to go about it. Perhaps that's why I chose to be outrageous.

Once alone with Niels, I approached him and started untying his tie. 'You don't need this,' I murmured in my softest voice, catching his eye.

He took a step back and thanked me while his left hand pulled on the tie to remove it. I checked his fingers for a wedding band and was pleased to see none. His reaction had been polite but encouragingly mild, and I kept up with the outrageous flirting during the entire driving lesson, grabbing his hairy hand to show me how to hold the steering wheel properly, brushing his leg while changing gear or playing dumb and using any available reason to invade his personal space.

The next day, I waited for the lesson with bated breath, wondering if he would return, which he did, wearing casual attire and looking more approachable. I showered Niels with attention, and he always showed indifference, but during the course, I noticed a few gradual changes in him. He took more care of his physical appearance, with his dark hair cut more fashionably, his three-day beard trimmed in a neat fashion, and his nails looked cleaner.

It was after a late driving lesson – to experience driving in the dark – that I invited him out for a drink.

'You shouldn't drink and drive, you know that!' He laughed, patting me on the back, and his hand stayed there a second longer than normal.

I looked back at the house. 'We could have a drink here.'

He nodded, followed me into the foyer, and Louise, our newly appointed housekeeper, greeted him with a warm smile before saying to me, 'Monsieur Timothy is out.'

She left with an abrupt turn and went back to her occupations. I missed Elise, our previous housekeeper. The woman had been with the family for almost her entire life and had practically raised me. She had been a warm and kind mother figure and had always taken my side when Grandfather and I argued, but she'd retired and moved with her husband to the south of France. This new housekeeper had quickly worked out where the power resided, and it wasn't with me, so she only gave me the minimal and necessary amount of her attention.

I'd intended to take Niels upstairs to my own sitting-room, but now I knew Grandfather was out, I was apprehensive, and we remained downstairs in the bar area tucked between the lounge and the library.

'What's your poison?' I asked Niels, who looked up at the large bookshelves in the library.

'I'll have whatever you're having.'

I grabbed a bottle of Old Forester Rye and poured us a glass each. The palms of my hands were sweaty. I rubbed them on my thigh and after making sure his attention was turned elsewhere, downed my drink quickly before pouring myself another.

He stared straight into my eyes as we clinked glasses, and he dipped his index finger into the alcohol before sucking it provocatively. My mouth felt dry, and I swallowed my drink with large gulps. He followed suit and downed his drink in a manly fashion, put his glass down, and took mine out of my hand; then he kissed me hard, so violently that I almost tripped over a footstool.

Although I had watched porn and made some preparations, nothing prepared me for the actual physical act, and Niels was more aggressive than expected. But I needn't have worried about my inexperience; Niels was an expert, and I was as malleable as putty in his hairy hands.

If the brain receives simultaneous signals of pain and pleasure, it will lessen the pain and let pleasure take over, perhaps as an instinctive coping mechanism; but once the pleasure was gone, the pain returned with a vengeance. The next day, I moved with difficulty.

I was still in bed when Niels turned up for the morning lesson. Despite sending the message that I was unwell and the lesson was therefore cancelled, he found a way to barge into my bedroom, looking confused and hurt.

'So that's how it's going to be now? You're cowardly refusing to see me? I can still separate the personal from the professional and do my job!'

It hadn't occurred to me that my behaviour could be misinterpreted. 'No, that's not—' I tried to get up, but pain burned down my legs, and I moaned.

'What's wrong?'

'What do you think?!' He gave me a blank look, and I couldn't believe I had to spell it out for him. 'You weren't exactly gentle last night. For a first time, it was a bit intense!'

He straightened up and blinked a few times. 'That's not even funny.'

My face must have displayed truth and innocence because his eyes filled with anger, and his mouth contorted as he hissed, 'That can't be right, not after the way you came on to me, *you* came on to *me*!' He paced toward the door and back. 'Is that even possible?'

'Why not?'

'I mean, come on! Look at you, you could have anyone you wanted!'

A knock at my door interrupted, and Louise's head peeked in. 'I'm sorry for disturbing you,' she said in French, looking at Niels and not looking sorry at all. 'Monsieur Timothy would like to see you in his office.'

It appeared Grandfather had got wind of what had transpired the previous night.

I tried to hurry after Niels, but pain was against me. After a quick but soothing hot bath, I marched into Grandfather's home office and slammed his door open.

His secretary was bent over some paperwork on his desk, offering a generous view of her cleavage, which he ogled with a contented expression. She was younger than half his age!

'You, out!' I said to her, and she collected the papers into a neat pile before leaving. I waited until the door was firmly shut behind her before turning back to Grandfather, glaring. 'Where is he?'

Grandfather leaned back in his chair with a tired sigh. 'Here we go again!'

It sounded unarguably similar to the incessant question he'd had to endure over the years – and it was perhaps for that very reason he never wanted me around – the one regarding his refusal to even mention them and demanding to know my parents' whereabouts.

He crossed his arms sternly. 'You will never see that man again. You don't need any more lessons anyway, you're ready to take your driving test.'

He picked up a pen and stared at the screen of his iPad to show the matter was over. I turned to leave, knowing he could not control me or watch my every move. If I wanted to be with Niels, the hell with him!

Grandfather raised his head. 'Oh, by the way, you remember my friend Keano Smet from Antwerp? He is sending his youngest daughter over for a while; she's a fine young woman, and she's about your age. I suggest you make her your girlfriend.'

I swallowed hard and shook my head. 'You are despicable, you know that?'

He stood up and threw the pen on the desk. 'And you are disgusting! I will not have my grandson be someone's little bitch, do you understand? Or you will be cut off from this family like your father before you, with no home and no financial support!'

'Fine! Am I really a member of this family, anyway? I hardly live here!' I left, slamming the door shut behind me.

My mouth has run dry. I lean away from Mouse and get up to put the kettle on.

'What happened?' asks Mouse when I return with two mugs of hot milky tea. 'Did you leave?'

'What happened was that my uncle Victor, Grandfather's favourite son and president of the New York branch, had been diagnosed with pancreatic cancer. The cancer had spread to the bones; he didn't have long, and Grandfather left to be with him, though he left me with quite the eighteenth birthday present.'

'Ah, and you were free to meet up with Niels.'

'I didn't. Truth was, and I know this makes me sound bad, but once I'd conquered him, I was not that interested. On top of that, I had just acquired shares in the company, a voting right of eight percent, a few board meetings a year to attend, and I had the Van Beers name to uphold. I might have continued to meet Niels only to challenge Grandfather's authority, but with him gone, it was game over. I didn't bother to go looking for him, and Grandfather may have paid him extra to stay away. I did get to meet that friend's daughter, though, my one-and-only best friend, Nikki. She's fantastic, you'll love her!'

'Will I?'

Mouse takes a sip of his tea, and his big blue eyes peer at me above the rim of the mug.

I remember how he last saw the two of us and laugh. 'There never was, nor will there ever be, anything more than friendship between us.'

Mouse puts his mug down, and his face turns serious. 'Listen, are you sure about going into Cunningham's house tomorrow?'

'Yes, Mouse, I am.'

He bites his bottom lip, and the gesture is sensuous. I want to kiss him and lean toward him, but he gets up stiffly. 'I won't be going with you.'

He walks away to his bedroom, and the door clicks shut behind him.

20

I WATCH ETHAN AND MAKAYLA walk up the path to the front door and realise why I barely remembered Makayla before. The eyes are pulled toward Ethan and seem to blur everything around him. It isn't just the flawless features of his face, which seem to have been drawn by a heavenly hand, but also his height and the stance of his perfectly proportioned body. I cannot help the grin on my face when he shakes my hand.

Once inside, he removes his jacket, hangs it on the back of a dining-room chair, and I am surprised at the ease people show when in Mouse's house. They all look comfortable and at home here. Ethan wears a tight-fitting turtleneck that outlines every single one of his muscles, and the shapes of his pecs look quite impressive.

'Blimey, you're as bad as Mouse! You two have more in common than just your looks!' exclaims Makayla beside me.

'Huh?' I realise I was staring and also have, unwillingly but rudely, ignored her. I try to cover up my mistake. '"Blimey"? That sounds awfully British; where is your American pride, girl?'

She laughs. I elbow her and whisper, 'I have a strange feeling of déjà vu here; what's going on? Where is Danny boy?'

'He's at work.'

'On Boxing Day?'

'There is no such thing here, and even if he didn't have to work, Daniel would never set foot in Cunningham's house. He hates the place.'

'And… doesn't he mind about…?' I ask, pointing my chin toward Ethan, who is now in the kitchen, leaning elegantly against the countertop and chatting with Mouse.

'Of course not; we are all friends here, and Dan and I have the kind of relationship where we trust each other. He's the one who suggested Ethan as soon as Mouse texted he wasn't going. He thought you might like a "strong male presence".'

I have to hand it to Daniel; he is a much better man than me, boldly leaving his girlfriend in the hands of an ex, especially one as gorgeous as Ethan.

Mouse and Ethan join us in the simile hallway, and Ethan gives me a pat on the shoulder. 'You're ready?'

'I'm ready.'

I give one last look at Mouse before leaving. His reason for not going was that he 'had bad experiences in that house.' Experiences, plural. A little detail that might have been overlooked, but I pick up on these things. There's obviously more than the being locked up incident he hasn't told me about.

Although Liam was Mouse's neighbour, each property comes with quite a substantial piece of land, and a tall wall separates both gardens. We have to walk out of Mouse's large front yard, turn, and follow the lane for another hundred yards or so before reaching Liam's gate. The gate is an old-fashioned wrought-iron affair with spikes at the top and a simple push handle. There's a lock, but I know from my brief time living here that it isn't used, the key having been long lost. I never thought about it before, but with only Liam living in this massive place, it would have been quite easy to rob him; not even a dog guarded it!

I'm about to push the gate open when a thought stops me, and I turn to Ethan. 'What about the cat? Did someone take it?'

'Don't worry, that cat is long gone. It was hanged on Halloween night three years ago.'

'Really? By whom?'

Ethan and Makayla exchange a look, and Makayla shrugs. 'We don't know, but apparently it's not uncommon to find murdered cats on Halloween nights.'

I nod and keep silent, forcing myself not to smile. This is the countryside and, unlike me, these people are animal lovers, but whoever killed that cat did me a favour. I hated it with its evil pointy head and baring sharp fangs whenever it hissed at me.

'Did you know, by the way?' she asks suddenly.

'What?'

'That Cunningham was gay? I suppose you did, but until that night, I didn't have a clue.' She turns to Ethan and adds, 'None of us did, did we?'

'No. Well… Jamie always suspected and…' He casts a quick glance at me. 'It seems he was always on point.'

I push the gate open and falter as a memory invades my mind. It does not happen like in the movies, with quick flashes of images suddenly hurting the character's head who cries out in pain, but it is more like sensations, feelings, knowing you are in a specific place without seeing it, like in a dream.

'Are you okay?'

I turn to look at Makayla as my head throbs. I feel dizzy for no more than two seconds, as if the brain has to readjust from the memory to the present time.

'Look, man, you don't have to do this today if you're not up to it; we can always come back,' adds Ethan.

'No, I'm fine. I was just wondering, had anyone from the village seen me or met me before Liam… before the incident?'

Makayla shakes her head. 'I didn't.'

'Neither did I,' says Ethan. 'And I would have seen if the shutters of your upstairs windows were open. We can just about make it out from here.'

I turn my head, look up at my house and see through the bare branches of the Paulownia trees that the shutters of the upstairs windows are closed. The memory is clearer now. I had been savagely beaten and could barely see; my left eye was swollen shut, while my right eye was blinded by blood. It was difficult to breathe, and someone strong had picked me up to carry me.

I feel funny as we walk to the front door but try not to show my distress. I don't want to give the other two cause for concern or they might sweep me away before I have a chance to investigate.

Makayla produces a key out of her pocket and lifts it up. 'Here it is! Cunningham never changed the lock. Daniel's parents used to work for the Mercers, the previous owners.'

She makes a sweeping gesture with her arm, and we look around the front yard. It might have looked grand at some point, but the garden is now just patches of bare soil, a grassy area that could almost pass for a lawn, one gingko tree, and an overgrown straggly rosebush.

My cheeks heat up with shame at the neglected garden and run-down house. I missed the foresight of Liam's alcohol dependency despite noticing his tendency to cover up smells with aftershave and the compulsive baking of excessive numbers of cookies. But Liam kept fit, taking care of his body, and alcoholics don't normally do that.

'Daniel spent a lot of time here when he was little, but I don't think his childhood memories were good ones,' says Ethan. I give him a questioning look, and he shrugs. 'His mother was very sick.'

I try to take the key from Makayla's hand, but she holds on to it.

'Are you sure about this?'

'Trust me, I studied psychology. It is best to exteriorise trauma and not let it fester, otherwise it becomes like cancerous cells sneakily developing until the damage is irreparable.'

She rolls her eyes and lets it go. 'A simple yes would have sufficed.'

We walk up the few remaining steps to the front door. I slip the key in the lock, and, though small, a part of me hopes it won't fit. It does fit, and the old door opens with a slight push. I throw a look over my shoulder at Ethan and Makayla, who nod their understanding. They will stay close.

We squint our eyes inside the dark room. Daylight comes through the small, barred window by the door, and although it is a mild sixteen degrees outside, the house feels much colder. I shiver with apprehension. Makayla presses the light switch, and the lights of the two massive chandeliers come on; the foyer is large, running from the front entrance to the back French doors. I suspect that, in the distant past, it might have been used for receptions or might even have functioned as a small ballroom.

Makayla crosses the room and opens the shutters of all four French doors to a magnificent view: an expanse of lawn with one cedar tree on the left and an Austrian pine on the right, both framing an uninterrupted landscape of lush green grass of the valley and the river winding its way east to west through part of the forest. The room has openings on all sides, leaving little space for furniture, and it is the only part of the house left uncluttered, with just a chest of drawers by the front door and two thin bookcases between doors.

There is no access to the upper floors from here, and that is the annoying thing about this house. The staircases are at either end, one behind the kitchen and utility room, the other in the living room, and you often have to walk through or around these rooms to go anywhere. I look at the three doors on my left: laundry/washroom with a toilet and basin, linen closet, and kitchen with utility room, two on the right: one leading to a corridor and the last one opening directly onto the living room.

I open the linen closet door first. According to Mouse, that is where he was detained. The light switch is on the outside, and my heart beats wildly as I click it on, but it is nothing more than a dressing room with shelves of linen. No padding in sight.

I walk through the old country kitchen and to the utility room to reach the staircase. On the left are the stairs leading up, on the right, a closed door with the stairs down to the cellar. The familiar scent of cookie-dough-turned-musty seizes my throat, and I take small breaths, swallowing saliva to counter its effects. I touch the handle of the door and hesitate.

'What's behind there?' asks Ethan.

'The cellar.'

Makayla shivers, and Ethan takes a step forward. 'I can go first if you like; reconnoitre the place before you go down there.'

I almost nod at him in agreement, feeling as fearful as a child, but stop myself and shake my head instead. I must do this. The electrical work has been done expertly, with no defective bulb and no scary shadows, and a range of powerful light strips turn on one after the other.

'Wow!' exclaims Makayla behind me as we enter the long, narrow room with its low ceiling. Barrels and shelves of wine bottles line the stone walls, and the floor is hard dirt.

'Jesus! No wonder we never saw him buy any wine.' says Ethan.

'Look at this! Chateau Barateau Haut-Médoc Cru Bourgeois 2009, that's over twelve years old!' says Makayla, holding out a bottle of wine.

'It probably came with the house; there's quite a fortune down here!'

The two of them excitedly go from shelf to shelf, reading the labels of wine bottles aloud, but I'm more concerned with checking the walls, running my hand along the stones for any unusual bump or crack that would reveal a secret room.

A palpable silence settles. I turn to look at Ethan and Makayla, who stand close together and watch me with raised eyebrows.

'What are you doing?'

'Nothing.' I rub my hands together to remove the blackish dust. 'Let's go back up.'

I walk ahead of them and open the corridor door. A few steps behind me, Makayla whispers to Ethan, 'I thought he was found in an upstairs bedroom?'

I pretend not to have heard her and holler, 'Come on! Aren't you interested to see the whole house?'

Appealing to their curiosity works. They rush forward to join me, and we go through every room on the ground floor as well as the attached garage before moving on upstairs via the living room.

We stand in a circle and look up at a hook in the ceiling. It doesn't look like much, and it's quite incredible that it managed to support Liam's weight. My palms turn clammy, and I rub them against my jeans. There used to be a chandelier lying near, which now hangs in my house. When I'd asked Liam why it was on the floor instead of being hooked up, he said it drooped too low, and he kept bumping his head on it. The floor is free of clutter, and a faint scent of bleach and lemon reminds me of my primary school days. I look at Ethan. 'Has somebody cleaned in here?'

He scratches his head. 'Church people, I think.'

I stride along and open every single door, slamming some of them into whatever lies behind in my haste, until the third to last, which opens to a south-facing room. The odour hits me. I take a giant step back, crash into the wall behind me, and fall, sitting on the floor with my knees up and my hands covering my mouth and nose.

Makayla runs to me. 'Tommy?'

'It's the smell, the smell!' I start hyperventilating.

'Breathe!'

I try to let air flow in and out slowly, but I get distracted by the sight of Ethan walking into the room, sniffing around, and saying, 'I can't smell anything.'

How can he not? I had to lie in that painful stench for hours, maybe days! I have to overcome this, I must. Makayla's hand touches my arm, and I open my eyes. She hands me a small plastic bag, and I realise she's had to rummage around to find it.

'Here, breathe into this.' She grabs Ethan's arm, pulling him toward me. 'Distract him!'

She enters the bedroom purposefully, unlatches the window, and pushes the wooden shutters open to let the breeze in. Ethan shuffles around, unsure of what to do, and leans on the doorjamb opposite me, arms crossed over his chest. He'd rolled back his sleeves above the elbows at some point, and I watch how the pose makes his muscles bulge. I can't help the thought that he has very sexy forearms, that a hundred push-ups are nothing to him, and I get a mental picture I really shouldn't be getting. I berate myself; should I really be thinking that when just the day before, I'd told Mouse I love him?

My breathing has returned to normal, and Ethan has had to do nothing more than just stand there; I guess the beauty of some people gives them magical power. My heart still races, my body feels weak, and I need a few more minutes before I can handle revisiting the horrible room.

'Have you ever considered acting?' I ask Ethan. It's a stupid clichéd question, but I need the distraction, and Ethan has the kind of face and body that would translate well onto the big screen.

He gives me a tired look; perhaps he's been asked too many times before. 'Have you?'

Fair point. He sighs and adds, 'I'm half Vietnamese; I don't really fit the common beauty standards.'

I find that hard to believe and wonder if he's fishing for compliments or if he means his words. No one would turn this heavenly creature down because of some stupid Western beauty standard; if anything, his difference makes him even more special. But what do I know? I have always lived in my predominantly white, privileged world.

'No, what I like is working with my hands, making connections, manipulating concrete things, feeling how they fit together or how to make them fit together—'

My phone beeps in my pocket; I take it out and read the message.

Everything okay?

It's almost lunchtime, and Mouse is getting worried; I key in a reply.

Fine, nearly done x

I take a deep breath, push myself up, and walk into the bedroom.

21

CHESTS AND CARDBOARD BOXES full of junk used to litter the floor, but they have all been pushed out of the way against the walls: somebody's been to clean up. Liam was a bit of a hoarder, leaving his finds helter-skelter all over the house, which was always messy.

I approach the double bed. The mattress has been cleaned, but I notice a faint outline of the stain and instinctively cover up the bottom half of my face. The window is open, but it's as if the stench is impregnated in my nose. I run my hand along the black frame of the metal bed and stop my fingers at slightly discoloured marks. This must have been where I pulled on my binds. 'Is this it? Surely, I could have escaped if I'd pulled harder!'

I grab the frame and pull to lift it, but it barely moves. It is heavier and sturdier than it looks. I keep trying like a madman until Ethan stops me and pushes the frame.

'Hey, it's okay, look, even I can barely move the thing! There was nothing you could do.'

I hadn't realised I had spoken my thoughts out loud. Tears slide down my cheeks, and I know it's not very manly, but I can't help it; I have always cried easily. Others used to tease me a lot at school, but I never minded my tears; thanks to them, I learned to fight.

I look around, but there's nothing more to see; it's just the bed and the stuff on the floor, and I leave. I wipe my face with my hand, creak my neck, and wait in the corridor for Makayla, who closes the shutters, the window, and the door behind her. We check other rooms and gather in the corridor.

'Let's check upstairs.'

I am grateful that they follow without question.

The last floor is just as before, almost completely empty: just a large expanse of wooden floor, rendered walls with un-shuttered windows on either side, and a low wood-panel ceiling. A small rickety ladder stands against the far wall, old pots of paint at its feet, all covered with a fine layer of dust. There are scuff marks in the dust, and I get closer, wondering what made those, when a red squirrel runs past.

I jump. 'Aaargh!'

Makayla giggles automatically then covers her mouth with her hand to stop herself, but this eases the tension, and I smile at her.

'Really?' she asks with a tilt of the head. 'Squirrels too? Squirrels are adorable!'

'Not to me; they leap like they're almost flying!'

We look around, but the squirrel has disappeared through a crack in the corner of the ceiling.

'Are there *any* animals you like?' she asks as we make our way back down to the ground floor.

'Sure! Lots of them: Birds, fish, sheep... goats... pigs... cows... horses... zebras... buffalos... basically anything that won't sneak up or jump on me.'

'So you'd rather be trampled.'

'Well, don't go putting that idea into his head!' exclaims Ethan.

I'm the one who locks the front door when we leave, and I ram the key in my pocket instead of handing it back to Makayla. She doesn't seem to notice. We part ways with Ethan at the gate – his house is the next one along on the other side of the lane – and he walks home in one direction while Makayla and I walk in the other, back to Mouse's house.

We went through every room in Liam's house, but no sign of a padded room. On the one hand, I am not surprised; the padded room doesn't match Liam's personality. From what I saw in my short time with him, he pretty much lived on a day-to-day basis, leaving things to the last minute, and making no actual plans. Only his exercise routine and his outings to church were regular.

The padded room, on the other hand, is something that had to be well thought-out and meticulously planned. Someone with a drinking problem who could barely take care of his own house couldn't have done this. Yet I remember Liam carrying me. I don't know why the memory had eluded me; it shouldn't have as I hadn't yet been drugged, but it has returned, making things a little clearer. Or not! Where is the padded room? And how did I get from it to one of Liam's bedrooms?

I exhale in frustration and run a hand over my hair. Makayla gives me a comforting smile. She has walked silently by my side, leaving me to my thoughts, and I realise that despite her bubbly and party-girl exterior, she is a very clever and sensitive girl. Daniel has hit the jackpot with her.

I stop to face her. 'Thank you.'

'Ah, come on!'

'No, I mean it. You were very helpful in there; Daniel is lucky to have you. You're quite an incredible woman.'

'I know.'

She smiles, and I bump elbow with her, joking, 'If I were into girls, I might have stolen you away from him.'

She laughs and takes my arm. 'And you'd have been welcomed to try!'

The smell of pizza reaches us as soon as we enter the house. Mouse and Daniel sit at the dining-room table, and although they face each other, the apparent closeness between them makes me grit my teeth. They both rise to greet us. Mouse knows I am not one for public displays of affection, and he squeezes my hand, but I grab it and pull him close in a proprietary gesture.

'Daniel has brought pizza.'

'How very generous of him.'

Nobody notices my sarcasm. Makayla and I go wash our hands at the sink, and we all sit down to eat.

'Did you buy my favourite?' Makayla asks Daniel, who opens up a pizza box.

'Yes, baby-doll, it's here: Kosher meat with pineapple.'

I turn a snigger into a cough at the 'baby-doll'. On appearance, the nickname fits her petite frame, cute freckles, and general American wholesomeness, but on the inside, Makayla is as poised and indomitable as a queen.

She grabs a piece of pizza and takes a bite while eyeing Mouse's open laptop. It displays some of his legal studies, and she asks with a mouthful, 'Hey, would you defend a guilty person?'

'Nobody's guilty until proven so.'

'But say someone asked you to defend them, and you know they're guilty, would you do it?'

'How would I know they're guilty?'

'I don't know! Say they've told you so; would you still take their case?'

'I suppose so. Guilty or not, everybody has the right to legal representation.'

'But what if they've committed a serious crime, like kidnapping or murder?'

'Then no, I plan on being a corporate lawyer, not a criminal one.'

I smile because that is a typical 'Mouse' thing to say, and I know that if Makayla doesn't let it go, this conversation can go round and round for a while. I switch off from it and try to get my thoughts and the newly returned memories in order.

On the third of December, Mouse kissed someone else and left me. Shocked and angry, I spent the next day on my own, waiting for his return. He had left most of his clothes and his laptop, and I thought he'd soon be back. When after the second day he hadn't returned, I went to his accommodation on campus.

I'd grabbed Mouse's khaki padded jacket to wear – it was a warm windbreaker – but found his room empty. The loud knocks disturbed a few neighbouring students, and I asked them if they'd seen him. One pointed out that his car was gone. Mouse hates driving, so I knew he could only have driven home, and I prepared to follow.

My fingers had barely closed around the door handle of the Volvo when a car stopped in front of me with a loud screech. Three muscular blokes jumped out and started punching me. I raised my arms to protect my face, but one blow hit the arcade of my left eyebrow. Blood spurted everywhere, and I fell to the ground. The young men left as quickly as they'd come, and I had no idea who they were.

Someone lifted me. Not someone, Liam. But it doesn't make sense! Liam lived an hour away from the university. How did I get from the campus to Les Vallées? Did I drive? I must be missing something because the only thing I remember after the attack is waking up in the dark, feeling hungover or drugged, but not yet knowing I had been incarcerated. And so far, no sign of a padded room anywhere.

I am not sure why strangers savagely beat me out of the blue, but it is possible someone saw me and Mouse together and decided it was time for some gay bashing. I try to think hard. Mouse kissed someone else and left me, but Mouse is here with me now; he cried yesterday, and Mouse never cries. He was upset about my meeting with Liam, and that's why he left me, I'm sure of it. Perhaps he thought something was going on between us as he'd found the baseball cap in my closet; he was fine until that point.

So what was that kiss about? I raise my head to look at Mouse. Daniel quickly looks away in the pretence of listening to the conversation, which I interrupt by asking Mouse, 'Why did you kiss him?'

'He didn't,' replies Daniel.

We all look at Daniel, who turns red and starts fidgeting, picking at a slice of chorizo on his pizza. I redden too, angry that Mouse would have told Daniel about Emilio while keeping me in the dark. Daniel, of all people! And as I glare at him, he swallows hard. 'Mouse didn't kiss me, I swear it.'

'Why would he kiss you?' asks Makayla, echoing my sentiment exactly because, well, why would *anyone* want to kiss Daniel?

Before Daniel has a chance to reply, Mouse puts a hand on my arm. 'Tommy, I can genuinely say that I've kissed no one but you.'

'Except that's not true! You kissed that biceps guy Emilio right under my nose!'

A look of confusion crosses Mouse's face, then he leans back in his chair and whispers, 'Enzo.'

'What?'

'His name is Enzo.'

'I don't give a fuck what his name is!'

I scowl at Mouse. In the corner of my eye, Makayla's head ping-pongs between Mouse and me. She turns to Daniel and whispers, 'Maybe we should leave.' Daniel doesn't look like he's going anywhere.

Mouse smiles, and I feel like I'm about to murder something. 'You find this funny?'

'No, it's just that you're not usually this expressive, it pleases me to see you so jealous: it shows that you care.'

'Of course I care! I told you yesterday, didn't I?'

'Tommy, I didn't kiss Enzo; he'd cornered me and forced that kiss on me.'

'What?!'

Shocked, I hang my head. When I look back at Mouse, it's written all over his face that I had completely misread the situation. 'Why didn't you push him away?'

'I tried. I did.'

'Mouse, I need to know these things! If anybody tries to kiss you against your will, let me know, and I will quite happily rearrange their face into pumpkin mulch!'

'O-kay, I think we should go,' Daniel declares, rising from his chair and helping Makayla up. 'I have to go back to work now, anyway.'

We all stand. Daniel is still fumbling with the chair, pushing it in awkwardly, looking nervous and urging Makayla on, and I suppose our spat has made him uncomfortable. Eventually, Mouse and I have the decency to send them off properly, the least we could do after the embarrassment of leaving them stuck in the middle of our quarrel.

When they've gone, I turn to face Mouse and look him straight in the eye. Not an easy thing to do. If I stare too long into his beautiful blue eyes, it is like drowning in a pool of longing and desire; my mind goes blank, and I forget what to say.

'Mini Mouse... I... you know what you said to me yesterday,' I explain. 'About wanting to know everything about me? It should go both ways; you shouldn't keep things from me; I also want to know everything about you.'

'Okay.'

'Okay? Okay! Is that really all you can say? You are so frustrating sometimes! And why is Daniel always hanging around here?!'

'Daniel is my closest friend. We were both born here, we grew up together. He has always shown only kindness to me, always supporting me, being there for me, especially when Mum died, and not once did he ever demand anything in return. He is and will always be welcome in this house.'

I feel shameful and realise I must learn to control my jealous streak. I had never known I was the jealous kind until the day I found Mouse in my parents' house.

I had not been pleased to see that some squatters had made themselves comfortable in my new home and had lain in wait, determined to catch the intruder. When Mouse broke in and I stared into his intense blue eyes – the same eyes that had looked so openly and so directly into mine in church – it was like floating through space, as if no longer shackled by gravity, feeling light and free. I knew him. The essence of him. That's how it had felt, like I'd always known him.

I had wanted to learn everything about him ever since the funeral, and when I'd asked his name, he infuriatingly took his time answering. I felt a strange pull to be close to him, but I was frustrated to see that I could not charm this boy who looked at me with both fear and defiance; then I saw the magazine in his hand. Every turn of the page was a stab in the heart, realising what he really wanted, knowing I could never be that, and I had the sudden urge to slap him to hurt him in return.

But hurting him was not what I had wanted to do at all. Ever since his ghostly appearance on the road, I'd wanted to slip inside his mind, read every thought he had ever had, crawl inside his skin, feel everything he felt, absorb him as a part of me and own him entirely.

He had put his hands on my arm and a strange electric current had run through me, making my heart race and leaving me confused; and suddenly I could no longer stand his touch or the sight of him because it was a pure moment of clarity, when you know that what you want is out of reach and yet, you could never be without it.

I look up at Mouse; he is within my reach now, and I have what I want. When we are intimate, it is a communion of two souls merging into one, and I am where I belong. But I cannot own him, and I should stop trying to. 'Yes, of course, you're right. He is your best friend, and he should be here as long as he wants.'

Mouse grabs my waist, pulls me into his embrace, and I rest my head on his shoulder.

He strokes the back of my neck with his thumb and whispers, 'You ought to trust me, Tommy; you are the one I want, and I will love no one else but you. I would die for you. I would kill for you.'

22

I AM LYING ON THE FLOOR of the padded cell, but it is shadowy light rather than complete darkness, and Mouse sits above me, smiling while massaging me. Everything is in black and white, but his eyes, which are an electric blue. Every time he blinks, his long lashes make the light of his eyes flutter, and it is like the warning of a lighthouse on a stormy, foggy day. He opens his mouth to speak, but suddenly he is no longer Mouse and has morphed into Liam. A scent fills up my nostrils, a mixture of wine and a citrus aftershave, and I feel like I'm drowning. I try to breathe through my mouth, but hands squeeze my neck, and words I cannot understand are whispered in my ear with an Irish accent.

I open my eyes, and it's the only thing I can do. My limbs are paralysed, and I cannot breathe. Something heavy pushes on my chest as I try to sit up, and things move and crawl inside my body: weighted shadows that keep me grounded. I have to breathe, but I am trapped inside my body, eyes bulging, moving frantically from left to right, and my lungs are desperate for oxygen. In this moment, I think, what a stupid way to die, when all I need is a bit of air, just a little, not much at all, and I let out a breath as if I had been holding it this entire time.

A warm body pulls me up, embraces me, and a hand wipes tears I hadn't realised were covering my face. 'Are you okay, my love? Why are you crying?'

'Huh? I just… I guess I had a nightmare.'

Mouse is fully dressed, and the sun shines bright through the white-linen curtains of the window.

'What time is it?'

'Almost half eleven. Should I make you breakfast?'

'Just a coffee, thanks.'

I rub my eyes with the palms of my hands. Wide awake all night and feeling a strange rush of adrenalin, I'd thought about watching something to calm me down, but the laptop was in Mouse's room, and there's only one TV, which is in his parents' bedroom. I didn't want to wake Mouse, and his parents' bedroom was out of bounds, so I'd grabbed my phone, watched a few videos, and spent a long time on my Instagram account chatting with Nikki – it was perfect timing for her in Tallahassee. Sleep had not come until the early hours of the morning.

I should put my ordeal of being locked up in the dark on paper. It's a method of exteriorising trauma I find therapeutic, cathartic, and it might rid me of this recent experience of sleep paralysis, but I'm not quite ready yet.

I still haven't found out what really happened or how it happened. For now, it is a shower and a shave, and when I come out of the bathroom, a steaming coffee awaits me. I take a sip and grimace at the taste; the coffee is instant, and Mouse has poured too much water. France is a country of coffee drinkers, but it appears Mouse and his parents never adapted to that particular custom and kept to their British tradition of milky tea.

Mouse sits at the dining table in front of his laptop, surrounded by three books on law. Someone rings the doorbell, and he shouts, 'Come in!'

An older woman with short platinum hair and two heavy carrier bags enters. 'Hi, Mouse,' she hollers with her head down, then she sees me. 'Hello love, how are you?'

'Fine, thank you... Mrs Byrne.'

I'm glad I remembered her name in time and move to help, but she goes directly to the kitchen. I can only watch as she unpacks a load of groceries, putting everything away herself as well as opening and checking kitchen cupboards for supplies.

'I've made a chicken pie for you. Just heat it up at gas mark four for thirty minutes, and there's also my famous garlic king prawns in the fridge,' she tells Mouse.

She smiles at me, and I'm about to thank her when Mouse, who hasn't moved and barely looked up from his laptop, replies, 'Tommy doesn't like seafood.'

'Oh, I'm sorry, love, I didn't know. But you will eat it, won't you, Mouse?' She doesn't give him time to reply and hardly draws breath before adding, 'I see that you're running out of blackberry jam. I'll send Andy later with the fig jam I made this autumn.'

'Okay.'

I look at Mouse and can't help but think he could sound a bit more grateful, but I suppose Mrs Byrne is used to his ways. She doesn't react but moves closer. 'Have you heard from your father?'

'I spoke to him on Christmas Day, his time.' Mouse lifts his head to look at her. 'He's fine.'

Mrs Byrne nods, and I have the feeling she already knows how Mouse's dad is; she probably gets in touch with him more often than Mouse does. She leaves with a wave, and I turn to Mouse. 'Does this happen a lot?'

'I suppose so. It happened a lot when my parents were around. I guess it's hard for some people to break the habit.'

I rub my chin and ponder for a few seconds. 'Maybe your father sent her; to check on you, make sure you're okay.' He snorts and turns back to tapping on the keyboard. I take his left hand to grab his attention. 'Does he know about me?'

'Yes.'

The reply came so quickly that I'm not sure if it's a lie or if he hates being interrupted when working. 'Are you sure? Because if he doesn't, I have a feeling he soon will.'

He stops and looks at me. 'Tommy, my father lives his life, and I live mine. It's always been this way, so you shouldn't concern yourself with him, but yes, he knows about you. He knows everything.'

I smooth my hair with both hands, and Mouse gets up to put the chicken pie in the oven. I'm not sure I like the 'he knows everything' part, but that's the problem with village life; nothing stays secret for long. I suppose the person who's entitled to know the most about me would be Mouse's father. I can still remember the look on his face the day he slammed my door open. He and Mouse have the same eyes, and they were not shooting bullets at me like the eyes of angry people usually do; they were more like the cold hard stare of a psychopathic killer. I shiver thinking about it, and I'm glad he's on the other side of the world.

After lunch, I suggest a hike as it is a beautiful Sunday afternoon, but Mouse is busy with his coursework. He can be a bit obsessive, and once he gets started on something, it is difficult to pull him away as he absolutely has to finish. I decide to take a walk to my house by myself.

When I reach the Woods' garden, Ethan and his dad are out sweeping and collecting fallen leaves. If Ethan wants to know what he'll look like when he's older, he only has to look at his dad; except for the eyes, they have the same face. They stop to greet me.

'You and Mouse, huh!' says Ethan's dad.

'Yes,' I reply, suddenly finding my toes very interesting.

'How long has this been going on, then?'

I look up, aware that he was with Mouse's dad when they barged into my house; everything is set to remind me of that day today. 'Not long; since November.'

'Right.'

It's not quite the truth, and my cheeks redden. Surely October 29 is almost November, and he doesn't need to know the exact details of our relationship, but Robert Wood leans his chin on both hands on the handle of the garden rake, and his stare makes me uncomfortable.

'Dad, how about grabbing a beer? This is thirsty work for an old man like you,' Ethan jokes.

Robert stares at me a few more seconds, then leaves to go indoors, and I give Ethan a grateful smile. 'That's what it was all about that day, wasn't it?'

'Yeah, I... yes.' I run a nervous hand through my hair. 'Mouse was way too young back then; for all I knew, he wasn't even gay.'

Ethan laughs. 'Mouse was born gay; it's the one thing about him we never had a doubt about. When he was little, he was always going on about liking this boy or that.' He nudges me playfully and adds, 'At some point, I was one of them, and he followed me around for weeks. I'm not surprised you had to run away; Mouse is as stubborn as he is dogged!'

He chuckles, then scratches the back of his head, turning serious. 'I had never seen his dad mad until that day, though; you should have seen the thumping he gave Mouse. It was so unexpected, even he was stunned by it.'

I nod and look toward my house; a tower of smoke climbs high above the roof, and I shudder in alarm. 'What the hell?'

'Oh, that must be Daniel, burning leaves or branches.'

'Can he do that? Isn't that dangerous?'

'Technically, it's illegal, but we all do it anyway. We try to compost everything but burning is the only solution when plants are diseased.'

So, Daniel is at mine. I suppose he does get his meagre monthly cheque from the Van Beers accountants for his work, so I shouldn't be surprised. In fact, it's perfect; not only should I play nice for Mouse's sake, but Daniel is also a talker, and you never know, he might let slip something important about the Liam/Mouse situation.

I leave Ethan to his work and continue up the lane. When reaching the barn, I see that the donkeys have been replaced by sheep and wonder who they belong to; I never cared to ask. Daniel's pickup is parked along the hedge on the outside of the property while my Volvo is in the driveway. I must have driven it here, but I don't think so, and I'm frustrated at not being able to remember how I got from the campus to the village.

The garden is an almost perfect rectangle, and I follow the smoke coming diagonally across from the other side of the house. Daniel has his back to me. He stands in front of the bonfire, smoking a cigarette with an ungloved hand. As soon as he hears footsteps, he turns around. With quick reflexes, he flicks the cigarette into the fire before greeting me with an embarrassed smile. I guess he's not supposed to be smoking, and the gesture makes me smile; he's not infallible after all.

Psychologically speaking, Daniel is a bit of a mystery to me, and I find it hard to trust his apparent kindness. He's been dealt a pretty rough hand, losing both parents through long illnesses and probably having to struggle financially as a result. It can't have been easy growing up seeing his peers happy with healthy parents and comfortable lives. He should be mad at the world, and it would make more sense to me if he were a mean, dissatisfied, and grumbling person rather than the male version of Mary Poppins.

'Mouse not with you?' he asks.

'He's studying.'

A silence follows. I'm not sure how to start the conversation, and perhaps he doesn't know what to say to me either. We stare at the fire until there's not much to look at, then he takes me around the garden, showing me the work he's done, asking me about the height of the hedges or whether he should prune the trees, or telling me about replacing the vine that runs along the front wall which is dead and no longer producing grapes. I tell him I'm happy with his work and invite him in for a beer.

I'm not even sure if I have beer and pray that someone – Mouse, who has a key – has stocked up my fridge so it isn't completely empty. When I pull on its door, I find two bottles of Perrier, a bottle of ketchup, a jar of Dijon mustard, a tub of butter, which has gone mouldy, and three 25cl bottles of *La Chouffe* that have just gone passed their sell-by date. I figure a few days isn't going to harm us and grab two out of the three bottles of beer. Most people are quite happy drinking straight from the bottle, but I rarely do that indoors and take two beer glasses out of the dresser.

'Can I ask you something?' I ask Daniel.

'I was there the day they found you.'

That's not what I was going to ask, but I nod and let him talk.

'I was working in Celia's garden and had taken a pause to chat with Andy Byrne. The Byrnes were on their way to Mouse's house. They were taking provisions in anticipation of Mouse's return for the holiday, and that's when we heard the ambulance. Two emergency vehicles drove past in quick succession and stopped at Cunningham's. Our first thought was that he was drunk again and that he might have hurt himself, so we walked closer to have a look and, as you can imagine, soon other villagers joined us at his gate.'

Daniel shakes his head. He is not looking at me but at his fingers, which draw circles on the glass he's holding. 'We were surprised when we saw them come out of the house with a body bag; that's when we realised it was serious, and someone asked if he was dead, but then a stretcher came out with a second—' He raises his head to look at me. 'I mean, with you. Your face was covered up, so all we saw was a bit of blond hair, and I immediately asked, "Mouse? It's not Mouse, is it?" because, as you now know, Cunningham had assaulted Mouse before. But just at that moment, Mouse drove past and stopped to ask what was going on. We said that we were sure glad to see him, and he asked why. Robert replied, "Someone's just gone inside that ambulance, and when we saw the blond hair, we thought he'd hurt you again." Mouse said something like "not me" or "not this time", I'm not sure. He just became frantic, scrambling to take his seatbelt off and falling out his car, leaving the engine on before running to the ambulance, shouting your name.'

I take a few seconds to digest the information. A part of me had still seen Mouse as the culprit behind the padded room, and I had never asked him how he'd learned of my abduction or what he did during the few days before I was found. How stupid of me! What had Mouse been up to? And if all they saw was a bit of blond hair, what made him so sure it was me?

I know Mouse and I are very blond, and we each had our past with Liam, so we were the likeliest victims, but Jamie's brother is also blond, and so is Jade; it could have been anybody. 'That was a good guess, then, shouting my name.'

Daniel's finger stills, and he lifts his head to look at me. 'I don't think it was a guess; he knew you were there because of your car.'

'My car?'

'Your car had been in Cunningham's driveway. None of us knew whose car it was, but...' Daniel gives me a shifty look, hesitates, and adds, 'Just the weekend before, I'd had a call from Mouse asking me if your car was still at Cunningham's, and that's when I knew the car belonged to you. Anyway, Mouse almost assaulted the ambulance driver, demanding to know what had happened. He told them they should take you to the clinic as per your request, he then pushed us all aside to get back in his car and follow the ambulance.'

'Wait a minute, my car is here now!'

'Mouse drove it here afterwards.'

I'm pretty sure I didn't drive from university; I was badly hurt, so how did my car end up there? Did Liam, *drunk* Liam, who may not have been allowed to drive, take it back to his? Had he really been on campus? Each time I learn something new, each time I am left with more questions. 'So Mouse wasn't in Les Vallées that whole time?'

'What do you mean? He was here, but he spent most of his time visiting you at the clinic.'

'I mean, you didn't see him in the village before that?'

'No, I don't think so; he was at uni. His holiday didn't start until the nineteenth.'

I look at Daniel. I have to tread carefully. He might be very loyal to Mouse since Mouse calls him his closest friend, and I take on a casual tone. 'I just thought he was here the first weekend of December, that's all.'

'Oh, you mean before Cunningham… you mean before? Yeah, I saw Mouse, that's right. It was strange because he stayed until Monday night, and I thought perhaps he'd had the day off. I was going to ask him, but he looked ill and seemed very upset about something that weekend; he refused to talk to anyone, not even me. He didn't stay long.'

Of course. Again, stupid me, because in these people's minds, I had been in Liam's house for only three days. It's probably for the best. They already know I was tied up and starved; they can't know I was also confined, drugged, perhaps even beaten and raped.

No, I wasn't raped; that's what the doctor said when I asked. And I had to ask because of the drugs: there are moments I don't remember, moments that seemed dreamlike, real but not real. But Dr Vargas was firm: 'There are signs of sexual activities, but they are not recent and no signs of violence or sexual assault.'

I stare at Daniel until he's looking right at me. 'Be honest, Daniel, what Cunningham did to me, were you surprised by it? Would you have thought him capable of doing such a thing?'

He is calm as he holds my gaze. 'No, I was not surprised by it. No one was, to be honest, not after the strange behaviour he had displayed. There's something not right about that house, something evil,' he whispers reflexively. 'And as for him being capable of doing such a thing, I have no doubt about it!'

'Liam's behaviour was strange? You mean he was drunk?'

'No, that's the funny thing; he didn't seem drunk that day. But now that we know about the drugs, perhaps he was high. He'd come out of his house to go knocking at Mouse's door like a maniac. The house was locked, but he kept calling out Mouse's name, asking why he'd suddenly disappeared. I kept telling him Mouse wasn't there, that he was at university, but Cunningham looked agitated. Eventually, I called Robert for help. The two of us walked him back to his house, but he kept asking where Mouse was, insisting that he was meant to help him, care for him, that he wanted to redeem himself. He said he was going to undo the hurt he'd caused… stuff like that… Robert said that it was all in the past, that he would see Mouse when he's back for the Christmas holiday, and he could ask for forgiveness then.'

Daniel takes a sip of his beer and throws me a suspicious look. 'But perhaps you already know all this?'

I blink a few times. 'I—what? Of course not! How could I possibly know all of this?'

'Because if your car was in Cunningham's driveway all that time, doesn't that mean you were there too?'

23

I RUMMAGE THROUGH THE KITCHEN cupboards in search of something sweet, ideally some kind of chocolate bar, but Mouse doesn't really eat junk food, and there is a choice of either homemade fruit preserves or a packet of shortbread biscuits. I put the kettle on and grab the biscuits, needing the sugar rush before speaking to Mouse.

It's not that it's difficult to talk to him, it's just that if Mouse wants to avoid an issue, he has a way of turning conversations around in so many circles that you eventually forget the topic you originally started with. However, if his answer is straightforward, I'll know right away if he's hiding something, as Mouse is a poor liar.

I set the tea and biscuits on the coffee table and call out. 'Time for a tea break!'

Mouse looks at me, yawns, and stretches his arms above his head before unfolding his tall body out of the dining-room chair. 'Perfect, just what I need.'

He sits on the floor and dips a biscuit in his tea before eating it. I munch on a few biscuits myself, watching Mouse. His hair is getting quite long again, grazing his shoulders, and it falls in scattered waves around his face like an eighties rock star. He used to have acne on his chin, but it's cleared up, and a hint of facial hair has appeared instead. He is incredibly handsome, but either he's not aware of it, or he simply doesn't care. Mouse's hands are delicate, and sometimes he looks so young that I can't imagine him snatching or hurting anyone, but I've seen him stripped bare – literally and figuratively – and in these moments, he is assured, assertive, and dominant. Not that I mind. I am, I must admit, a bit of a lazy lover, someone who prefers the other to take charge.

I check my phone. 'Fourteen. That's the number of calls I got from you between the fifth and nineteenth of December, and I never answered any of those calls. Didn't you wonder where I was?'

He takes a biscuit and rolls it between his fingers before looking at me. 'Of course I did; that's why I called. But you never picked up, and I just thought you'd done another one of your disappearing acts. Your phone location showed that you were here, your car was in Cunningham's driveway, yet no one had seen or heard from you. There was no activity on any of your social media, and the post was piling up in both your houses.'

Mouse then dips the biscuit in his tea and swallows it, showing no sign of panic or nervousness.

'Didn't you wonder what my car was doing at Liam's?'

'I was mad at you, Tommy. I couldn't believe you'd gone straight to see Cunningham after I'd left you, right after I'd just discovered you were meeting with him on the day of your parents' crash. You were with him instead of trying to talk to me to patch things up. You were with that bastard instead of me... well, that's what I thought.'

He kneels on the floor before me, takes my hands in his, and looks at me with a pained but tender expression. 'You have no idea how much I regretted not being there for you, my love. I knew Cunningham could be violent, but I didn't realise he'd be crazy enough to go as far as drug you and tie you up to keep hurting you. I really didn't!'

Mouse isn't lying, I can tell. You'd have to be an Oscar-winning actor to pull it off, and Mouse doesn't have that kind of skill, which leaves me still confused over what happened. If Mouse isn't the culprit, then Liam was, and I have to go back to his house to find the padded room. I must have missed it. I should go at night, I decide, when nobody will notice; the key is still in one of my pockets, and lately, I find it hard to sleep, anyway.

Mouse notices the distant look in my eyes. 'You haven't forgiven me; tell you what, how about I cook your favourite tonight, *carbonade flamande* with gingerbread, just like you like?'

I smile at him. 'That's a bit ambitious, even for you, and would you have all the ingredients? I don't think Mrs Byrne brought any beef this morning.'

'Where there's a will, there's a way. I'll go ask around the village right now for some beef… and gingerbread.'

He's up quickly and I rise to grab hold of his arm. 'There's no need, really.' I give him a tight hug, and he gives me a quick peck on the cheek.

'Just give me two seconds.'

My phone rings and the displayed number is unfamiliar. I'm tempted to just leave it, but Mouse is out the door, and I take the call. 'Hello?'

'Hi, Tommy! How about going shopping in town with me tomorrow morning? Then we could grab lunch somewhere; I know a restaurant that does kosher,' says Makayla's upbeat voice in my ear. 'It's the last day of my vacation. I'm back at work on Tuesday, unfortunately.'

'Shopping?'

'Yes.'

'Are you stereotyping me right now? There are plenty of girls in this village who'd go with you; what about Anna? I thought she was your best friend?'

'I'm not stereotyping you, and a lot of men enjoy shopping. And Anna *is* my best friend, but I don't want to go with her, I want to go with you.'

'Why?'

'Because I like you, and you must have noticed how close Mouse and Dan are. I thought you and I should stick together while you're here; give us a chance to get to know each other better, get close too.'

I can see where she's coming from, and it's not a bad idea, but I had planned to go to the mayor's office and ask for the cadastral survey of the village. I can't have someone looking over my shoulder when I go, especially someone who's already witnessed my suspicious behaviour in Liam's house.

'Hang on, let me check something,' I reply. I go on the town hall's website to see what time it opens, and that's when I learn you can't just turn up, you have to make an appointment. 'Sure, okay, I've got time,' I tell Makayla. 'I'll pick you up at ten.'

Mouse has successfully found both beef and gingerbread – though he moans that the couple who owns the bed and breakfast charged him a fortune for the beef – and we are in the kitchen preparing the food. Cooking with Mouse is always enjoyable: he follows recipes right down to the letter, and I often make fun of him. We end up mock-arguing when I inevitably make adjustments, adding a condiment here or a bit more beer there, and declare that cooking is an art. He would try to push me out of the kitchen for messing with his work, and as he always has to be right, blame me for not sticking to the recipe if the food turns out bad, but we always end up laughing it off.

The pot simmers on the stove, and I help Mouse out of his apron. He takes me into his arms, and I could swear he's grown again. He's now slightly taller than me and almost as tall as Ethan. He kisses me, and as the food is slow cooking, we find our own way to pass the time.

Dinner was delicious, and I nod off against Mouse on the sofa like an old man. He nudges me awake. 'You should go to bed.'

I nod and kiss him goodnight before brushing my teeth and settling in my room, but I don't go to sleep, instead, I read the news on my phone, watch videos, play a few games, and stay awake until later in the night.

When Mouse is fast asleep in his room, I put on a pair of his trainers – they are quieter than my Chelsea boots – and tiptoe out of the house. I've put on a jumper under my hoodie, but it is cold out, and I sprint all the way to Liam's front door. The moon is almost full, and I barely need any light to insert the key in the lock.

Once inside, I look around the vast room with my phone light and try to calm my heartbeat. Instinct makes me want to turn on the lights, but I force myself not to; it would draw attention. Eyes open, brow creased, I focus and listen to the silence, but old houses, even when empty, are never truly quiet: walls move, pipes and floorboards creak, shutters, slightly loose, rattle in the wind.

Being here on my own is spooky, and I fight the urge to turn back. The shutters are closed, and the windows are double-glazed, but narrow vents above them filter the muted sound of a heavy engine backfiring somewhere on the main road. An owl hoots nearby, and dogs bark in the distance. Were it raining, I'd hear the patter of raindrops hitting the slabs or water running down the gutters. But in my cell, there was nothing. No rain, no wind, no thunder, no animal cries, no engine sounds. Nothing. Except for that one time when there was a hammering sound, but perhaps that wasn't even real, which means I may have been buried underground.

The quietest place in this house is indeed the cellar, and I make my way to it. At least it's safe to switch the lights on; the grilled vents are small squares that will barely be seen from outside. Though the room is big, it feels claustrophobic, and my heart beats hard inside my chest. The ceiling is low here, but in my cell, I could just about graze it even if I stood on my toes and raised my arms, and I sigh with frustration.

I work systematically, from one end of the room to the other, running my hand along every stone, every nook and cranny, taking bottles out of their shelves and moving heavy barrels out of the way. When I have covered all four walls, I start again, desperate to find something, anything, and I even hurt my knees when I go down on them to check the floor.

My clothes are filthy with blackish dust, and I brush them with both hands before sitting on the first step of the concrete stairs to think. Although Liam's house is big, the layout is pretty simple. On the ground floor, a massive hallway, a closet, a large kitchen with utility room, and stairwell. On the other side of the hallway: a corridor in the middle with a study, a bedroom, and shower room on one side, and a large sitting and dining room on the other. A door at the end opens onto the garage.

The garage is an add-on, built with breeze blocks rather than stones and rendered on the outside to match the rest of the house; it has no ceiling but just a roof with visible beams. Could there be another room underneath it? I have to check and should hurry as I am getting cold but find myself unable to move. Here, everything is lit, and the lighting feels safe. Up above, I will have to use only the minimal lighting from my phone if I want to stay inconspicuous. I am not looking forward to that.

So far, I have avoided thinking about my time in the cell; it was too horrible and upsetting to contemplate, but I must force myself now if I want answers to my questions. I was drugged; that's a fact. Even I knew it as everything felt more or less dreamlike, that's why I refused to drink the bottled water back then, but somehow, I was drugged anyway, with potent psychotropic and hypnotic drugs, perhaps even mixed with codeine as I was always sleeping. What made me think I was with Mouse? It was my first thought. As soon as I woke, I thought he was beside me, like he had been ever since his eighteenth birthday, and I was enjoying his touch. Was that a dream? Was this initial thought a misconception? Something that subsequently warped the reality of the entire situation.

Because the smell... The smell belonged to Liam, or Liam's house: cookie dough and wine and the citrus scent of his aftershave. Not the murmured words, though, even if some of them had had his Irish accent. Liam would never have whispered words of love; he hated me. I had diverted his peaceful path as a kid, tricked him into meeting me as an adult, made him witness my parents' death, used his sense of guilt to blackmail him into housing me – treating him no better than a butler – and even forced him into getting me a temporary car.

Were the whispered words also a hallucination?

I take my head in my hand in confusion. Eventually, and even though I don't want to, I close my eyes, imagining myself back in the cell. I had to rely on smell and touch; it was pitch black in there, complete darkness, except for the small blue light in the shower and toilet cubicle. Shower and toilet... this requires plumbing. The water has to come from somewhere, and the waste has to evacuate. As it happens, there are two water tanks, one is in the utility room just above me, and the other is in the garage; I'm sure I saw it there the other day. Now I have something to do, follow the pipes.

I get up stiffly and dust my knees; my hands are frozen, and my body shakes with cold. Back on the ground floor, I see through the small entrance window that it's bright out and let out a sigh of relief; the moon is on my side.

I turn on my phone light, which thankfully is powerful, and check the water tank in the utility room. The pipes are buried in the wall and seem to travel upwards to the bathroom immediately above.

I jog to the garage. Liam's car takes up much of the space, as well as a lawnmower, a weightlifting bench with various weights, a workbench, a box of tools on the floor, tubs of assorted sizes at the feet of gardening tools leaning against the wall, a coiled hose, sacks of lawn fertiliser, plastic sheeting material, pieces of softwood, and two jerry cans of fuel.

The floor is smooth cement, and there is no trap door, no pull-hook, and no opening of any kind. I check the pipes of the water tank; they lead to the en-suite shower room on the ground floor, and I follow them in reverse back to the garage to make sure.

My phone slips through my fingers, stiff with cold, and goes sliding under the car. Darkness engulfs me, and I become panicky. A scratching sound breaks the silence, and I frantically crawl on the floor with an outstretched arm to retrieve my phone before pointing it in all directions around me.

Outside, I raise my head and exhale with relief. The moon illuminates the landscape with a dull grey light, like on a cloudy day. I check the time on my phone, it's just gone past 4 a.m.

In Mouse's garden, palm fronds and flax plant leaves glisten with frost and form stiff architectural shapes. I've almost reached the front door when the phone vibrates in my hand, making me jump. Grandfather's face appears on the screen.

'Grandfather?'

'Tommy, will you be here for New Year's Eve or not? I think it's important you come.'

'Grandfather, it's four in the morning!'

'I couldn't sleep.'

Typical of Grandfather to think that just because he couldn't sleep, it was perfectly acceptable to call me in the middle of the night; however, there is something in his urgent tone.

'Is everything all right?' I ask.

'Yes, everything's fine,' he replies, irritated, and I smile because I'm much more used to this tone. 'Just make sure you come.' He hesitates. 'It's important to me.'

I falter. That is a bit of a clincher: Grandfather is the only family I have, and we only have each other. The Bakker side of the family has always refused to see me or acknowledge me in any way. When, at fourteen, I'd ambushed Otto Bakker, telling him I was his daughter's son, he'd kept a stoic face and replied that he didn't have a daughter.

Grandfather and I rarely see eye to eye, and he has sent me off out of his sight more times than I can count, but the fact is, and especially after losing his sons – two of them in quick succession – he is the only one who's ever been there for me. At the very least, I should have a sense of reciprocity.

'I'll bring someone.'

'I suppose that "someone" being a girl is too much to hope for?'

'You suppose right.'

The tinkling sound of ice cubes dropping into a glass suggests he's pouring himself a drink. He sighs and whispers, 'Fine.' He then ends the call.

The front door opens, and Mouse sticks a dishevelled head out. 'There you are! What are you doing outside?'

'I couldn't sleep.'

I dash inside the warm house; Mouse pulls me toward him and exclaims, 'Jesus, you're like ice!'

He grabs a blanket and wraps me in tight, embracing me from the back to share his warmth, and the gesture feels familiar.

'I was on the phone with Grandfather,' I tell him. 'I'm going to go to his New Year's Eve party, and I'd love it if you came too. Will you?'

'Of course! I'll go wherever you go.'

'Good, it will be the perfect opportunity to introduce you. I'm sorry if I woke you.'

Mouse shakes his head. 'You didn't wake me; I was thirsty and got up to fetch a glass of water. I went to check on you on my way back, only you weren't in bed, and I went through the house looking for you. When I couldn't find you, I panicked. You shouldn't disappear like that, silly, you scared me.'

I stiffen because these last four words, these *exact* words – I've heard them before.

24

I TOSS AND TURN IN MY BED. I've heard the words before, only the last time they had Liam's voice and Liam's Irish accent. Didn't they? Simple coincidence? I don't know. I had just accepted the fact that Mouse's presence in the cell might have been a hallucination, and now I'm not so sure. This keeps happening. Every time I go in one direction, getting closer, I am pulled in another; it is so frustrating!

For now, I will ignore the words, work under the assumption that Liam was the culprit, and take it from there. Who knows? Perhaps the house next door isn't the only property he owns; perhaps that's why he needed my car – to transport me from one place to the other. Carrying me around would have been much easier to do for Liam than for Mouse, and I fall asleep with the thought.

I wake up late and skip breakfast, hurrying to get ready for my morning with Makayla. I make a call to the mayor's office while walking to my house to get my car. I explain what I want and get lucky; they will have papers ready for me when I go that morning.

The weather has turned cold, and I tighten the belt around my long coat. The icy breeze sweeps through my hair and ears, stings my face, and helps revive me.

Makayla's family's home is on the east side of the village, close to the park and right next to the B&B. The house is wooden framed, set back, and surrounded by a few tall oak trees. A porch swing hangs by the entrance, and two wooden deck chairs sit forgotten on the lawn.

I knock on the door, and two cute, dimpled kids open it wide, giving me a full view of a long corridor with wooden floors and purple walls.

'Hello,' I singsong. 'I'm Tommy, here to pick up Makayla.'

'We're not supposed to let strangers in,' replies the boy, the eldest, who looks to be around eight or nine.

'But can he, Joshua? He's so pretty, and I want to see his magic trick again,' says the little girl next to him.

I don't understand what magic trick she means. I'm about to tell her I can't do magic and that her brother is right, when I drop my phone and let out a string of expletives just as a smaller boy appears with a plastic gun in his hand. He was making shooting sounds as he tried to kill an invisible enemy when he saw me, and perhaps he thought I looked like a child abductor because he screams and cries, running away in absolute terror.

The eldest turns and yells, 'Auntie Kay, that wasn't me! It's your man Terry who made Adam cry!'

'No, my name is Tommy.'

He runs to the door where the little boy has disappeared, immediately followed by his sister, and I can do nothing more than stand at the threshold with my hands behind my back. There is sniffling and the indistinct, gentle voice of someone consoling the crying child.

Makayla appears, sees me standing there, and bursts out laughing. 'Oh my God, no wonder; what are you wearing?'

I look down at my long black coat. 'What's wrong with it? It's Emporio Armani.'

'Very elegant. Does it really come with a belt?'

'Nah, I'm just a bit thin these days, and I thought it looked good. What do you think?'

She gives me a mischievous smile and takes a red padded coat out of a closet before putting it on. She is still smiling when we're sitting in the car buckling our seatbelts, and I exclaim, 'What?'

'You've just met my niece and nephews here on vacation. Guess what game they were playing before your arrival?'

'How could I possibly know that?'

'They were playing at WWII, shooting Nazis. And here you come with your short blond hair and your long belted coat and your hands behind your back.' She laughs, leans close to me, and adds, 'Adam said you shouted in German. He thought you were a Nazi for real.'

'That is incredibly offensive, and that wasn't German, that was Dutch!'

My cheeks burn as I had been cursing. I take the thin belt off, throw it on the back seat, and start the engine. 'Bloody kids!' I grumble as we set off.

Shopping with Makayla isn't really shopping; she knows almost everybody regardless of age or gender, and a lot of our time is spent chatting in this shop or that. I take advantage of one of those long chats to pop to the town hall. There's the familiar system of taking a seat outside reception and waiting for my number to be called.

When it's my turn, I have an excuse ready: a sheep has lost its way into my garden, and I'd like to know the owner, but I don't need it. As soon as she sees me, one secretary asks if I'm Elaine Robbins' boy, and without giving me a chance to reply, she produces a load of cadastral maps that she takes out back to copy. She rolls the lot before handing it out to me.

'How's your father?'

'Fine, thank you.' I leave quickly before she has a chance to realise her mistake and bump into a man outside the door of the waiting area.

I am about to apologise when he says, 'My dear child, how are you?'

'I'm fine, thank you,' I reply, thinking another person has mistaken me for Mouse.

'I daresay you look much better than when I found you, and I'm glad to see you survived. Are you living well?'

He is the local priest, and I hadn't recognised him in his normal clothes. My free hand slips inside my pocket so as not to give him a chance to grab it – I have distrusted men of the cloth ever since Vicar Watson – and my palms sweat, embarrassed to have come face to face with the person who found me tied up, naked, and lying in my own filth. I am eager to leave, but the least I can do is show gratitude. He saved me after all. 'Yes, Father, thank you for saving my life.'

'Do not thank me, my boy, I should have done more; I knew Liam had his demons. He was sober when he said he was on his way to make amends, and I thought perhaps this time he meant it, but when he returned and declared he had brought the lad home and was going to care for him, I could smell the alcohol on his breath. I thought it was just the drink talking but went there to check. There was an unfamiliar car in his driveway, but no one inside the house, though, nothing amiss.' He sighs and shakes his head. 'I left someone of trust with him for a while, kept with the regular visits, and I thought he had been doing well, getting better. I'm so sorry, my boy. I didn't realise it was something he was planning to do rather than something he'd done.'

'He told you that? That he'd taken a lad home?'

He nods and I want to ask if he remembers when the conversation happened, but he gets called in and leaves me with a quick farewell.

It appears Liam was the culprit after all, and I will have to speak to the priest again. If only I could find tangible proof!

Makayla is waiting in the square, phone in hand, and she waves at me when she sees me.

'I was just about to call you; what's that?' she asks, pointing at the papers under my arm.

'Just a bunch of papers.'

She takes my arm, and we resume shopping. I buy a shirt for myself, a new pair of hiking boots, a pair of sunglasses and some T-shirts for Mouse – Mouse is a T-shirt kind of guy, whatever the weather he has a T-shirt on; if it's cold, he adds a hoodie with a front zipper and/or a coat. We spend a lot of time at the shoe shop; Makayla wants a pair of shoes for work, and they have to be 'comfortable but gorgeous'. She finds the perfect pair, and we have lunch at a small restaurant.

We sit outside on a heated terrace, and by lunchtime, the weather is much warmer.

'How long have you known you were gay?' asks Makayla.

I tilt my head, eyebrows raised. 'Seriously, we're going to talk about that?'

'If we are to become close friends, we need to know everything about each other, don't you think?'

I laugh. 'Okay, you start then; how did your family end up here?'

Appetisers are put on our table by a smiling waiter, and she picks at them with manicured fingers. 'My father works for the forestry and agricultural company in town; that's how we ended up here.'

'That must have been quite the change from… wait, where are you from?'

'Cedar Rapids, Iowa. We lived there until I was nine, but my family is originally from Chicago.'

'I know Chicago. I've just spent three years there, doing a degree in finance and business management.'

'Wait, what?' she exclaims excitedly. 'I just did a business degree at Booth University. Are you saying we were in Chicago at the same time?'

'Most of my lectures were online because of the pandemic, and I didn't go out much. I was at Saint Xavier's.'

'Oh my God! I can't believe it! See, we already have something in common. If I'd known you were there, we could have met. I'd have introduced you to my brother and sister. Actually, a lot of my relatives are there.'

'Me? The Nazi boy?' I joke.

'Ouch! You're still upset about that.'

We share experiences of a few places and haunts from Chicago. The conversation gets quite animated with funny stories, and the first and second courses are eaten quickly.

Nazia Jesberger

'If your family is still in Chicago, how did you end up in Cedar Rapids? Was that also for work?'

Makayla gives me an awkward smile. 'That's enough about me for now, I have a question for you.'

'Ask away.'

She wipes her mouth with a napkin before putting it down, both hands on the table. 'Do you have a problem with Daniel?'

The question catches me by surprise, and I run a hand through my hair, momentarily speechless. 'No, no, of course not. What makes you think that? Did he say something?'

She shrugs. 'No, it's just the way you look at him sometimes.'

'What way do I look at him?'

'With irritation and… suspicion, maybe?'

I nod. 'Okay, he's been through a lot, right? Does it make sense for him to be so sensible and cheerful and kind all the time?'

'It's exactly because he's been through a lot that he is sensible and kind all the time; he had to mature early. Daniel doesn't take life for granted, and he doesn't want to waste time on unnecessary hate or anger. He understood quickly that it wouldn't get him anywhere.'

Jesus, the guy's a fucking saint!

'You're doing it right now.' She laughs. 'I guess I'll just have to bear with it.'

'You care about him a lot, don't you?'

'I do! It's still early days, but the truth is, I've always been a bit in love with him, and I can already see our future together.' She exhales. 'It's not going to be easy. If we're to stay together, he'll have to make quite the sacrifice… or I will.'

I think about Daniel flicking his cigarette in the fire. 'You're a goddess; what real sacrifice would he have to make?'

'His way of life, his eating habits, maybe even his religion.'

Oh. I hadn't thought of that.

'Daniel might be on his own here, but he has quite an extensive family, *Irish Catholic* family, scattered throughout the UK. Imagine what they'll say when he brings home a Jewish girl.'

We keep silent for a few moments, contemplating the situation as we go through our dessert, and I cannot help but think that Mouse and Daniel have a few things in common. They both live on their own, financially independent, while the rest of their family lives abroad. They even speak the same quirky language. I suppose they all do to an extent, especially the ones who were born here and learned English through their parents, but Mouse and Daniel share a similar vocabulary.

Makayla looks lost in her thoughts, and I say, 'Well, not that it's any consolation, but there's always worse: I'm a Catholic too, and on New Year's Eve, I'll be bringing home an atheist *boy* to my grandfather.'

We laugh as we order our coffees.

Makayla has fixed her gaze at a point just above my chest, and I look down to see her staring at my pendant.

'I knew you were with Mouse before he told us.'

I shift uncomfortably in my chair. 'Oh?'

'That was around his neck before Christmas; did he give it to you? Was that a Christmas present?'

'He did give it to me, yes.'

I lick my lips and take a sip of my coffee, uneasy about this partial answer. The truth will come out eventually, and if we are to get close, I'd better come clean now rather than have her feeling betrayed later down the line. I had already deceived a town hall official earlier in the morning, and it wasn't a good feeling. I grab hold of the pendant, look down at it, and sigh. 'He gave it to me not at Christmas this year but a few months before his fifteenth birthday.'

She looks at me without expression as I stare at her.

My teeth scrape my bottom lip as I wait, letting the words sink in, wondering if she will spring up from her chair and leave me alone at the table like in a bad break-up when a smile lights her face.

'I'm glad you told me. I already knew there'd been something going on with you two.'

'You did? How?'

Her smile turns sheepish. 'Sorry, Daniel is a blabber-mouth; but he told only me, no one else.'

I rub my head with a hand, feeling tense but relieved; at least now I can be completely honest with her. We argue over who is going to pay the bill. I'm determined to pay, and she calls me sexist, but I win when I say: 'How often am I going to get the chance to treat a woman?'

After settling the bill, I tell her I treat my friend Nikki often, and she gives me a light punch on the arm. I pretend to be hurt, and we are laughing when someone exclaims, 'Makayla!'

We turn to face a young woman caked with make-up; she wears an enormous scarf around her neck and carries a handbag that seems too heavy for her. I may be thin, but she looks positively anorexic.

'What a pleasure to see you!' she says in Parisian-accented French with a fake smile.

Makayla copies her tone, replying, 'You too.' She does not look pleased to see her at all.

'Look at you! You've traded your short, plain boyfriend for a tall, handsome one.'

'Not at all. Daniel and I are still together. This is my friend Tommy.'

She sees the woman get closer to me, acting flirtatious, and adds, 'Mouse's boyfriend, in fact. You remember Mouse, don't you?'

'Yes, yes, the little albino.'

'What? He's not an albino!' I exclaim in shock, appalled at this girl's rudeness.

'Joking, darling, just a schoolkid moniker. Well, I'd better run, bye-bye!'

I watch her leave and if my eyes could shoot bullets, she would be shot in the back twice (one shot for the way she spoke to Makayla and one shot for calling Mouse an albino) and shot again in the face to shut that awful mouth of hers. I shake my head and look at Makayla. 'Who the hell was that?'

'Ugh! A former classmate of mine, she thinks she's all that since she's started working for a famous *Maison de couture* in Paris.'

'Albino, how rude! You've never called Mouse that at school, have you?'

'No way! We'd never do that to one of our own.' She's putting leather gloves on as she adds, 'Others might have, though. Mouse was short, he was a bit of a pedantic nerd *and* openly gay, he got called quite a few names behind his back.'

I am always astounded at the meanness of mankind; they should see how tall Mouse is now! And he's always been good-looking, but apparently, no matter what you look like, it is never good enough, and someone will find ways to make you appear flawed. Isn't that what famous actors say sometimes? That they were bullied for looking like this or acting like that.

We are on our way back to Les Vallées, and Makayla berates me for leaving my house unoccupied. 'If you're going to be living with Mouse, you might as well rent the place! A house has to be lived in. I know two of the realtors in town, and I could put you in touch.'

I snort; I have had my problems with estate agents.

'Who's your home insured with?'

'Are you going to give me a sales pitch?' I mock.

I frown as she's hit a nerve, and I cannot actually remember if the house is insured. When I got the house, the primary concern for the accountant was to decide whether I should inherit according to Belgian law, with a fixed inheritance tax of three percent, or French law with no inheritance tax under one hundred thousand euros. The problem was the estate agents, who each valued the house at different prices.

'No sales pitch, just something for you to consider,' Makayla replies. 'I have insured most villagers; they'd rather have me visiting their home than some random stranger.'

I glance at her. That's interesting information; to value the contents of people's homes, Makayla would have seen the interior of most houses. 'Did you ever come across anything unusual on your visits?'

'Not really. There are a couple of places I wouldn't want to return to; some people clearly don't know what soap is. There was even this one house infested with cockroaches; they were crawling around as if they owned the place!'

'Yuk! Is Mouse insured with you?' I ask distractedly.

'Of course, he's very loyal; him and his father both.'

'His father?'

'Yes. Mouse owns the house, but the cars and the workshop are in his father's name; he has quite a few valuable motor parts too.'

The workshop!

I can't believe I completely forgot about it.

25

I HAVE SPREAD OUT THE CADASTRAL papers on the dining table in my house, and each property or land is labelled with its owner's name. There are four isolated properties, including mine, and the workshop is kind of one of them. Situated right opposite Liam's house, at the corner of the junction, it is easy to forget it's there because of the trees surrounding it. I guess the east side of the village was originally part of the forest, and it seemed to be up to each landowner whether to remove the entire trees to build or clear only the necessary area.

The workshop appears to be one of the latter, with access from the other lane, opposite the Woods' house and neighbouring the Byrnes' vast property. Definitely worth investigating. At the north end of the village, the Petersons' farmhouse is surrounded by paddocks, a large greenhouse, and a small vineyard, but it's also full of activities and noisy animal life, and I dismiss it, which leaves a farmer's barn at the edge of farmlands to the north-west, all belonging to a certain Rousseau. The name appears whenever there are fields, and I assume he's a big farmer around here.

The small barn and paddock before my house also has a French owner by the name of Pintureau, whose house lies in the next village.

Outside, the wind picks up. Some of the window frames rattle, and I look up in concern. I don't enjoy being here on my own, and I don't think I ever did. Why my parents chose this house, I will never know, probably because it is isolated, and the landscape was the perfect inspiration for my mother. But even years ago, though I kept pushing Mouse away, I was always grateful for his presence. There is something too exposed about being here, and the only reason I didn't sell the house was that my parents had lived in it.

Mouse's house, on the other hand, feels comfortable. I like where it is situated, right on the edge of the village with magnificent views on two sides, yet not too far from other dwellings. It's strange, but I also like how other people just walk in and feel as relaxed as if they were in their own homes.

I look through the window in front of me; the leafless trees bend, pushed toward the house by a cold eastern wind, and a grapevine branch scrapes along the wall. I link my phone to the Bluetooth speaker output and put the radio on to cover the howling and rattling sounds.

I am not sure what I'll find when visiting the workshop, and in truth, I'm not sure what I want to find. A part of me really wants Mouse to have been with me in the cell. I don't like the alternative – that it was mostly hallucinations; it diminishes me, somehow. As a former student of psychology, I should be able to tell what's real and what's not. I can't bear the idea of Mouse thinking his boyfriend is crazy, and I don't want the look in his eyes to change since, right now, he looks at me with awe, love, and desire.

An old song by French singer Francis Cabrel plays on the radio, and it keeps repeating: '*Je l'aime à mourir.*' – I love her to death. I smile, as it expresses my feelings for Mouse, then I grimace and turn the radio off. I can't believe I'm as bad as my grandfather, and yet I'd vowed never to become like him, who gave his heart to only one person and could never find love again after that person was gone.

There was a time of happiness; when my grandmother Renée was alive, my parents had not yet deserted me, and we all lived together in the mansion in Brussels. Memories of that time are few: Grandmother would look after me while my mother was out painting. She would take me to the kitchen where Elise baked, and we would knead dough for biscuits, or she would give me baths and wrap me in a large warm towel while singing French nursery rhymes. Grandmother was a Walloon; she only spoke French, and her voice seemed exotic, but what I remember most was her love of horse riding.

There had been a country house somewhere, with stables, horses, fields, and a forest nearby. I would follow both Grandmother and my uncle Lucas to the stables and watch them get the horses ready for a ride. Uncle Lucas was a teenager of about fifteen years old, and he often played with me. I remember him as a golden-haired boy with a radiant smile. He was always pushing large unruly curls out of his face. A memory sticks with me: him laughing while I struggled to put yellow wellington boots on before helping me out, then the two of us marching to the vegetable garden to dig and plant radishes. He loved horse riding just as much as Grandmother, and the two of them taught me how to ride.

Then disaster struck. The stables were on fire, and I remember feeling relieved on learning the horses were out and safe – I'd grown quite fond of them – but Grandfather had looked teary and panicked, and he was so beside himself he had to be held back by firefighters. Some of them eventually came out carrying what I later learned were two lifeless bodies. No one had noticed my presence. I had stood under a tree watching the entire scene when the house cat leapt from a branch onto my shoulders, its claws scratching my skin, drawing blood, and I had run back to the house crying in fear.

When I awoke the next morning, I walked barefoot to the kitchen but found it deserted. I walked around the unfamiliar house looking for everybody and found them all in tears in front of a locked door. People took turns to call Grandfather's name through the door, asking him to open up, and Grandfather kept telling them to go away with a trembling voice I barely recognised. I asked for my grandmother – who had always made me breakfast – but got blank wet stares and no reply until Elise took me back to the kitchen, sat me down, and laboured to tell me I would never see Grandmother or Uncle Lucas again because they had gone to heaven and were resting in peace with God. Grandfather had stayed in his room without eating for two days, then my father was in there with him for a long time. Shortly after, my parents disappeared, and Grandfather came out.

We drove back to Brussels. I was dressed in a dark suit and black tie for the funeral and met Uncle Victor, who had just started working in New York. There was no sign of my parents, and Grandfather harshly rebuked me whenever I mentioned them. He was fifty years old, and he never remarried, never even had a girlfriend; instead, he kept hiring a string of personal assistants, always young, always female, and rather unnecessary.

Thinking about that time now, I regret not giving Grandfather a chance to be at my parents' funeral. My old resentment toward him had resurfaced and flared: I had been so close to meeting them. I wanted to keep them to myself – my parents were finally mine, only mine

– and I had pushed Nikki away when she had tried to convince me he had a right to know.

'What right does he have?' I'd shouted. 'When he cast them out a long time ago! And who do you think you are to tell me what I should or shouldn't do? I don't want you here! Go home, this has got nothing to do with you, and I want to be alone with them!'

The next day, I had walked into Grandfather's office to find him leering over yet another PA – this one was Brazilian, and I had to admit she was incredibly beautiful – and without looking up, he'd said, 'Have you got yourself a girlfriend yet?'

As I stood there silently, he sent his PA away, leaned back in his seat, and sighed tiredly. 'No, I do not know where your parents are.'

'I do!' This had grabbed his attention, but he pretended indifference, and I continued. 'I've just come from burying them.'

His body stiffened, and his eyes blinked; he stared at my watery eyes, and his right hand shook. 'What are you saying?'

'There was an accident. They're buried in a small town in France, in case you're interested.'

I walked away, leaving him with this minimal information, and stood for a long time staring at my mother's paintings, which still adorn the walls of the house, until the tears that had uncharacteristically refused to fall finally appeared. Grandfather had once again locked himself away for a full day, but I knew he wouldn't move my parents; they would not be buried with the rest of the Van Beers family. The day I discovered my parents' whereabouts was also the day I discovered the reason for their sudden departure and my abandonment.

Searching for my parents hadn't been a simple task; there were people with the Van Beers name all over Europe, and after my eighteenth birthday, I had pretty much given up. I had my own life to live; Grandfather was finally trying to get to know me properly, and my parents had never actually been 'parents' to me. If they wanted nothing to do with me, the hell with them!

I was in the south of France, helping a friend with the repairs of his roof, and when the work was done and the summer was over, I gave Elise and her husband Alain a surprise visit before starting my third year at university.

I had just reached their front door when Elise came out. She jumped in surprise, and her face lit up with a big smile when she recognised me. She gave me a hug and dropped what she was holding, which was a letter. I picked it up, and that's when I saw the name and address of my father. 'You found them?! You found my parents!'

I was so excited that I squeezed her in my arms before giving her a kiss on each cheek, and she invited me in.

She opened a back door and called Alain, who was trimming a bush in the back garden. 'Alain! Tommy's here.'

'So?'

'Not the neighbour's cat, our Tommy, Tommy Van Beers!'

She looked at me with an apologetic smile. It was ironic, she'd said, that their neighbour's cat had a name similar to mine – apparently it was spelled Tomi – when I hated cats so much.

'I'll ask my father when I see him if he named me after a cat.' I laughed as we sat at the kitchen table, and Alain walked in noisily, tapping his feet on the outdoor mat unnecessarily, as it was a dry, sunny afternoon.

'You've met your father, at last, and he told you everything?' he asked as he put the tap on at the sink to wash his hands.

I gave Elise a look of confusion, and she smiled awkwardly before replying, 'He hasn't met his parents yet.' She turned to look at me and added, 'You haven't, have you?'

I cast a glance at Alain, who was leaning against the sink, drying his hands with a small red hand towel he had picked up from a hook. He was a tall Frenchman with a balding head and a thick grey moustache, and he'd been with Elise since my eleventh birthday. It was a second marriage for both, and they each had two grown-up children.

'Not yet,' I replied.

'I thought you said you'd be seeing him?' asked Alain, and I saw Elise trying to shut him up with a warning look.

I looked at the letter, which lay on the kitchen table, picked it up, and read the address before asking Elise, 'How did you find them?'

'They've been back in Europe for two years now, ever since your eighteenth birthday; they wanted to make it easy for you to find them.'

I looked at both of them, nodding, all the while processing the words I'd just heard. Elise had stopped working for my grandfather in May, three months before my eighteenth birthday, and it appeared I had wasted my time searching for Van Beers around Europe if they had been on another continent. How did she know about that? My parents had finally been ready to meet me just as I had given up on them, but they had not come to me. They expected me to go to them.

I glanced down at the letter, flipping it over in my hands, and looked back up at Elise. 'How long have you been in touch with them?'

She swallowed and licked her lips, unable to meet my eyes, confirming my suspicion. Elise gave Alain a helpless look.

'You haven't given the poor boy anything to drink! I'll grab us a beer,' he said.

He opened the fridge, turning his back to me, and I stared back at Elise. 'Elise, it has been more than two years, hasn't it?'

She nodded, and I choked, trying to keep my anger at bay. There was so much I wanted to say, but the emotions and sense of betrayal were overpowering. She'd known. All that time she had seen me search for my parents and she'd said nothing.

I watched her eyes fill with tears; she closed them and took a deep breath. 'I sent them photos and news of you every year, the old-fashioned way, via post.'

She rubbed her eyes with both hands and covered her mouth with a trembling hand. I shook my head, tears threatening to run down my face.

'I'm sorry, Tommy, I'm so sorry, but they forbade me from telling you where they were; they didn't want you to know. They made me promise.'

Alain put an opened bottle of beer in front of me before sitting next to Elise. He held her hand in comfort. 'I wasn't yet with Elise when the fire happened, but she told me everything.'

I blinked in confusion. The fire? A foul taste filled my mouth, and I grabbed the bottle of beer hard, took a large swig while keeping my eyes on Elise – who wiped running tears from her face – before putting the bottle down so hard I cracked the edge of its bottom. 'Elise!'

'He killed them, Tommy. You know, don't you? He didn't mean to, but your father killed them. His own mother, his beautiful little brother, he killed them!'

She sobbed as old grief resurfaced, and Alain moved his chair in a protective stance, watching me like a hawk as if I were about to hurt her – which may have crossed my mind for a split second. She was right; deep down, I had always known, always suspected, and I sat struggling to breathe as my heart pounded in my chest.

Alain took the bottles of beer away and took three tumblers out of a kitchen cupboard. He grabbed a bottle of whisky and poured us all some before handing me a glass, which I swallowed quickly.

'What happened?' I asked brusquely. 'Now is no longer the time to hide anything; what happened exactly?'

Elise was hiding her face in her hands, and she did not look like she was in any condition to answer, but she grabbed a tissue to dry her tears, blew her nose, took a sip of whisky, and said to Alain, 'Give us a minute.'

He looked at me and hesitated; she nodded and squeezed his hand, but he said, 'Elise, I'm not moving an inch!'

'Fine,' she replied before looking at me. 'You should really hear this from your father, not from me. I only know my side of the story.'

'Which is what?'

'Your father was young, don't forget that; he and Renée had an argument about...' She looked away and hesitated.

'About what?'

'About you, about your horse riding lessons. Peter was against it, and he'd shouted he'd had enough of hearing about the bloody horses, that your grandmother spent more time with them than with her own family, that she was favouring Lucas and abandoning Peter because of one mistake he'd made in his youth, that sort of thing…'

She took another sip of her drink. 'Peter has always been hot-headed, and he used to be quite capricious. He didn't like Renée's reply that if he didn't want his son to be raised a certain way, then he should raise him himself, otherwise he should not interfere, and nothing was going to stop her from teaching you to ride if that was what you wanted. Anyway, in anger or in retaliation, he burned down the stables, making sure the horses would be able to escape. What he didn't know… what none of us knew except your grandmother was that Lucas would often visit the horses at night and… sometimes, he'd even fall asleep on a makeshift bed of hay hidden in a corner.'

She finished her drink, and Alain put more in her glass while I was having a vision, a memory re-emerging of my uncle Lucas. He was sitting on a tartan rug in a hay corner as he raised a finger over his mouth in a silencing gesture and winked at me.

'Renée must have known he was inside; as soon as she saw the stables on fire, she ran in to try to get him out…'

A silence followed; we all knew the outcome. I kept my head down, and tears ran down my face and onto the table.

Elise sniffed and kept blowing her nose, then started crying again as she tried to speak. 'Peter—' She choked, put a hand on her chest, and tried again. 'Peter had not only killed his mother and baby brother, but he'd also turned his father into a criminal. Timothy covered up your father's crime and made Renée the culprit, the person he loved the most in the world... Your grandfather was destroyed, yet he said that's what she would have wanted... Peter thought it best to disappear. He took his wife, and he left.'

I had been crying silently and let the tears run for a long time, then I repeated with a small voice, 'He took his wife, and he left... he took his wife but not his child.'

I raised my head to look at Elise and shouted, 'He took my mother, but not me!'

She got up from her chair to hold me. 'Oh, my poor boy, my poor beautiful boy! Your parents thought they did what was best for you. They wanted you to be happy, to have a comfortable life, not wanting for anything. They didn't want you to live on the run with a murderer for a father.'

I was supposed to fly straight from Nice to Manchester that day, but I changed my flight and instead flew to Brittany. Grandfather was on a golfing holiday returning from a day out with friends, and I hugged him tight as soon as I met him. The gesture surprised him, and he asked what was wrong. I whispered, 'I know now.'

I gave him one last pat on the back and walked away, leaving him with a quizzical look on his face.

Grandfather had loved only one person, and I had followed in his footsteps, which wasn't very smart. It would be best to get some distance from Mouse, but I had done that already, and my three years away from him had been miserable. I had tried to date other people to get him out of my thoughts, but he was always in my head, no matter what I did.

I hadn't planned on returning to Europe, exile being self-punishment for my transgression and the unnatural feelings I seemed to have toward Mouse, but when hearing of his mother's passing, I remembered how he had stood by me at my own parents' funeral and the comfort it had given me. I just had to be there.

Now, it is my job to protect him, make sure he is safe; nothing bad should ever happen to him.

The vine branch scraping against the wall breaks, and the noise startles me. I grab my phone, push on the switch to close all the shutters, and put my coat on. Mouse's house is only half a mile away, but the wind is strong, and I take the car.

'I'm back,' I shout as soon as I walk through the door.

I take my coat and boots off and look around, but there is no reply from Mouse. I walk toward the bedrooms, and he comes out wearing nothing more than a leather cap and his underwear. Immediately, I laugh. Just seeing him has already made me feel better.

'You got them then?' I ask.

He takes the cap off to look at it. 'Delivered this morning. I love them, thank you.'

He gives me a kiss on the cheek.

Mouse often wears caps, and I had ordered a few of them: a Stetson and a US Airforce design with folded ear flaps, both of them made of leather, and a blue Mayser with UV protection, half linen and half denim. Hopefully, I'd be killing two birds with one stone, giving Mouse a belated Christmas present as well as the incentive to stop wearing the Iowa cap.

'And that's not all,' I say as I lift the shopping bags. 'I got you some T-shirts as well.'

He peeks inside the bags. 'Should I try these on, too?'

'Not just yet.'

I grab him by the waist to pull him against me, and I love the immediate effect I have on him.

26

ACCESS TO THE WORKSHOP is through a large wooden gate; the path leading to it might look like a tractor track but for the fine dark gravel, which screeches under our boots as we walk. The green tin building stands solitary in a small clearing, and the woodland surrounding it hides the view over the valley. It looks rather creepy, and I would not want to be here alone at night.

Mouse puts the key in, lifts the garage door, and I see that there is no place for concealment here. It's just tin walls with a concrete base, a car lift, a massive fuel heater, a small makeshift office in the back with tools of all kinds, and the familiar smell of oil, grease, and pneumatics. There are four cars in total, but according to Mouse, only one of them is fully functional.

'This is my dad's pride and joy, a Renault Alpine A110,' he says as he runs his hand along the metallic blue body of the car. He points at a beige carcass. 'That one over there is a Peugeot 404, and that's part of a Triumph TR4. Sixties cars.'

'What's this thing, then?' I ask as I stand by a roofless car that seems to be missing only its wheels.

'Citroën Mehari, sort of popular in hippie days, I guess.'

'I didn't know you knew so much about cars.'

Mouse snorts. 'I know nothing about cars! I'm not really that interested either; my knowledge stops here.'

I take some time looking around the place while Mouse sits in his father's desk chair and plays on his phone. I am sitting inside the Mehari, running my hand along the old dashboard and feeling the rough leather of the enormous steering wheel, when Mouse joins me.

His hand comes resting on my knee. He gives me a kiss on the neck, starts getting quite hands on, and I rebuff him gently.

'What are you doing? This is your father's place!'

'And?' He laughs. 'You're such a prude sometimes, you know that.' He takes his long body out of the car, jangles the keys, and signals for us to go. 'No one would walk in on us here,' he says cheekily as he closes the garage door.

He is referring to what happened earlier, just after lunch, when Mouse and I were chatting in the kitchen while sipping tea. I was leaning against the kitchen counter, and Mouse was standing by the fridge when someone rang the doorbell and did not wait to be called in but entered straight away. It was only the cleaner, Irene Barrow, from number four, but there was something in the way she had entered, as if she'd planned to catch us off-guard or would have been only too pleased to report some kind of ungodly behaviour.

I had glanced at Mouse, and though his face is usually impassive, there had been something playful in the twitch of his lips. I had straightened with apprehension; he was, after all, still a teenager: rebellious, daring, and provocative, but he'd just put a hand on my shoulder and whispered, 'Let's get out of here.'

I'd immediately suggested coming to the workshop, the perfect opportunity handed to me on a silver platter.

We now leave hand in hand, and the display of affection does not bother me; the village feels strangely safe. There might be haters – there always are – but this community seems full of oddballs and is strongly supportive of each other. I don't think there will be any gay bashing here.

It's the one thing I've always been conscious of, even before my attack on campus. I'm not sure if my demeanour gives off a gay vibe, but I like to dress smart and sophisticated, and sometimes it doesn't take much. I was once in a pub in Manchester having a drink with Nikki when some bullfrog of a guy started a fight. He was likely drunk and kept wanting to smash my face for the only reason that I 'look like a Ken doll'.

Good looks are usually an asset, people smile more easily or grant favours more readily, but put me in a nice tuxedo, and I might act a little conceited. I like the way I look; envious people might hate that, and sadly, for a man, beauty must come with strong masculinity.

A murmur of voices disrupts the tranquillity of the village, and once we've reached the T-junction, we see that a few women have gathered at Liam's gates: Anna and her mother Kellie, Ethan's mother, Mai Lin, Juliet, and even Celia Smith.

Mouse lets go of my hand. A voice calls out behind us, and we turn to see Daniel with a game console under his arm. He gives me a quick pat on the back and shares one of their special handshakes with Mouse. 'What's up?'

'No clue!' replies Mouse with a shrug. 'What are you up to?'

'I was on my way to see you guys; I thought we might have a game or two together.'

Juliet and Anna detach themselves from the group of women to greet us. Anna wears a Peruvian hat that gives her a cute puppy look, and Juliet twirls one of her ginger curls.

'It looks like the house might go for sale,' she says. 'Nowak is going around the place taking photos, and he's with some woman, either a buyer or a seller, not sure which.'

Daniel spits. 'They should burn the bloody place down!'

I am surprised at the vehemence of his words; I didn't realise he felt so strongly about the place. Mouse puts a hand on his shoulder and squeezes it with a little smile. At this moment, Nowak, one of the estate agents in town, comes out of the house, camera in hand, and is immediately followed by a short woman.

'That's Cunningham's wife,' murmurs Mouse, and I look at him.

'Are you sure?'

'I saw a photo, and I never forget a face.'

We all gaze in her direction, and she instinctively looks up at us. She speaks to Nowak before walking purposefully toward us, and we gather closer as a group in a reflex action. Questioning glances are cast around as she draws close, and she eventually stops in front of Mouse, peers at him for a quick moment, then stares at me. She opens her mouth but hesitates and takes a breath. 'I heard. I'm sorry.'

'You should be!' replies Mouse before I can say anything, and I look at his angered face in surprise.

'Funny, isn't it?' he adds, arms crossed over his chest. 'That in the ten years he's lived here, he's never had any visitors, not once. It's our first time seeing you here, and you're his wife!'

'We were divorced.'

'And yet, here you are claiming his house; the man wasn't good enough for you, but his money is.'

'Mouse!' I interject while putting a hand on his arm to stop him from being so rude, but he brushes my hand away, stands directly in front of her, and blurts out, 'No! If there is one thing I hate more than anything, it's hypocrisy! It's okay for you to get a divorce despite your religion, but it wasn't okay for him to be gay?!'

Mouse is rarely angry, and when he is, he tends to turn his anger toward inanimate objects. When it comes to people, he is generally passive-aggressive and never confrontational. But something about this woman seems to have ticked him off, and I don't think he realises how threatening his tall figure might look to the short woman standing in front of him.

I try to pull him out of her personal space, but he grabs my hand. 'The two of us happen to be together; now what do you think about that? Are we "holding hands with the devil"? Are we "beyond redemption"?'

He makes quotation marks with his free hand at the last two questions, and she opens her eyes wide in shock.

'I-I don't… look, this was a long time ago… I was hurt; I was young, okay, and—'

'No! That's no excuse, I am young! I am eighteen years old!' he shouts. 'And I would never abandon someone I love like you did! Wasn't he your husband? Didn't you make a vow to love him, to cherish him for better for worse instead of this exile you put him in? Do you know why he drank? He could not accept himself. He beat

people up because he had to hide who he was, and you…
you just rejected him, made him feel like he was a sinner.'

I try to pull Mouse away from her before he says
something he might regret. There are things he doesn't
know about her after all, like the stillborn baby, and
Cunningham's ex is looking rather aghast at the
unexpected verbal abuse, but Mouse pushes back,
determined to finish what he has to say.

'Perhaps if you'd helped him, if you'd supported him
in accepting himself for who he was rather than just
abandoning him, none of this would have happened. This
is as much on you as it was on Cunningham, and it's too
late to apologise now!'

He walks away in angry strides, leaving only silence
behind him, and I look apologetically at Maeve
Cunningham's crestfallen face.

'I'm sorry,' I say gently. 'It seems he is more upset
about Liam's death than I thought.'

I leave the job of comforting her to others – it is not
my place to do so – and follow Mouse. After a few steps,
I look back but no one has made a move toward her;
instead, they just keep staring, speechless. Perhaps they're
still in shock after seeing a middle-aged woman being
admonished by a teenager rather than the other way
around, and Maeve Cunningham looks at everyone in
turn before walking back to her car with her head down.

Mouse is pacing in the living room, fists tightly closed
and looking rather agitated. I embrace him from the back

to still him, resting my head on his neck. A moment passes, and when he is calm, I say, 'That was a bit harsh.'

He unlocks himself from my embrace and turns around to face me. 'Was it though?'

'There are things you don't know… she lost a baby; that can't have been easy to deal with, and grief makes you do all sorts of things.'

Mouse does not look convinced; he sighs and runs a hand over the back of his neck. 'I don't get religion, I really don't!' he exclaims.

'You don't *get* religion, that's the point. You either have faith or you don't,' I reply with a smile.

'Well, I don't!'

'I know.'

He raises his big blue eyes to look at me. 'Is that a problem? Is this ever going to be a problem between us?'

'No, I don't care about that, I care about you.'

There is a knock at the door, and Daniel's head peers in. 'Is everything all right?'

'Everything's fine, come in!' replies Mouse. He goes to the kitchen, grabs three cans of beer from the fridge, and hands one to Daniel first, who promptly opens it, takes a sip, and settles himself on the sofa; Mouse and I follow suit. We sip our drink for a while in comfortable silence. Daniel and Mouse sit side by side while I have settled sideways in the armchair. Mouse's feet rest on the low table, and Daniel makes figures of eight on the can with his index finger.

'Will you guys be around in mid-January?' asks Daniel. 'It's Makayla's birthday on the fifteenth, and I want to throw her a surprise party.'

Mouse looks at me with uncertainty, and I quickly say, 'I'm not going anywhere; wherever you are, that's where I'll be.'

We stare at each other for a few seconds, both of us knowing that when Grandfather turns seventy, I will have responsibilities and will no longer be free to do as I please.

'Then I'm counting you in,' says Daniel cheerfully.

The three of us spend the rest of the afternoon together. We move the TV to the living room and play video games until Daniel leaves to join Makayla's family for dinner. Mouse and I share a curry, and we start packing for our trip to Belgium the next day.

It seems I have only just closed my eyes when Mouse's body comes snuggling against me. I have moved so low in the bed that my head rests against his bare chest.

'You smell like barbecue,' I whisper, still half asleep.

A strong smell of smoke transports me back to my youth, and I jump out of bed, fully awake, to see an orange glow in a dark foggy sky. I open the window; thick smoke fills my nostrils, and I cough. I shake Mouse awake, shouting, 'Fire!' He rubs his eyes and coughs while I search the house for the source of the fire.

'It's not here!' he shouts from the living room and points to the flashing blue lights outside. We dress hastily but warmly before getting out of the house and are met with what seems to me like chaos.

A shower of ashes falls on our heads, and the burning smell is overpowering. Police officers push an increasing crowd of villagers with dishevelled hair and unwashed, unshaved faces away from Liam's house, forming some sort of barrier with their vans to block access while a fire truck gets through. Meanwhile, firefighters work hard to put out the fire. The flames climb high in a sky darkened by smoke, and there is no longer a roof on the house. The second-floor windows have exploded, and the walls, covered in black soot, crumble from the top.

Robert Wood has spotted us and runs toward us. 'Are you two all right? I thought you might have gone already; I'm surprised you didn't hear anything sooner.'

'We went to bed late. What time is it?' says Mouse.

'What happened?' I ask.

'Thick smoke blew towards our house an hour ago, waking us around four, and there were flames rising high out of Liam's house; I immediately called it in.'

'Do they know what caused it?'

'Not yet.'

We exchange looks silently, all of us knowing the house had been empty, and the suggestion that the fire was deliberate is left unspoken.

We join the rest of the crowd, all gathered in the Woods' lit front yard, and Mai Lin hands me a paper cup of black coffee. The Byrnes, still in their pyjamas and dressing gowns, stand in the centre of a large group of adults as if they were the authority of the village. A few people have anticipated the rain of ashes and huddle together under umbrellas. Celia Smith appeases her ginger cat in her arms, and I stand as far away from her as possible. Anna, Ethan, Jamie, Owen, and Leah have gathered under the porch, most of them taking videos with their phones, and Daniel covers a shivering Makayla with a blanket next to them.

Every head is turned toward Liam's house. People speak in hushed tones while watching the firefighters, in fascination, do an efficient job of putting out the fire, and soon, only a dripping blackened carcass is left standing.

Two gendarmes have joined the crowd. They were given coffee and are not actually interrogating anyone, but they surreptitiously gather information by seemingly conversing naturally, deflecting people's inquiries while asking their own unassuming questions.

If the fire turns out to be a criminal act, I know it will not be long until suspicious looks are cast my way; not only have I been involved in an incident with Liam, but I'm also a relative newcomer to the village. Being an outsider makes me an easy target, and I have no doubt fingers will be pointed at me.

I brush ashes from my hair nervously and look behind me at Daniel. He has always seemed to hate the house, and I cannot help but think of his strong words only a few hours ago: 'They should burn the bloody place down!'

Could he have something to do with this?

He stands on his own a few feet away from the others, Makayla no longer by his side, and stares intensely at what remains of Cunningham's home. I try to read his face, but there is no hint of pleasure or satisfaction in his features, just shock and something else, something I can't put my finger on.

My arm is pulled hard, and Makayla has grabbed both Mouse and me to steer us toward the others under the porch.

She gathers us together with a waving hand. 'I just spoke to Florian Massé.'

'Who's that?' I ask.

'One of the firefighters.'

'Is he the one married to Pelletier?' asks Jamie, and she nods.

'Anyways, he said it was rather strange; they think the fire started in the roof. Apparently, there was highly flammable material there. They're not saying what it is yet, but they're adamant there was a loft room or something up there that would have been unusually warm when the house was inhabited, as it was located between the chimneys.'

My breath catches as I turn to look at the void that used to be Liam's roof. I can't believe I missed it! Why didn't I check to see if there was an attic? I had seen no trap door, and most houses around here have roofs built with tightly packed rafters; they are too shallow for anything. I know because I'd helped a friend fix a similar roof once, but Liam's house was different: his roof was big and high.

Why the fuck didn't I think of that?!

I am mad at myself and shift on my feet, trying hard not to hyperventilate. Is that where I was detained? Convinced to have been kept underground, I'd made a stupid, careless mistake and overlooked the roof.

Highly flammable material. It could have been the mattresses and padding: probably soundproofing material and probably flammable. I rub my face with both hands, run them through my filthy hair, and try not to scream with rage and frustration. I lift my head and close my eyes, taking deep, calming breaths.

A big part of me is disappointed that I didn't get to see the room for myself, that the proof I'd been searching for has literally disappeared in a cloud of smoke, but another part of me is somewhat relieved. If the padded room was in the roof of Liam's house, then the search is over, and it means he had been my jailer for sure. A weight lifts off my shoulder, and I realise the stress of the confounding situation I'd found myself in had been bearing on me ever since I came here. I blow air through my mouth, letting out a heavy sigh.

Mouse turns to look at me, eyes unfocused, and I think he is about to give me a comforting hug when he does the strangest thing: he walks straight past me to go embrace Daniel, who I hadn't realised had been watching Liam's house beside me, face wet with tears.

Mouse whispers in his ear, 'It's over now. It's over.'

Daniel sobs and grips Mouse's hoodie. I look at Makayla questioningly, but I am the only one close enough to have heard Mouse's whispers, and she is just as surprised and confused as I am; so are the others.

Eventually, Daniel stops crying and lets go of Mouse's jacket. He wipes his tears with a sleeve and grabs hold of Makayla's hand. 'Come,' he says to her. 'I need to tell you something.'

27

'WHAT WAS THAT ABOUT?' I ask Mouse, who immediately looks around. Though our little group is at a distance from the others, there are still too many ears, and I change tack. 'We have to be at Poitiers train station in less than three hours,' I say louder. 'We should really go get ready!'

Man, I really want to stay in the village and wish I had not made plans to go home for the New Year. I need to get to the bottom of this, but I promised Grandfather, and it's too late to back out now.

Once back at the house, I repeat the question.

'It's not my place to tell you,' Mouse replies. He disappears inside the bathroom, locks the door behind him, and leaves me standing in the corridor with a stunned expression.

We sit in the first-class carriage on the train, opposite each other, and Mouse isn't talking. His head leans

371

against the window, pretending to be asleep when he coughs and asks for water.

I hand him a small bottle. 'Are you going to tell me or not?'

'Not.'

'Mouse, come on! After what I've suffered in that house, I think I have a right to know!'

'Like I said, it's not my place to tell you.'

'Mouse!'

'Look, just know that it has nothing to do with you or with Cunningham.'

Mouse's ears turn red and his jaws clench.

I force him to look me in the eye. 'Mouse, I know you think you're being loyal to Daniel, but believe me, if it were the other way around, Makayla would already know by now.'

He sighs, scratches his ear, looks needlessly around the carriage – there is no one near us – and hesitates. His head moves closer to mine, and his mouth opens; he's about to tell me everything when he exhales and looks away. I feel frustrated but try not to show it; instead, I grab hold of his hand and press it gently with mine. It is a gesture of comfort to let him know that we're on the same side, that he will always be safe with me, and he can tell me anything.

'Daniel was abused as a child,' he blurts out.

Mouse looks like someone's caught him in mischief, and it's unusual to see such a powerful expression on his face; he must really hate that I made him reveal such a major secret, and not just anyone's secret, but Daniel's.

I squeeze his hand. 'Thank you for telling me. What's it got to do with Liam's house?'

'That's where it happened; Mercer abused him when his parents were working there. I remember my mum saying he always had to be dragged to the house. He told his parents things about being a bad boy, a monster that would come get him, hurt him, punish him, and… some other sick stuff… but he was a small boy, and they believed the stories were made up: he kept describing a place they'd never seen, a place of torture he called "the felt pencil-case room".'

'Jesus Christ!' I exclaim. 'Poor Daniel, no wonder he hated the place!'

The pieces are now falling into place: the padded cell existed before Liam owned the house. I glance at Mouse, who bites his bottom lip. There is something so sensual about seeing his white teeth rub against the pink lip that my thoughts divert. I blink away quickly, wondering what the hell is wrong with me. How could I let myself get so easily distracted? Especially in view of what I had just heard.

'Daniel told you this?' I ask Mouse, who nods his head and flicks a strand of hair away from his eyes.

'When I was little, I gave him… I found photos… I wasn't sure what I was looking at, at the time. I was the only one who knew. His parents… they came to know the truth a few months after Mercer had moved south and got arrested for child abuse.' Mouse blows air through his mouth in anger. 'I suppose everyone will know now anyway! Poor Daniel.'

'You found photos of him? Of... that? How? Mouse, how old were you? Were you also—'

'No. I just found the photos, that's all.'

Mouse turns to look out the window, and I know it is as much as I'm going to get from him today. I squeeze his hand before letting it go and lean back in my seat. I think about what Daniel has gone through: he really was dealt a shit hand. Yet you wouldn't know it from his positive and generous attitude, but his kindness makes sense now. While some victims might repeat the cycle of abuse, others become survivors who understand pain and suffering; they put such value on life that they become incredibly kind and composed. He is going up quite a few notches in my esteem.

Daniel had known about the padded room, but he was just a child, and his parents had not believed him. Had he doubted the room's existence all that time? Or did Daniel know exactly where it was? Did he burn down the house because of what had happened in it? Couldn't he have done this anytime? Or did he wait until the house was no longer inhabited?

I shake my head. Maybe it had nothing to do with him: arson does not fit his personality, and I find it hard to visualise Daniel doing anything out of line. Come to think of it, he had been eager to hand me the key to Liam's house, encouraging me to go there quickly, as if he knew I would search the place. Was he expecting me to find anything? Were we both looking for the same thing? If so, he could not have known the location of the padded room for sure.

I recall the intense look that had passed between him and Mouse during the Christmas lunch; Mouse knew Daniel was using me to his own end. No wonder he had been angry; both his boyfriend and his closest friend had gone directly against him and disregarded his opinion.

I glance at Mouse and see that he's nodded off – for real this time. We have had little sleep; I feel drained, and it's going to be a long day. I lean my head back and close my eyes.

We stop to take a few pictures at La Grande Place in Brussels. It is Mouse's first time in Belgium, and he makes me walk to a small shop determined to buy chocolates – a box for me and a box for Grandfather. He falls asleep again, and once the Uber has reached home, I gently shake him awake. 'We're here,' I whisper.

As soon as we're out of the vehicle, Mouse runs one hand over his neck while stretching the other arm high above his head. He looks around. 'Are we staying in a hotel?'

'No, this is home.'

Mouse throws me an incredulous look, then stares back at the house. The sun is low behind it, making it look even bigger than it already is.

'This is…' He shakes his head and whistles. 'This is not what I was expecting.'

'What were you expecting?'

'An apartment in a building, I guess.' He spins around. 'Are you sure we are in the city? That looks like a woodland right there!'

I laugh as we mount the stairs to the entrance. Once inside, Louise greets me in French with a smile – she had changed her attitude as soon as I'd become a shareholder. 'Welcome home, Monsieur Tommy, it's—'

'Is Grandfather home?' I interrupt, taking my coat and gloves off before handing them to her.

'Yes, indeed, he has asked me to prepare the lilac room for your guest.'

'Taylor Robbins, *enchanté*,' says Mouse with the biggest grin I have ever seen on his face as he hands her his coat. He watches how they are discreetly handed, along with our suitcases, to maids who disappear quickly. 'You have servants?' he whispers to me with an astonished smile. 'You're actually very rich!'

I point out that there is more staff than usual because of the party, trying to downplay Grandfather's wealth, and Mouse chortles quietly. He looks around in awe at the grand staircase, and there is a little boy look of wonder on his face. His ears have turned red, and I suddenly feel very shy. This is my family home, so I have never thought much about the grandeur of the place, but it must feel new to him; he has mostly seen me in the context of my parents' modest house. I am reminded of Niels readjusting his tie nervously, looking ill-at-ease, and wonder if Mouse feels just as uneasy. 'Are you nervous?'

Mouse shrugs with a devil-may-care attitude.

'This way!' I say as I direct him through the lounge to the bar. 'I'll make us a cocktail; it will take the edge off, and then I'll show you the house.'

Mouse stands in front of the large lounge window, watching the sunset, while I filter the Rob Roy liquid over two martini glasses.

Grandfather walks into the room, head down, looking through his gold-rim spectacles at a sheet of paper in his hand. 'You're finally here,' he says. 'There are a few things I'd like to discuss with you before the party and—'

He looks up above the rim of his glasses just as Mouse turns from the window. Grandfather stops dead. 'Sweet Jesus!'

He crosses himself as his face blanches and looks aghast: it's as if he's seen a ghost. He fumbles to take the glasses off, knocking them off, and they go flying at Mouse's feet, then he takes hold of himself and utters with a cavernous voice, 'You're not my grandson; who are you?'

Mouse doesn't understand Dutch and faces Grandfather placidly.

I rush toward them and greet Grandfather with a hello and a half-hug-half-pat-on-the-back sort of embrace. 'This is Mouse, my boyfriend; he lives in France, but he's also English.'

'How do you do,' says Mouse before picking Grandfather's eyeglasses and handing them to him.

Grandfather takes them automatically, still frowning. 'Mouse? As in Mickey?'

'No, just Mouse.'

'Well, what kind of stupid name is that?! Are you scared of everything, boy?'

Grandfather has regained his composure; he sounds stern as he tries to intimidate Mouse, but Mouse remains as inexpressive and unfazed as ever and just shrugs.

'No more stupid than Timothy, I suppose. Do you honour the gods?'

Grandfather pauses, then chuckles. 'At least this one is both witty and handsome; there's improvement there!'

'Actually,' adds Mouse, 'only people who know me well or who are close to me use the nickname. You are Tommy's grandfather, so you may call me Mouse, but my official name is Taylor.'

'Then perhaps it is time to lose the silly nickname and grow up!'

Mouse's eyes catch mine before staring back into Grandfather's eyes. 'Isn't that the point I was just making?'

I cannot keep a straight face and let out a snigger; sometimes Mouse really cracks me up. He can deliver a truth or a sarcastic comment with both a deadpan face and an innocent tone, and he has just asserted himself, throwing the ball back in Grandfather's court. It is now up to him to decide whether he wants to get close to Mouse or keep his distance.

Grandfather appraises him, and I don't need to wonder which name he will decide to use; he doesn't let people in easily. He stares hard at Mouse, yet there's a glint in his eyes, and I can't help the feeling that they seem to connect somehow. Grandfather folds the piece of paper he is holding in half, sits himself in one of the lounge chairs, points at Mouse to sit in another opposite him, looks toward the bar, and turns to me. 'I see you were making drinks; I'll have a Whisky Sour.'

I make Grandfather's drink, set all the drinks on the coffee table, and sit in a chair at an angle right between Mouse and Grandfather. They both lean forward to grab their glass, taking a sip and mirroring each other's gesture, and I watch the two of them with apprehension.

'Tell me, young man, what do you do for a living?' asks Grandfather.

'Nothing yet, I study law. I'm in my second year.'

'A second-year student, you must be around twenty years old?'

'Eighteen.'

Grandfather tilts his head and looks at me with disapproval. 'First a thirty-year-old when you're yourself just a teenager, and now a teenager of your own, there's something wrong with you!'

'Most likely,' I reply with a smile. 'It appears to run in the family.'

Grandfather shakes his head and looks back at Mouse. 'What about your parents?'

Mouse stares blankly, and I see we have hit the first glitch; the question is too vague. Mouse has this funny quirk where if you're not exact with your words or specific enough when questioning him, he does not answer. Luckily, Grandfather doesn't take his silence as disrespect.

'What do they do?' he asks.

'My father used to work in marketing and is now retired; he's recently moved to Brisbane to live with his brother.'

Grandfather smooths his hair with his right hand, and Mouse watches him with an amused smile.

'So you live with your mother?'

'No, she passed away last summer.'

Mouse is a man of few words. His replies are so curt and direct that Grandfather is a little dazed by them, and he gives me a sideways glance – he is not used to this. Grandfather may be approaching seventy, but he looks younger; his hair may be white, but it looks thick and healthy, and though he's lost some of his height, he still stands lean and proud. He is used to people buttering him up, complimenting him, sucking up to him with fake praises and phony voices. Mouse's directness must be unfamiliar, and he clears his throat. 'I'm sorry to hear that, it must be tough.'

Mouse nods. 'It was a hard blow for my father, but he's getting better, I think, now that he's surrounded by family.'

'And you?'

Mouse looks at me and gives me such a gentle smile that Grandfather whispers, 'I see.'

He pushes on his knees to stand up. 'You've had a long journey, and you must be famished; I'd better not keep you, there will be plenty of opportunities to talk later.' He faces me. 'Come find me before the party, Tommy; I would like a word.'

Mouse and I have a snack, and I take him on a tour of the house. I show him the lilac room, which is, incidentally, the furthest from my room. The lilac room is thus called not because of its colour but because of the large painting that hangs above the bed: a reproduction of Monet's *Éternels Éclairs* with strong lilac hues that apparently took my mother several years to finish.

I lend Mouse one of my tuxedos – the party is black tie – and leave him to settle. I shower, put on my own tuxedo, and go in search of Grandfather. If I'm to be reprimanded or hear some Mouse bashing, I might as well get it over quickly.

I find Grandfather in the conservatory tending to a tall bonsai tree; he does not turn when he hears me enter. 'Tell me, Tommy, have you ever thought of having children?'

A knot forms in my throat and a thousand thoughts run through my head. The one that sticks is that Grandfather will want me to produce an heir, and my palms start to sweat. I rub them against my thighs and look out at the lit garden outside. 'I'm only twenty-four,' I emit lamely.

Grandfather puts the pair of clippers away into the small drawer of a walnut chest, sits in a chair and gestures for me to do the same. 'It's not a question of age.' He crosses a leg over the other. 'You could be twelve and already know that someday you'll want a family. I was just wondering, and especially in view of your different lifestyle, if—'

'It's not a lifestyle, Grandfather! It's who I am!'

He raises a hand. 'Wrong choice of words. Considering who you are, then, do you think you will ever have children?'

I knew one day this moment would come: the moment where I would have to tell Grandfather that his last name and his legacy would die with me, but I did not think it would come so soon. I had hoped to be in my thirties, at least, and I take a deep breath while looking Grandfather straight in the eye. 'No, nothing to do with my sexuality; I have never wanted children.'

Grandfather does not wince like I expect him to; instead, he nods, runs a hand through his white hair, and sighs. 'I don't blame you, Tommy. I know you've not had an easy childhood, and I know I am to blame for that; believe me, I have many regrets.'

I swallow with difficulty, unable to speak as emotions threaten to overcome me. A long silence stretches while the two of us stare into each other's eyes, words unnecessary.

Grandfather snorts. 'It seems like the men in our family are cursed, anyway. My father was the only sibling alive to repatriate from Congo, my only brother died in infancy, and my sons died before reaching middle age.' He chuckles. 'Perhaps you should have been given only your mother's name, eh? It might save your life.'

I give him a little smile; not long ago, I was on the brink of death, and it's a good thing he doesn't know. I want to tell him I will be careful, but guilt weighs heavily on my mind. 'It's my fault,' I whisper, but Grandfather does not seem to be listening to me.

'Perhaps women will have more luck,' he muses, and I get side-tracked.

'Women? Do you mean Joanna?'

Louise enters and hands Grandfather a leather folder before leaving quietly.

Grandfather clears his throat and moves forward in his seat. 'Anyway, it is best that everything's in order.' He raises the folder. 'This here contains my will.'

'Grandfather…'

Grandfather raises a hand. 'Relax, Tommy, everything's fine, and I certainly intend to enjoy my retirement; there's no need for concern.' He hands me the leather binder. 'I'd like you to take a look.'

I take the document and stare at Grandfather; there is an unusual expression on his face, one I've only seen once, on the day that Grandmother died: a look of fear. I let the document rest on my lap and lean back into my seat. I am reluctant to look at it, and I'd rather he told me straight. 'Is this about Joanna? She's getting the company.'

Grandfather smiles, but he still looks tense. 'You were always smart, Tommy, but not much of a businessman. Part of my shares will be transferred to her, yes, which means her shares will slightly exceed yours, but, for you, not much will change except all of this…' He raises his hands to the sides. 'Everything I own will be yours.'

That Joanna will oversee the company is a relief; she always has done. She has dedicated her life to it, moving up the ladder ever since she started working as a twenty-two-year-old. She has a keen business sense and has seen the company through several financial crises, always coming out on top. Joanna is also an accomplished woman with a devoted husband and three successful children. If Grandfather decides the company is hers, then I will not stand in the way; like he said: business was never my thing, so I am not sure why he looks scared.

'Are you afraid I will fight it? Because I have a stronger claim?'

He points at the document with his chin, and I see I was wrong about the look in his eyes; it is not just fear, it is fear of disappointing me.

I open the flap and read the pages on top; it is a DNA test analysis.

'You do not have a stronger claim, Tommy. Joanna is not a distant cousin like you thought; she is my daughter, your aunt.'

28

GRANDFATHER REALLY KNOWS how to deliver a blow. The blood drains from my face, and I stare at him in shock. His eyes avoid mine, and he runs a hand through his hair.

'Keep reading,' he commands.

I turn the pages – the ones that say Joanna Harriet Marshall née Jensen and Timothy Van Beers are a 99.993% DNA match – and I see that the will is not complicated: I am to inherit Grandfather's fortune and the entirety of his estate.

I look up in surprise. 'She gets nothing?! She is your daughter, and you leave her nothing?'

'She gets the company, that's what she wants; that's what she's always wanted, nothing more.'

I look back at the DNA test and check the date. It was done fifteen years ago. I slap the folder down on the side table near me; I cannot help the feeling of betrayal that overwhelms me. 'Who else knew about this?'

Grandfather sighs and stands to look out the window before turning toward me. 'You have to understand, Tommy, when Joanna came to find me as an eighteen-year-old claiming her mother had just disclosed the truth that I was, in fact, her father, there were no DNA tests in those days; it was not so easy to prove paternity. Because of what she told me, I took it in good faith that she was indeed my daughter, conceived before my wedding to your grandmother, and I tried to give her the best opportunities. She refused, stating she already had a family. All she wanted was a place within the company and a chance to prove herself.'

'But still—'

'She's not my family, Tommy. Not really, not officially, you are! You are a Van Beers; you are my grandson! I didn't raise Joanna.'

You didn't raise me either, I nearly said, but thought it best to keep my mouth shut.

'Joanna already has everything, anyway; she comes from a wealthy family, is married to a big American financier, and she will be chairwoman of my company. She will not have anything more. Joanna will not take anything more from you!'

Grandfather turns his back to me, visibly upset, and I rise from my seat to stand by his side. He puts his hands in his pockets and clicks his tongue. 'There's always the chance she might contest the will. I don't think she will, but I've taken precautions and transferred parts of my estate to you; I'll just need your signature.'

'Grandfather—'

'I'm sorry, Tommy. I'm sorry I hated you for so long when none of it was your fault. Your father—'

'Yes, it's my fault! It's my fault he died!' I blurt out. 'My parents, your son, they died because of me. If only I hadn't gone to meet them, they'd still be alive! They were so surprised when they saw me, they wouldn't have had the stupid accident if I'd left them well alone! I'm sorry, Grandfather, I'm so sorry.'

'No, Tommy, none of this was your fault. Don't you dare apologise to me! It was perfectly normal for you to want to meet your parents, and I'm the one who sent them away. I was such a stupid man, such a stupid, stubborn man! Abandoning you when I should have been there for you, always being harsh on you even though you were such a good boy, always complying to my every whimsical demand. I just wanted you out of my sight, and my darling Renée...' Grandfather shakes his head. 'My poor Renée... how many times must she have turned in her grave... she adored you...'

Grandfather turns to face me and takes a hand out of his pocket to put it on my shoulder. 'It is time to right the wrong, and I am proud of you, Tommy, of the person you are. I don't care that you're gay or that you'll never want children. I don't care that you don't want to run the company, and if you do, I will—'

'I don't!'

'And it doesn't matter, you understand me? All that matters is your happiness; I owe you that much. I know it's too late, but I promise to do my best for you from now on.'

The look of determination and sincerity in Grandfather's eyes shakes me to the core; a strong knot of emotions is stuck in my throat, and tears threaten to spill. I force myself to breathe steadily before saying with a shaky smile, 'It's not too late, it's never too late.'

Louise knocks at the door. 'The guests are arriving now.'

Grandfather gives me one last smile and grabs my arms with both hands. 'You are my grandson, Tommy, my family, and I love you.'

He leaves, and the declaration has my feet stuck to the ground. My head turns to watch him go, but my body cannot move. I have never heard the words before, not from him, and I can only stand there in shock. I feel light-headed and take a seat while the tears that were held back are liberated and roll down my face.

Shortly after, the door opens, and the blurry figure of a very elegant Mouse enters; he rushes to crouch in front of me and takes my hands.

'I'm sorry,' he says.

I almost laugh because it is unusual to hear the words in his mouth – Mouse never apologises. It really is an evening of firsts!

'I never make a good first impression, and I know that!' he adds. 'I will make more of an effort, I promise.'

He lets go of my hands and wipes my tears with his thumbs. 'Does your grandfather really hate me that much?'

I shake my head and let out a small cackle; he has misinterpreted my tears, and I am about to tell him when he sees the title page sticking out of the folder. The Dutch words are so similar to English that he immediately understands them. He pulls my forehead against his. 'Don't cry, I will take care of you, my love, I promise. Everything I have is yours; it doesn't matter if you have nothing. I will get my master's and get an excellent job. I will work really hard and make sure you never want for anything; just trust me, okay?'

I put my hand on his cheek, and he presses it with his. 'It's not what you think,' I whisper with a smile. 'Everything's fine.'

'Are you sure?'

I nod.

Mouse hesitates, stands, and hands me a bow tie. 'Then would you mind helping me with this? I tried to follow the directions on YouTube but still made a mess of it!'

I laugh as I grab the tie and stand to put it around his neck. I attempt to make the knot and Mouse looks so handsome that a wave of euphoria runs through me, followed by an irrational fear that I am too happy and will soon lose everything. My hands freeze. No, it is not an irrational fear, it is a particular scent: baby powder and antiseptic, a scent that reminds me of my time in captivity.

'Do you have perfume on?' I ask Mouse.

'No. You sure you're okay?'

I nod and stop my hands from shaking as I make the knot of the bow tie, trying not to show any distress.

'Everything's going to be fine, and no one will ever hurt you again,' whispers Mouse as if he could read my thoughts. He catches my eye, and the blue of his irises is so intense that I quickly look away; this could get quite dangerous, and we are already late for the party.

I clear my throat. 'I need to straighten myself up; I must look quite the mess.'

I leave Mouse behind as I take long strides to the bathroom and take deep, calming breaths. I stare at my reflection, feeling uneasy as my mind swirls with strange senses and recollections, but I cannot trust myself. Things would have been so much clearer if only I had not been drugged.

Once calm and presentable, I look for Mouse in the conservatory, but the room is empty. I rush to the large reception room where Grandfather has already greeted all the guests, and the party has started; the small orchestra is playing Beethoven's Symphony No. 6. I worry that I have left Mouse all alone to face a room full of strangers but find him in an animated conversation in English with a small group of board members.

***

It is the first day of the New Year, and I walk to the breakfast room unsteadily, head slightly hungover and body still sluggish with sleep and weariness. It is a holiday for the staff and the house is quiet. I find Mouse and Grandfather sharing breakfast, sitting opposite each other at the kitchen table, and the two of them are chatting companionably. Grandfather bites into a piece of bread topped with ham and cheese while Mouse dips a croissant into his tea. The soaked, drooping pastry coming out of the cup looks disgusting and turns my stomach, but I manage to croak a morning greeting.

'Tommy, still not a morning person, I see,' says Grandfather cheerfully. 'Mouse and I have been up for a while; your boyfriend is contrary! He hands me expensive chocolates at the same time as admonishing me for the company not making full use of the "excellent potential of the AI team".'

They both smile as they share a conspiring look, and I raise an eyebrow; not only do they seem to get on, but Grandfather is even using Mouse's nickname now. I shake my head, wondering if I am dreaming, and pour myself a cup of strong coffee before joining them at the table.

'Don't just have coffee, eat something! You're too thin, even more so than usual. A few people remarked on it last night, and we wouldn't want them to think you've got AIDS now, would we?' says Grandfather as he rubs his hands clean. 'Anyway, I'll leave you boys to it as I have a previous engagement this morning.'

'On New Year's Day?' I remark.

'Yes. I'll be back before luncheon, and we could take Mouse on a tour of Brussels this afternoon.'

Grandfather has a strange expression on his face as he rises from his chair, and I watch him leave with a frown: he is hiding something.

I turn to Mouse, who has moved from croissant to buttered toast. 'You alright?' I ask gently.

'Yes, very hungry for some reason.'

'Did you sleep okay?'

'I slept fine; the bed was comfortable.'

'Thank you for last night.'

Mouse nods. Grandfather's party had been more enjoyable than expected. Having Mouse around had really made a difference; he not only kept to his promise of 'making an effort', but he exceeded my expectations. He was almost the star of the party. Mouse was able to carry any conversation, whether it was about finance, politics, or social events, and I realised last night that he is extremely knowledgeable. He once told me he can remember anything he hears or reads with ease, and it appears he was not exaggerating.

When I had walked into the reception room, a small group had gathered around Mouse and was hanging on his every word. Leon Donkin had slapped Grandfather's back.

'Where did you hide this one, Tim? Is he another grandson we knew nothing about?' he asked.

Grandfather laughed. 'Almost, he's my grandson's boyfriend. Isn't he handsome?'

'He certainly is clever!' ejected Asif Khan.

'But not perfect; he doesn't speak Dutch!' added Leon, and they all laughed.

I stood rooted on the spot. Grandfather had beaten me to it, but I should have been the one to introduce Mouse and deal with the possible repercussions. I was as discomfited as I was proud.

Grabbing a flute of Champagne, I started navigating the room, greeting the guests with a smile and a kind word, calling them by their name and asking about their family and dog/health/latest sports car/golf handicap.

At the other end of the room, Joanna was deep in conversation with her husband. Did she look like Grandfather? There did not seem to be much resemblance. Her fiery hair was done up into a sophisticated bun, and she appeared to be one of those women who didn't bother to cover the grey; perhaps someone had told her it softened her face, making her look less icy. She was stick thin for a woman her age, and that seemed to be a Van Beers family trait, and maybe there was something familiar in the way she moved. Joanna noticed me staring and moved closer; her step faltered when Mouse appeared by my side and whispered in my ear. 'By the way, you look very dashing.'

The old-fashioned expression made me smile. When Joanna reached us, I turned to Mouse and said, 'Mouse, this is Joanna Marshall…' I stared straight into her eyes as I added, 'My aunt.'

There was the slightest lift of the eyebrows before she smiled at Mouse. 'Pleasure to meet you.'

Mouse did not get the chance to introduce himself, as he was dragged away by the head of the AI team to join their little group. He seemed to be rather popular, the new shiny toy perhaps, but the AI team was a group of young people.

'You two make a beautiful couple, kind of like twins; what's his name?' asked Joanna as she watched him.

'His name is Taylor.'

'It fits him, he is very handsome.' She took a sip of her drink and looked back at me. 'So… you know.'

'I know.'

'It won't change anything; my father will always be the man who raised me.'

I thought about all the interactions Grandfather and Joanna had over time, and nothing in their behaviour could have indicated some sort of rapport between them other than the mutual respect of two people sharing a common goal, yet they must have gotten close. They shared the same dream, did they not?

I wanted to make sure she didn't see me as a threat and nodded. 'You're right, it changes nothing… and I'm always on your side.'

Just then, laughter erupted from Mouse's little group. Mouse was not only laughing, but he also seemed to be the source of everyone's joviality, and I saw him in a whole new light – almost as if he were a stranger, someone I had never seen before. A warm wave of affection had run through me as I joined him and the others.

I watch Mouse as he butters toast before handing it to me. He can appear standoffish, arrogant, and entitled, and I always thought that was the reason he was a loner, but it appears I was wrong. He's not a loner because he's an outcast or socially awkward, as he demonstrated last night, but rather, he keeps to himself out of choice.

God, how much I love him!

The feeling comes out of nowhere and overwhelms me. I grab hold of his wrist, and the surprise gesture makes him drop the knife, but he has no time to react, and we are suddenly both on our feet. My mouth presses hard on his while my hands run along his body, searching for openings in his clothes to access his skin.

Mouse is a healthy young man, and his body reacts immediately. The need to have him is urgent, almost violent, and I have half a mind to bend him over the kitchen table, but Mouse is not the submissive kind, and his body is hard as stone. I pull him with me toward the nearest bedroom – his – and it is a chaotic journey of two bodies entwined, crashing against walls, and tripping up the stairs until I tear his clothes off and pin him on the bed with strong unyielding arms.

We're still breathing hard as we lie facing each other, and Mouse's shiny blue eyes stare into mine. 'That was… unexpected.'

I give Mouse a worried look; I don't usually take charge, and I wonder if I've put him off when he adds with a laugh, 'For a moment, I thought you were going to fuck me right there in the kitchen!'

'Yes, the thought crossed my mind.'

Mouse whispers 'naughty' as he leans over me with a mischievous smile, and that's when I see the blood running down his neck.

'Shit!' *Could I really have bitten him so hard?*

'What?'

'You're bleeding.'

I slide my hand over the wound, and he sees the blood on my fingers; he sits up and checks himself with his phone.

'It's no big deal,' he says with a shrug. 'I have something for that. Tell me something,' he asks as he rummages through his toiletry bag. 'You don't seem to have any qualms about having sex anywhere here, so why are you such a prude when you're in my house?'

Because I'm not in someone else's home here, I am about to reply when the familiar smell once again reaches my nose. Heat rushes to my head.

'What is that?' I ask, pointing at the tube he is holding.

'Healing gel.'

'Can I see?'

Mouse hands me the gel. I put it under my nose and really wish I hadn't, my head spins, and my vision blurs. It is the scent from last night, and it's not that the acidic smell is unpleasant, it's just that it transports me straight back to the black cell where I had imagined Mouse's warm hands massaging me. 'I'd better go.'

I dress quickly and almost run to my bedroom, lean heavily on the door after closing it behind me, and take a breath.

That had not been a hallucination; it couldn't have been! The smell is too strong: a strange mixture of antiseptic and baby powder. Hands really had tried to ease the pain away. The question is, whose hands? The padded room had been in Liam's house. Liam had told the priest he'd picked up a lad and was going to care for him, but I remember the massage was followed by a kiss... and only one person had ever kissed me that way.

29

I HAVE BEEN HOLED UP in my bedroom for quite a while, pacing back and forth, thinking, trying hard to remember. I thought I was done with this padded cell business; clearly not! And who burned it down? Could Mouse possibly have something to do with the fire? He spent the night with me, and sleep has been restless recently. I'd have heard him if he'd left. I must stop evading and have a serious one-on-one talk with Mouse.

I find him in the library. He has settled in an armchair by the fire, with a steaming cup of tea on the side table near him and an open book on code-breaking on his lap. The sight of him is so lovely and picture-perfect that my heart quivers, and I hesitate at the threshold. Perhaps I should forget about the past, leave it well alone and take it from here.

No, I need to know.

Mouse is engrossed in the story and does not hear me approach; I gently grab the book out of his hand, and he looks up at me. 'We need to talk.'

He blinks, and though his face remains impassive, his body curves in on itself. 'Is this about what happened upstairs earlier? Have I… disappointed you?'

I shake my head and grab the nearest chair to place it in front of him, as close as possible, before sitting on it, body leaning forward, and I am about to speak when Grandfather appears.

'Here they are! This one is my grandson Tommy, and that's his boyfriend Taylor, but we call him Mouse.'

Grandfather is not alone; he has entered the room with a tall and smiling older woman on his arm whom he introduces. 'Lisanne, my girlfriend.'

Mouse and I are suddenly on our feet.

'Girlfriend?' I ask.

'Indeed. You've introduced me to your boyfriend; I thought it was only fair that I should do the same and introduce you to my girlfriend. We've been seeing each other for quite a while, and Lisanne is an absolute gem. She made me see the error of my ways, and I'm a new man thanks to her.'

I am surprised at his affectionate tone: I have spent my youth watching Grandfather leer at younger women and never realised he had it in him to form a proper relationship with a woman his age. Distracted, I fail to give the newcomer a proper greeting.

A tense silence follows until Lisanne nervously leans toward Grandfather. 'Perhaps I shouldn't have come,' she whispers.

'Nonsense! I didn't get to see you last night, already!' replies Grandfather as he glowers at me, and I suddenly remember my manners.

'Not at all, it's lovely to meet you, Lisanne, and Happy New Year!'

'Perfect, let's all have lunch together,' declares Grandfather cheerfully before slapping me once on the back. He pulls Mouse along so they walk to the dining room side by side. I smile at Lisanne, but the smile does not reach my eyes; I am too preoccupied with other thoughts.

Lunch is a tense, awkward affair, and only Grandfather seems to enjoy his meal. He seems oblivious to the strained atmosphere and hasn't realised that Mouse is unusually stiff and quiet, casting confused glances at me. The obvious hurt on his face shakes me to the core, and I hate myself for the pain it's causing him, but I can't seem to make any gesture toward him until I have definite answers.

Lisanne is more perceptive than Grandfather and is probably stressed with the whole situation. She tries hard to keep conversations going, filling the blanks with questions and small talk. I try to focus on her, but my thoughts keep wandering; that's most likely why I fail to stop the train wreck that follows.

'Where did you two meet?' she asks, but I'm distracted, and Mouse eventually replies.

'In church.'

'Oh, that's nice, at least you know you share the same beliefs.'

'Not at all, I'm afraid; it was a funeral.'

'Oh, I'm so sorry. Was it someone close?'

'Not to me... Tommy's parents.'

Grandfather stills. He looks like an animated toy that has run out of batteries while I am yanked from my trance with such a shock that I can't find the right words to defuse the situation. There's not enough air circulating around the room, as if we're drowning as we look at each other.

Mouse blinks, his ears turn a bright red, and he stutters, 'I-I... I wasn't thinking... That-that was so tactless, I should... leave, please forgive me.'

He gets up suddenly, almost falling from his chair, and walks away as unsteadily as a drunkard. I am too stunned to react, and from the corner of my eye, I see Grandfather slowly putting his cutlery down. I turn to look at him, and his eyes lock on to mine with a fierce scowl.

'What did you do?'

My guilty conscience takes over, redirecting my thoughts, and I misunderstand his question. 'I—nothing! Nothing happened between us back then, I promise you!'

Grandfather frowns, uncomprehending; then his eyes open wide as he puts two and two together while a voice in my head calls me a liar. I had kissed Mouse. I had molested an underage kid!

Heart filled with anger, I had walked around the village trying to step in my parents' footsteps, trying to get a sense of them. The house had given me nothing, so I'd gutted it, and no matter how far I went or which lane I chose, my parents were nowhere to be found. I was so angry! Angry at God, who had not only robbed me of my parents once again but also made me witness their death. So when I heard that little girl making fun of Mouse, it had felt like she was attacking me. There was such a powerful sense of kinship with him I'd immediately thought he was a message sent from my parents: their deaths had brought me to him, my mother had even reached out to him in her final moment. I was *supposed* to look after him, and if he wanted to be kissed by a boy, then his wish was my command.

Except I was not a boy anymore but a man! Stupid! Stupid! I'm the one who sent Mouse down this path, and he had every right to lock me up.

'Sweet Jesus! I should certainly hope not; it's bad enough that he's still a teenager!' exclaims Grandfather. He runs a hand through his hair, exhales heavily and leans back against his chair. 'I meant: what did you do in the three hours I was gone? Because Mouse was perfectly fine when I left! The two of us were chatting and laughing quite happily, but now he can barely string two words together. He tried to look dignified during the meal, but it's obvious the poor chap is broken-hearted. So what was all this about, exactly, Tommy? Why put him through the trouble of introducing him if you're only going to discard him? Is it because I like him? Is this a way to get back at me? Or do you actually enjoy being cruel?!'

If Grandfather's words are like arrows to the chest, it is the expression of hurt and disappointment on his face that tasers me, rendering me momentarily speechless and paralysed. It's as if he is the lover I've betrayed and let down rather than my grandfather, and I really should run after Mouse.

'I do not enjoy being cruel, and I'm not discarding anyone! I have to talk to Mouse.'

Rising from my seat, I catch Lisanne's eyes and suddenly remember her presence; she's been quite a black hole in my vision. Perhaps she's one of those unassuming women. I give her my most gentle smile. 'You didn't get to see me at my best today; I've been rather preoccupied. I'm sorry we met under such strained circumstances, but when matters are resolved, I promise to give you my full attention. Excuse me.'

I leave and rush to the lilac room, but Mouse isn't there. I find him in the library exactly where he was earlier, and something pulls at my heart: he really looks like he belongs here.

'I just had to finish it,' says Mouse as he closes the book and puts it down on the table by his side. He gestures to the chair I'd moved earlier. 'You wanted to talk?'

I nod and take the seat opposite him. I run a hand through my hair; now that I'm here, I'm not sure where to start. 'You knew about the padded cell.'

Mouse looks at me with big blue innocent eyes; he has such an open face that, for the first time, I see the resemblance with his mother. I remember who I'm talking to; I have to be coherent and make my questions clear. It crosses my mind that I might get better results if I fire random questions in quick succession to surprise and destabilise Mouse before I get to the core of the matter. I rub my sweaty palms against my thighs and start over. 'The padded room… any idea who burned it down?'

'Quentin Rousseau.'

'…'

I wasn't expecting a straight answer, and it is like whiplash; I was supposed to destabilise him, not the other way around! I stare at Mouse with astonishment. 'You know this for a fact?'

'Not exactly. Quentin is a pyromaniac; he's been burning things down ever since he was eleven years old, and he was one of Mercer's victims.'

'So it might not be him.'

'It is him; I'd dropped one of those old photos in his mailbox just the day before.'

'You—You did what?! Jesus Christ, Mouse, what the fuck is wrong with you?! You can't go messing with someone's head like that! And do you realise how dangerous that was? Someone could have died in that fire!'

'I didn't start the fire! And nobody died; the house was empty.'

I am so appalled that I am speechless and just stare at Mouse in horror.

That was probably what my father was thinking when he torched the stables, and two lives had been lost. History has a funny way of repeating itself, and Mouse is much more like his mother than I thought. It wasn't easy to see, but she'd been quite a manipulative woman. She'd had the whole village wrapped around her finger and had people do her bidding regardless of the consequences.

Mouse shrugs and leisurely checks his nails. 'I owe it to Daniel; he's done so much for me, and it's clear he wanted the place gone, he needed to be free of his past and… I did it for us too…' His eyes meet mine, and the intense look pins me down. 'You seem strangely attached to Cunningham and his house, and don't think I didn't know where you'd been that night I found you outside. You were covered in dust, that same dust that was stuck on your clothes after you and Makayla had been there. What I can't understand is why. Why go back there? Why did you even stay there in the first place? After what he'd done to you? Why didn't you just leave?'

I am confused. Is Mouse really under the impression that I was in Liam's house of my own accord, or is he deflecting?

'Are you saying you weren't the one who locked me up?'

'Lock you up! What is this obsession with being locked up? Twice you've mentioned it, now. Is this some kind of fetish? Is that why you let that madman tie you to a bed?' Mouse reddens – we're both remembering the same thing, him tying my hands behind my back. 'Look where that got you, you nearly died!' He looks irritated and angry with me, and he resembles a parent who scolds their child after they've recklessly put their life in danger.

I lower my head, pinch the bridge of my nose, scrunch up my eyes and let out a defeated sigh. 'I just want to know exactly how and why I was confined to that padded cell.'

Mouse watches me silently, and I wonder if wheels and cogs are turning inside his head; it is difficult to tell with him. He frowns. 'You don't remember.'

I raise my head and give him a piercing stare; there's something in the way he says this that makes me think he knows. 'No, I don't remember, I was drugged, Mouse! So why don't you tell me? How did I end up in that cell?'

'I carried you all the way up there.'

'What! Why?'

'To protect you.'

'Protect me? Protect me from what?'

'From Cunningham!' he replies angrily. 'Have you any idea what it did to me to see you lying on his sofa, naked and semi-conscious, covered in blood and bruises and with eyes so swollen you couldn't even open them? It broke my heart! I wanted to kill him! How could he do that to you? How could you let him?!!'

I blink, trying to get my head around what he's telling me. 'Mouse, when was that?'

'Saturday fifth December, eleven fifty-three.'

Saturday fifth was the day I was assaulted on campus, and it seems Liam really had taken me to his house. Had he driven my car? Why did he take me there instead of the hospital? Was it really to take care of me?

Mouse had immediately assumed Liam was the one who'd attacked me, and it's no surprise; he'd found me in Liam's house, and Liam had assaulted Mouse before.

I take a calming breath and raise a hand in a halting motion. 'Hold on, let's start at the beginning, Mouse. You said you'd tracked my location, and you told the police I might have been in Liam's house longer than three days. When exactly did you find out I was in Liam's house?'

'That day. When I saw Cunningham come out of his driveway in your car, I thought, "Why is he driving Tommy's car?" You didn't answer when I called. I called you a few more times, but you never picked up, and I must admit I was angry.'

'What did you do?'

'Nothing… for a long time. Then I tracked your phone, realised you were next door, and I went to see you there.' Mouse shakes his head slowly and rubs his neck. 'Seeing you in that terrible state… that was… I just wanted to take you home, take care of you, so I grabbed you as gently as I could, but Cunningham returned, and he wasn't alone. The priest and another guy were with him. Instinct took over: I didn't want them to see you like this! I took the stairs to the first floor, realised they were searching the house, and I kept moving up, desperately looking for a place to hide, and that's when I remembered the secret room.'

'Then what?' I whisper.

'We stayed there until they stopped the search. I wanted to carry you home, but one guy stayed behind, and you were too noisy to be moved. You kept moaning in pain, and it was lucky they hadn't heard anything when I was carrying you. I had to cover your mouth to silence you. You fell asleep after I cleaned your wounds, embraced you, and kept you warm. I didn't want to wake you, you needed to recover. I discreetly left to grab a few medical items that might heal you more quickly, and it wasn't easy! I don't know who that guy was, but he had eyes like a hawk! I was so stressed and in such a rush to get back to you that I completely forgot the change of clothes.'

I shake my head in disbelief, speechless. It does explain how I got to the padded cell, but why lock me in? And if he'd planned to take me home, why did he abandon me there?

'You said you were angry; is that why you abandoned me?'

'But… Tommy, I didn't abandon you, you threw me out. You fought me. Hard. Don't you remember?'

I shake my head again, but I do remember fighting; it's just that my reality had been warped by drugs.

Mouse's hand goes to his neck, rubbing it. 'In fact, you nearly strangled me, and I had no choice but to fight back. You kept shouting that I should leave you alone, that you wanted to be free; you pleaded with me to free you… It broke my heart. You didn't love me like I love you. You had made your choice.'

Mouse's mouth grimaces in pain, eyes reflecting sorrow.

'No, you're wrong. I have always loved you; always. I wasn't in Liam's house by choice, and you shouldn't have locked me in that room; I didn't deserve it!'

'For goodness' sake, Tommy, how could I lock you in that room? There is no lock; that big wood-panel door is a simple push–pull mechanism!'

My eyes shift and glaze over. I remember falling through it onto the wooden floorboard of the second floor. I cover my face with my palms and let out a moan. I was convinced I'd searched the entire room inch by inch; had I inspected the floor thoroughly? It was black, complete darkness. No, wait, my eyes had also been swollen shut, that's why they were so painful. Eventually, I could see: the day I dreamed I'd been fed cookies, I had looked into the padded cell and saw that it was empty. And after falling, I'd been able to see my reflection in the upstairs window; it had looked dark because it was nighttime.

Fuck! Really?!

I'd really thought I'd been imprisoned. When I could have actually just left. Was it the effect of the drug? Was it down to my guilty conscience? Or was I such a twisted person I'd imagined the worst of Mouse?

I had passed out, and I guess Liam found me. He must have heard me when I fell because everything changed after that. Why did he tie me to a bed? Had I fought him? Had I yelled? Had his intent been malicious?

He had dried my body, had placed patches over my eyes, had also cut my hair and shaved me. Did he realise who I was then? Is that really why he killed himself?

All the information I was given – by Officer Ahmed, Father Prichet, Daniel, and finally, Mouse – comes together. My eyes refocus. 'He thought I was you! Liam thought I was you.'

Mouse frowns uncomprehending, and I add, 'I was wearing your khaki jacket that day and came out of your dorm, my face was covered in blood from the assault, and perhaps he didn't recognise me; he thought I was you.'

'He thought he was assaulting *me*?'

'No, Mouse. Liam isn't the one who attacked me.'

'Jesus Christ! Are you still defending him?!'

'No, I'm telling you the truth. Three muscly blokes suddenly attacked me on campus, nothing to do with Liam. But he did find me, and I guess he took my car to drive me to his. I think he was on his way to see you; he'd told Father Prichet he needed to redeem himself and make it up to you.'

'But... are you sure? He didn't attack you?'

'Yes, I'm sure.'

Mouse has a baffled expression; he looks like an elementary schoolboy stuck on a simple calculus problem.

His face turns red, and he puts both hands on my arms, grabbing hold of my shirtsleeves. 'But Cunningham hurt you, didn't he? He drugged you and tied you to a bed; he starved you, and you nearly died! He did harm you, didn't he?'

Mouse is putting pressure on my arms, and there's something desperate in the tone of his voice. It seems the whole padded cell business was a misunderstanding – my drugged and confused mind had not worked properly – and I don't want to fill Mouse with guilt. Liam *had* drugged me. Perhaps he thought he was medicating me, but he had also gagged me, hooded me, and tied me to a bed. Unfortunately, he's no longer around to explain his

Nazia Jesberger

actions, and unless I remember, I will never know why he did it.

Deep down, I'm not sure what Liam's intent was, but I almost died.

'Yes. He did harm me,' I reply.

EPILOGUE

I CANNOT SLEEP. Eyes haunt me. Different eyes but always the same look, the look of people who know they haven't got long, who know they are dying.

The haunted eyes of Tommy's mother. *My* mother. Did she really know she was going to die? She had that look as she blew kisses at me.

Cunningham.

I thought I was okay here, in the serenity of Tommy's house; last night was the best sleep I'd had in weeks, no nightmares, no haunted eyes. But after Tommy's revelations, I cannot sleep. Guilt eats at me: I'm the one who got Tommy hurt. I know who assaulted him. I think I know. And if I'm right, Tommy's assault was a direct consequence of my actions. They were not after him but me.

Bloody Hell! I throw punches at the pillow, over and over, and put it over my mouth to muffle a groan. I cover my face with my hands, slide them in my hair, and rub my stiff and sweaty neck.

I don't think Tommy and I look alike – our resemblance is only superficial – but a month ago, we had a similar haircut, and in the early hours of a December morning and especially as he was wearing my jacket, it might have been easy to mistake him for me.

Those fuckers wouldn't let go of what I did to their precious teammate. But I'd been angry and hurt after leaving Tommy, and Enzo had started it first, anyway, by forcing his mouth on mine. There was no way I could let him get away with that.

So what if I erased his registration and all traces of him with the lacrosse team? Boo hoo, he's not going to be able to compete this year, big deal! My blood boils when I think of what they did to Tommy; my head spins with ideas and ways of exacting revenge, but I take a deep breath and try to calm my mind.

Breathe. Inhale. Exhale.

Revenge is definitely not the best course of action; it leads to death. Tommy was right about that; he nearly died because of it… his parents died… my mother died… Cunningham died.

I watched him die.

Those eyes again.

This has to stop! I'm only eighteen years old, and I've witnessed so many deaths already. Too many.

Cunningham: was I wrong about him? Did I get it all wrong?

No, Tommy did. He says Cunningham wanted redemption, and he doesn't think that he had bad intentions towards me, but then Tommy tends to see the good in people. Case in point: he's with me.

Whatever intentions Cunningham had, the fact was that as soon as he'd found me in his house, he became violent. He wasn't about to apologise or ask for forgiveness!

And he was supposed to find me in his house; that was the plan.

I had hidden Tommy away, protected him, soothed his pain, and tried to comfort him as best as I could, yet he'd brutally rejected me. That hurt. How did I not see he'd been drugged?

I was expecting it, I suppose, his rejection. That's what he'd done in the past, before abandoning me altogether, and no one had ever cared or stuck up for me. I had always been nothing more than a hindrance.

I'd left him with a heavy heart and rushed back to university in time for some of my end-of-term exams, but I knew I'd be back to deal with Cunningham. He was not only a waste of space – no longer a contribution to society – but he'd also spiralled downwards ever since his time at the clinic. Not only was he not cured, he'd somehow been given access to drugs, and now he'd also attacked the person I love… or so I thought. He had to be eliminated, and a plan was set in motion.

It was a simple one: Cunningham was to attack me, and I was to kill him in self-defence. Even so, the finer details had to be perfect. First, it could not look like it was planned, and the murder weapon had to be something on-hand. That is why I had taken his Swiss Army knife with me and made sure Cunningham would find me near the upstairs bathroom. Second, I needed a good reason to be in his home, and Daniel had given me two. He'd called me one day to tell me a strange story about Cunningham going to my house looking for me, and he'd later confirmed the presence of Tommy's car in Cunningham's driveway. I could use either excuse: I was there because Cunningham had asked for me, or I was there to see Tommy, even if, at the time, I thought Tommy was long gone. None of the locals had seen him, and he wasn't answering any of his calls. I'd genuinely thought he'd disappeared on me again. I couldn't blame him; who'd want to stay around Cunningham?

It never occurred to me that Tommy could be tied up to a bed somewhere. Cunningham was renowned for being violent in anger but not sadistic. I am ashamed of this oversight on my part. He had left my fifteen-year-old self in the laundry closet for hours, but I'd thought that was his way of disciplining a naughty and annoying child, nothing more.

How wrong I'd been.

I'd made such a racket when I broke into Cunningham's home that if anyone else had been there, they'd have come running; Cunningham certainly had, and he was exactly where I wanted him. He was still very drunk, and I had smiled at the sight of him.

I guess he didn't like me smiling because he immediately slapped me hard and, of course, I let him. Despite what others might think, I did not put myself in danger. I could totally overpower him. There is one major assumption people always make about me; they think I am weak. Even now I'm tall.

It started at school. Back then, I was shorter than everyone else. I excelled in sports, but I wasn't interested in team sports and was considered a tech nerd. The label came with its own stereotype, and I perpetuated the lie by being generally lazy, disliking violence, and letting myself be easily pushed around.

I was not weak, though; I was a spy. And to be a spy, you have to be strong enough to push or carry heavy things out of the way, swift enough to evade capture, nimble enough to crawl through tight places, robust enough to climb up awkward surfaces, fast enough to outrun angry animals, and fervent enough to endure any potentially dangerous situation. To this day, I am still as efficiently trained as a US Marine; it's just that no one knows it, and the deception pleases me. Deception takes time, commitment, and sacrifice, and I enjoy feeling like the heroes of my favourite movies. The only person who might know is Tommy. I barely struggled to carry him up two flights of stairs, but maybe even he isn't aware as I am always gentle with him, even on the rare occasions he turns angry or violent.

Because I despise violence, no one fears me. Cunningham did not fear me; his eyes only reflected anger and hate. When he'd slapped me, I let my body fall on the floor on purpose and smirked, needing to enrage him further so he would beat me quite badly, but when I noticed the rope in his hands, I knew I needed to act fast, this was not part of the plan. Whichever way you looked at it, there's no way one could justify strangulation as self-defence, and I could not allow myself to be in a vulnerable position with him behind me. I had to take the rope from him. My hand had reached into my pocket to grab the Swiss Army knife, and I was about to get it out when he threw me in the bathroom. Tommy's bloodied clothes distracted me, and Cunningham had the opportunity to subjugate me, but his angered face slackened.

'You killed Grayson,' he slurred.

'Yes,' I replied.

I didn't know who Grayson was, but that wasn't important; Cunningham was delusional, and that was a good thing. He had to be mad, he had to attack me. But Cunningham stood still, no longer violent, hunched over, looking sad, pathetic, and helpless, and my will to hurt him rapidly waned. I thought of Tommy's beaten face, and a surge of anger erupted.

I rose, got so close to Cunningham I'd stepped on his toes and, keeping a sardonic smile on my face, repeated slowly, 'Yes, I killed him... and now I'm going to kill you.'

I was expecting a set of punches and had tightened my abs, hoping he wouldn't hit my head in such a way that I'd collapse, but there was no reaction from him, not even a slap. Instead, he looked up and pointed at the hook in the ceiling with a trembling hand. 'You hanged him up there.'

Grayson was not a person; it was his cat.

I looked up at the hook, looked back down at Cunningham, and it became clear I could not kill this man, however much I had hated him. I was a coward; I'd always been a coward.

I had hanged his cat but had not killed it. It had drowned in the Byrnes' pond, its head and front paws submerged under water. Hanging its dead body had only been a threat, a psychological manoeuvre to destabilise him.

I could never kill a cat! And if one wasn't capable of killing a cat, how could one possibly kill a human being?

Perhaps if I'd known that, only a few metres away, Tommy was shackled to a bed and fighting for his life, I wouldn't have lost my resolve; but I didn't know, and I watched Cunningham remove a pile of towels from the metal chair before grabbing it and placing it under the hook.

He climbed on it, unsteadily, to attach the rope, and I taunted him. 'If you want me to meet the same end as your cat, you'll have to catch me first.'

Cunningham peered down at me as if he'd just remembered my presence and the look in his eyes troubled me; there was something familiar about it.

'You've come for him, haven't you?'

What? I've come for his dead cat?

'But you'll never win,' he whispered.

Well, I knew that! I had lost the minute I realised I could not kill him.

'I know this because you and I are the same. No one needs us.'

My upper lip twitched. The truth of his words hit me harder than any punch he could have thrown. I stared at his face – a door swinging open onto my future.

I'd thought myself superior. Unlike him, I'd never denied who I was, but we had been the same; both desperate for validation, and that's why we had connected all those years ago. I had turned to tormenting him the same way he had turned to drugs and alcohol, seeking comfort the only way we knew how. My ears turned red with shame, and I clenched my fists with determination. I would not end up like him!

I'll do whatever it takes, but I will never end up like you.

Irritated, I turned my back to leave and marched towards the staircase. The chair fell with a crash, there was a snapping sound, and I whipped around to see Cunningham hanging from the rope. The Swiss Army knife rested in my pocket, and I could have cut the cord, but it was obvious Cunningham's neck was broken, and, once again, I ran.

I toss and turn in bed, trying to find a comfortable position, but I know I will not sleep. My hands grope about in the dark to find the light switch. I turn the lamps on and sit up, rub dry eyes with closed fists and comb my hair back with my fingers, then check the time on my phone: 00:09

A knock rasps at my door, so light that I think I imagine it; then Tommy comes in. He wears midnight-blue silk pyjama bottoms with a silk robe open over his chest and holds a highball glass of water.

'Can't sleep?' he asks. 'I thought you might get thirsty, and I brought you water.'

I look at the jug and tumbler on the small round table by the window, and Tommy's eyes follow my gaze.

'Oh.'

'Thanks,' I say as I reach out a hand, and he carefully places the glass in it before sitting by me on the bed. I take a sip; the cool water is refreshing.

As soon as I put the glass down on the bedside table, Tommy's hand is in my hair. He affectionately pushes wild strands away from my eyes, looking lost in his own thoughts. He's not been sleeping much lately, and I wonder if something troubles him.

'What's wrong?' I ask. His eyes shift, and he looks at me.

'Nothing's wrong.' He gives me a gentle smile, but I wonder if he's lying; sometimes it is difficult for me to read people. Tommy leans his head against mine, foreheads touching, and murmurs: 'You should never doubt my love, mini Mouse, never. Even if I don't say the words, you will forever be here.'

He grabs my hand and presses it on the tattooed mouse on his chest, then he lets go, leans back and puts his hands on either side of my face. 'I just have one final question, and then I promise I will never mention his name again.'

His eyes look straight into mine. Such captivating eyes! Such mesmerising eyes! The colour of honey with a green tinge around the pupil. Ask for the moon, and I will give it to you. Ask for my soul, it is yours.

'How exactly did Liam die?' he asks.

'He hanged himself,' I reply.

Tommy stares at me a little longer, then slowly looks down and nods.

He takes off his robe, gets into bed with me, turns the light off, nestles against me, and now that he is in my arms, there are no other eyes than his.

I feel serene, and a moment later, I am asleep.

THE END

Printed by Amazon Italia Logistica S.r.l.
Torrazza Piemonte (TO), Italy

46113810R00244